**As I bowed my head, all the doubts, fears, apprehension—everything—melted away, and I was aware only of the heat rising to the surface, the dragon finally breaking free.**

*Oh, man, it's been way too long.*

With a ripple and a snarl of pain, I shed my weak human body at last, letting my real form uncoil like a spring. My spine lengthened, stretching out with tiny pops and cracks, as if trying to shake off the stiffness. My face tightened as human skin and teeth melted away, forming a narrow muzzle with razor-sharp fangs, bony eye ridges and pale horns twisting back from my skull. Scales covered my body, overlapping miniature shields, the color of flame and sunset and as hard as steel.

Rearing onto my hind legs, I gave a defiant roar as my wings finally unfurled, snapping open in the wind like crimson sails. A fierce, savage joy filled me as I gave them a few practice flaps, lifting myself off the ground to hover on the wind. Yes, *this* was what I'd been missing!

**Books by Julie Kagawa**
**available from Harlequin TEEN**
**(all listed in series reading order)**

**The Talon Saga**

*Talon*
*Rogue*
*Soldier*

**Blood of Eden**

*The Immortal Rules*
*The Eternity Cure*
*The Forever Song*

**The Iron Fey**

*The Iron King**
"Winter's Passage" (Ebook Novella)**
*The Iron Daughter**
*The Iron Queen*
"Summer's Crossing" (Ebook Novella)**
*The Iron Knight*
"Iron's Prophecy" (Ebook Novella)**
*The Lost Prince*
*The Iron Traitor*
*The Iron Warrior*

*Also available in *The Iron Fey Volume One* anthology
**Also available in print in *The Iron Legends* anthology along with the exclusive *Guide to the Iron Fey*

# TALON

JULIE KAGAWA

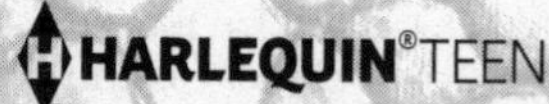

ISBN-13: 978-0-373-21215-6

Talon



This edition published by arrangement with Harlequin Books S.A.

For questions and comments about the quality of this book, please contact us at CustomerService@Harlequin.com.

**Printed in U.S.A.**

To Laurie and Tashya, who dreamed of dragons with me.

# AS ONE, WE RISE

# PART I

## Observe. Assimilate. Blend in.

# EMBER

"Ember, when did your parents die, and what was the cause of death?"

I stifled a groan and tore my gaze from the car window, where the bright, sunny town of Crescent Beach shimmered beyond the tinted glass. The air in the black sedan was cold and stale and, annoyingly, the driver had engaged the child safety locks so I couldn't roll down the window. We'd been stuck in the car for hours, and I was itching to get out of this moving prison and into the sun. Outside the glass, palm trees lined the road, and charming villas shared the sidewalk with weathered gray shacks advertising food, T-shirts, surfboard wax and more. Just beyond the pavement, past a strip of glistening white sand, the Pacific Ocean shimmered like a huge turquoise jewel, teasing me with its frothy waves and countless beachgoers splashing freely in the glittering water.

"Ember? Did you hear me? Answer the question, please."

I sighed and settled back against the cold leather. "Joseph and Kate Hill were killed in a car accident when we were seven years old," I recited, seeing the driver's impassive gaze watching me from the rearview mirror. Beside him, Mr. Ramsey's dark head bobbed in affirmation.

"Go on."

I squirmed against the seat belt. "They had gone to see a Broadway musical, *West Side Story,*" I continued, "and were struck by a drunk driver on the way home. My brother and I went to live with our grandparents, until Grandpa Bill developed lung cancer and could no longer take care of us. So we came here to stay with our aunt and uncle." I snuck a longing gaze out the window again, seeing a pair of humans on surfboards, gliding down the waves. My curiosity perked. I'd never gone surfing before, not in my dusty little corner of desert. It looked nearly as much fun as flying, though I doubted anything could compare to soaring the air currents, feeling the wind in your face and beneath your wings. I didn't know how I was going to survive the summer completely earthborn. Humans were lucky, I thought, as the car sped on and the surfers were lost from view. They didn't know what they were missing.

"Good," muttered Mr. Ramsey, sounding distracted. I imagined him scanning his ever-present tablet, scrolling through our files and background. "Dante, what is your real objective while in Crescent Beach?"

My twin calmly pulled his earbuds down and hit the pause button on his iPhone. He had this uncanny ability to zone out to music or television and still know exactly what was going on around him. I did not have this talent. My teachers had to smack me upside the head to get my attention if there was anything remotely distracting around. "Observe and blend in," he stated in his cool, unruffled voice. "Learn how to engage with humans, how to *be* human. Assimilate into their social structure and make them believe we are one of them."

I rolled my eyes. He caught my gaze and gave a small

shrug. Dante and I weren't really twins, not in the truest sense of the word. Sure, we were the same age. Sure, we looked very similar; we had the same obscenely red hair and green eyes. And we'd been together as far back as I could remember. But we didn't come from the same womb. We didn't come from a womb at all, really. Dante and I were clutchmates, which was still highly unusual because our kind normally didn't lay more than one egg at a time. Making us strange, even among our own. But Dante and I had hatched together and were raised together, and as far as anyone was concerned, he was my twin, my sibling and my only friend.

"Mmm." Apparently satisfied that we had not, in fact, forgotten the made-up backstory drilled so deep into my head that I could recite it in my sleep, Mr. Ramsey went back to scrolling through his tablet, and I went back to staring out the window.

The ocean receded, the sparkling horizon dropping from view as we turned off the main stretch and entered a subdivision with impressive white-and-rose villas lining the streets, surrounded by perfectly manicured lawns and palm trees. Some of these dwellings were truly enormous, making me stare in amazement. I'd never seen such huge houses except on television, or in the documentaries the teachers made us watch years ago, when we were first learning about humankind. Where they lived, how they acted, their behavior and family units and language—we'd studied it all.

Now, we would be living among them.

Excitement rose up again, making me even more impatient. I wanted out. I wanted to touch and feel and see the things beyond the glass, to finally experience it. My world, up until now, had been a large underground facility that I never saw the outside of, then a private school in the middle of the Great Basin, with no one around for miles, and only my brother and teachers for company. Safe, protected, far from prying human eyes…and possibly the most boring spot on the face of the planet. I squirmed against the seat again, accidentally hitting the back of the chair in front of me.

"Ember," Mr. Ramsey said, a note of irritation in his voice, "sit still."

Scowling, I settled back, crossing my arms. *Sit still, calm down, be quiet.* The most familiar phrases in my life. I was never good at sitting in one place for long periods of time, though my teachers had tried their hardest to instill "a little patience" into me. *Patience,* stodgy Mr. Smith had told me on more than one occasion, *is a virtue that holds especially true for your kind. The best-laid plans are never conceived in a day. You have the luxury of time—time to think, time to plan, time to calculate and see everything come to fruition. Talon has survived for centuries, and will continue to survive, because it knows the value of patience. So what's the blasted hurry, hatchling?*

I rolled my eyes. The "blasted hurry" was that I rarely had any time that was truly my own. They wanted me to sit, listen, learn, be quiet, when I wanted to run, shout, jump, fly. Everything in my life was rules: can't do this, don't do that, be here at this time, follow the instructions to the letter. It had gotten worse as I got older, every tiny detail of my life regulated and laid out for me, until I was ready to explode. The only thing that had kept me from going completely nuts was looking forward to the day I turned sixteen. The day I would "graduate" from that isolated corner of no-man's-land and, if I was deemed *ready,* begin the next stage of training. I'd done everything I could to be "ready" for this, and it must've paid off because here we were. *Observe, assimilate and blend in,* that was our official mission, but all I cared about was that I was out of school and away from Talon. I'd finally get to see the world I'd studied all my life.

The sedan finally pulled into a cul-de-sac of smaller but no less elegant villas and rolled to a stop in front of a driveway in the very center. I peered through the window and grinned with excitement at the place that would be home for an indefinite length of time.

The structure looming above us sat across a tiny lawn of short grass, scrub and a single palm tree encircled in brick. Its walls were a cheerful, buttery yellow, the tiled roof a deep red. The top floor had huge glass windows that caught the afternoon light, and the front door stood beneath an archway, like the entrance to a castle, I thought. But best of all, through the gap between the house and its neighbor, I could just make out the silvery glint of water, and my heart leaped at the thought of the ocean right in our backyard.

I wanted nothing more than to yank open the door, jump out and go sprinting down the sand dunes until I hit the ocean waiting for me at the bottom. But Mr. Ramsey, our official escort for the day, turned in his seat to eye us, particularly me, as if he knew what was going through my mind. "Wait here," he said, his rather large nostrils flaring with the order. "I will inform your guardians you have arrived. Do not move until I return."

He opened his door, letting in a brief, intoxicating rush of warmth and salt-drenched air, slammed it behind him and marched up the worn brick path to the waiting villa.

I drummed my fingers against the leather seat and squirmed.

"Wow," Dante breathed, peering over my shoulder, craning his neck to see the whole house. I could feel his presence behind me, his hand on my back as he steadied himself. "So, it's finally happening," he said in a low voice. "No more private school, no more getting up at 6:00 a.m. every single day, no more being stuck in the middle of nowhere."

"No classes, no study hall, no evaluators dropping by every month to see how 'human' we are." I grinned back at him. The driver was watching us, listening to us, but I didn't care. "Sixteen years, and we finally get to start our lives. We're finally free."

My twin chuckled. "I wouldn't go that far," he murmured, gently tugging a strand of my short red hair. "Remember, we're here to blend in, to study the humans and assimilate into the community. This is just another phase of training. Don't forget, at the end of the summer, we start our sophomore year of high school. But more important, our real instructors will show up, and they'll decide where we fit into the organization. This is a brief respite, at most, so enjoy it while you can."

I made a face at him. "I intend to."

And I did. He had no idea how much. I was tired of rules and isolation, of watching the world go by without me. I was tired of Talon and their endless string of policies, laws and restrictions. No more of that. The summer was mine, and I had big plans, things I wanted to do, before it ended and we'd be forced back into the system. This summer, I was going to live.

*If* I was ever allowed out of this stupid car.

The front door opened again, and Mr. Ramsey waved us forward. But instead of disengaging the child locks, the driver himself got out of the sedan and opened the doors for us. Of course he let Dante out first, and I almost slid across the seat to exit the car behind him. I was literally bouncing with impatience by the time the driver walked around to my side and *finally* let me out.

When my feet hit the ground, I stretched both arms over my head and yawned, breathing in the sun-soaked air, letting it warm my skin. I already loved how this place smelled. Ocean and sand, surf and hot pavement, the sound of distant waves caressing the beach. I wondered what Mr. Ramsey and my future guardians would say if I blew them all off and went skipping down to the ocean without looking back.

"Ember! Dante!" Mr. Ramsey stood in the shade of the archway, beckoning to us. I sighed and had taken one step toward the trunk to get my bags when the driver stopped me.

"I'll bring in your luggage, Miss Ember," he said solemnly. "You go on up to the house."

"Are you sure? I can get it." I stepped forward, holding out a hand, and he cringed back, averting his eyes. I blinked and stopped, remembering that some humans in the organization—the ones who actually knew what we were—were afraid of us. Our teachers had told us as much; though we were civilized and had slipped perfectly into human society, we were still predators, higher up on the food chain, and they knew it.

"Come on, sis," Dante called as I stepped back. He stood at the edge of the walkway with his hands in his pockets, the sun gleaming off his crimson hair. He already looked perfectly at home. "The sooner we meet everyone, the sooner we can do what we want."

That sounded good to me. I nodded and followed him up the walk to Mr. Ramsey, who ushered us into a charming, well-lit living room. Through the large bay windows off to the side, I could see a rickety picket fence and, beyond that, the beach, a long wooden dock and the ever-tempting ocean. A pair of humans stood in front of a green leather sofa as we came in, waiting for us.

"Ember, Dante," Mr. Ramsey said, nodding to the pair, "this is your aunt Sarah and uncle Liam. They'll be taking care of you until further notice."

"Nice to meet you," Dante, ever the polite one, said, while I hung back and observed our new guardians curiously. With a few distinctions, all humans looked basically the same to me. But our teachers had instructed us that it was crucial to see the differences, to recognize the individual, so I did that now. "Uncle" Liam was lanky and wind-burned, with russet hair and a neatly trimmed beard peppered with white. He had a stern face and unsmiling, swamp-water eyes that swept over us critically, before he gave a short, brisk nod. "Aunt" Sarah was plump and cheerful looking, her brown hair pulled into a neat bun, her dark eyes watching us with hawklike intensity.

"Well," Mr. Ramsey said, tucking his tablet under an arm. "My job here is done. I'll have Murray deliver your bags to your rooms. Mr. O'Conner, you know who to call if there is an emergency. Ember, Dante…" He nodded to us, fixing me with a firm glare. "Obey your guardians. Remember your training. Your evaluators will be in to check on you in three months."

And, just like that, he swept from the room, out the front door and was gone. He didn't say goodbye, and we hadn't expected him to. Sentiment was not a big thing among our kind.

"Ember and Dante Hill, welcome to your new home,"

Uncle Liam announced, sounding like he'd done this speech before. He probably had. "I'm sure your instructors have informed you of the rules, but let me remind you, in case you forgot. While you are here, Sarah and I are your guardians, thus we are responsible for you. Meals are served at 8:00 a.m., noon and 6:30 p.m. You are not required to be home for mealtimes, but you are to call to let us know where you are. You should already have the numbers memorized, so there is no excuse not to. Talon has provided you with a vehicle—I understand you both have driver's licenses—but you must ask permission before taking it out. Curfew is strictly at midnight, no exceptions, no questions asked. And, of course, the most important rule." His green-gray eyes narrowed. "Under no circumstances are you to Shift into your true forms. And you are *never* to fly, for any reason whatsoever. With the amount of people, technology and hidden threats, the risk of being seen is far too great. Your old school was on Talon property and they controlled the airspace around it, so the risks were minimal if you needed to Shift, but that is not the case here. Unless you receive a direct order from Talon itself, flying around in your true forms is strictly, one hundred percent forbidden. Is that understood?"

I managed a brief nod, though the thought made me physically ill. How did they expect me to never fly again? They might as well just tear my wings off.

"If you fail to comply with these rules," Liam continued, "or if we deem you unfit for human society, Talon will be informed at once, and you will be evaluated to see if reeducation is necessary. Other than that, you are free to come and go as you please. Do you have any questions?"

I did. I might be completely earthbound, but that didn't

mean I had to stay here. "So, the beach," I said, and he arched an eyebrow at me. "Can we go down there any time?"

Sarah chuckled. "It's a public beach, Ember. As long as you're home by curfew, you can spend as much time down there as you want. In fact, it's a good place to meet the locals—a lot of kids your age go there to hang out." She turned, beckoning to us with a chubby hand. "But here, let me show you to your rooms and you can unpack."

Music to my ears.

My room was on the top floor, light and airy, with bare but cheerful orange walls and large windows. It had a fantastic view of the beach, as if I needed any more encouragement. As soon as Sarah left, I dug a green two-piece bathing suit and cutoff shorts out of my suitcase, not even bothering to unpack my clothes. Talon had provided us with a wardrobe for sunny Cali, so I had plenty of suits, shorts and numerous pairs of sandals to choose from. I guessed they really did care about us fitting in.

But before I did anything else, I carefully dug my jewelry box out from where it was nestled within a pile of shirts and set it on my new dresser. Talon had provided us with everything—clothes, food, entertainment—but this small wooden box, fashioned like an old chest, was where I kept all my personal things. I unlocked the box with the hidden key and gently pushed back the lid, peeking in. The bright sunlight sparkled off a collection of small treasures: a couple of rings, a gold necklace, an assortment of old coins collected over the years. I picked up a piece of quartz I'd found in the desert one afternoon and held it up to the light, letting it glitter in my palm. Hey, I couldn't help it. I liked shiny things; it was in my blood.

Replacing the crystal, I closed the box and checked myself in the mirror above the dresser. A short, somewhat spiky-haired human girl gazed back. After what seemed like an eternity, I had become used to her face; it had been a long time since the human in the mirror seemed like a stranger.

Whirling around, I strode to my door, flung it open and ran straight into Dante.

"Oof," he grunted, staggering backward as I tried not to trip and fall over him. He had changed into shorts and a loose sleeveless shirt, and his red hair was mussed as if already wind tossed. He gave me a rueful look as he caught himself on the railing, rubbing his chest. "Ow. Well, I was going to ask if you wanted to go check out the beach, but it looks like you beat me to it."

I shot him a grin, the same as when we competed against each other in school, defiant and challenging. "Race you to the water."

He rolled his eyes. "Come on, sis. We're not in training any—" But I had already rushed past him down the hall, and heard him scramble to catch up.

Bursting out of the house, we flew down the steps, leaped the picket fence and broke into a flat-out run toward the ocean. I loved running, or anything that involved speed and exertion, feeling my muscles stretch and the wind in my face. It reminded me of flying, and though nothing could compare to the pure thrill of soaring through the clouds, beating my twin in a footrace, or anything really, ran a very close second.

Unfortunately, Dante and I were pretty evenly matched, and we reached the water's edge at the same time. Splashing into the turquoise sea at last, I gave a breathless whoop, just as a wave came out of nowhere and smashed into me, filling my mouth with salty water and knocking me off my feet.

Wading over, Dante reached down to pull me up, but he was laughing so hard he could barely stand. Grabbing the offered wrist, I gave it a yank, and he toppled in after me as another wave came hissing in and covered us both.

Sputtering, Dante rolled upright, shaking water from his hair and wringing out his shirt. I staggered to my feet as the water receded, sucking at my ankles as it swept back to the ocean. "You know," my twin muttered, giving me an exasperated half smile, "you typically take off your regular clothes before you decide to do a face-plant into the ocean. That's what normal people do, anyway."

I grinned at him cheekily. "What? Now you have an excuse to take off your shirt and show everyone the manly six-pack you've been working on all year."

"Ha-ha. Hey, look, a shark."

He pointed behind me. I turned, and he shoved me into another wave. With a shriek, I sprang up and tore after him as he took off down the beach, the foaming seawater lapping at my toes.

Sometime later, we were both drenched, hot and covered in sand. We'd also traveled pretty far down the beach, passing sunbathers and families, though the strip was emptier than I'd thought it would be. Farther out, I could see surfers on their colorful boards, gliding through waves much larger than those close to shore. I wondered, again, what it was like to surf, if it was anything like flying. I made it a priority to find out.

Closer to the edge of the beach, a volleyball net stood

in the sand, and several teenagers bumped a ball back and forth over the net. There were six of them, four boys and two girls, all wearing shorts or bikinis. They were very tan, as if they'd spent a lifetime out in the sun, the girls slender and beautiful, the boys shirtless and muscular. A pair of sleek yellow boards lay nearby, showing that at least a couple of them were surfers. Curious, I stopped to watch from a safe distance away, but Dante nudged my shoulder and jerked his head in their direction.

"Come on," he murmured, and started ambling toward the group. Frowning, I followed.

"Um. What are we doing?"

He looked back at me and winked. "Fitting in."

"What, right now?" I glanced at the humans, then back at my brother. "I mean, you're just going to walk up to a bunch of mortals and talk to them? What are you going to say?"

"I figured I'd start with 'hi.'"

A little apprehensively, I trailed after him. As we approached the net, one of the boys, his dark hair bleached blond at the tips, leaped up and spiked the ball toward one of the girls on the other side. She instantly dove into the sand to save it, sending the white sphere flying in our direction.

Dante caught it. The game paused a moment as all the players turned in our direction.

My brother smiled. "Hey," he greeted, tossing the ball to one of the girls. Who, I noticed, nearly missed the catch from gaping at him. "Need a couple extra players?"

The group hesitated. I noted the way the girls were staring wide-eyed at Dante, and bit down a snort. By human standards, my twin was charming and extremely good-looking, and he knew it, too. It wasn't by accident. When choosing the form that would be ours for the rest of our life, everyone in Talon was groomed to the highest standards of human beauty. There were no ugly "humans" in the organization, and there was a very good reason for that. Mortals responded to beauty, wealth, power, charisma. It made them easier to sway, easier to control, and Dante was a natural at getting what he wanted. *This* was sure to go to his already inflated head. But at least three of the guys were staring at me, too.

One of the boys, lean and tan, with blond hair down to his shoulders, finally shrugged. "Sure, dude." His voice was light, easygoing. "The more, the merrier. Come on in and pick a side." He flashed me a grin, as if hoping I would choose his side of the net. I hesitated a moment, then obliged him. *Fit in, make friends, adapt.* That was what we were here to do, right?

The other girl on my side, the one who'd dived for the ball, smiled at me as I joined her on the front row. "Hey," she said, pushing long brown hair out of her face. "You're new around here, aren't you? Come for summer vacation?"

I stared at her and, for a second, my mind went blank. What did I say? What did I do? This was the first human, not counting my teachers and guardians, who had ever spoken to me. I wasn't like my brother, who was comfortable around people and knew how to respond regardless of the situation. I stared at the human, feeling trapped, wondering what would happen if I just turned around and sprinted back home.

But the girl didn't laugh or tease or give me a weird look. "Oh, right," she said as Dante was tossed the ball and encouraged to serve. "You have no idea who I am, do you? I'm Lexi. That's my brother, Calvin." She nodded to the tall blond human who had smiled at me earlier. "And that's Tyler, Kristin, Jake and Neil. We all live here," Lexi continued as Dante walked to where a lone sandal sat several yards from the net, marking the back line. "Except for Kristin." She nodded at the girl on the other side, blond and tan and model-gorgeous. "But her family owns a beach house and comes down every summer. The rest of us have been here forever." She shot me a sideways look as Dante prepared to serve. "So, where did you two move from? Ever played volleyball before?"

I was trying to keep up with the endless string of words, to find time to respond, when Dante tossed the ball, leaped gracefully into the air and hit it with a resounding whack that propelled it over the net and behind my head. It was expertly bumped to the blond boy, who hit the ball with his fingertips, setting me up for a spike. I *hadn't* ever played volleyball before, only studied it on TV. Thankfully, my kind were naturals at picking up physical activities, and I instinctively knew what to do. I bounced into the air and smacked the ball right at Bleach-tips. It shot toward him like a missile, and he dug for it frantically. The ball struck his hand at an angle, bounced off and rolled merrily toward the ocean. He cursed and jogged off after it, while our side cheered.

"Nice shot!" Lexi grinned, watching Bleach-tips scoop up the wayward ball and come striding back. "Guess that answers my question, doesn't it? What was your name again?"

The tightness in my chest deflated, and I grinned back. "Ember," I replied as Calvin smiled and nodded in approval. "And that's my brother, Dante. We're here for the whole summer."

★ ★ ★

We played until the sun began to sink over the ocean, turning the sky a brilliant shade of orange and pink. At one point, Dante had to borrow someone's phone to call Uncle Liam, as we'd both forgotten ours in the mad dash to the beach. When the light began to fade and the group finally split up, Lexi and Calvin invited Dante and I to the burger shack on the edge of the beach, and we accepted eagerly.

As I sat beside Lexi, munching greasy fries and sipping a mango smoothie, something I'd never experienced before (nor had my stomach, though our digestive tracts could handle just about anything), I couldn't help but be amazed. So *these* were normal teenagers, and *this* was what summer was supposed to be. Sand and sun and volleyball and junk food. No trainers. No evaluators with their cold hands and even colder eyes, watching our every move. The two surfboards I'd seen earlier lay propped on the table beside us; they actually belonged to Lexi and Calvin, and both had offered to teach me. Yep, I'd say my first day of being human was going swimmingly.

And then, sitting at an outdoor table with the sun fading into the ocean and the sky dotted with stars, I felt a strange prickle on the back of my neck. The same feeling I'd get whenever I was being observed by an evaluator, all tingly and disconcerting. It always meant someone was watching me.

I turned in my seat, scanning the parking lot, but I didn't see anything unusual. A pair of girls walking back to their Camaro, drinks in hand. A family with two toddlers heading to the door. None of them were staring at me. But that tingle rippling across my neck hadn't gone away.

And then, a dragon pulled up on a motorcycle.

Not in its real form, obviously. The art of Shifting—changing into human form—was so widespread it was common dragon knowledge now. All our kind knew how to do it. And those that couldn't were either taught very quickly, or they were hunted down by the Order of St. George, the terrible cult of dragonslayers whose only purpose was our destruction. Shifting into human form was our best defense against genocidal dragon killers and a world of unsuspecting mortals; one did not just wander about in full reptile form unless one had a death wish.

So, the dragon who cruised casually to the edge of the lot appeared human, and a fine specimen of humanity, too. He was slightly older than us, lean and tall, with a tousled mess of black hair and a leather jacket over his broad shoulders. He didn't kill the engine, but sat there staring at me, a smirk stretching his full lips, and even in human form, there was an air of danger about him, in his eyes that were so light a brown they were almost gold. My blood heated at the sight of him, and a flush rose to my skin—instant reactions to another of our kind, and a stranger at that.

Lexi noticed me staring at the parking lot, and her gaze followed mine. "Oh." She sighed, sounding dreamy all of a sudden. "G double B is back."

"Who?" I whispered, wondering when Talon had planted him here. It was highly unusual to run into another dragon anywhere; Talon never placed their charges in the same town, for safety reasons. Too many dragons in one spot attracted St. George to the area. The only reason Dante and I had been placed here together was because we were true siblings, and that was almost unheard of in the organization.

"Gorgeous Biker Boy," Lexi replied as the strange dragon continued to stare at me, almost challenging. "No one knows who he is. He showed up a few weeks ago, and has been coming around all the popular hangouts. He never talks to anyone, just checks the place out, like he's looking for somebody, and leaves." Her knee bumped mine under the table, making me jump, and she grinned wickedly. "But it seems like he's found what he was looking for."

"Huh? Who?" I tore my gaze from the strange dragon as he revved his bike and cruised out of the parking lot, vanishing as quickly as he'd appeared. "What do you mean, he's found what he was looking for?"

Lexi just giggled, but I suddenly caught Dante's eye over the table and burger wrappings, and my stomach dropped. My twin's expression was cold, dangerous, as he glared at the spot where the other dragon had been moments before. His pupils contracted, shrinking down until they were black slits against the green, looking inhuman and very reptile.

I kicked him under the table. He blinked, and his eyes went normal again. My stomach uncoiled. *Jeez, Dante. What was* that *about?*

"We should go," he announced, standing up. Lexi made a disappointed noise and pouted, but he didn't relent. "It's our first day here, and our aunt and uncle will worry if we're not back soon. We'll see you around, right?"

"Dude, it's cool." Calvin waved him off. "We practically live on the beach. Ember, meet us here tomorrow afternoon, yeah? The waves are supposed to be sick."

I promised I would, then hurried after my brother.

"Hey," I whispered, lightly smacking his arm as I caught up. "What's with you? You nearly went psychopathic lizard on me, right in front of two very normal humans. What's the deal?"

He shot me a guilty look. "I know. I'm sorry. It's just..." He raked a hand through his hair, the salt making it stand on end. "Do you know what that was, in the parking lot just now?"

"You mean the other dragon? Yeah, I kinda noticed."

"Ember." Dante stopped and met my gaze, grim and a little frightened. Which, in turn, scared me. Dante was always the calm, collected one. "That wasn't anyone from Talon," he said solemnly. "That was a rogue. I'd bet my life on it."

My insides shriveled.

*Rogue.*

The stranger was a rogue. A dragon who, for reasons beyond comprehension, had broken away from Talon, severing all ties and going on the run. This was the one unforgivable crime in the eyes of Talon; dragons who went rogue were immediately pronounced traitors and criminals, and offered one chance to turn themselves in. If they refused, the infamous Vipers were sent to bring them back, to whatever punishment awaited them for such betrayal.

A rogue dragon, hanging around Crescent Beach. Staring right at me. Like he'd known I would be there.

"What do we do now?" I asked. "How long do you think he's been out of Talon?"

"Probably not long," Dante muttered, watching the last of the humans on the beach with an intensity that hadn't been there before. "I can't imagine he'll be around much longer. Ember, don't tell Liam and Sarah about this when we get home, okay?"

Puzzled, I frowned at him. "Why?"

"Because they'll inform Talon," Dante answered, making my stomach clench. "Because the organization might call us back if they suspect a rogue is in the area." He must've seen my look of horror, because he placed a hand on my arm and smiled. “It’s all right. Let me handle this. I’ll take care of everything.”

I believed him. Dante always accomplished what he said he would. I should’ve been relieved.

But I remembered the strange dragon’s eyes, the look on his face as he’d stared at me, the way my blood had warmed at the sight of him. I remembered the heat of his gaze, the instant awakening of something fierce and primal inside me when our eyes met.

The rogue dragon was trouble. Plain and simple.

And I was intrigued.

★ ★ ★

The next day started off perfectly. I slept in for maybe the first time in my life, waking up close to noon to find Dante had already gone down to the beach. I found him with several of our new friends from yesterday, and we spent the afternoon talking, swimming, playing volleyball and eating more junk food from the Smoothie Hut. It was easier this time, to mingle, fit in and be part of this group, though some of their mannerisms were strange. Touching, for example. Lexi was very touchy-feely, and the first time she grabbed my arm, I had to force myself not to pull back, hissing. She and Kristin giggled a lot and talked at length about subjects completely foreign to me. Clothes and shoes and shopping and boys. Especially boys. It was baffling, this obsession with other humans. Clothes I could understand; shoes seemed to be the humans’ equivalent of shiny things and treasure. Maybe they hoarded boots like we did gemstones. That was something I could comprehend. But every time Lexi snatched my arm and pointed to some random human on the beach, I would nod and agree that he was "gorgeous," as she put it, but I couldn't see the attraction.

By the end of the day, however, the ebb and flow of human conversation was starting to sink in, and I felt I was starting to "get it." I confirmed with Lexi that she was willing to teach me to surf, and she promised to take me to a "secret spot" farther down the beach, where it was never crowded and the waves were constant. As evening approached and the sun dipped lower over the ocean, we went back out on the sand and Calvin dug a shallow pit, filled it with driftwood and started a fire. Entranced, I buried my feet in the cooling sand and stared into the flames. Beside me, Lexi chatted away as a boy who had brought a guitar picked at the strings with deft fingers. The fire snapped against the wood, beautiful and glorious, seeping into my skin and warming my face. Oh, yeah. Life was good. At the moment, it was perfect.

And then, my phone chirped sharply in the quiet.

Digging it out of my pocket, I held it up just as Dante's phone went off, too. We shared a glance, then gazed down at the screen. There was a new text from Liam and Sarah, and a cold knot settled in my stomach as I read it.

Come home, it ordered, simply. Now.

Dante immediately rose to his feet, dusting himself off. "We gotta go," he told the group, who "aahed" at him in protest. He grinned and shrugged. "Sorry, family calls. Ember, come on."

I didn't move. It wasn't curfew. Liam and Sarah had said we could go where we pleased as long as they knew where we were. They were only human. What were they going to do, come out and drag us home by the ear? "I'm not ready yet," I told him, making his eyes widen. "You go ahead. I'll catch up."

His eyes narrowed to dangerous green slits as he glared down at me. I knew what he was saying, just from that stare. We knew each other so well, it almost echoed in my brain.

*We have to go,* it told me. *We have to obey the guardians, because Talon put them in charge. Don't screw this up for us.*

I glared back. *I want to stay. I'm just getting the hang of this.*

His gaze sharpened. *You're going to get us in trouble.*

*You go, then.* I shrugged, settling back on my elbows, my intent crystal clear. *I'm staying right here.*

All this passed between us in a heartbeat. But then, Dante stopped glaring, and his expression turned pleading as he mouthed, *Please.*

I slumped. Angry Dante I could handle, but scared, beseeching Dante always got to me. "Fine," I muttered, and got to my feet, dusting sand from my clothes. "Let's go, then." I gave my twin one last glower that said, *You owe me,* and he smiled. With a last longing look at the bonfire and the flames licking gloriously over the wood, I turned my back on the group and stalked up the beach with my brother.

Aunt Sarah and Uncle Liam were waiting for us in the living room, but they weren't the only ones.

As soon as we walked through the door, my primal instincts flared, hissing and cringing as a pair of cold, unamused gazes met mine. They were dragons; there was no mistaking that aura of power and the way my own dragon shrank away, wanting to flee from another, stronger predator. Yeah, Talon might be superorganized and spread all over the world, but centuries of survival instincts could not be forgotten just because we were "civilized" now. And when a hatchling was faced with two scary-looking, fully mature adult dragons, even in human form, it was hard to stay put when all her survival instincts were telling her to slink away with her tail between her legs.

"Hello, students." One of them stepped forward, acid-green eyes piercingly bright. She was actually the scarier of the two—a tall, elegant woman in a black Armani suit, her blond hair pulled into a tight bun. Her male companion, also dressed in black Armani, watched with his hands folded in front of him. His dark hair was slicked back, his eyes flat and cold, but it was the female who radiated danger, even as she smiled at me. Her three-inch heels clicked over the tile as she stopped at the edge of the living room and regarded me as if I were a curious bug that had crawled from beneath the door. "There's been a change of plans."

# GARRET

I crouched in the damp, steamy undergrowth of the Brazilian rain forest, insects humming around me, feeling sweat trickle down my back beneath my combat armor. Beside me, another soldier knelt motionless in the ferns, his M-16 held in both hands, muzzle slanting down across his chest. The rest of our squad, eight in all, were scattered behind us, silent and watchful.

About a hundred yards away, up a narrow gravel road through a sparse, dying lawn, the low earthen walls of the hacienda shimmered in the afternoon heat. Guards wandered the perimeter, AK-47s slung over their shoulders, unaware that they were being watched. I'd counted six outside; there were twice that number indoors, not to mention an unknown quantity of servants. And, of course, our target. The guards and servants were unimportant; casualties were expected on both sides. Taking out the target was our first and only priority.

I spoke quietly into the headset at my jaw. "Bravo in position."

"Good," muttered the staticky voice in my ear. "Alpha will advance as soon as the first shell hits. Hold your ground until the target has shown itself."

"Understood."

The soldier beside me took a deep, quiet breath and let it out slowly. He was a few years older than me and had a shiny burn scar that covered nearly half his face. He'd seen action before; everyone on this squad had. Some were venerable veterans, having several kills under their belt. No green soldiers here, not with what we had to do. Everyone knew what was expected, from the assault team out front to Tristan's snipers waiting in the trees. I looked over my team, feeling a brief ache of resignation and acceptance. Some of us would fall today. When facing an enemy as powerful as this, death was almost certain. We were prepared. All of us were ready to die for the Order. No hesitation.

"Get ready," I told the squad. "We start in thirty and counting."

They nodded, grim and silent. We huddled in the thick jungle, blending into the vegetation. I counted down the seconds in my head, my gaze never leaving the hacienda walls.

*Three,* I thought as a whistle sounded overhead, faint at first, then growing louder and louder, until it was almost deafening. *Two...one...*

The mortar shell struck the hacienda with an explosion of fire and smoke, sending pieces of the roof in every direction. Instantly, the squad waiting on the edge of the clearing in front of the house opened fire, filling the air with the roar of machine guns. Cries of alarm came from within the building as enemy soldiers rushed into the front yard, diving behind cover and returning fire. A grenade flew over the wall, thrown by one of the guards, and an explosion of dirt erupted where it landed.

I could feel the tension in the soldiers behind me as we watched the scene play out. *Not yet,* I thought as one of

Alpha's soldiers jerked and collapsed to the lawn. *Hold your position.*

Alpha squad pressed forward, firing short, precise bursts as they advanced on the house. Shots ricocheted off trees and plaster, men screamed and the roar of gunfire echoed above the hacienda roof. Reinforcements rushed out, joining the firefight, but the target did not appear.

*Come on,* I thought, looking up toward the estate walls. Another Alpha soldier jerked and went down, bleeding in the grass. There was little cover on the flat expanse to the estate, while the enemy guards crouched behind the low wall and poked their muzzles over the top. Another soldier fell, and I narrowed my eyes. *Come on, take the bait. We know you're in there. Where are you?*

Alpha was halfway up the lawn when the roof exploded.

Something dark, scaly and massive erupted from the hacienda, sending tile and wood flying as it launched itself into the air. My heart jumped as I watched the monster soar above the canopy. It was huge, a full-grown adult, the height of a bull elephant and three times as long. Curved horns spiraled up from its narrow skull, and a mane of spines ran down its neck to a long, thrashing tail. The sun glinted off midnight scales, and leathery wings cast a long shadow over the ground as the dragon hovered in the air, glaring down at the battle below, then dove to attack.

Wings flared, it landed on the lawn with a roar that shook the earth, then sent a cone of flame blasting through the ranks of soldiers. Bodies fell away, screaming, flailing, as hellish dragonfire consumed armor and flesh like tinder. The dragon pounced, scything through the ranks with its claws, crushing soldiers in its teeth before flinging them away. Its tail whipped out, striking an entire group coming up behind it and knocking them aside like bowling pins.

*Now!* I leaped to my feet, as did the rest of my squad, and opened fire on the huge reptile. The M-16s chattered in sharp, three-round bursts, and I aimed carefully for the dragon's side, behind the front foreleg where the heart would be. Blood erupted along the armored hide, and the dragon roared as some of the shots pierced through scales, though not enough to kill it. It staggered, and I pressed forward grimly, concentrating fire on its weak points. The quicker we killed it, the less damage it could do and the fewer lives it would take. There could be no hesitation on our part; it was either us or the dragon.

Directly across from us, a black jeep with a mounted .50-caliber Browning M2 burst from the bushes, and machine-gun fire joined the cacophony as the vehicle sped toward the huge reptile. Caught in a deadly crossfire, the dragon roared. Bounding away, it opened its leathery wings and launched itself into the air with a powerful downward thrust.

"Aim for the wings!" the commander barked in my ear, though I was already switching targets, methodically firing at the sweeping membranes. "Bring it down! Don't let it fly away."

But the dragon had no intention of fleeing. It turned and swooped from the sky, dropping fifteen tons of scales, teeth and claws onto its target. It smashed full force into the jeep, halting the vehicle's momentum, crushing the hood and causing the driver to smash into the windshield. The gunner flew from the back and tumbled to the ground, sprawling limply in the ferns. With a triumphant bellow, the dragon overturned the vehicle, crushing metal and glass and turning the jeep into a mangled wreck. I winced, but there was no time to think on the lives lost. We would pay our respects to the fallen when the battle was won.

My squad switched fire back to the dragon's flank. Streaked with blood, the dragon jerked, and that long neck snapped around, a murderous gleam in its red eyes as it glared in our direction.

"Hold position!" I snapped to the rest of my squad as the dragon roared a challenge and spun, tail lashing. "I'll draw it off. Keep firing!"

A couple of them glanced at me, grim and resigned, but they didn't argue. Better one soldier fall than the entire team. I was squad leader; if I died so that my brothers could keep fighting, the sacrifice would be worth it. They knew that as well as I did.

I left my hiding place and started forward, firing short, controlled bursts as I did, heading around the dragon's side. Spotting me, the dragon reared its head back and took a breath, and my pulse spiked. I dove away as fire erupted from its jaws, searing into the jungle and setting the trees ablaze. Rolling to my feet, I looked up to see the huge lizard coming for me, maw gaping wide. My heart pounded, but my hands remained steady as I raised my gun and fired at the horned skull, knowing the thick breastplate would protect its chest and stomach. The dragon flinched, shaking its head as the shots struck its bony brow and cheekbones, and kept coming.

I threw myself to the side as the dragon's head shot forward, jaws snapping shut in the spot I had been. Quick as a snake, it whipped its neck around and lunged again, teeth that could shear through a telephone pole coming right at me. I avoided the six-inch fangs, but the massive horned head still crashed into my side, and even through the combat vest, pain erupted through my ribs. The ground fell away as the force hurled me into the air, the world spinning around me, and I rolled several paces when I struck the earth again. Clenching my jaw, I pushed myself to my elbows and looked up…

…into the crimson eyes of my enemy.

The dragon loomed overhead, dark and massive, its wings partially open to cast a huge shadow over the ground. I stared into its ancient, alien face, saw myself reflected in those cold red eyes that held no mercy, no pity or understanding—just raw hate and savage triumph. It took a breath, nostrils flaring, and I braced myself for the killing flames. There was no fear, no remorse. I was a soldier of St. George; to die honorably in battle against our oldest foe was all I could hope for.

A single shot rang out from somewhere in the jungle, the sharp retort echoing loudly even in the chaos. The dragon lurched sideways with a roar, a bright spray of blood erupting from its side as the armor-piercing .50-caliber sniper round struck behind its foreleg, straight into the heart. The precision perfect shot that Tristan St. Anthony was known for.

The blow knocked the dragon off its feet, and the ground shook as it finally collapsed. Wailing, it struggled to rise, clawing at the ground, wings and tail thrashing desperately. But it was dying, its struggles growing weaker even as the soldiers continued to pump it full of rounds. From where I lay, I watched its head hit the ground with a thump, watched its struggles grow weaker and weaker, until it was almost still. Only the faint, labored rise and fall of its ribs, and the frantic twitch of its tail, showed it was still clinging to life.

As it lay there, gasping, it suddenly rolled its eye back and looked at me, the slitted, bright red pupil staring up from the dirt. For a moment, we stared at each other, dragon and slayer, caught in an endless cycle of war and death.

I bowed my head, still keeping the dragon in my sights, and murmured, *"In nomine Domini Sabaoth, sui filiiqui ite ad Infernos." In the name of the Lord of Hosts and his son, depart to hell.* An incantation taught to all soldiers, from when they believed dragons were demons and might possess you in a final attempt to remain in the world. I knew better. Dragons were flesh and blood; get past their scales and armor, and they died just like anything else. But they were also warriors, brave in their own way, and every warrior deserved a final send-off.

A low rumble came from the dying dragon. Its jaws opened, and a deep, inhuman voice emerged. "Do not think you have won, St. George," it rasped, glaring at me in disdain. "I am but a single scale in the body of Talon. We will endure, as we always have, and we grow stronger even as your race destroys itself from within. You, and all your kind, will fall before us. Soon."

Then the light behind the crimson orbs dimmed. The dragon's lids closed, its head dropped to the ground and its whole body shuddered. With a final spasm, the wings stilled, the tail beating the earth ceased and the huge reptile went limp as it finally gave up its fight for life.

I collapsed to my back in the dirt as cheers rose around me. Soldiers emerged from the trees, shaking their weapons and letting out victory cries. Beyond the massive corpse, bodies from both sides lay scattered about the lawn, some stirring weakly, some charred to blackened husks. Flames still flickered through the trees, black columns of smoke billowing into the sky. The crumpled remains of the jeep smoldered in the middle of the field, a testament to the awesome power of the huge reptile.

The firefight with the guards had ceased. Now that their master was gone, the last of the enemy was fleeing into the jungle. No orders were given to track them down; we already had what we'd come for. In a few minutes, another crew would chopper in, clean up the debris, raze the hacienda and make all the bodies disappear. No one would ever know that a monstrous, fire-breathing creature of legend had died here this afternoon.

I looked at the lifeless dragon, crumpled in the dirt while the squads milled around its body and grinned and slapped one another on the back. A few soldiers approached the huge carcass, shaking their heads at the size, disgust and awe written on their faces. I stayed where I was. It was not the first dead dragon I'd seen, though it was the largest I'd ever fought. It would not be the last.

I wondered, very briefly, if there would ever be a "last."

*Dragons are evil;* that was what every soldier of St. George was taught. *They are demons. Wyrms of the devil. Their final goal is the enslavement of the human race, and we are the only ones standing between them and the ignorant.*

While I wasn't certain about the entire *wyrms of the devil* part, our enemy certainly was strong, cunning and savage. My own family had been murdered by a dragon when I was just a toddler. I'd been rescued by the Order and trained to take the fight back to the monsters that had slaughtered my parents and sister. For every dragon I killed, more human lives would be spared.

I'd fought enough battles, seen enough of what they could do, to know firsthand that they were ruthless. Merciless. Inhuman. Their power was vast, and they only got stronger with age. Thankfully, there weren't many ancient dragons in the world anymore, or at least, most of our battles were against smaller, younger dragons. To take down this huge, powerful adult was an enormous victory for our side. I felt no remorse in killing the beast; this dragon was a central figure in the South American cartels, responsible for the deaths of thousands. The world was a better place with it gone. Maybe through my actions today, some little kid wouldn't have to grow up an orphan, never knowing his family. It was the least I could do, and I did it gladly. I owed my family that much.

My ribs gave a sharp, painful throb, and I gritted my teeth. Now that the adrenaline had worn off and the fight was done, I turned my attention to my injury. My combat vest had absorbed a good bit of the damage, but judging from the pain in my side, the force of the blow had still cracked a rib or two.

"Well, that was amusing. If you ever get tired of the soldier life, you should consider a career as a dragon soccer ball. You flew nearly twenty feet on that last hit."

I raised my head as a mound of weeds and moss melted out of the undergrowth and shuffled to my side. It carried a Barrett M107A1 .50-caliber sniper rifle in one shaggy limb, and the other reached up to tug back its hood, revealing a smirking, dark-haired soldier four years my senior, his eyes so blue they were almost black.

"You okay?" Tristan St. Anthony asked, crouching down beside me. His ghillie suit rustled as he shrugged out of it, setting it and the rifle carefully aside. "Anything broken?"

"No," I gritted out, setting my jaw as pain stabbed through me. "I'm fine. Nothing serious, it's just a cracked rib or two." I breathed cautiously as the commander emerged from the trees and slowly made his way across the field. I watched him bark orders to the other squads, point at the dragon and the bodies scattered about, and I struggled carefully upright. The medic would be here in a few minutes, taking stock of the wounded, seeing who could be saved. I didn't want to give the impression that I was seriously hurt, not when many other soldiers lay on the brink of death. The commander met my gaze over the carnage, gave a tiny nod of approval and continued on.

I glanced at Tristan. "Killing shot goes to you, then, doesn't it? How big was the pot this time?"

"Three hundred. You'd think they'd figure it out by now." Tristan didn't bother hiding the smugness in his voice. He gave me an appraising look. "Though I guess I should give you a portion, since you were the one who set it up."

"Don't I always?" Tristan and I had been partners awhile now, ever since I'd turned fourteen and joined the real missions, three years ago. He'd lost his first partner to dragonfire, and hadn't been pleased with the notion of "babysitting a kid," despite the fact that, at the time, he was only eighteen himself. His tune had changed when, on our first assignment together, I'd saved him from an ambush, nearly gotten myself killed and managed to shoot the enemy before it could slaughter us both. Now, three years and dozens of battles later, I couldn't imagine having someone else at my back. We'd saved each other's lives so often, we'd both lost count.

"Still." Tristan shifted to one knee, grinning wryly. "You're my partner, you nearly got yourself eaten and you might've set a world record for distance in being head-butted by a dragon. You deserve something." He nodded, then dug in his pocket and flourished a ten-dollar bill. "Here you go, partner. Don't spend it all in one place."

★ ★ ★

The long campaign was finally over.

And we'd survived.

Or some of us had. The lucky ones. Myself, Tristan and his

fellow snipers, and Bravo—my squad—had come out mostly unscathed. However, there were numerous losses within the other squads, especially Alpha, the ones responsible for luring out the dragon. The casualties were high, but not unexpected. A strike that large was atypical for the Order; we were normally sent after dragons in teams, not a whole army. Because of the nature of the raid, the best soldiers from several Order chapterhouses had been pulled in to take out the dragon and its followers, Tristan and I included. The operation had required the full might of St. George, especially because we were dealing with the rare adult dragon, and the Order had taken no chances. We could not let the dragon escape and disappear into Talon. After the battle had been won, the army had dispersed, and we'd returned to our home bases to await further orders.

For Tristan and I, that meant returning to the States and St. George's western chapterhouse, a lonely outpost deep in the Mohave Desert near the Arizona/Utah state line. The Order had several chapters set up in England, the United States and a few other countries, but this was home for me and my teammates. Those who had fallen in South America were given a hero's burial and laid within our barren, sprawling cemetery, their graves marked with a simple white cross. They had no family to attend their funeral, no relatives to lay flowers at their grave. No one except their commanders and brothers-in-arms would see them laid to rest.

The ceremony was simple, as it always was. I'd attended many funerals before, watched soldiers I'd known for years buried in neat ranks through the sand. It was a constant reminder and an accepted fact among the soldiers—this was what awaited us at the end of the road. After the ceremony, we returned to the barracks, several cots emptier now, and life in the St. George chapterhouse continued as it always did.

About a week after the raid on the hacienda, Tristan and I were called into Lieutenant Martin's office.

"At ease, boys." Martin waved to a couple of chairs in front of his desk, and we took a seat obediently, myself moving a little stiffly as my ribs were wrapped and still tender. Gabriel Martin was a stocky man with brown hair graying at the temples and sharp black eyes that could be amused or icy cold, depending on his mood. His office was standard for most Order chapterhouses, small and sparse, as the Order didn't believe in extravagance. But Martin had a red dragon hide hanging on the wall behind his desk, his first kill, and the hilt of his ceremonial sword was polished dragon bone. He nodded at us as he sat behind his desk, his lined mouth curved in a faint, rare smile.

"Tristan St. Anthony and Garret Xavier Sebastian. Your names are making quite the rounds among the men lately. First off, I want to congratulate you both on another successful mission. I understand the killing shot went to you, St. Anthony. And, Sebastian, I watched you lead the beast away from your squad. *And* survive. You're both among the best we have, and the Order is lucky to have you."

"Thank you, sir," we both said at roughly the same time. The lieutenant studied us for a moment, steepling his fingers together, then lowering them with a sigh.

"Because of this," he went on, "the Order wishes to send you on another mission, one slightly different than what you've been used to so far. You are both exceptional in the field—we hope you will do as well in a more…delicate environment."

"Sir?" Tristan asked, furrowing his brow.

Martin smiled grimly. "Our intelligence has informed us of possible Talon activity taking place in Southern California," he said, eyeing us each in turn. "We believe they are using this spot to plant dragon sleepers into the population. As you know, sleepers are insidious because they appear completely human, and Talon has trained them to assimilate to their surroundings. Of course, we cannot simply march in and take out a suspect without proof that it is a dragon. The consequences for such actions would be dire, and the secrecy of the Order must be maintained at all costs. But you both know this."

"Yes, sir," I replied when he looked at me. He waited a moment, and I added, "What would you have us do, sir?"

Martin leaned back, rubbing his chin. "We have done extensive research around the area," he went on, "and we believe that a new sleeper will be implanted there soon. We have even narrowed it down to the town, a place called Crescent Beach." His gaze sharpened. "More important," he went on, "we have reason to believe that this sleeper will be female."

Tristan and I straightened. Destroying all dragons was the Order's holy mission, but the females of the breed took top priority. If we could take out a female—a dragonell—that meant fewer eggs would be laid, and fewer dragons would be hatched each year. Talon jealously guarded their dragonells; there were rumors that most of Talon's female population was kept locked away for breeding purposes and never saw the outside world. To find one away from the organization was a rare, golden opportunity. Killing it would be a huge blow to our enemies, and another step in winning the war.

"Yes," Martin said, noting our reactions. "So you both know how crucial this is. Talon's sleepers begin their assimilation in the summer, observing, blending in and making contacts for the organization. You will both go undercover and be on the lookout for any dragon activity, but, Sebastian, we want you to get in close and flush the sleeper into the open."

I blinked. "Me?" I asked, and Martin nodded. Tristan sat up straighter; even he seemed stunned. *Go undercover?* I thought. *To a normal town, with civilians? How? I know nothing about…that. Being normal.* "Permission to speak freely, sir."

"Granted."

"Sir, why me? Surely there are others more qualified for this kind of work. I'm not a spy. I'm just a soldier."

"You're one of our best," Martin insisted quietly. "Killed your first dragon at fourteen, led a successful raid on a nest at sixteen, more kills under your belt than anyone your age. I've heard what the others have been calling you lately—the Perfect Soldier. It fits. But there is another reason we chose you. How old are you now, Sebastian?"

"Seventeen, sir."

"Most of our soldiers are too old to pass for a teen in high school. That, or they're not experienced enough. We need someone who will fit in with a group of adolescents, someone they will not suspect." Martin leaned forward again, regarding me intently. "No, when the captain asked who was the best to send for this job, even though I'd rather keep you both in the field, I recommended you and St. Anthony." His hard black eyes narrowed. "I know you won't disappoint me, or the Order. Will you, soldiers?"

"No, sir," Tristan and I answered together. Martin nodded, then picked up a thick manila file and regarded us over the edge. Briskly, he tapped it against the surface of the desk three times, then held it up.

"Everything you need to know is in here," he said, handing me the folder across the desk. I took it and flipped it open to reveal fake birth certificates, social security cards and driver's licenses on the first page. "You have seventy-two hours to memorize everything in that file, and come up with a plan for exposing the sleeper. When you find it, take it out. Call in reinforcements if you have to, but make sure it does not escape."

"Yes, sir."

"Good." Martin nodded. "I suggest you hurry. There is no set time for eliminating your target, but you will want to flush it out before the end of the summer. Otherwise, Talon could relocate it, and the opportunity to kill another of the devils will be lost." His black eyes narrowed. "I also do not need to remind you boys to be extremely cautious when dealing with civilians. They can never know of us, or the existence of Talon. Secrecy is crucial. Is that understood?"

"Yes, sir."

"Very well." Martin waved a hand, and we rose with twin salutes. "You depart for California at the end of the week. Good luck to you both."

# EMBER

The ocean wasn't cooperating today.

I glared at the deep blue water, scowling as it lapped against the fiberglass board I straddled, bobbing me gently on the surface. I'd been sitting here for twenty minutes, the sun beating down on my head, and the only "waves" I'd seen weren't fit for kiddie pools. I should've listened to Calvin yesterday when he'd said the water was going to be flatter than the caterwauling Lexi called singing. That had earned him an annoyed smack from his sister, but he did have this sixth sense about the ocean, when the waves would be highest and the water perfect for boarding. Today was not one of those days.

*Oh, come on,* I thought at the ocean, at Triton or Poseidon or whatever fickle sea god happened to be listening. *One wave. Give me one proper wave and I'll admit defeat. I'll leave you alone if you just give me one good ride. Preferably before the sun goes down and I have to go home.*

The sea gods laughed at me, and the ocean remained calm.

I sighed, carefully lying back on the slim board and gazing up at the sky. Like the ocean, it was a flat, perfect blue. A seagull soared past, its black-tipped wings spread wide to catch the breeze, filling me with nostalgia. I remembered swooping the air currents, the sun warming my wing membranes, my tail streaming behind me as I flew above the clouds. Running, skating, surfing—they were all a blast, but nothing compared to flying.

Though riding a fifteen-foot wave as it roared onto shore was the closest I'd ever come to that pure adrenaline rush.

I'd be happy if I could get an eight-footer today.

Another pair of gulls glided overhead, mocking me with their high-pitched calls, and I wrinkled my nose. What I wouldn't give to forget everything and go soaring through the clouds with the gulls and the pelicans. Especially now. Ever since *her* arrival, exactly one month ago, when Dante and I had come home that evening to find two adult dragons in our living room.

★ ★ ★

"Change of plans?" I managed as the female dragon continued to watch me, a faint smile on her full red lips. "Are… are you here to take us back?"

The woman's smile grew wider, and slightly evil, I thought. "No, my dear," she said, making me slump in relief. "But, in light of recent events, the organization has decided it would be best to accelerate your training. We—" she gestured back to the dragon behind her "—will be taking over your education for the summer."

"What!" No, that couldn't be right. The summer was supposed to be ours—three months of freedom with no trainers, lessons, rules or responsibilities. The final stage of training was supposed to happen *after* the assimilation process, when Talon deemed us ready for human society on a permanent basis. "I thought the organization sent us here to blend in,"

I protested. "How are we going to do that while learning… whatever we're supposed to be learning?"

My voice came out high-pitched and kind of desperate, and the woman raised an amused eyebrow. I didn't care. The walls were closing in and my freedom, tiny and fragile as it was, was slipping out the window. I wasn't ready for this, not yet. I didn't know much about the last stage of training, only that it lasted several years and was specifically tailored to whatever position Talon had chosen for you. I could be destined to become a Chameleon, the dragons who occupied positions of power in human society. Or I could be shunted in with the Gilas, the grunts and bodyguards to important Talon officials. There were other positions, of course, but the important thing was every dragon had one. *Ut omnes sergimus,* was Talon's motto. *As one, we rise.* Every dragon had a place, and we all had to work together for the good of the organization and our own survival. Only, we didn't have a choice in where that place would be. I couldn't even speculate what I wanted to do when I "grew up." There were a few positions within the organization that sounded okay, that I wouldn't completely hate, but it was useless to hope for anything outside of Talon. I was a dragon. My whole life had already been mapped out.

Which was why I had so been looking forward to the summer, one final hurrah before I had to become a responsible member of the organization. Before I became a full member of Talon for life, which was a very, very long time for us. Three months, that was all I wanted. Was that too much to ask?

Apparently so. Scary Talon Lady gave me an amused look, as if she thought I was being cute. "Don't worry, my dear." I didn't like her smile at all. "I will make certain you stay on the right path. You and I will be spending a lot of time together from now on."

That ominous smile lingered a moment before she turned to my guardians, waiting rigidly nearby. "And remember, humans." Her poisonous green eyes narrowed. "Absolute discretion is key. Be certain that they use the alternate exit to the rendezvous point tomorrow. We want nothing tracking their movements, or questioning where they go every morning. No one is to see them leave, or return. Is this clear?"

Dante and I exchanged a look as Liam and Sarah quickly uttered assurances. *Great, more rules,* was my first thought, followed almost immediately by, *Wait, what alternate exit?*

Scary Talon Lady turned back to me, smiling once more. "I will see you tomorrow, hatchling," she said, and it almost sounded like a threat. "Bright and early."

When they left, I turned immediately to Liam, who sighed, as if he knew what I was going to ask. "This way," he said, motioning us both to follow. "I'll show you where you need to go tomorrow morning."

We trailed him down to the basement, which was cold and mostly empty: cement floor, low ceiling, washer and dryer on the far wall and an ancient weight-lifting machine collecting dust in the corner. Beside the machine sat an inconspicuous wooden door, looking like the entrance to a bathroom.

Liam walked up to the door, pulled out a key and unlocked it, then turned to us.

"Under no circumstances are you to tell anyone about this, is that understood?" he said, his voice low and firm. We nodded, and he put a hand on the doorknob, then pulled the door back with a creak.

I blinked. Instead of a bathroom, a long, narrow tunnel

stretched away into the darkness. The walls and floor were rough cement, not natural stone or earth, so someone had obviously built this, maybe as an escape route. I shouldn't have been surprised. Our old "school," the place Dante and I had grown up, had several secret exits, in case we were ever attacked by our ancient enemies, the Order of St. George. We never had been; I'd never seen a soldier of St. George except in pictures, but there were surprise "emergency escape practice runs" every month or so, just in case.

"Tomorrow morning, I expect you both to be here at 6:15 sharp. Now listen, you two. Where you are going, and what happens when you get there, is strictly confidential. This tunnel doesn't exist—do not mention it to *anyone.* In fact, from the time you step through this door until whenever you return, you are to speak to no one outside the organization, for any reason. Leave your phones at home—they won't be necessary where you're going. Is that understood?"

"Yes," Dante said immediately, but I wrinkled my nose, staring down the tunnel to where it vanished into the dark. A hidden passageway in our own basement? What other secrets were hiding in these walls? I wondered. And was this level of paranoia normal for Talon, or were Dante and I special for some reason?

Curiosity flared, and I stepped forward, but Liam quickly shut the door again, locking me out. I frowned and watched the key vanish into his pocket, wondering if he would ever leave it sitting unattended on a dresser. It would probably be too much trouble to "borrow" the key and slip down the passageway alone, especially if I had to wait only till tomorrow to find out where it went. Still, I was curious.

"Where does the tunnel go?" I asked as he shooed us up the stairs again.

Liam grunted. "There is no tunnel," he said briskly as we stepped into the kitchen. "This is a perfectly normal household."

I rolled my eyes. "Fine. The nonexistent secret passageway that we're not supposed to talk about, I get it. Where does it go?"

"You'll see tomorrow."

And I did. The next morning, I hurried downstairs with Dante to find the door already unlocked for us. Pulling it open with a creak, I peered into the corridor, lit sparsely with bare bulbs every twenty or so feet, then grinned back at my brother.

"Do you think it'll take us to a secret underground cave full of dragons and treasure?"

He smirked. "What is this, a Tolkien novel? I very seriously doubt it."

"You're no fun at all."

We followed the straight, narrow passageway for maybe three blocks, until it ended at a flight of stairs with another simple wooden door at the top. Eager and curious, I pushed it open, but there was no looming cavern beyond the frame, no circle of dragons waiting for us, no bustling, underground facility with computer terminals lining the walls.

Through the door sat a clean but very plain-looking garage. It had cracked cement floors, no windows and was wide enough to hold at least two vehicles. The double doors were shut, and the shelves lining the walls were filled with normal garage-y things: tools and hoses and old bike tires and such. Not counting the secret tunnel we'd just come through, it was disappointingly normal in every way. Except, of course, for the pair of black sedans already humming in the center of the carport.

The drivers' doors opened, and two men stepped out, dressed in identical black suits with dark glasses. As one, they turned and opened each of their passenger doors, then stood beside the cars, hands folded in front of them, waiting.

I eyed the men warily. "I guess we're supposed to go with you?"

"Yes, ma'am," one of them answered, staring straight ahead.

I suppressed a wince. I hated being called "ma'am." "And, there's two of you because…?"

"We're to drive you to your destinations, ma'am," the human answered, as though that was obvious. Though he still didn't look at me. I blinked.

"Separately?"

"Yes, ma'am. That is correct."

I frowned. Dante and I never did anything separately. All our classes, schoolwork, activities, events, everything, had been done together. I didn't like the idea of my brother being taken away in a strange car with a strange human to a place I knew nothing about. "Can't we drive there together?" I asked.

"I'm afraid that is impossible, ma'am." The human's voice was polite but firm. "You are not going to the same place."

Even more wary now, I crossed my arms, but Dante stepped up behind me, brushing my elbow. "Come on," he whispered as I glanced at him. "Don't be stubborn. Talon ordered this—we have to do what they say."

I sighed. He was right; if Talon had set this up, there was nothing I could do. "Fine," I muttered, and looked back at the drivers. "Which car is mine?" I asked.

"It doesn't matter, ma'am."

Before I could reply, Dante stepped around me, walked over to one of the cars and slid into the back. His driver briskly shut the door, walked around to his side and shut his own door behind him.

That left me. Swallowing a growl, I walked to the remaining car, ignoring my driver, and plopped into the backseat. As the garage doors lifted and we backed out into the sunlight, I turned to watch the other car, hoping for a final glimpse of my brother in the backseat. But the windows were tinted, and I couldn't see him as the sedans pulled onto the road and sped away in opposite directions.

The drive was short and silent. I knew better than to ask where we were going. Resting an elbow on the door, I gazed out the window, watching the town flash by, until we pulled into the parking lot of a plain-looking office building. It was several stories high, with lots of dark glass windows that reflected the cloudless sky.

The driver pulled around the building and came to a stop in front of a loading dock in the back. The metal door was tightly sealed, but an entryway stood open beside it, dark and beckoning. I sighed.

Leaving the car and the driver, who still said nothing to me, I walked into the building and followed the long tile hallway until I came to an open door at the end. Beyond the frame was an office, with a metal stool sitting in front of an enormous wooden desk. A plush leather chair swiveled as I came in, and the blond woman in black Armani smiled at me across the floor.

"Hello, hatchling," Scary Talon Lady greeted, lacing perfect, red-tinted nails under her chin. "You're late."

I swallowed hard and didn't answer. One did not talk back

to one's elders, especially if one's elders had a few hundred pounds advantage and the knowledge of several mortal life spans to back them up. The woman's poisonous green eyes watched me a moment longer, and her lips curled faintly in amusement, before she gestured at the stool. "Sit."

I did. The metal stool was hard and uncomfortable, probably on purpose. Scary Talon Lady leaned back in her chair and crossed her long legs, still continuing to watch me with the unblinking stare of a predator.

"Well, here we are," she said at last. "And I bet you're wondering why, aren't you?" She raised an eyebrow at my continued silence. "Don't be afraid to talk to me, hatchling. At least, not today. Talon's senior vice president himself asked me to take over your training, but right now, this is just an introduction. Student to teacher." The faint smile vanished then, and her voice went hard. "Make no mistake about it—after today, things will become much more difficult. You are going to struggle, and you are going to get hurt. It is not going to be easy for you. So, if you have any questions, hatchling, now is the time to ask them."

My stomach twisted. "What am I being trained for?" I almost whispered.

"Survival," Scary Talon Lady answered without hesitation, and elaborated. "To survive a world that, if it knew what you really were, would stop at nothing to see you destroyed." She paused to let the gravity of that statement sink in, before continuing. "All our kind must learn to defend ourselves, and to be on the lookout for those who would do us harm. Who would drive us to extinction, if they could. They almost succeeded, once. We cannot let that happen again." She paused again, appraising me over the desktop.

"Tell me, hatchling," she said. "What is the greatest threat to our survival? Why did we nearly go extinct the first time?"

"St. George," I answered. That was an easy question. From the moment we hatched, we were warned about the terrible Order of St. George. We were taught their entire blood-filled history, from the first dragonslayers, to the fanatical Templar Knights, all the way up to the militaristic order they were now. We were told stories of St. George soldiers murdering hatchlings, shooting them in cold blood, even if they were children. We were warned to always be wary of strangers who asked too many questions, who seemed unnaturally interested in our past. St. George was ruthless and cunning and unmerciful, the enemy of all our kind. Every dragon knew that.

"No. That is incorrect."

I blinked in shock. The woman across from me leaned forward, her eyes intense. "We nearly went extinct," she said slowly, "because we couldn't trust one another. We were more concerned about our possessions and defending our territories than our survival as a race. And so, the humans hunted us down, one by one, and nearly destroyed us. Only near the end, when our numbers had dwindled to almost nothing, did one dragon—the Elder Wyrm—gather us all together and force us to cooperate. We learned to become human, to hide in plain sight, to disappear into the throngs of humanity. But most important, we learned that we *must* work together for our survival. A single dragon, powerful as he or she may be, cannot stand against this human-infested world. If we are to thrive, if we are to have any hope for a future, we must all accept our place in the organization. Alone, we fall. As one, we rise." Scary Talon Lady narrowed her eyes, her acidic gaze cutting right through me. "Everything we do, everything I teach you, will be for the good of us all. Can you remember that, hatchling?"

I nodded.

"Good." My trainer sat back once more, her lips curling in a small, evil smile. "Because it's not going to get any easier from here."

★ ★ ★

She was right. From that day forth, starting at 6:00 a.m. every morning, I'd wake up to the sound of my alarm beeping in my ear. I'd change, stagger downstairs to grab a bagel or a doughnut, and then Dante and I would meet our drivers at the end of the secret tunnel and separate. Once I reached the office building, I'd walk into that same room, and Scary Talon Lady—she never told me her name, ever—would be waiting behind her large wooden desk.

"Report," she would bark at me, every morning. And I'd have to go over what I'd done the previous day. Who I'd met. Where we'd gone. What we'd done. She'd ask me specific questions about my friends, demanding I explain why they'd said a particular thing, or reacted a particular way. I hated it, but that wasn't the worst part of the morning.

No, the worst part was after the "debriefing." She'd order me to the storage room of the building, which was huge and vast and mostly empty, with hard cement floors and iron beams crisscrossing the ceiling. And then the real fun would begin.

"Break down these boxes," she would snap, pointing to a huge pile of crates, "and stack them in the opposite corner."

"Drag these pallets to the other end of the room. And when you are done, bring them back. Be quick about it."

"Carry these buckets of water around the building ten times. When you are finished, go ten times the other way."

"Stack these tires into pillars of eight, one in every corner of the room, as fast as you can. No, you cannot roll them, you must carry them."

Every day. For two hours straight. No questions. No talking back or complaining. Just stupid, monotonous, pointless tasks. All the while, Scary Talon Lady would watch my progress, offering no explanation, never saying anything except to snap at me to move faster, to work harder. Nothing I did was good enough, no matter how hard I worked or how quickly I completed the task. I was always too slow, too weak, too lacking in everything, despite her absolute, number-one rule: no Shifting into my true form while I did any of it.

This morning, I'd finally snapped.

*"Why?"* I snarled, my voice echoing into the vastness of the room, breaking two of her rules at once. No talking back, and no questions. I didn't care anymore. The brick I'd dropped had landed on my foot, sparking a curse and a flare of temper. And Scary Talon Lady, always there, always watching, had barked some kind of pithy insult before telling me to keep moving, faster this time. I was sore, my arms were burning, sweat was running into my eyes and now my toe was throbbing. I'd had enough.

"This is pointless!" I exclaimed, shouting across the room. "You're always telling me to go faster, to be stronger, but I'm not allowed to change?" I gestured wildly to the mountains of bricks on both sides of the room, imagining how easy this would be if I could fly. "I could get this done ten times as fast in my real form. Why can't I do this as me?"

"Because that is not the point of the exercise," was the

cool, infuriating reply. "And you just earned yourself another hour of carting bricks back and forth, only now I want you to count them. I will be keeping track, as well, and if you lose count, you will start all over again from the top. Is that understood?"

I seethed, wishing I could Shift into my real form and blast through one of the skylights in the ceiling. Leave my sadistic trainer and her pointless exercises behind for good. Of course, I could never get away with something so crazy, especially in broad daylight. If even one human saw me, there would be chaos and panic and bedlam and doom. Even if no one believed what they'd seen, Talon would have to step in and try to mitigate the damage, which was generally expensive and something they didn't care to do. The Order of St. George might show up, as they always seemed to appear when the unexplainable occurred, and then someone would have to be called in to deal with that mess. Bottom line, I'd be in a world of trouble.

Setting my jaw, I bent down and grabbed the brick, then hefted it to my shoulder as I'd been ordered. One more hour. One more hour of this torture, and then the day was mine.

"I don't hear you counting," Scary Talon Lady sang from across the room. I gritted my teeth, swallowing the flames that wanted to burst free, and snarled back.

"One!"

★ ★ ★

I couldn't get out of there fast enough. When the torture finally ended and I came out of the secret tunnel, I raced to my room, grabbed my board and instantly headed down to the water. I needed something to clear my head, and riding the waves was the perfect distraction.

Only, the ocean was being obnoxious today, too. It was a conspiracy.

The surfboard bobbed gently on the water as I continued to stare at the sky. A lone cloud, a tiny cotton ball far overhead, hung in the endless blue, far, far away. Closing one eye, I raised my hand and imagined cupping my claws around it as I soared by on the wind. I remembered the sun warming my back and wings, the rush that filled me when I dove and swooped and soared on the currents. Surfing was the closest I'd come to that thrill, and it was a pale comparison. I wanted to fly.

*I bet that rogue dragon can go flying whenever he wants.*

I folded my hands on my stomach, thinking of him. It had been nearly a month since that brief glance in the parking lot, and since then, I'd seen neither hide nor hair of the rogue dragon or his motorcycle. Not that I hadn't looked for him. I'd kept my eyes open, scanning the beach crowds, the parking lots, even the dark corners of the Crescent Beach mall. Nothing. Dante never spoke about the incident, either, becoming evasive and busy when I asked about it. He wouldn't tell me what he'd done, or if he'd even done anything, and it annoyed me that he was being so secretive. If it wasn't for Lexi's confirmation that G double B had, in fact, existed, I might have thought the whole incident some kind of lucid dream.

I frowned. Dante was being cagey about a lot of things, lately. Not only with the rogue dragon, but he didn't like talking about his own training sessions, either. I'd asked him, several times, what he and his trainer did all morning, and his answers were pretty vague. Politics and Human Sciences, learning the different governments and names of world leaders and such. I suspected he was keeping his answers deliberately boring so I would lose interest and not want to discuss it. I didn't know why; I'd told him everything Scary Talon Lady made me do, and he was appropriately sympathetic, but he rarely spoke of his own sessions.

Something moved past me in the water, and I sat up, my nerves prickling for a different reason. The sea was calm, nothing had changed, but I could have sworn I'd felt movement off to the right....

A dark, triangular fin broke the surface about a hundred yards away, and my heart gave a violent lurch. Quickly, I pulled my legs out of the water and kneeled on the surfboard. The fin vanished for a moment, then reappeared, closer than before. Definitely stalking, circling. I could see the long, sleek shadow below the water, the dark torpedo-shaped body coming right at me.

I smiled. Not that I'd be scared any other time, but this morning, I was keyed up and ready for a fight. As it neared, I planted my palms on the board, lowered my head and gave a low growl.

Abruptly, the shadow veered away, the tail slapping a fine spray of mist into the air in its haste to turn around. I watched the fin slice through the water, growing rapidly smaller before it vanished into the depths again, and grinned triumphantly.

*Ha. Bet you've never run into an even nastier predator floating on a surfboard before, have you?*

I sighed. Well, unexpected visitor aside, nothing much was happening on this side of the ocean today. And I'd promised to meet Lexi at the Smoothie Hut. She, more intelligently, had heeded her brother's advice and decided to spend the afternoon sunbathing and checking out boys with Kristin. Never mind that Kristin had a boyfriend back home in New York. She liked to "window-shop" while on vacation, and Lexi was more than happy to join in. The testosterone-ridden part of our group, Dante included, had gone to check out a truck-pulling event or something, so it was just us girls tonight. And though I thought sunbathing and gossiping about human boys the epitome of boring, it was better than sitting out here doing nothing, with no company except gulls and curious sharks.

Lying on my stomach, I paddled back to shore, catching a pathetic little four-footer close to the beach and gliding the rest of the way in. There was a good crowd of people splashing in the too-calm water today, some of them families with toddlers. I thought back to my unexpected meeting in the deep ocean, and though I thought my visitor was probably long gone, I didn't want to take the chance that it could still be hanging around. Not with fat little kids scampering through the shallows, happily oblivious.

"Shark!" I yelled as my feet hit the wet sand. "There's a shark out there! Everyone get out of the water!"

Man, you want to see humans move fast? Scream *that* on a crowded beach and watch what happens. It's amazing the fear people have for a scaly, sharp-toothed predator. I watched the water empty in seconds, parents scooping up their children and fleeing to shore, desperate to get out of the ocean, and found it a little ironic. They were so terrified of the big nasty monster out in the water, when there was a bigger, nastier, deadlier one right there on the beach.

★ ★ ★

After talking to a pair of lifeguards, and explaining that, yes, I did see a shark out in the water, and no, I wasn't causing a panic just for fun, I found Lexi and Kristin farther up the shore, at the edge of the parking lot. They were standing next to a yellow Jeep and talking to a trio of shirtless guys in swim trunks, none of whom I'd seen before. As I approached, that strange prickle teased the back of my neck, and I gazed around, searching for dark hair and a motorcycle. Nothing. I must be getting paranoid.

"There you are!" Lexi grabbed my arm like she was afraid I would fly away. "We were just about to go look for you. People are saying there's a shark in the water!"

"Oh," I said. "Um. Yeah, there is. I mean, that's why I came out. It's probably nothing, though." I glanced at the three strange guys. They were a little older than us, college age, maybe, and not from around here. Except for their tanned arms, their skin was pale and pasty, as if this was the first time they'd taken off their shirts. One of them caught me looking at him and winked. I bristled, but decided not to comment.

"Lexi," I said, turning away from Winky-guy. "Your new friends. Are you going to introduce me or what?"

"Oh, yeah. This is Ember, the one I was telling you about." Lexi waved at me like a game show attendant showing off the day's prize. "Ember, this is Drew, Travis and Colin. They just got here from Colorado State, so Kristin and I were going to show them around the beach."

"Ah." I glanced at Kristin, sitting casually against the hood of the Jeep, one long tan leg resting on the bumper. Two of the three guys couldn't stop staring; you could almost see the drool hanging down their chins. "Well, I don't think you'll want to go anywhere near the water today," I said. "You know, with Jaws hanging around out there."

She pouted, but I was relieved. I didn't like the way these three were staring at us, or the way that Travis casually put an arm around Lexi's shoulders. My dragon growled uneasily, recognizing another predator, as Colin's gaze lingered on me.

"That's okay," Travis said as Lexi blushed. "There are other places we can go. I heard there was this supersecret spot you locals go to hang out, am I right? Pirate's Cove, Dead Man's Cove…something like that?"

"You mean Lone Rock Cove?" Lexi asked, smiling up at him. I wanted to kick her. Lone Rock was a little-known inlet several miles down the beach. You had to take a dirt path from the road to get there, so it was pretty isolated. It was also where "questionable things" happened, according to Liam. Dante and I had been cautioned not to go there alone, and never after dusk.

The boys' grins widened. "Yeah, that's the one," Colin chimed in. "Would you ladies care to show us where it is? We have beer and Doritos. It could be a picnic."

*No,* I thought. *We wouldn't.* "Let's go to the Smoothie Hut instead," I offered. *Where there will be lots of other people around.* "I'm starving, and I've been craving curly fries since lunch."

"Oh, Ember, where's your spirit of adventure?" Kristin sighed, sliding lazily off the hood, making sure to rub her smooth thigh muscles down the metal. If the Jeep were a boy, it would've spontaneously combusted. Flipping her hair back, she gave the guys a sultry smile. "We can take you there," she purred as Lexi bobbed her head in agreement, "if you agree to buy us something later tonight."

The boys grinned at one another like they'd won the lottery. "Well, you drive a hard bargain, gorgeous," Colin said. "But I think we can accept those terms."

I stifled a groan. I didn't want to go; I didn't like these three for some reason. I'd seen how males acted around girls; they often got very stupid and possessive. I still wasn't an expert on the nuances of human behavior, especially when it came to their mating rituals. Maybe this was normal?

I really should've listened to my dragon.

# GARRET

I wasn't terribly fond of these clothes.

When fighting creatures with fangs that could sever ligaments, claws that could rip you open like a paper sack and breath that could melt the skin from your bones, armor was essential. A good flak jacket could take a lot of heat and damage and was better protection than a Kevlar vest when dealing with a dragon's natural weapons. Over the years, however, our enemies started to realize that firearms were just as efficient, and now were just as likely to shoot us as blast us with flame. Still, when forced into their natural forms, dragons always fell back to their deadliest weapons. Our black-and-gray combat uniforms were made of flame-retardant fabric and lined with steel plates; they couldn't protect us from everything, especially a direct blast of dragonfire, but it was better than going into battle with nothing.

The point was, I was comfortable in armor. The more padding and steel between me and my enemy, the better. I'd been through missions where my armor had been ripped to shreds, burned and cut to pieces, and if I hadn't had it on, I would have been dead. I didn't like feeling vulnerable or exposed. And there were few things flimsier than shorts and the loose black tank top I was wearing at the moment. I might as well have walked around this beach stark naked.

"You're sulking again," Tristan remarked from the driver's seat, not looking up from the window. Like me, he wore shorts and a tank top, the picture of a fist with the thumb and pinkie held out gracing the front. Unlike me, it didn't seem to bother him.

"I'm not sulking."

"Right. Brooding, then." He fell silent as a young couple walked by the Jeep, close enough to touch his arm dangling out the window, but he didn't even glance their way. His gaze hadn't left the group at the edge of the parking lot. "We've been here over three weeks, partner," he informed me, as if I'd lost track. "You're going to have to get used to it sometime. This is where that whole adapting-and-blending-in thing applies. Can't walk around the beach in full combat armor, even if there is a dragon nearby."

I knew that. I also knew the Order required us to finish this mission, regardless of my personal feelings. Guns and dragons and fighting and death: that was what I was good at. Long stakeouts in a cheerful town surrounded by civilians, less so. "Do you still have the targets in sight?" I asked, already knowing the answer.

He snorted, again without looking back. "Garret, I can hold the crosshairs on a target for two hours without moving it or dropping the scope," he said irritably. "I think I can keep an eye on a bunch of teenage girls."

I let the jab slide. It had been a frustrating three weeks. Three weeks of research, of watching the beach 24/7, observing the different groups, weeding out tourists, family units, the poor, the employed. From the intelligence we'd received, we knew that the sleeper dragon was young, well-off and it would be drawn to the popular, pretty crowd in order to fit in. The clique that "owned" the beach, so to speak. After countless hours of investigation, we'd finally narrowed it down to a group of teens who were out here nearly every day, and usually together. Any one of them could be our target.

Phase one, complete. Now, we were almost ready for phase two, the part I'd been dreading. The part where I'd have to infiltrate the group, get them to trust me and discover which of them was a fire-breathing monster of legend.

I had no idea how I was going to do that.

"Well, well," Tristan muttered, causing me to glance across the lot again. "Looks like they're about to take off with a bunch of frat boys. That could be problematic."

I followed his gaze to where a Jeep similar to our black one was pulling out of its parking space. Two of the girls, the blond and the brunette, sat wedged between a pair of strange guys in the back. All four were laughing and talking, and had beer bottles in their hands. The other, the small redhead, sat up front, her eyes trained out the window like she really didn't want to be there. Her surfboard stuck precariously out of the back as they squealed off down the road.

I glanced at my partner. "What now?"

He put the Jeep in Reverse and backed out of the lot. "Easy. We follow them."

# EMBER

It was late afternoon when we got to the cove, which was flanked on two sides by a wall of windswept cliffs that sheltered it from waves and casual tourists. The small white beach leading down to the water was completely empty, though if we waited a few hours for the sun to set, that would change. Lone Rock Cove was not a place normally visited during the day, as the broken bottles, trash and *other* things lying in the sand indicated. A single large boulder sat in the center of the beach halfway between the cliff walls and the ocean, giving the alcove its name.

I made a face. I didn't want to be here. The three guys had been drinking most of the way, ignoring the fact that this was very illegal, and had encouraged Lexi and Kristin to do the same. They'd tried to get me to drink, too, and under normal circumstances I would've joined in. But they still made me nervous, and I didn't think getting tipsy around them was a good idea. One of the guys, Colin, kept trying to put his hands on me, and I kept squirming out of his grip, my temper fraying thinner with every attempt. If he only knew the true face of the girl he was feeling up so intently...he'd probably wet himself.

*Keep it together, Ember. You do not want to cook this idiot like a marshmallow s'more, even if he is asking for it.*

"Hey," Drew said, shielding his eyes from the glare of the sun and squinting at the far cliffs. "Is that…a cave?"

"Oh, yeah." Kristin shrugged. "Not much of a cave, really. Just a big hole that fills up with water when the tide comes in."

"Let's go check it out."

"Uh, let's not," I said firmly. No way was I letting my two friends go marching into a dark, lonely cave with these guys. My mind was made up; I definitely didn't like them. Pulling back from Colin, I grabbed Kristin's arm and steered her away from Drew, who scowled. "Thanks, but we really should get home now. I promised my aunt I'd be back by six." A lie, but I wanted to get out of here. "Come on, Lex."

Kristin pulled out of my grasp and rubbed her arm, frowning. "I want to stay," she said. "You two can go on. I want to show Drew the cave."

*So* not going to happen. I glared at Kristin, wondering what she would do if I dragged her out by that pretty but empty head of hair. "We came here in one car, genius. You're looking to hitchhike home if you stay."

"Hey, now." Thick arms wrapped around me from behind, and Colin pulled me back to his chest. "Relax," he breathed in my ear. "You're so uptight. Let them see the cave—what's going to happen? You can wait here with me."

I stiffened, arching away from him. He chuckled, and his grip tightened. "Come on. Don't be like that."

"Get off me," I growled, pushing at his chest. *Don't Shift, Ember. If you Shift and eat this troll, Talon will lock you away for the rest of your life. Plus, you'd probably get food poisoning.*

"Let her go, dickwad," Lexi snapped, finally sensing the danger. *A little late,* I thought, trying to keep his lips away from my face and his hands off my butt. "She said she doesn't want to, so leave her alone. Kristin, come on. Let's get out of here."

The other boys protested. Colin ignored them all and clutched me tighter. "Just relax, beautiful," he murmured, nuzzling along my neck. "We'll have more fun if you relax." Raising his head, he pressed thick, sloppy lips to mine.

My temper and disgust flared. Planting my feet, I shoved him. Hard.

He flew backward and landed on his butt in the sand, a startled grunt escaping him. For a second, he stared at me in shock. Then his face went red, and he leaped up with a snarl.

"Bitch!"

I didn't see the slap coming. I mean, I did, but I wasn't expecting it. In my sixteen years, no one had ever hit me. Annoyed swats upside the head, or taps with a ruler when I wasn't paying attention, but they'd never really struck me. Not even Scary Talon Lady had ever laid a hand on me. I wasn't prepared for the explosion of pain behind my eyes, the world tilting violently, feeling sand under my hands and knees when I fell.

The instant rush of fire through my veins, my dragon surging up with a roar, ready to blast this puny human to cinders.

Lexi and Kristin screamed. I clamped down on my fury, gritting my teeth with the effort not to Shift, not to erupt into scales and teeth and claws and show this human true fear. My fingers crushed the ground beneath me, the nails elongating into curved talons, and I buried them in the sand. My nostrils flared, and my lungs burned with heat as I bowed my head, fighting to stay in control. I knew my eyes had gone slitted and reptilian, and didn't dare lift my head as the disgusting human stepped closer. I trembled and squeezed my eyes shut. If he so much as touched me, there would be nothing but a pile of bones and ash when I was done.

"Hey!"

The shout came from behind us. I raised my head just as something slammed into Colin from the side, pushing him off. He flew backward again, tripped and went sprawling in the sand. Blinking, I craned my head up and looked into the face of a boy.

My heart gave a weird little flutter. I'd been around Lexi for over a month, listening to her gush about boys, watching her point out the "gorgeous" ones. I understood human beauty now, and I'd even reached the point where I could nudge Lexi toward a cute guy, and she would agree that he was hot, but I still didn't get the fascination.

Maybe all that boy-watching had finally sunk in, because this stranger was, to use two of Lexi's favorite words, *absolutely gorgeous*.

He was about my age, maybe a little older, with cropped hair that glinted a pale gold in the sunlight. He was tan, lean and muscular, as if he spent most of his time out in the sun and the rest at the gym. And his eyes. They were the brightest shade of gray I'd ever seen. Not silvery, more...gunmetal. Metallic. They pinned me with a vivid stare, and my heart leaped as he extended a hand. "You okay?"

I nodded. "Yeah," I almost whispered. Making sure my digits were free of scary-looking claws, I placed my hand in his, and he gently pulled me upright. Those brilliant eyes gazed into mine, and my stomach danced. "Thanks."

"What the hell!"

Colin had leaped to his feet and was stalking toward us, his friends in tow. They did not look friendly or charming now. But then, another stranger appeared, taller than my rescuer and just as fit. He had short black hair and midnight-blue eyes, and his lips were curled in a dangerous smirk as he stepped up beside us. Colin and the others halted at his arrival, no longer outnumbering the new boy three to one, and everyone stared at one another for a moment.

"Well." The other stranger's voice dripped sarcasm, and he raised an eyebrow at the three goons in front of him. "Yet another fine example of evolution in reverse. Good thing we decided to take a walk, huh, Garret? We would've missed the monkey show."

The light-haired boy, Garret, didn't move, but his mouth twitched into a grim smile. "And they say chivalry is dead."

"Who asked you?" Apparently, Colin had recovered, though not enough to come up with anything witty. Squaring his shoulders, he stepped forward, and Garret deftly moved me behind him. "You're messing with my girl, *kid,*" Colin said, his face pulled into an ugly scowl. "This ain't your business. Get lost, before we send you to the E.R."

"I'm not yours!" I snapped before either of them could reply. "And if you bring that nasty, slobbery excuse for a mouth anywhere near me again, I'll kick you where the sun don't shine!"

Colin blinked, possibly too thick to realize what I meant by that, but the gray-eyed boy in front of me chuckled. It sounded…rusty, somehow. Out of practice, as if he didn't laugh very often and I had surprised it out of him.

His friend snickered, too. "Sounds like she doesn't want you around anymore," he said as Colin swelled with outrage. "At least, that's how it looks to me. What do you think, Garret?"

Garret's voice went cold, soft and lethal. "I think they need to leave. Now."

Colin lunged, swinging a savage fist at his smaller opponent. I jumped, but Garret somehow caught the arm and twisted it so that Colin flipped over and landed square on his back in the sand, his breath leaving his lungs in a startled *oof!* I blinked in shock, and Colin's friends gave howls of fury and leaped into the fray.

I scrambled back, retreating with Kristin and Lexi, away from the sudden brawl. I wanted to help; my dragon was urging me to get in there and start blasting away, but of course I couldn't do that. Besides, the two strangers were doing fine on their own. I didn't know if they took some kind of martial art, or if they were just badasses, because they dodged, blocked and countered punches with no problem, moving seamlessly with and around each other. The dark-haired stranger blocked a vicious hook, lunged in and drove his knee into his opponent's stomach, bending him over. Garret ducked a nasty right cross, then returned with a fist under the chin, snapping the other's head back. I whooped in encouragement.

In a few short seconds, the scuffle was over. The taller stranger landed a blow across his opponent's jaw that sent him crumpling to the sand, and Garret caught Colin in the temple with a savage elbow, knocking him down. Colin tried to get up, failed and slumped back, cradling his head.

Straightening, the two boys looked at their fallen opponents, then back at us. The dark-haired one grinned. "Well, that was entertaining," he said dryly, rubbing his knuckles.

"Reminds me of so many good times we've had together, right, cousin?" The other boy shook his head and turned to me.

"Do you need a ride?" he asked in his quiet voice, and for some reason, those bright gray eyes sent another quiver through my stomach. "We can take you home, or back to the main beach, if you like. I promise we're much better behaved than these idiots. Even Tristan over there."

The other boy sniffed. "I'm not even going to dignify that statement by taking offense."

I shook myself, needing to stay focused as Lexi and Kristin looked a bit shell-shocked. Lexi clung to me, shaking, and Kristin stared wide-eyed at the bodies sprawled in the sand. "Back to the main beach would be perfect," I told Garret.

He gave a somber nod, but at that moment, Colin groaned and staggered to his feet. He swayed, glaring poison at the two strangers, then, shockingly, turned his furious gaze on me. "You *bitch,*" he spat, and Lexi gasped with outrage. "You West Coasters are all the same. You ask for it, beg for it, then refuse to put out. You're nothing but a whore! You're nothing but a slut—"

Releasing Lexi, I straightened, marched up to the reeling jock, and kicked him where the sun didn't shine.

"That's for stealing my first kiss," I told him as he made a strangled noise and dropped to the sand again, clutching his groin. I didn't know if it was really that important, but all the movies seemed to think it was, and besides, he didn't know how easy he'd gotten off. I turned to the strangers, both staring at me in amazement now, and raised my chin. "Well? Are we leaving or not? I think we're more than done here."

# GARRET

We drove to the main beach, Tristan and I in the front, our three passengers and a surfboard in the backseat. The girls, especially the blonde and the brunette, talked consistently in excited, high-pitched voices, speaking so quickly it was difficult to follow the conversation. Not that I was trying very hard. I already knew a lot about these girls, beginning with their names. Kristin Duff and Alexis Thompson I remembered from the long hours spent watching their group, learning their routines and their habits. And, of course, Ember Hill. I knew several facts about her, too. She was sixteen. She knew how to surf. She spent a lot of evenings at the Smoothie Hut with her friends. But nothing could have prepared me for this afternoon, when she had marched right up to the bigger, heavier frat boy, and kicked him "where the sun don't shine."

At the time, it had been amusing, though I had been too stunned to do more than wince. Tristan had cackled like a hyena. But looking back, I cursed myself for not reacting, for just standing there as Ember Hill marched up to that civilian and slammed her foot between his legs. Not that the boorish frat boy didn't deserve it, but my hesitation could have gotten us killed. For just an instant, with her eyes flashing and her lips curled back in a snarl, I'd thought the girl was our target. That her slender body would ripple and explode into a mass of hissing teeth, claws and scales before she bit the civilian's head off. And that we would be next, because I had foolishly left my Glock in the Jeep and had nothing to defend myself from a raging, fire-breathing dragon except my flip-flops.

*Ember Hill,* I mused, turning her name over in my head. The signs were all there: her status, her arrival in Crescent Beach, even her name. Everything about her pointed to a possible sleeper, except for one thing.

She had a brother. A twin, in fact. And despite their wealth, power, influence and global domination, our enemies only produced one offspring at a time. Dragons did not have siblings, but Ember and Dante Hill were definitely brother and sister. They were comfortable with each other; they argued and teased and fought like normal siblings, but they also looked out for the other, stood up for each other even to their friends. It was obvious they had grown up together. And they looked too alike not to be related. Which meant, despite her fierceness and fiery demeanor, the red-haired girl in the backseat could not be our sleeper.

She seemed perfectly human now, talking excitedly to her friends, sometimes asking me or Tristan a question when the other two let up. All three were extremely curious, wanting to know our ages, where we lived, if we were residents of Crescent Beach or just visiting. I didn't speak much, letting Tristan fill them in on our fabricated history: that he and I were cousins, that his dad's job had brought us to Crescent Beach for the summer, that we had an apartment farther down the main strip. When they pressed me further for information—where I came from, where *my* parents were—I had the answers ready. I'd come here from Chicago. My dad was a disabled veteran, and my uncle had invited me here for the summer. The lies flowed smoothly and easily, though the boy in the story—the one who attended Kennedy High and lived on Mulligan Avenue and had a beagle named Otis—was a complete stranger to me. An imposter, living a made-up life.

I wondered if any of these three were doing the same.

We finally pulled into the parking lot along the main stretch of beach, and the girls piled out, Lexi and Kristin stumbling a bit as they exited the vehicle. Ember smoothly grabbed Lexi's arm and steered her aside, preventing her from walking into another beachgoer, then turned to me.

"Um." Her green eyes appraised me, boldly direct. "Thank you," she said, "for today. For getting rid of those trolls. You and Tristan both. Lexi and Kristin are a little too tipsy to know what could've happened down there, but...thanks."

"You're welcome," I replied, meeting her gaze. "We were happy to help."

She smiled, and I felt a weird twist in the pit of my stomach. Odd. At that moment, though, Kristin's face appeared in the window, smiling as she leaned in.

"So, it's my birthday this week," she told us in a breathy, slightly slurred voice. Ember rolled her eyes and walked to the back of the Jeep to get her surfboard, but Kristin continued to lean against my door. "And I'm having a party Saturday, no parents on the premises. They'll be gone for the whole weekend, so...yeah. Pool table, hot tub on the patio, open unlocked bar?" She peered at me from beneath her lashes, blinking rapidly. I wondered if she had something in her eye. "You guys wanna come? I'll give you the address."

"Ooh, yes, you totally should!" Lexi added, peeking in over her shoulder, crowding the window. I leaned back to give myself some space. "Come party with us. It'll be great!"

Saturday. Today was Monday; that was five days from now, plenty of time to do more legwork on these three, find out more about them. I shared a glance with Tristan. He raised both eyebrows, and I turned back to the girls with a shrug. "Sure, sounds good to us."

They beamed. Kristin gave us the address, then all three strode across the parking lot toward the emptying beach and the sun setting over the waves. I waited until they were out of earshot, then muttered, "What now? What's the plan?"

Tristan smiled grimly and put the Jeep in Reverse. "Now, the real mission begins."

# EMBER

From the edge of the parking lot, I watched the black Jeep pull onto the road, pick up speed and cruise out of sight. Garret's pale hair glimmered once in the dying afternoon sun, and then he was gone.

I sighed.

"Man." Lexi echoed my sigh, leaning against my shoulder. Not long ago, the unexpected contact would've made me shrink back. Now, I planted my feet to balance both her and my surfboard on the other side. "There go two smoking-hot human beings. Think they'll come to the party like they said they would?"

"I don't know," I muttered. In the weeks I'd been here, I'd seen pretty humans come and go. From lean fellow surfers, to suntanned volleyball players, to charismatic boys and sultry girls on the prowl for summer romance or a good time. The three trolls we'd run into today were very much in the "icky" category of the good time, but they weren't unusual. They were here for a finite number of days, and then they'd be gone like everyone else.

Garret was probably no different. A pretty face that I would see only once, before he vanished into the unknown, never to be glimpsed again. I knew that. All the locals in

Crescent Beach followed an unofficial rule: don't get attached to tourists. Summer flings were fine. Kissing and long walks on the beach, making out under the stars, going to parties and doing it in the hot tub, all fine. But never promise, or let them promise, "forever." Because no matter how much you liked them, no matter how perfect everything was, at the end of the summer they would always return home. And you'd be left with beautiful memories and the longing for what had been and what could never be again. Of course, I didn't understand that attraction, how someone could get so attached to someone else. I figured it was a human thing and didn't worry much about it.

Though there was something about Garret that was… strange. Something I couldn't quite pin down. The way he held himself, perhaps, so careful and controlled. Or that split-second look in his eyes right before Colin attacked him: flat, hard and dangerous. He exuded confidence, but at the same time, there was an uncertainty to him, like he wasn't quite sure what to do, how to act. I sensed that the calm, stoic front he put up was a wall, and if I dug a little deeper, I would find a completely different person on the other side.

I wondered if I would ever see him again. And if I did, I wondered if I could somehow break through that dignified shell to the person beneath.

I gave myself a mental shake. What was I thinking? Garret was a stranger and, more important, he was a human. I would not ruin the rest of the summer pining over the—admittedly gorgeous—ghost of a human boy. Especially if I had to deal with Scary Talon Lady for the next two months. My summer was already short enough.

"Probably not," I told Lexi, who gave another heartfelt

sigh and straightened, tossing her hair back. I picked up my surfboard and turned toward the beach, just as Kristin wandered back from grabbing her purse from her car. "Come on," I said to both of them. "Walk me to the Smoothie Hut. I need a Mango Swirl to get this taste out of my mouth."

Later, with the evening sun setting over the water, we sipped our drinks and chatted about the day's adventures, a basket of cheese sticks between us on the table. We talked of Garret and Tristan's valiant rescue, and joked about Kristin's bad taste in guys. Of course, Lexi agreed with me that the three frat boys were absolute creepers, and vehemently denied that she'd thought any of them were cute. But when she expressed her desire to castrate Colin with a pair of rusty pruning shears for hitting me, my stomach went cold at what had almost happened.

*What would Talon do to me,* I wondered, *if I'd killed that human? If I'd Shifted right there and bitten his head off? Blasted him to cinders, right in front of Lexi, Kristin and everyone else?* I remembered the smoldering heat in my lungs, the way my back had itched, ready to burst open with wings and scales. The way my human body had suddenly felt very tight and confined as I'd clamped down with everything I had, trying not to change. The blaze of fury as my dragon had surged up with a roar, wanting to shred that human into bloody confetti.

I shivered, appalled at my own violent thoughts. And, even more frightening, annoyed that I hadn't gotten to Shift into my natural form and pop the human like a balloon. *Wonder if I should tell Dante about this,* I thought, as Kristin said goodbye and left for a "lame-ass family event" and Lexi excused herself to go to the restroom. *I guess I should; he'll probably hear about it from Lex or Kristin, anyway. I just hope he doesn't do the whole overprotective twin-brother freakout.*

And then, I got that weird tickle on the back of my neck, a second before the rogue dragon slid into the seat across from me.

"Hey, Firebrand."

The cool, sarcastic voice rippled through me, stoking a flame to life. It was as if my dragon had never died down, never settled into sleepy compliance. At the rogue dragon's presence, it perked up again, instantly awake and aware. My eyes widened, and I sat back in my seat, staring at him.

The boy across from me smiled and casually helped himself to a cheese stick, oblivious to the heat singing through my veins. "Mind if I sit here?"

I could see the dragon in him, in his near-golden eyes, in the slightly dangerous grin he flashed me over the table, the smile of a predator. I could feel the flames burning within, my own dragon rising up to either challenge or accept, I wasn't sure which. I did know one thing: talking to the rogue could get me in a lot of trouble, both from my trainer and Talon itself. And I didn't care one iota.

My dragon snapped and flared, wanting out. I took a deep breath to cool myself off, and smirked back. "Free country." I shrugged. "Do whatever you like."

"Interesting choice of words." The other dragon cocked his head, one corner of his lip twitching. I noticed he had a tattoo half-hidden beneath the collar of his shirt, some sort of Celtic knot or design. "But it's not entirely free for us, is it?"

I blinked and frowned slightly. "Um, hi, I'm Ember. It's nice to meet you, weird, cryptic statements aside." My dragon snorted at me, disgusted. She knew exactly what he was talking about.

He grinned, and it made my skin flush. "You don't know what I am, do you?"

"You're a rogue," I answered, abandoning all pretense of ignorance. Subtlety was never my strong suit. His grin grew wider, showing even white teeth, and I lowered my voice. "I don't care that you're a rogue, but why are you here? You could get in a lot of trouble if Talon found out. Aren't you afraid the Vipers could be looking for you?"

He actually chuckled at that. "I'm sure they are. But what about you, Firebrand? You realize *you* could get into a lot of trouble just by talking to me, right? If Talon ever found out their vulnerable little hatchling was conversing with a big dangerous rogue, they might pull you back to the nest. Or they might see you as a collaborator, and then the Vipers would come after us both. That doesn't scare you?"

"I haven't told you to go away, have I?" I asked, avoiding the question. Though the answer, of course, was *yes*. No one in their right mind wanted a Viper after them. There were dark rumors surrounding Talon's most mysterious agents, and all of them were terrifying. I certainly wouldn't want a Viper on my tail, though I wasn't about to tell *him* that.

The rogue raised an eyebrow, appraising me, and I met his stare head-on. Vipers or no Vipers, I was curious. Except for my brother and our trainers, who didn't count, I hadn't seen another dragon in years. "Who are you?" I asked, determined to satisfy some of my curiosity. "What's your name?"

"My name?" He leaned back, still appraising, and gave me a lazy smile. "I don't know, Firebrand. That seems like an awful lot of faith to put in a complete stranger. How do I know you won't turn me in? Run back to the organization and tell them you saw a rogue hanging around the Smoothie Hut?" He snatched another cheese stick and waggled it in my face. "That wouldn't go well for me."

"I won't turn you in," I promised. "I didn't before, when I first saw you last month." He ignored me, biting into the cheese stick with a grin, and I frowned. "You were looking for me, weren't you?" I guessed, remembering the way he'd stared at me, golden eyes piercing even from across the parking lot. "Why?"

"You ask a lot of questions."

"And you're not answering any of them." I swatted his hand away from the last of the cheese sticks. "Stop playing games. If you were scared I was going to turn you in, you wouldn't have sat down in the first place. So what do you want?"

He laughed, his deep, low voice sending tendrils of heat curling through me. "All right, you have me there. I'll stop beating around the bush, then." Shaking his head, he gave me an appraising look. "Let me ask you a question. How much do you really know about Talon?"

I cast a furtive look at the other tables, making sure no one could hear us. Or that Lexi was not returning from the bathroom. "What kind of question is that?" I said, lowering my voice. "I know as much as the next, um, person. The organization exists to ensure our safety and survival. Every member has a place, and everything they do is to help our race grow stronger."

The rogue sneered. "Textbook answer, Firebrand. Bravo, you know exactly what they want you to say."

I bristled. "Says the traitor who ran away from Talon and

is living on the run like a criminal. For all I know, everything out of your mouth is a lie."

"Don't kid yourself." The rogue's voice was suddenly grave, his expression darkening. "I know things about…*them*…that you don't. I've seen the inside of the organization. I know how they work. And I'm here to warn you, little Firebrand. Be careful. What they show you is barely scratching the surface."

I thought of my sadistic trainer, her intense gaze following me around the office building, and shivered. "What do you mean?"

"You want answers?" He rose with a shifting of leather and bike chains, gazing down at me. "Meet me at Lover's Bluff tomorrow at midnight." His near-golden eyes danced, and he smiled evilly. "That's past curfew, so you'll have to play rogue yourself if you want the truth."

I crossed my arms. "So, you want me to meet a complete stranger out on a lonely cliff in the middle of the night? Seems like you expect an awful lot of faith from *me*."

The rogue smiled. "Touché." Putting one hand on the table, he leaned in and lowered his voice so that only I could hear him. "My name is Riley," he said, and his nearness made my insides churn. He smelled of dust and chains and leather, and, beneath that, the faintest hint of wind and sky. Impossible to sense unless you'd actually been there. "That's my human name, anyway," the rogue continued. "If you want my real name, I'll tell you tomorrow…if you decide to show. If you're too scared, just don't show up, and I'll know where we stand. You'll never see me again."

"And if I do decide to show?"

He chuckled. "Firebrand," he murmured, his voice going

even softer, "think about it. Two dragons, on an isolated cliff overlooking the ocean, with no humans around for miles and no Talon to stop us. What do you think we're going to do?"

If my dragon was excited before, she could barely be contained now. My back itched beneath my shirt, wings straining to break free, to unfurl and flap away into the sky right then. The rogue—Riley—grinned, as if he could sense my reaction, and straightened, gazing down at me.

"Tomorrow night," he whispered, and then he sauntered away without looking back. Deep inside, something in me mourned to see him go.

"Oh. My. God!" Lexi squeaked, dropping onto the bench across from me, her eyes big and round. "Was that *Gorgeous Biker Boy* that just left? Did he actually talk to you? What did he say? What did he want?"

I shrugged. "Nothing, Lex," I said, feeling bad for lying, but of course, I couldn't tell her the truth. What had happened between Riley and me was dragon business; humans had no part in it. She gave me an incredulous look, and I sighed. "Fine, but don't yell at me for bursting your bubble. He asked if I wanted to take a ride on his power machine." I paused. "Not the motorcycle."

"Oh." Lexi thought about that for a second, then wrinkled her nose. "Ew! So he was just a disgusting perv, after all, huh? That's too bad, he was really, *really* hot."

"Yeah," I agreed softly, standing up, thinking of the rogue dragon's last words. His challenge to meet him after curfew, to *fly* with him, when he knew how dangerous that was, for both of us.

I shouldn't. I should inform Talon that the rogue was still hanging around. That was what I was supposed to do.

Rogue dragons were dangerous; everyone in the organization knew it. They were unstable, unpredictable and put the survival of our race in jeopardy. The rogue could be lying about Talon, just to get me out in the open. My rational, logical side warned me not to even *think* about sneaking out, breaking curfew and meeting a total stranger on an empty cliff after midnight.

Unfortunately, my dragon had other plans.

# GARRET

"You still haven't told me the plan," I told Tristan as we walked through a pair of sliding glass doors. After we'd left the girls at the beach, he'd driven to the nearest gas station and headed to the hugely advertised "beer cave" at the back. I followed him into the chilly interior, letting the doors shut behind us. "The girl's party is only a few days from now. What's the objective for this weekend?"

"Garret." Tristan looked back at me. "Relax. It's a party. There is no set objective. You're just there to hang out, fit in, get them to trust you. Surely you can do that."

"I have never been to a party," I said in a flat voice, which was true. The Order saw such things as frivolous, and anything that took time away from training was not only considered wasteful, it was dangerous. "I'm not sure what constitutes 'hanging out.'"

"I'm sure it'll come to you." He headed to the back corner, stacked floor to ceiling with boxes of alcohol. I continued to glare at him, and he sighed. "Look, just think of it as an exercise. Observe and blend in. Try to think like the enemy. You've done that before, right?"

"Yes."

"It's the same thing. Adapt. Engage in conversation. Smile

sometimes." He grabbed the nearest twelve-pack and tossed it at me. I caught it, and my partner shook his head with a grin. "Poor Garret. He can face down fire-breathing dragons and leap from a helicopter at two hundred feet, but stick him with a bunch of adolescents and he falls apart."

I ignored the jab, holding up the twelve-pack of beer. "What's this for?"

"Forget torture and interrogation. You want someone to spill their guts, share a secret or reveal they're actually a twenty-foot winged lizard that can breathe fire?" Tristan smiled wickedly and picked up another case. "This is the quickest way. Besides, most parties nowadays are BYOB."

"What?"

"Bring your own booze." Tristan rolled his eyes. "Seriously, partner. We do have a television in the bunkhouse. Sometimes, too much training is a bad thing."

"I don't drink." Not that the Order didn't allow it; in a profession as dangerous as ours, they recognized the soldiers' need to unwind, as long as it didn't devolve into drunken stupidity. But alcohol muted the senses and made people do silly, incomprehensible things. I wanted to be fully in control of myself, always.

"Everyone at this party does, I guarantee it," Tristan said. "And you, my friend, are going to, as well, if you want to blend in." He shouldered the case and turned toward the exit. I followed, grabbing a two-liter of Coke for the drive home.

Back at the apartment, I put the beer in the refrigerator and sat down at the laptop on the kitchen table. Opening a secure link to Order Intelligence, I paused a moment, then typed, Requesting subject analysis into the subject line at the top. Continuing to the body of the email, I wrote, Garret

Xavier Sebastian, ID 870012. Requesting detailed background information on potential targets: Alexis Thompson, Kristin Duff and Ember Hill. Location: Crescent Beach, CA. Importance: high. Response: immediate.

Clicking the send button, I closed the laptop and leaned back in the chair, thinking of the encounter this afternoon. My mind kept drifting back to the red-haired girl, Ember. The other two girls I'd nearly forgotten, though I knew I shouldn't write them off so quickly. But Ember was the one that mattered. When she'd first looked at me on the beach, my entire body had seized up for a moment, something I'd never experienced before. I couldn't catch my breath; I couldn't do anything except stare at her. And for a split second, I'd wondered if she knew who I was, why I was there.

Fortunately, Tristan had appeared, and the fight with the college students had cleared my head, though I was still fairly annoyed with myself for losing focus. I was a soldier. What had happened between me and the girl, whatever that was… it was a fluke, something that wouldn't happen again. I knew my mission. I was here to find and kill a dragon. Nothing else mattered.

I had to stay focused. I would not let myself be distracted by thoughts of a red-haired girl with bright green eyes, even though she'd surprised me today and made me laugh. Even though I admired her fierceness in standing up for herself and her friend.

Even though, hours later, I could not seem to get her out of my head.

# EMBER

"Hey, Dante, do you ever miss flying?"

My twin looked up from his desk and open laptop. We were hanging out in his room with me sprawled on the bed, flipping through a surfing magazine while he streamed videos on his laptop. The window was open, and a cool breeze filtered through the curtains, smelling of sand and seawater. The digital clock on his dresser read 11:22 p.m. Late, but I was too nervous and excited to sleep, despite the somewhat exhausting day I'd had. Determined to make up for yesterday's dud waves, I'd dragged Lexi out past the reef this afternoon, and we'd surfed until the sun went down. Of course, this was *after* my training session with the dragon from hell, hauling bags of compost around the building for two hours straight. It took a thirty-minute shower and three scrubbings of shampoo to wash the stench from my hair, and I was positive my instructor got the extrarank bags just to spite me.

Dante gave me a strange look. "Yeah," he answered, swiveling in his chair to face me. "Occasionally. Why? Do you?"

"All the time," I admitted, closing the magazine. "I mean, that's why I love surfing—it's the closest thing I can get to flying, but it's not the same."

"Oh? I thought it was because you loved getting pounded by waves and bashed against reefs and nearly drowning." Dante grinned and shook his head at me. "Typically, you're supposed to start with tiny waves and work up to the monsters. You're not supposed to go charging into eighteen-foot surf on your first lesson."

"Calvin said I was a natural."

"Calvin nearly got his ear chewed off by Aunt Sarah when she heard what happened." My twin's expression darkened. "This was *after* he nearly got his head bitten off by your furious brother when they dragged you out of the water that day."

"I said I was sorry about that." We were getting off topic, and I held up my hands. "Anyway, the point is, I miss flying. A lot. Do you…" I fiddled with the edge of the blanket. "Do you ever think about…breaking the rules?"

Dante frowned. "What do you mean?"

"Well…sneaking out. Finding some lonely corner of the beach, where no human could possibly see us, and… Shifting. Just for a few minutes, just enough to go flying around—"

"No."

Dante's voice was sharp. I blinked in surprise, looking up at him. His face was grave, worried, his brows drawn together in a serious frown. "We can't do that, Ember. Ever. Tell me you're not thinking about it."

My stomach twisted, but I shrugged. "Sure, I *think* about it sometimes," I said, keeping my voice light, uncaring. "But that doesn't mean I'd actually *do* it."

"Good." Dante relaxed. "Because if we ever did something like that and Talon found out?" He shivered. "At best, they'd call us back for reeducation. At worst, they might think we went rogue. Like that dragon we saw on our first day here. You don't see *him* around anymore, do you?"

I studied a loose thread on the blanket. "No."

Guilt prickled. I hated lying to my brother, but there was certainly no way I was telling him about the rogue. The first time we'd seen him, Riley had disappeared and, coincidentally, our trainers had arrived the very next day. Dante never spoke of the incident in the parking lot, evading the question or ignoring it completely when I asked. I strongly suspected he had done something, informed Talon about the rogue dragon, and Riley'd had to get out of town before the Vipers came for him.

Now, not only was he back, he had challenged me to come flying with him, defying Talon and all their rules, daring me to do the same. And, though my dragon practically jumped out of my skin at the chance, the situation with Dante made me a little sad. I'd always told my brother everything before, but there was no way I was letting him in on *this* little secret. Riley could vanish, for good this time. I wasn't going to let him get away again.

Maybe sensing my mood, Dante rose, walked over and dropped beside me, putting a hand on my back. "I know it's hard sometimes," he said as I picked morosely at the string. "But it won't be forever. We should just enjoy this while we can. I don't want to risk losing what we have here. And… I don't want to risk us getting separated. So, we have to follow the rules for now, okay, sis?"

"Easy for you to say," I muttered. "You don't have to go to class with the sadistic dragon from hell. I bet you've never had to haul bricks or tires or bags of dung around the room while your trainer yells at you to go faster. And you're always home before me, it seems." I glared up at him, almost a challenge. "What do you *do* every morning, anyway?"

Dante shrugged. "I told you," he answered, his voice way too casual. "Boring stuff. Politics and Human Sciences. Learning the names of world leaders and their laws and what they had for breakfast. Nothing nearly as exciting as your mornings."

He ruffled my hair, knowing how much I hated that, and I swatted his arm away. It ended in a short scuffle on the mattress, with his arm wrapped around my head, mussing my hair, while I snarled and yelled at him to get off.

"Ember. Dante." There was a short tap on the door, and Uncle Liam peered in, eyes narrowed. "We're going to bed," he stated, which meant it was now 11:30 p.m., on the dot. "Keep it down if you're going to be awake much longer."

"Yes, Uncle," we answered together, and Liam looked at me.

"Also, Ember. Your instructor called. She wants you at your session earlier than normal tomorrow, so set your alarm back an hour."

"What? That means I'll have to get up at *five!*"

"Then you'd best go to bed soon," Liam replied briskly, and shut the door.

I shoved Dante off, stood and ran my fingers through my hair, fuming but still afraid he would hear my sudden, rapid heartbeat.

"Guess I'll turn in, too," I muttered, frowning at my twin to hide my unease. "Since I have to get up at the butt crack of dawn. And don't give me that look. I don't see your trainer dragging you out of bed at ungodly o'clock." He just grinned unsympathetically and watched me from the nest of rumpled blankets. I sighed. “What about you? When are you going to bed?”

Dante snorted. “I don’t know, *Aunt Sarah*. But I’ll be sure to tell you when I’m getting sleepy so you can read me a story.”

“Oh, shut up.” I turned and opened the door. “Smart-ass. Good night, Tweedledum.” A stupid nickname I’d latched on to when we’d first watched *Alice in Wonderland* as kids. I remembered being fascinated by the fat, bumbling cartoon twins, and started calling my brother by that name, just to annoy him. It had stuck ever since.

“Wait.” Dante looked up with a fake pleading expression. “Before you go, could you turn on my night-light and bring me a glass of water?”

I shut the door.

The house was quiet, cloaked in shadow. Normally, a pale, silvery light shone through the large bay windows from the moon outside, but tonight, the rooms seemed darker, more foreboding. I tiptoed across the hall to my room, making sure the light to Aunt Sarah and Uncle Liam’s bedroom was turned off. Dante’s light remained on, of course, but Dante wouldn’t barge into my room in the middle of the night.

Shutting my door, I flipped off the light and leaned against the wall for a second, my heart still pounding wildly. Up until this moment, I hadn’t really known if I was going to do this. Sneak out, break curfew, meet with a dangerous rogue dragon on a lonely bluff. Now, it wasn’t a question. Riley said there were things about Talon that I didn’t know, and I was suddenly very curious what those things were, but that wasn’t the only reason I was doing this. I was tired of Talon, my instructor, my training and their endless rules. I needed to fly, to feel the wind under my wings, or I was going to snap.

Climbing over the sill, I dangled for a moment, then dropped, landing with a soft thump in the cool sand. Straightening, I hugged the side of the house, making my way around to where my bike lay slumped against the corner of the fence. I couldn't take the car, of course, and the spot I was headed was only about five miles away. Not too far. I just had to get home before sunrise.

As I pushed my bike to the brightly lit sidewalk, I paused to look back at the house. Dante's light was still on, but if I knew him, he would be glued to the computer screen. The guardians were both in bed, lights off, curtains drawn. No one would see me creep down the road and disappear into the night, to go flying with a complete stranger after midnight.

*You know you're breaking about a dozen sacred rules here, Ember.*

I shook off my fear. No, no second guesses. I'd followed their rules long enough. Tonight, I was going to fly.

Taking a deep breath, I swung my leg over the bike and pushed off down the street, feeling my doubts get smaller and smaller with every cycle. By the time I'd reached the corner, and my house had been swallowed up by the darkness, they were gone entirely.

# GARRET

"Come on," Tristan muttered from the edge of the roof. "Put some clothes on, man."

I paused in the doorway that led to the roof of our apartment complex, wondering if I shouldn't turn around and go back inside. Every night from the time we arrived, we'd take turns on the roof of this building, scanning the sky, watching for glimpses of scales or wings. A long shot, to be certain, but better than sitting around doing nothing.

Sighing, I closed the door and walked up behind him. He stood at the corner, peering through a pair of binoculars, gazing at the darkening horizon. "Anything?"

"Other than a guy grilling on the balcony in his birthday suit, no." Tristan didn't lower the binoculars, didn't even move as he said this. "Did you get a chance to read the report that came back?"

"Yes," I answered, having just come from the kitchen and the open email file on the laptop. Re: Requesting subject analysis, the subject line read. The body of the email contained the names of the subjects I'd designated and a little information about each of them: age, parents, addresses, where they were born. Everything looked pretty ordinary… except for one thing.

Ember Hill: Age 16. Mother: Kate Hill, deceased. Father: Joseph Hill, deceased.

Both parents, dead. In a fatal car accident, apparently. Everything below that was fairly normal. Ember and her brother, Dante, were born at St. Mary's Hospital in Pierre, South Dakota. Their birth certificates listed them as twins, with Dante being born three minutes ahead of his sister, making him the eldest. They appeared to have had a normal childhood, though there was little information beyond where and when they were born and how their parents had died. Though that might mean any number of things, most Talon sleepers had one thing in common. They were all "orphans," living with relatives or guardians, or adopted into another family. Their human records meant nothing; all Talon operatives had birth certificates, records of where they were born, social security numbers, everything. Talon was nothing if not thorough, but the orphan thing always stood out.

"So," Tristan went on as I picked up the second pair of binoculars and joined him at the edge. "I've been thinking. Of those three girls we met yesterday, did any of them scream 'dragon' to you?"

"No," I replied, raising the binoculars. "They all seemed perfectly normal."

"Yes," Tristan agreed. "And Talon has taught them to blend in. But of those three, who would be the one you would pick for the sleeper?"

"Ember," I said immediately. There was no doubt in my mind. She was pretty, she was intelligent and she had a fierceness that the other two lacked. "But she has a sibling," I went on, glancing over at him. "And dragons only lay one egg at a time. So it can't be her."

"That's true," Tristan said slowly. "But here's the thing, Garret. There are exceptions to the rules. Just because it's highly improbable for a tiger to have a white cub doesn't mean it hasn't happened. Just because whales only have one calf at a time doesn't mean they've never had twins. There are anomalies in every species, so who's to say that a dragon can't lay a pair of eggs at once? We know that dragons are loners, and that they plant only one sleeper at a time. But our own understanding could be holding us back." Tristan lowered the binoculars and finally looked at me dead-on. "What if we accepted the idea that there could be more than one dragon in Crescent Beach? Now how does that girl look to you?"

A chill ran up my spine at the thought. "Are you saying that Ember is our sleeper?"

"No." Tristan sighed. "Not yet. We can't make a move, of course, unless we're absolutely sure. That means you have to see the sleeper in its true form, or have indisputable evidence that it's a dragon. If we guess wrong and expose the Order to the public, or worse, take out a civilian..." He shuddered. "Let's just say we'd better be damn sure we have the right target."

"I'm still not entirely sure how I'm going to do that," I admitted, finally voicing the concern that had been plaguing me since I'd received this mission. "Yes, we have a few leads, but I have no idea how I'm going to convince a dragon to show its true self. I mean, isn't that exactly what Talon trains them not to do?"

I felt very weak then, admitting that I was unsure, hating that there wasn't a tangible enemy I could take down. I wasn't like Tristan, patient, calculating, willing to wait as long as it was required for the target to show itself. I wanted to see the target right then, to know what I was up against, what I could shoot at.

Tristan shook his head and returned to scanning the sky.

"Trust," my partner murmured, "is a very powerful thing. If you can get them to trust you, they'll share their thoughts, their fears, their friends' secrets, anything. They'll tell you if their best friend can sometimes breathe fire, or if they saw some strange creature flying across the moon one night. Everyone slips up, makes a mistake. We just have to be there when they do."

I didn't say anything to that, and for several minutes, we scanned the horizon in silence. I thought about what Tristan had said and wondered, vaguely, how I could get a perfect stranger to open up and trust me when I could never reciprocate.

Suddenly restless, I stepped back from the edge, causing my partner to frown at me. "Where are you going?"

"This is useless." I gestured to the sky. "We don't need two people looking over the same spot. We'll have better luck if we split our efforts. You stay here, keep an eye on the beach. I'm going out to scan the cliffs."

"By yourself? And if you see the sleeper flying around, you'll...what? Take it down alone?" Tristan shook his head. "Even hatchlings are a two-person job, Garret."

"If I see the sleeper, I'll observe quietly from a distance and inform you immediately."

"Charred corpses have a notoriously difficult time placing a call."

"It's not going to attack me right out in the open. And when did you get to be such an uptight pain in the ass?" I walked back toward the stairs, pulling keys out of my pocket.

"I'm going. If you see something, let me know, and I'll call you the instant I spot anything remotely interesting." Opening the door, I glanced over my shoulder. "I'll be back at 0500. If you don't hear from me in a couple hours, I've probably been eaten by a dragon."

"Fine. If you don't hear from me by then, it's because I hope you were," was the reply as the door slammed shut behind me.

# EMBER

Lover's Bluff, as it was called by the locals, was a lonely outcropping of rock that jutted over the ocean, several miles past the main beach and in the middle of nowhere. In the daylight hours, it was a sightseeing and picture-taking spot. At night, it was known as the place where couples would go to prove their love, joining hands and leaping to the foaming waters below. If their love was strong enough, rumors went, they would survive. If not, one or both would drown.

Lexi claimed it was wonderfully romantic. I thought it was pretty stupid myself.

I rode my bike down the narrow road until I reached the tiny parking lot in the shadow of the bluff. At the end of the pavement, a flight of steps zigzagged to the flat outcropping of rock overlooking the waves. A guardrail hemmed in the perimeter, and a large danger sign warned you back from the edge. Not that it did much good.

I left my bike by the railing and climbed the steps to wait. Overhead, a huge full moon peeked through the clouds, keeping silent company. I wondered if the rogue would show; if he would really risk discovery to go flying with a virtual stranger. Maybe he was testing me, gauging how serious I was about breaking the rules, making certain I wouldn't expose him to Talon. Or maybe he was just playing the stupid hatchling, having a good laugh at her expense.

As the minutes ticked by, that worry grew. I'd checked my watch a dozen times on the way here; one more glance showed that it was fifteen minutes past midnight, with no rogue dragon in sight.

*Well, what did you expect, Ember? He's a rogue, after all. Untrustworthy, just like Talon said.*

Angry now, I walked to the end of the pavement and, in defiance of the ocean, hopped onto the rail and leaned over, peering into the roiling water.

*Well, now what? Do I go home? Or do I say "screw it" and go flying by myself?* The thought was tempting. After all, I'd snuck out, broken curfew and had come all this way; it seemed a waste to go back home just because some lying stranger wasn't here like he'd said he would be....

A cry echoed over the distant waves, and my heart stopped.

Backing away from the railing, I stood rigid, counting the seconds, scanning the darkness for any signs of movement. The cry came again, closer this time, and I held my breath.

And then, a massive winged creature exploded through the waves beyond the rail, surging into the sky in an eruption of foam. It rose above me, beating the air with powerful wings, the downbeats whipping violently at my hair, before it dropped to the ground with a crash and another bellowing cry.

I staggered back, even as my dragon surged up with a joyful shriek, nearly bursting out of my skin. I barely kept myself from Shifting right then and pouncing on the stranger just ten feet away.

He was older than me, probably by a couple decades, given

his size. Dragons aged slower than humans and remained hatchlings until our fiftieth year, when we became young adults. In my true form, I topped out at maybe five hundred pounds, about the size of a large tiger. This dragon had a few hundred pounds on me, all sleek muscle and sinew, and though he wasn't nearly as huge as a full-grown, bus-size adult, he was still impressive. His scales were a deep navy blue, the color of the ocean depths, and his eyes gleamed a brilliant gold in the darkness. A sail-like fin ran from between sweeping ebony horns, all the way to the tip of his slinky tail. Which he wrapped around his clawed feet as he sat down, catlike, and watched me.

I gazed up into the narrow, scaly face, and realized he was *smirking* at me. Looking very Riley-like, even in dragon form. Annoyance quickly replaced excitement, and I crossed my arms. Here I was, gaping like a stunned human at my own kind. If Dante knew, he'd never let me live it down.

"That was quite the entrance," I said, only now realizing that I was completely soaked from the explosion of seawater caused by beating dragon wings. Which were now folded neatly over his back, dripping puddles onto the rock. "Would you like me to applaud?"

The dragon—Riley—grinned, showing a set of sharp white fangs. "Did you like that, Firebrand?" he rumbled, his voice low and mocking, and if I'd had any doubts that this was the same rogue, they would be gone now. "Frankly, I wasn't expecting you to show."

"You don't know me very well."

"I guess not. Though it's nice to hear you haven't forgotten everything about being a dragon."

He'd been speaking in Draconic, I realized, the native

language of all our kind. I'd grown up speaking Draconic, only learning English when our human education had begun, years later. I hadn't been *answering* in Draconic, because not only did the language consist of verbal communication, but many words and phrases required complex and subtle nuances to get the point across. It was physically impossible for the human body to mimic important things like tail position and pupil width, so speaking flawless Draconic in human form wasn't possible. But I understood it perfectly.

"You're one to talk," I challenged. "You're the rogue, the one who abandoned everything Talon stands for. Are you even going to tell me your real name? Or was that just a lie to get me out here?"

"It wasn't," the rogue said mildly. "My real name is Cobalt, or it is when I'm in this form. And don't spout Talon's garbage at me. I've forgotten more about Talon than you'll ever know, *hatchling.*"

*"Rnesh karr slithis,"* I hissed back, which was Draconic for *Eat your own tail,* the dragon version of *Go screw yourself.* No extra translation needed.

He laughed. "Ouch. Language, Firebrand." The rogue rose to his feet like a cat and spread his wings. Leathery and blue-black, they cast a dark shadow over me and the rocky ground, making me feel small beneath them. "So, are you all hot air and talk?" Cobalt wondered, and his head rose on a long graceful neck as he looked down his snout at me. "Or are we actually going to fly?"

I raised my chin, feeling my dragon squirming with excitement, with impatience. Turning, I walked a few paces away and then spun back, breathing deep. But I noticed the blue dragon still watching me from the edge of the cliff, wearing that careless grin. I scowled at him.

"Uh, a little privacy, please?" I snapped, and the rogue blinked in surprise. I tapped my foot and waited, but he didn't seem to get the hint. "Okay, I'll be a bit more clear. Turn around."

He cocked his head, frowning. "Why?"

"Because I'm not going to ruin a perfectly good pair of shorts when I change, and I don't feel like biking home in the nude." He still looked baffled, and I rolled my eyes. "I'm taking off my clothes, genius, but I'm not here to give you a show. So, turn around."

"You do realize that we are both dragons, right? I don't care about your human concerns of modesty."

"Well, that's too bad, because I do." I crossed my arms, staring him down. He glowered back. Maybe I was being "too human," but my old instructors had pounded modesty into my head at school, claiming that we could not prance around buck naked in normal society, even if we never wore clothes in our natural forms. "Glare all you want, but I'm not Shifting a hair if you're watching me. So if you want me to go flying anywhere with you tonight, turn around!"

With a snort, the blue dragon stood and, with a display of great dignity, turned around. Sitting with his back to me, he curled his tail around himself again and turned his snout toward the ocean.

"And no peeking!" I called.

No reply, but his wings opened, flaring out to either side, a leathery curtain separating us. Triumphant, I kicked off my sandals and stripped out of my shorts and top, placing them in a neat, folded pile under a bush. Shivering with excitement,

I walked to the middle of the bluff, sparing a quick glance at the rogue to make sure he wasn't cheating. His back was facing me, dark wings outstretched, so he was still behaving himself. Now it was my turn.

The wind hissed over the bluff, cold sea spray hitting my bare skin as I closed my eyes, breathing deep once more. As I bowed my head, all the doubts, fears, apprehension—everything—melted away, and I was aware only of the heat rising to the surface, the dragon finally breaking free.

*Oh, man, it's been way too long.*

With a ripple and a snarl of pain, I shed my weak human body at last, letting my real form uncoil like a spring. My spine lengthened, stretching out with tiny pops and cracks, as if trying to shake off the stiffness. My face tightened as human skin and teeth melted away, forming a narrow muzzle with razor-sharp fangs, bony eye ridges and pale horns twisting back from my skull. Scales covered my body, overlapping miniature shields, the color of flame and sunset and as hard as steel. Rearing onto my hind legs, I gave a defiant roar as my wings finally unfurled, snapping open in the wind like crimson sails. A fierce, savage joy filled me as I gave them a few practice flaps, lifting myself off the ground to hover on the wind. Yes, *this* was what I'd been missing! I felt like I'd been stuffed into a box for far too long and had finally broken free.

Dropping to the cliff, I shook myself and turned to the rogue, surprised to see him still facing the ocean. "Done yet?" he asked, the tip of his tail thumping the ground impatiently. "I would hate to offend your human sensibilities, after all. Oh, and in case you've forgotten, those things in the center of your back are called *wings*. You use them for flying, in the event that we actually get off the ground tonight."

I would've answered, but a blast of salt-laced wind buffeted said wings, teasing them open, and I couldn't stand there any longer. Bounding forward, I leaped the railing, passed the still-sitting rogue, and launched myself off the cliff. "Keep up if you can!" I bellowed over my shoulder as the wind filled my wings and I shot skyward.

Waves crashed below me, sending up fountains of foam and spray as they churned against the rocks. Intimidating from the ground, perhaps, but not from the sky. I climbed quickly, rising into the night, until I flew higher than even the gulls dared to soar. Stars hung like diamonds overhead, and the air up here was thin and cold. Below me, the vast, endless expanse of the ocean stretched on forever, as did the glittering lights of the towns and cities spreading out from the beach. I'd never flown over a vastly populated area before, and was amazed at the amount of lights, buildings, cars and, of course, people. So many humans. And none had any idea that, far, far above, a dragon was soaring over their heads, watching them all.

Something shot by me with a screech and a blast of wind, disrupting my flight and making me wobble in the current. Catching myself, I looked up to where a sleek-winged form wheeled lazily around and glided back, eyes glowing like yellow stars.

"Not bad, hatchling." Cobalt spun and dropped beside me, shockingly graceful. His grin was challenging. "But let's see if *you* can keep up now!"

Tucking his wings, he dove toward the water, leaving a blast of cold wind in his wake. With a determined flap, I plunged after him, and we fell from the sky like rocks, the air shrieking around me. As we neared the ocean, my third membrane slid across my eyes, protecting me from spray and salt, but Cobalt still didn't slow down.

We were seconds from hitting the water when a swell rose up behind us, a wall of water nearly fifteen feet high. Cobalt's wings finally opened a few feet from the water, pulling him up at the last second, skimming the surface. I snapped mine open, too, barely managing to keep from diving snout-first into the churning sea. But we were both in the shadow of the huge wave, and it was starting to curl, an avalanche of foam and seawater and pounding surf, descending right on us.

Cobalt gave a screech of defiance and pumped his wings, shooting ahead of the wave. I flapped after him, keeping ahead of the swell just like I did when surfing, skimming the surface of the wall. As the wave began to break, we banked to the left, following the curl of the wave, and suddenly, I was *flying* in the pipe. Thrilled, I stuck out a claw and traced the wall of water, letting it slide through my talons just as I did while surfing. I could see the end of the tunnel, starting to collapse with water and foam, and gave my wings a final push.

Cobalt broke from the pipe, rocketing into the air with a triumphant bugle. I was right behind him, shooting through the curtain of white just as the wave collapsed with a roar, churning furiously as it pounded at nothing. I howled in pure glee, spiraling into the air after the rogue, every fiber of my being surging with adrenaline.

"That. Was. Awesome!" I panted, switching to English for the last word, as there was nothing in Draconic that actually meant *awesome*. Cobalt, grinning as he hovered in the air, beating his wings in rapid, downward sweeps, didn't argue or even taunt me. "Why hasn't anyone ever tried that before?"

The rogue laughed. "I don't think Talon wants it catching on, Firebrand. They'd have a coronary if they knew we were out here tonight." He snorted, rolling his golden eyes. "But screw what Talon thinks. This night is ours. Ready for another go?"

I flashed him a toothy smile. "Race you to the water!"

★ ★ ★

We "wing surfed" for the rest of the night, cruising above the ocean until a wave rose up behind us and we raced it to shore, breaking away just before it collapsed into pounding foam and surf. It was amazing. It was just like surfing, only better, because now I was *flying.* Cobalt stayed right with me, even through the waves where I thought I'd wipe out. He was shockingly graceful, twisting and looping through water as easily as air, and some of his aerial stunts were pretty impressive, though I didn't tell him that. He'd obviously been doing this a long time.

Still, I was no slacker when it came to flying, either, and didn't wipe out once, though I came really close a few times. It helped that I wasn't bound to a surfboard when racing monster waves in dragon form and could always fly away when I thought I might eat it.

Finally Cobalt broke away to perch on a boulder jutting up from the water, beckoning me over with a claw. Reluctantly, I flapped up to join him, digging my talons into the jagged stone and sinking to my haunches, facing the rogue.

"What's the matter?" I teased as waves crashed into the

rock, drenching me with spray. I didn't want to stop. I hadn't had nearly enough. "Getting tired already?"

He flashed me a knowing smile and folded his wings comfortably behind him. "Don't get too big for your fire gland, hatchling," he warned, though it lacked the bite of before. "I just wanted to point out that sunrise is about two hours away. And that if your guardians are early risers, you should probably flap on home soon, before they wake up."

I jumped and looked to the eastern horizon, where a faint blue glow had snuck up and chased away the stars. The dragon bravado shriveled a little, and my human sensibilities rose up to take its place. "Oh, crap! What time is it? Did we really stay out all night?"

"And then some." Cobalt regarded me with intense, half-lidded eyes. "And I bet you've never had so much fun breaking the rules. So, what were you saying about rogues again?"

I scowled at him. "You never answered any of my questions, either. Or was that your plan all along?"

"Pretty much." The rogue's grin was smug, and I bristled. "Don't glare at me, Firebrand. You know asking questions was the last thing on your mind. Now you have an excuse to do this again."

*Again?* Could I do this again? Once was risky enough; I had snuck out of the house, Shifted into dragon form and had gone flying after midnight with a rogue. Just one of those offenses was enough to get me sent back to Talon. "What makes you think there will be a next time?" I challenged.

"Because I know you're curious." Cobalt's voice turned somber. "Because you're exactly like me—you don't want your whole life planned out. You're tired of following Talon's rules, of not having any say in your future. You want to know who Talon really is, but it's even more than that, isn't it? You want to be free." His eyes gleamed, golden and brilliant in the shadows. "And I can show you how."

A chill crept up my spine. Sneaking out was one thing, but this? "That's treason," I whispered. Cobalt shrugged, making his wings ripple.

"You're sitting here in your real form talking to a rogue. I think we're a little past breaking the rules."

He had a point. Still, I wasn't about to let him get the upper hand. I'd come here for a reason. It had been forgotten in the thrill of flying and breaking a half dozen Talon rules tonight, but I wasn't about to give up.

"You promised me answers," I insisted, well aware of the passing of time, of every second that ticked by. I had to go soon, or I'd be in a world of trouble. "You said you had information about Talon. Were you telling the truth, or was that just a ploy to get me out here?"

"I do have information," Cobalt said. "This was more of a test to see how badly you wanted it. Congratulations, hatchling, you passed. Next time, I just might share some of it."

"I don't believe you," I shot back. "If you're really so well informed about Talon, tell me something I don't know."

"How about the code to the secret room in your guardian's basement?"

I snorted. "You mean the tunnel out of the house?" I asked. "The one we use every day to meet our trainers? I already know about that. Nothing earth-shattering there."

The rogue's grin stayed smug. "I'm not talking about the tunnel, Firebrand," he said quietly. "I'm talking about the command room. Every Talon base has a secret room where the guardians report in, receive orders from the organization and keep them updated about your progress. That's their real job—to report any suspicious activity to Talon. If you set one toe out of line, it goes straight to the organization, and Talon swoops in faster than you can blink." I stared at him, and he settled back on the rock, watching me lazily. "The room is behind a secret door in the basement, and the only way in is to punch in the special code on the panel beside it. If you ask nicely, I'll give it to you."

"*How* do you know all this?"

He chuckled. "I told you, Firebrand. I've been around." I gave him a skeptical look, and he held my gaze. "I have my ways, don't worry about that. But that doesn't answer my question. Do you want the code or not? It changes every few weeks, so you'll have to move fast if you want to use it."

I debated with myself a moment longer, wondering if he was telling the truth or pulling my leg. But if there *was* a secret room… I was curious. I wanted to know what Liam and Sarah were telling Talon behind closed doors. "Let's hear it," I growled at last.

Cobalt recited a string of numbers and made me repeat them a couple times to make certain I remembered. "And are you sure this will get me in?" I asked when we were finished.

He shrugged one scaly shoulder. "Go check it out yourself if you don't believe me. Just make sure they don't catch you snooping around. Talon doesn't like that." He bared his fangs in a brief, humorless smile before sobering. "I can tell you more, of course. This is only the beginning. But if you want me to share all Talon's dirty little secrets, you're going to have to meet me again."

"When?" I asked, impatient. "Tomorrow?"

"Not tomorrow," Cobalt said. "Or the next night, or any

night this week. We don't have to set a time or a place. Just promise that you'll meet me again, one dragon to another. I'll tell you everything about Talon then."

I snorted. "Fine. But you'd better not up and vanish into thin air again." He just grinned, and I narrowed my eyes. "How will I know where to meet you if you won't tell me where you are?"

"Oh, don't worry, Firebrand." Stepping back, the rogue dragon opened his wings, casting a dark shadow over the rocks. His eyes gleamed yellow as he gazed down at me. "I'll find you."

And he launched himself into the air, his wings blasting me with wind and spray. I craned my neck up, watching his sleek form get smaller and smaller, as the blue dragon soared over the pounding waves and vanished into the night.

# GARRET

No luck.

Lowering the binoculars, I tossed them to the seat beside me, put the Jeep in Reverse and pulled away from the railing, heading back to the road. That was the third lonely cliff I'd staked out tonight, scanning the sky with the night vision lens, and the only movement I'd seen belonged to planes and a lone pelican swooping over the water. No hint of a flying reptile anywhere.

My phone rang as I pulled onto the main road; I snatched it from where it lay on the dash and held it up. Tristan's voice buzzed in my ear. "Anything?"

"Negative. I tried three different spots, but there was no movement. If the sleeper is still out there, it won't be flying around in the daytime."

"All right." Tristan sighed, sounding frustrated. "I didn't see anything, either. Come on back."

I hung up, feeling frustrated, as well. We'd been here nearly a month and still had no real leads. And the summer was flying by quickly. If it ended without a kill, the sleeper could be relocated and our target would be lost. I couldn't allow that. I'd never failed a mission before, and I wasn't about to now.

As I turned onto another street, movement in the headlight beams caught my attention. A body was jogging down the sidewalk on the right, pushing a bicycle. Bright red hair gleamed in the headlights, and my heart jumped.

*Ember?*

I shook my head, annoyed with myself. The girl had been on my mind most of the day. In fact, one of the main reasons I'd decided to leave the apartment tonight and hunt for dragons was to focus on something else. Something that wasn't her. I didn't like this instant excitement, the sudden hope in seeing a random civilian and thinking that it might be the red-haired girl I'd met yesterday afternoon.

But, just to be certain, I pulled alongside the girl and slowed, then blinked in surprise. It *was* Ember, striding down the sidewalk with a mountain bike, looking like she was in a hurry. The bike's front tire was flat, and the girl did not look pleased.

Suspicion flared then, replacing everything else. Why was she out so late? Why was she alone? One possible answer rose to mind: she was the sleeper dragon, returning from a night of flying around. Yes, she had a brother but...perhaps that was Talon's newest ruse. A ploy to throw us off. Or an anomaly, like Tristan said. And if that was the case, then Ember Hill suddenly demanded a lot more attention.

I eased over to the curb, slowing even more. A Corvette swung around me with an irritable beep, but I ignored it. "Ember," I called. "Over here."

She looked up, green eyes widening. "Garret? Oh, wow, small world!" She did not slow down, and I tapped the gas pedal to keep up. "What are you doing up so early?"

*I could ask you the same.* "Couldn't sleep." I did not specify why. "Went for a drive. What about you?"

"Me? Oh, I like to go biking early, before I hit the water. Clears my head, you know?" The answer was swift and immediate, no hesitation on her part, even as she quickened her pace. "Nothing worse than being distracted when a twelve-foot wall of water is crashing down on you. It's nice to get up early, work everything out of your system."

Except I'd never seen her out in the early morning, biking, on the beach with her friends, anywhere. Until about 9:00 or 10:00 a.m., she was nowhere to be found.

"Unfortunately," Ember continued, oblivious to my suspicion, "I blew out a tire, so now I have to hurry home, before Dante yells at me for taking his bike without permission, again."

*Perfect opening.* "Hop in," I told her, jerking my head at the rear seat. "Put the bike in the back, it should fit. I'll take you home."

"Really?" Her eyes lit up. "Are you sure?"

I nodded, pulling to the curb. Ember beamed, wrangled the bike into the back, then slid into the passenger seat. I quickly hid the binoculars in the glove compartment before she got in, and we started down the road.

"Thanks for this," she said, after giving me the address of her house, which I already knew but of course didn't mention. "Jeez, that's twice now you've shown up to rescue me. Are you some sort of knight in training or something?"

I shifted uncomfortably, as that statement was closer to the truth than she knew, and didn't answer. Ember watched me a moment, then smiled. "Where's your cousin?" she asked, tilting her head. "Did he not want to go sightseeing?"

"He's back at the apartment," I replied. "Sleeping."

"Not an early bird, I take it." She gazed out the window, toward the coastline, and I snuck a glance at her. "Well, his loss. I wish I could get out on the ocean more often. It's so peaceful right before the sun comes up. Just you and the waves." She looked back at me, smiling again, and something in her eyes made my stomach twist. "Oh, well. Sleeping in is nice, too, and I'm kinda glad it was just you who showed up this morning."

I gazed down the road, not knowing what to say. My whole life, I'd been trained to fight; I knew guns and weapons and combat, how to kill a man twenty different ways, how to shoot a dragon's fire gland to cripple it. I even had special training in infiltration: blending in, being invisible. But this was completely different. Nothing had prepared me for talking to a teenage girl in the front seat of my car.

*Adapt,* Tristan had told me before. *This is no different than any other mission. Talk to them. Engage in conversation. Get them to trust you.*

I groped for something, anything, to keep her talking. Remembering the surfboard in the back of the Jeep yesterday, I asked, "So…you like surfing?"

"Oh, yeah," was the eager, sincere reply. "I love it. The wind, the waves, the excitement of barreling down a huge wall of water before it pounds you into the sand. Nothing compares, really."

"It sounds pretty amazing," I said, not having to lie about that, because it did. "I've always wanted to try."

And then, I had an idea. One that Tristan, had he been here, would have been proud of.

"Could you teach me?" I asked the girl.

Ember blinked. "To surf?" she asked, and I nodded. "I guess so, I mean…" She cocked her head at me with an appraising look. "You really want me to teach you?"

"Is there a reason I shouldn't?"

"No, it's just…" She shrugged. "It's not like I'm an expert. I've just been surfing about a month myself. I'm not sure how great of an instructor I'll be. You should really ask Calvin, he teaches this stuff for a living."

"I'd rather it be you," I said. Calvin and Lexi had lived in Crescent Beach their whole lives and were no longer on our suspect list. Ember was an unknown, a mystery. If I could get her to trust me, enough to let me into her house or room, we'd be one step closer to finding the sleeper.

That was the reason I told myself, anyway.

"Well…" She pondered the question a moment more, then grinned, making her eyes flash. "All right. I'll do it, but don't say I didn't warn you. If Lexi were here, she'd be telling you all kinds of horror stories about me and surfing."

"How much?"

She frowned. "What?"

"The surf shop next to our apartment offers lessons," I explained to her confused expression. "It isn't free. They charge a hundred and fifty an hour for a private session."

"Really?" For just a moment, a thoughtful, eager look crossed her face, as if she was imagining all the money she could make with this information. Dragons were extreme acquisitionists, power hungry and eternally greedy. Acquiring wealth was the only thing they cared about.

But Ember shook herself, and the eager look faded into one of disgust. "Don't be silly," she said, waving it off. "Calvin and Lexi taught me with no strings attached. I'm not going to charge anything for teaching something I love to do."

That surprised me, but I kept my expression neutral. "All right, fair enough." I nodded. "When can you do it?"

"Hmm." She scrunched up her forehead, thinking. "How about this afternoon," she said as we pulled into a well-kept subdivision close to the main beach. "Meet me at the Smoothie Hut at two, no…better make it three o' clock, and I'll give you your own private surf lesson. That is, if you're not afraid of getting pounded a few times." She grinned, looking sly. "You're a good swimmer, right?"

I glanced at her. "Yes, but isn't it customary to start small and work your way up to the big waves?" She continued to flash me that slightly evil grin, and I raised an eyebrow. "Or is this free 'lesson' just to watch me make a fool of myself?"

"No, it's to see if you really want to do this," she answered, abruptly serious. "Surfing isn't for the faint of heart. You're going to wipe out, and you're going to get your ass kicked by the ocean a few times. But don't worry." She smiled, and her green eyes sparkled as she looked up at me. "I'll be gentle."

"I look forward to it."

She grinned, but then a shadow crossed her face and she pointed to the sidewalk. "Um, you can let me off at that corner," she directed, looking nervously up the road. "No need to drive me all the way to the house. I can make it home from here."

I was puzzled but didn't argue. Pulling to a stop at the corner, I hopped out and grabbed the bike from the backseat, then set it before her on the sidewalk.

"Thanks." She reached for the handlebars, but one of her hands came to rest over mine before I could pull back, sending a jolt racing up my arm. "I owe you one. You're a lifesaver. Really."

My heart pounded, and I swiftly drew my arm back, all my senses buzzing like crazy. Ember didn't seem to notice and started pushing the bike down the sidewalk. "I'll see you this afternoon at three," she called over her shoulder. "And if you don't show, I'll just assume you got scared of the big bad waves and chickened out."

"I'll be there," I replied. Waves didn't scare me. They were big, they were violent, and if you made one wrong move they could easily crush you. Very much like a dragon. I wasn't afraid of dragons. I respected them, and I knew that, one day, one of the savage creatures would probably kill me, but I wasn't afraid of them. Ancient reptiles, fighting, killing and death, odd as it might seem, were familiar and comfortable.

What *wasn't* familiar was the way my skin prickled when Ember smiled at me, the odd pulling sensation in my stomach when her gaze met mine. The way my throat was suddenly dry as she walked away, her lithe body swaying as she broke into an easy jog, loping down the sidewalk. I watched her, unable to tear my eyes away, until she turned a corner and was gone.

With a mental shake, I hopped back in the Jeep and wrenched the key in the ignition, trying to gather my thoughts. Dammit, what was wrong with me? That was twice now I'd lost my focus around that girl. It had to stop. This was a mission, and Ember was part of the objective. I could not lower my guard. I wasn't here to surf, or go to parties, or talk to an intriguing red-haired girl who didn't hesitate to kick bullies in the crotch or tackle giant waves. I was here to find a dragon, flush it into the open and kill it.

And if Ember was the sleeper…

*Remember your mission, soldier. Do not lose sight of it again.*

Putting the Jeep in Drive, I headed home.

★ ★ ★

"That took longer than expected," Tristan said as I walked through the door of the apartment, tossing the keys on the counter. "Did you get lost on your way back? Maybe take a detour to the Smoothie Hut?"

"No," I muttered, though mention of the Smoothie Hut made my stomach clench with nerves…and anticipation. "But I think I have a lead."

# EMBER

*Made it.*

The house was still dark as I ditched the bike, unlocked the front door and crept down the silent hallway, sparing a quick glance at the clock on the wall: 4:52 a.m. Close, but I was home free. Liam and Sarah weren't up yet; all I had to do was climb the stairs, slip into bed, and they would never know what had happened.

At the edge of the kitchen, however, I stopped. The basement door was just a few feet away, taunting me. The secret room was down there, hiding any number of secrets about Talon, my trainer, maybe even me.

I slipped across the linoleum to the basement door, hesitated and put a hand on the knob.

Just as something grabbed my arm.

I jumped a foot in the air and whirled around. "Dante!" I squeaked as my twin stared back at me, a grave look on his face. "Jeez, give me a heart attack, why don't you?" My heart pounded, but I forced myself not to panic. "What are you doing up?" I whispered. "You're supposed to be asleep, stalker."

"Come on, sis. It's me." Dante's voice was low, angry. "You've never been able to hide anything from me. I don't know why you thought you'd be able to sneak out unnoticed. I just hope your illegal midnight flight was worth it." His eyes flicked to the basement door and narrowed to green slits. "Shouldn't you be trying to get upstairs right now, before Liam comes out and sees you?"

I hesitated. Should I tell him about the secret room and the code to open it? I'd never hidden anything from my brother before. But if I did tell him, he'd want to know where I'd gotten that information, and I wasn't ready to admit my association with a rogue dragon just yet. Getting caught sneaking out was bad enough.

"That's what I was doing, before you shaved a couple years off my life," I whispered, moving away from the door, back toward the stairs. I kept my head down as we climbed the steps so he wouldn't see I was lying. "Are you going to tell Liam?"

I heard the irritation in his voice as he answered. "You know I wouldn't do that. You're an idiot, but you're still my sister. We stick together, no matter what." I relaxed, and his tone sharpened. "Even when I think you did something completely stupid and dangerous tonight, just because you wanted to fly."

I stopped outside the door to my room. "It isn't that bad."

"Ember. It's the one thing that can get us called back to Talon. Or get *you* called back to Talon. I don't want us to be separated, and I sure as hell don't want to go back." Dante shook his head with a frustrated sigh, before giving me a half angry, half pleading look. "You can't do that anymore, okay, sis? This one time, I understand. But we have to follow the rules or risk losing everything we've worked so hard for. Sixteen years of preparing for this, all gone in an instant. Am I making any sense to you?"

I slumped. "Yeah," I whispered. He was right; I'd been stupid and stubborn and had taken a huge risk tonight. I'd endangered not only my time here but Dante's, too. My actions affected both of us, and I'd forgotten that. I might be okay with risking my own neck, but I wouldn't risk my brother's. "Okay, fine," I said. "I was a moron. No more flying around after midnight, I promise."

Even though something inside me shriveled a bit in misery. My dragon, perhaps, mourning the loss of her wings, and knowing she would never see Cobalt again. She already missed him.

Dante nodded. "Good," he said, and gave me a lopsided little grin. "Because I'm going to be a zombie today, thanks to you. Next time, at least have the courtesy to sneak out on a weekend when I don't have to be up in an hour."

I snorted. "Good night, Tweedledum."

He smirked and turned down the hall, and I went through my own door, letting it click shut behind me. Walking to my bed, I did a face-plant into the mattress, replaying the events of the day.

*Busy night.* And it wasn't done yet. I still had to meet Garret later this afternoon for surf lessons. The thought sent a little thrill through me; the human was gorgeous, mysterious, and those metallic gray eyes made my tummy squirm. I was definitely looking forward to seeing him again. Though, I had to admit, flying the waves with Cobalt, feeling that surge of pure adrenaline as we soared the wind together, was just bliss. The rogue was cocky, arrogant and exasperating, but he certainly knew how to live.

And, if what Cobalt said was true, there was still the matter of the hidden room in the basement. There was no time to search for it now, of course, but I *would* get down there soon and see if the rogue knew what he was talking about. If Talon was keeping secrets, I wanted to know why.

My eyes flickered shut, the tired contentment of soaring the wind stealing over me. No matter what I promised my brother, tonight had been amazing. And I knew I wouldn't forget it—or the mysterious rogue—anytime soon.

*Worth it,* my dragon side whispered smugly.

Just as the alarm buzzed.

★ ★ ★

"You look tired, hatchling." Scary Talon Lady eyed me critically across the desk, arms crossed as she looked me up and down. "Did you not get enough sleep? I told your guardians I wanted you here early today."

"It's five-thirty in the morning," I said, knowing how I must look—eyes bloodshot, hair spiky with wind and salt. "The sun isn't even up yet."

"Well, this should perk you right up." My instructor smiled in that way that chilled my blood. "We're doing something a little different this morning. Follow me."

Nervously, I trailed her down to the storage room, then blinked in surprise when she opened the door. The normally vast, empty space was filled wall-to-wall with crates, pallets, steel drums and ladders. Some were stacked nearly to the ceiling, creating a labyrinth of shadowy aisles, hallways and corridors, a gigantic maze inside the room.

"What's this for?" I asked, just as something small and fast streaked from the darkness and hit me right in the chest. With a yelp, I staggered back, clutching my shoulder. Thick liquid spread over my clothes, and my hand came away smeared with red. "What the hell?" I gasped.

"It's paint," my trainer said calmly, easing my panicked confusion. "But, make no mistake, had that been a real bullet, you would most assuredly be dead." She waved an arm toward the labyrinth of boxes looming before me in the darkness. "There are a dozen 'St. George soldiers' hiding in that maze," she continued, smiling down at me. "All hunting you. All looking to kill you. Welcome to phase two of your training, hatchling. I want you to go in there and survive as long as you can."

I stared into the room, trying to catch glimpses of my attackers, these "soldiers" of St. George. I couldn't see anything, but I was quite certain they could see me and were probably watching us right now. "How long is long enough?" I asked quietly.

"Until I say so."

Of course. With a sigh, I began walking toward the maze, but Scary Talon Lady's voice stopped me before I took three steps.

"What do you think you're doing, hatchling?"

Annoyed, I turned back, wondering what I'd done wrong this time. "I'm doing what you told me to. Go into maze, get shot at, survive. Isn't that what you want?"

My instructor gave me a blatant look of disgust and shook her head. "You're not taking this seriously. If you are trapped in a warehouse with a team of well-trained, heavily armed St. George soldiers, do you really think you are going to survive as a human?"

I stared at her, frowning, before I got what she was really saying. "You…you mean I can do this in my real form?"

She rolled her eyes. "I do hope your brother catches on faster than you. It would be a shame to lose you both to stupidity."

"Yes!" I whispered, clenching my fist. I barely heard the insult. I could finally be a dragon without breaking the rules. That almost made this whole crazy exercise worth it.

My trainer snapped her fingers and pointed to a large stack of crates in the corner.

"If you are concerned about modesty, or your clothes, you may change over there," she ordered in a flat voice. "Though you are eventually going to have to get over that. There will be no time to find a bathroom if you are being chased by snipers in helicopters."

I hurried over and ducked behind the boxes, then shrugged out of my clothes as fast as I could. My body rippled as the dragon burst free again, wings brushing against the wooden crates as they unfurled for the second time that morning. It was still liberating, still completely freeing, even after a whole night of flying around.

My talons clicked over the concrete as I stalked back to the maze, feeling comfortable and confident in my dragon skin. Even Scary Talon Lady didn't look quite so scary anymore, though she eyed my dragon self with as much bored disdain as she did my human self.

"Hold still," she ordered, and pressed something into my ear hole, right behind my horns. I snorted and reared back, shaking my head, and she cuffed me under the chin. "Stop that. It's just an earbud. It will allow me to communicate with you in the maze, and to hear everything that is going on around you. So stop twitching."

I curled my lip, trying not to think about it, even though it was uncomfortable. My trainer didn't notice. "On my signal," she continued, pulling out her phone, "you have two minutes to find a good position and prepare for the hunt. If you are shot, you are 'dead.' Which means you have two minutes to find another position before the hunt starts again, and I add another fifteen minutes to the overall game. How long we are here depends on how long you survive, understand?"

Crap. That meant I just would have to avoid getting shot. No way I was staying here all afternoon, not with Garret waiting for me. Dragon or no, I'd promised him a surf lesson, and I still wanted to see him. "Yes," I answered.

"I will be observing your progress from up top," she continued, "so do not think you can lie about being killed. We *will* stay here all day if that is what it takes until I am satisfied."

Double crap. How long would I have to stay alive before this unappeasable woman was "satisfied"? Probably much longer than I thought.

"Two minutes," Scary Talon Lady reminded me. "Starting…now."

I spun, claws raking over the cement, and bounded into the maze.

I didn't see any soldiers as I wove my way through the endless corridors, peeking around crates to make sure the aisles were empty. Everything remained very quiet, save for my breathing, and the click of my talons on the cement. As I crept farther into the room, no one shot at me, nothing moved in the shadows, no footsteps shuffled over the ground.

Where were these so-called soldiers, anyway? Maybe this was an elaborate hoax my trainer had cooked up to make me paranoid. Maybe there was no one here at all....

Something small and oval dropped into the corridor from above, bounced once with a metallic click and came to rest near my claws. As I stared in confusion, there was a sudden deafening hiss, and white smoke erupted from the tiny object, spewing everywhere. I backed away, squinting, but the smoke had completely filled the aisle and I couldn't see where I was going.

Shots erupted overhead, and several blows struck me from all sides. As the smoke cleared, I looked up to see six humans standing atop the aisle, three on either side. They wore heavy tactical gear and ski masks, and carried large, very real-looking guns in their hands. My whole body was covered in red paint, dripping down my scales and spattering to the concrete. I cringed as the realization hit. I'd stood no chance against them. I'd walked right into their ambush, and if these were real St. George soldiers, I'd be blown to bits.

"And you're dead," buzzed a familiar voice in my ear as the figures slipped away and vanished as quickly as they had appeared. "A very dismal start, I'm afraid. Let us hope you can turn this around, or we will be here all day. Two minutes!"

A little daunted now, I hurried down another corridor, attempting to put as much distance between me and the six highly trained soldiers as I could.

* * *

Sometime later I crouched, exhausted, behind a stack of pallets, my sides heaving from the last little scuffle. I'd been running from the soldiers for what seemed like hours, and they always seemed one step ahead of me. I'd slip away from one only to be shot by another hiding atop the crates overhead. I'd enter a corridor to find it blocked by two soldiers, and when I turned to run, two more would appear behind me, boxing me in. I was almost completely covered in paint; it seeped between my scales and dripped to the floor when I moved, looking very much like blood. And each time I was hit, my trainer's bored, smug voice would crackle in my ear, taunting me, telling me I had failed again, that I was dead.

I had no idea how much time had passed from the last time I'd been shot. Minutes? Hours? I didn't think it mattered, not with my sadistic instructor keeping track. Curling my tail around myself, I huddled in the dark corner, breathing as quietly as I could and hoping that maybe the "hide and hope they don't notice you" method would allow me to survive long enough to get out of here.

A small oval object sailed over the stack of crates, hit the wall and bounced toward me with a clink. I hissed and shot out of the corner before it could go off. Most of the projectiles lobbed at me had been smoke grenades, which, while I didn't have to worry about things like smoke inhalation, made it very difficult to see in the tight corridors. Death by paint usually followed as I thrashed around in confusion. But the last grenade had exploded in a blinding burst of light, and the soldiers had pumped me full of rounds as I'd stood there, stunned. *Not going through that again, thanks.*

I darted for another shadowy corner and ran into a bullet storm. The bastards were lying in wait right outside my hiding spot and had trapped me inside a funnel of death. Cringing, I closed my eyes and hunkered down as I was bathed in red paint, again.

"Pathetic," snarled a familiar, hated voice when the ambush was done and the soldiers had slipped back into the maze. "Let us pray that you are not ever hunted by the real soldiers of St. George, because your head would be mounted over their fireplace in no time. Two minutes!"

Anger blazed, and my fraying temper finally snapped. With a snarl, I turned and lashed out at a pile of crates, ripping a huge chunk of wood from the boxes with my claws.

All right, enough was enough! Why should I be the hunted? I was a freaking *dragon.* The apex predator, according to Talon. If survival meant not getting shot at all costs, maybe I should be the one doing the hunting.

I crouched, then leaped atop one of the crate piles, landing as quietly as I could. The labyrinth spread out before me, looking much different from up top. *All right, you bastards,* I thought, lowering myself into a stalking position, my belly scales nearly brushing the crates. *We're changing the rules a bit. This time, I'm coming for you.*

I prowled along the top of the maze, keeping my body low and straight and my wings pressed to my back, all senses attuned for the sights, sounds and smell of my prey. Slithering over the narrow aisles, my steps light so my talons wouldn't clack and give me away, I felt a savage, growing excitement. *This* felt natural, easy. The fear I'd had before disappeared, and everything seemed sharper, clearer, now that I was on the hunt. I could sense my enemies, lurking in the shadows and darkness, waiting for me. But now, they were the ones in danger.

I caught a whiff of human ahead of me and froze, one claw suspended above the crates. Holding myself perfectly still, I watched a soldier creep along the top of the maze without seeing me, then drop silently into the narrow aisle below.

Crouching even lower, my chin just a few inches from the wood, I stalked noiselessly to the place the soldier had dropped out of sight and peered over the edge. He stood almost directly below, his gaze and the muzzle of his gun pointed at the end of the corridor, where another two soldiers waited, I saw. None of them had noticed me.

*Hello, boys.* I grinned, and felt my back haunches wriggle as I tensed to pounce. *Payback's a bitch.*

"Death from above!" I howled, leaping toward my opponents with talons and wings spread. The soldier jerked and looked up, just as I landed on him with a snarl, driving him to the cement. His helmeted head struck the back of a pallet and he lay there, dazed.

The other two soldiers instantly whipped around and raised their guns. I roared, baring my fangs, and went for them, barely avoiding a paintball to the face as I lunged. Bounding toward the first soldier, I leaped sideways, catapulted off the wall to avoid the spray of bullets and drove my horned head into his chest, flinging him back several feet. He crashed into a stack of crates, which collapsed on top of him, and struggled to rise. The last soldier swiftly backed away as I spun on him, growling, and tensed to pounce.

"Stop!"

The command rang in my ear, but also directly in front of me, and I stumbled to a halt a lunge away from the last opponent. Shouldering the gun, the last soldier reached up and pulled off his helmet and mask, revealing Scary Talon Lady's face in the dim light. I blinked in surprise and quickly stepped back.

"Finally." My trainer raked a hand through her hair, long golden strands falling down her back. Her acidic eyes regarded me over the hall. "About time, hatchling. I was wondering if the purpose for this exercise would ever penetrate that thick skull of yours. I was certain we'd be here until midnight, chasing you around the building, before you finally figured it out."

Confused, I shook my head. "You…you *wanted* me to attack," I guessed. "To go on the offensive. That was the whole point, wasn't it?" My trainer raised a mocking eyebrow, and I scowled. "You weren't going to let me quit until I started fighting back, no matter how long I survived down here."

She lowered the gun and nodded. "Exactly. Dragons are never *prey,* hatchling. Dragons are *hunters.* Even to the soldiers of St. George, we are deadly, intelligent, highly adaptable killers. We are not to be taken lightly. If you are ever trapped in a building with a soldier of St. George, his life should be in just as much danger, do you understand? Because you'll be hunting him, as well. And one more thing…"

Faster than thought, she raised the gun and fired it, point-blank, at my chest. The paint bullet exploded in a spray of crimson, making me flinch even though it didn't hurt. My instructor smiled coldly.

"*Never* hesitate to go in for the kill."

# GARRET

Fifteen twenty-two, and still no Ember.

I resisted the urge to check my watch again and leaned back in the hard booth seat, staring out at the parking lot. The orange smoothie I'd gotten in an effort to look normal sat melting on the edge of the table, condensation pooling around the foam cup. Around me, the small fast-food restaurant was fairly packed; people sat at tables or in booths, talking and laughing, while I sat quietly by myself and waited for a girl who might be a dragon.

An ancient white Volkswagen with several surfboards strapped to the roof wheeled into the parking spot next to my Jeep, and Ember hopped out almost before the car stopped moving. All my senses went alert as the girl, dressed in shorts and a loose top with a bikini underneath, scurried up the walk and ducked through the glass doors.

She spotted me almost instantly and hurried over, smiling. "Garret! Hey, sorry I'm late. I, uh, lost track of time. Thanks for waiting—were you here long?"

*Since 1400.* "No," I said, but movement outside caught my attention. Two more people were emerging from the car now; Lexi Thompson, whom I'd met the other day with Ember, and a taller boy with blond hair pulled into a ponytail.

Ember followed my gaze. "Oh, yeah. Lexi and Calvin will be joining us. They were the ones who taught me to surf, after all, and Calvin knows all the best spots on the beach. Hope you don't mind." She gave me an apologetic smile and leaned in, resting her palm on the corner of the table. My stomach jumped as her face hovered close to mine. "Actually, they kinda invited themselves," she whispered. "I made the mistake of telling Lexi, and when she heard I was going to teach you, she had to come. And then Calvin didn't want us hanging out with some strange guy after the creepers from the other day, so…yeah. Sorry."

Well, this was…unexpected. But surmountable. There was no reason the others shouldn't come; my objective was to fit in with the whole group, after all. And if Lexi was Ember's friend, she likely knew a lot about her, secret things, perhaps. If I could get her to open up and share what she knew, that would bring me one step closer to my objective.

So why did I feel like they were intruders?

"That's fine," I said, shrugging. "Not a problem."

"Hey, Garret!" Lexi bounced up and slid into the booth across from me. "So, you're actually going to put your life in Ember's hands today, huh? Did she tell you what she did on her very first day of surf lessons?"

"Lexi." Ember sighed as I leaned back to give myself a little more space away from the other girl. "We want him to come with us, you know. Not run away screaming."

I tilted my head at the girl across from me. "What happened?"

"She almost drowned," Lexi went on, cheerfully oblivious. "Got the basics down really quick, then decided to brave an eighteen-footer all by herself. It was a pretty spectacular wipeout."

I glanced at Ember and raised an eyebrow, and she actually colored a little. "Don't worry," she said with an exasperated glare at her friend. "I'm not going to throw you at eighteen-footers on your first day. We'll start with baby waves and work our way up. I'll go easy on you, I promise."

Calvin sauntered up, a trio of smoothies in hand. "Dude," he greeted, setting the drinks on the table, where they were pounced upon by the girls. "Garret, right? So you'll be joining us today, huh? Ever gone surfing before?"

"No."

He smirked, but it was without malice, lazy and knowing at the same time. "Well, it's gonna be interesting, I can tell you that."

★ ★ ★

We didn't drive far. I sat in the backseat with Ember, gazing out the window, while Lexi craned her neck around to talk to us both, chattering nonstop. I didn't say much, but I didn't need to, as the two girls more than made up for my silence. I began to have serious doubts that the friendly, cheerful girl sitting beside me could be anything but a normal teen. She certainly didn't fit the normal dragon model: vicious, ruthless, power-hungry. Then again, all the dragons I'd encountered had been trying to kill me, and vice versa. I'd never really seen a dragon in human form for an extended amount of time, never encountered one that was trying to fit in. Still, I wondered if I wasn't wasting my time pursuing this.

Oddly enough, I found that I didn't care. The backseat of

the Volkswagen was very small, and Ember's slim leg was brushing against mine, a fact I was acutely aware of as the car trundled down a narrow back road. At one point, the tires hit either a rock or a log and bounced so hard the top of my head struck the roof and Ember nearly ended up in my lap.

"Sorry." She shifted away, but her hand came to rest on my thigh, and all my nerve endings snapped to attention. I noticed her cheeks were slightly pink as she drew back, and felt the heat radiating from my own skin. Embarrassment or...something else? I hadn't been around many civilians, certainly not many females my own age. There were women in the Order, but they occupied the jobs outside of combat—gathering intelligence, handling paperwork, saving a soldier's life when he got himself incinerated by a dragon. They were crucial to the Order, but there were no female soldiers in St. George. Tristan had no problems talking to girls, especially when he'd had a few, but when faced with a member of the opposite sex I usually found myself with nothing to say, so I avoided them when I could.

*The mission,* I reminded myself. *Focus on the mission.* I could not be distracted by this girl. I couldn't let myself think of her as anything but an objective. And I certainly couldn't let myself think of touching her again, of feeling her skin against mine, her warm fingers on my leg.

I stared out the window, deliberately forcing my thoughts elsewhere. Anything to keep myself distracted and my mind off the girl beside me.

The Volkswagen finally came to a bouncing, shuddering halt in the shadow of a grove of palm trees. Through the space between two giant thornbushes, an empty strip of sand and the ocean beckoned, white-capped waves breaking in the distance. I exited the car and felt the heat of the sun beating on my bare shoulders. Ember climbed out behind me and yawned, covering her mouth with one hand.

"Pull another all-nighter, Em?" Lexi teased as she helped Calvin unstrap the boards from the roof. "You know, if you went to bed before dawn, we could actually go surfing before noon sometimes. Just a thought."

"Oh, like you're ever up before noon," Ember scoffed. She didn't give any outward signs of alarm, but I caught the discrepancy with what she'd told me this morning. Ember didn't get up early; even her friends knew this, though they probably thought she was sleeping. No one ever saw her, or her brother, until afternoon.

So why was she out this morning, alone? Where was she coming from?

"Here," she went on, tugging a blue board from the roof and handing it to me. I took it with a puzzled look, and she smiled. "That's yours for today. Be nice to it. It's been through a lot."

I nodded and tucked the surfboard under my arm as I'd seen Ember do. It was surprisingly light and had more than a few dents and scratches on the surface. Calvin swung a pristine white board under his arm and headed down toward the water, moving with lazy confidence. The rest of us trailed behind, Ember and Lexi walking to either side of me, explaining the basics of surfing.

I tried to listen, but both were talking at the same time and one tended to finish the sentence the other girl began, so it was difficult to follow along. Nothing really stuck until we reached the edge of the beach, and Ember turned to me.

"Okay!" she announced, and dropped her board into the sand with a soft thump. "This is where we start."

"Here?" I glanced at the ocean, where Calvin was striding into the surf, not looking back. "I was under the impression that surfing was done in the water."

Lexi giggled, and Ember frowned at her. "It is, of course. But there's a whole lot of things to learn before you can ride a wave. Paddling, balance, timing, things like that. It's easier to start on solid ground first."

"Or you can be like Ember and keep falling off the board into the water," Lexi added. "Because you're too impatient to start on the beach."

The other girl huffed at her. "You shush. I only agreed to let you come because you promised you'd let me do this." She glowered fiercely, and Lexi giggled again. I found myself wishing she was gone, that it was just me and Ember in this empty little cove. I'd be able to better concentrate and learn more if I had just one teacher and Lexi wasn't peering over our shoulders.

That's what I told myself, anyway.

Ember sighed. Turning back to me, she pointed to my board. "Here. Put your surfboard next to mine. I'll show you how to paddle out, catch a wave and stand up when you do. After that, you're on your own. The balance part comes with time and practice."

I followed her lead. Under Ember's tutelage, I learned to lie on my stomach and paddle my arms when trying to catch a wave, then quickly spring into a crouch to ride it down. I learned the best way to stand when surfing, keeping my knees bent and my weight balanced, and how to steer the board when I did catch a wave. Ember was a very patient teacher, gently correcting my stance when I needed it, answering any questions I had. Once, her hand came to rest on my arm as she demonstrated a technique, and the prickle from her fingers lingered on my skin a long time afterward. Lexi would comment occasionally, either to confirm what Ember was saying or tease her teaching methods, but by the end of the lesson, I'd nearly forgotten about her.

"All right," Ember announced, giving me an appraising stare. I caught a flash of admiration in those green eyes as she smiled at me. "I think you've got it. In fact, I'm pretty sure you're either a natural, or you've been pulling my leg this whole time about not ever having done this before. I'm going to feel awfully stupid if you're some surfing champion from Waimea or something."

I met her gaze. "You don't have to wonder. I've never done this before." She gave me a dubious look, and I held up my hands. "I promise."

"Then why do I have the feeling you're going to catch a wave and dazzle us on your very first try?"

"Maybe I just have an exceptional teacher."

She snorted. "Flattery will get you nowhere, sir. I have a brother that tries the same thing at home, so I am immune to such charms." But she was blushing while she said it, and I resisted the urge to smile.

"Moment of truth, then," Lexi stated, picking up her board and grinning at us. "Time to let him try the real thing."

# EMBER

Garret picked up his board and turned to me, waiting. And for about the hundredth time this afternoon, my stomach gave a weird little jolt. His hair shone in the sun, and his sculpted arms and shoulders were highly noticeable without his shirt. As was the lean, tanned, washboard stomach and chest. The boy definitely worked out or did something strenuous in his free time. One did not get a body like that from sitting around.

And even though he denied it, I couldn't help but think he had done this before. He was so graceful, knowing exactly where to put his feet, how to balance himself on the board. Even on land, with the board stationary, I could tell he would do fine in the water, maybe more than fine.

Maybe I was wrong. Maybe he would wipe out, as I had on my first day of surf lessons. Granted, I wasn't going to let him try the monsters just yet, but one did not just pick up a board and surf merrily down a wave on the very first try.

"Come on," I told him, grabbing my board. "I've shown you everything you need. Now you just have to do it."

He followed us into the water without hesitation, paddling about a hundred yards from shore. As always, while floating on my board in the middle of the sparkling ocean, I felt a familiar rising excitement. Maybe I couldn't fly anymore, but this—the rush, the prickle of danger, the adrenaline—certainly came close. At least I didn't have to give this up just yet.

I remembered Cobalt, soaring with him over the crashing ocean, racing the waves, and felt a twinge of sadness and regret. I'd never do that again. Which meant I'd probably never see him again, either.

"Ember?" Garret's voice broke through my melancholy. He sat very close, bobbing on the surface of the water, and his metallic gaze was fastened on me. "You all right?"

That same prickle again, but I ignored it. "Yeah," I said, giving him a bright smile. "I'm fine. Just...looking for waves."

"That's a relief." He actually smiled back. "Because I'm depending on you to show me how to do this. The lesson isn't over yet, I hope."

Those eyes. I felt like they pierced right through me; that if I didn't break away now, they would peel me open to see what lay beneath. Deep within, the dragon stirred, growling. She didn't like this human, I realized. Maybe he scared her, or the intensity of his gaze reminded her of a predator. Or maybe she felt that, if I stared at him much longer, I would lose myself in those stormy eyes and forget all about a certain golden-eyed rogue, waiting for me in the darkness.

"Here comes a good one!" Lexi announced.

I tore my gaze away and stared out over the water. Coming right at us, getting larger as it approached, was the familiar swell of our next ride. And, by the looks of it, it wasn't a small one. Not gigantic, per se, but definitely not the "baby" wave I'd promised Garret.

Oops. So much for easing him into it.

I jerked my board around as Lexi did the same, and Garret followed our example. "When I say go," I told him, lying flat on my stomach, "paddle just like I told you. Paddle like your life depends on it, and don't look back."

Briefly, our gazes met. I didn't see any fear or doubt on his face, just confidence, excitement and trust. My breath caught under that look, but then the swell loomed over us, and I hollered for everyone to go.

We paddled. I hit the top of the wave first, and for just a moment, I perched on the rim of a mountain, my board teetering on the edge. Then the nose of the board plunged downward, and I leaped upright as we began to fall.

Wind and spray whipped around me, buffeting my hair. I didn't see anything but the ocean and the front of my board as it sliced through the water.

And then, Garret sliced past me, his board sending up a spray of foam. Startled, I nearly fell, but quickly regained my balance and watched him from the corner of my eye. He stood on the board just as I'd taught him, knees bent, arms slightly raised, the wind whipping at his hair as he careened down the wave. A thrill of pride zipped through me, and I steered my board in his direction, pulling alongside him.

"You're doing it!" I called, though my voice was probably drowned out by the roar of the wave behind us. But then Garret looked over with a brief, dazzling smile, and my heart nearly stopped. I'd never seen him smile before, not a real one, and it transformed him completely. He was a creature of light, of energy and power and adrenaline, and absolutely beautiful.

Behind us, the wave curled over and crashed in a roar of foam and spray, losing fury as it petered out in the shallows. Still on our boards, we cruised toward the beach until our momentum gave out and Garret hopped off the board into waist-deep water. He was panting, breathing hard, his whole face lit up again with an eager, excited grin as he spun to me.

"That was amazing," he exclaimed as I grinned back and splashed beside him, our boards bumping noses as they floated behind us. "I never felt… I mean…" He shook his head, sending droplets flying from his wet hair. "Just… Wow."

I laughed. It was good to see him like this, unguarded and free. He was normally so reserved, I had wondered if he'd ever had any real fun in his entire life. "Beginner's luck, I think. No more going easy on you—next time we'll catch a real ride."

"Hey, guys!" Lexi floated over, straddling her board. "What's the holdup? Are we going again, or what?"

I looked at Garret. He grinned, looking eager and boyish as he grabbed his board and turned toward the waves. "Yeah. Let's go again."

*Birth of a new surfer,* I thought smugly, following them into the water. *Let's hope I haven't created a monster.*

★ ★ ★

We surfed the rest of the afternoon. Garret was an incredibly quick study, learning to spot approaching waves, eventually passing on those that were too small. He did wipe out a couple times, but we all did, and he fell off his board much less than I expected, especially on the bigger waves. Even after a particularly nasty wipeout, he bounced to his feet, shook water from his hair and waded dauntlessly back into the surf.

The sun was hanging low and red over the water when we finally stopped, Calvin returning from farther down the alcove to join us. I was starving, tired and a little sore from being tumbled through the surf a few times, but Garret seemed reluctant to head back. He was insatiable. I really had created a monster.

"Can we do this again?" he asked, quite seriously, as we loaded the boards onto the roof of the car. I looked at him, at the way his eyes stayed trained on me, the calm, happy look on his face, and my stomach danced.

"Sure!" I grinned and tugged down a strap. "When did you have in mind?"

"Tomorrow," was the immediate reply. "If that's okay with you."

I would've liked nothing better than to meet him again, maybe alone this time, but unfortunately... "I can't tomorrow, Garret," I said. "It's Kristin's birthday, and we're meeting at the mall that afternoon so we can watch her buy things, I mean...so we can hang out and stuff. Sorry." At least, I hoped I'd be able to make it. Scary Talon Lady had really screwed up my mornings, so the important things like surfing and hanging out with friends had to be moved to the afternoon. Thankfully, neither Kristin nor Lexi were early risers.

"Come with us!" piped Lexi from the other side, poking her head over the roof. "Kristin won't mind, and I think she's bringing someone, so you won't be the only guy there. Sadly, my deadbeat brother won't be joining us."

Calvin didn't even look up from his surfboard. "Walk around the mall with a bunch of girls squealing at clothes and other dudes? Yeah, you have fun with that."

I ignored him, focused on Garret. "Anyway, that's where we'll be tomorrow afternoon. You're welcome to come along."

"To the mall?" A faintly troubled look crossed his face,

that wariness settling back on him like a second skin. "I… don't know. Maybe."

"Well," I said, trying to sound nonchalant, "if you make up your mind, you're welcome to join us. If it's lunchtime, just look for me at the Panda Garden in the food court, or at the Cinnabon next door."

"If it's before lunch, just follow the sounds of Ember complaining that she's hungry," Lexi added, and dodged the pebble I hurled at her.

It hit Calvin instead, earning a very exasperated, "Dude!" and the order to get in the car before he tied us to the roof with the surfboards. I obeyed, a little sad that such an awesome day had come to an end, but the genuine smile Garret gave me as we slid into the back made it all worth it.

Back at the Smoothie Hut, we pulled into the spot next to Garret's black Jeep, and I gazed mournfully at our gorgeous tagalong. "Well." I sighed as Lexi exited the front and pushed her seat forward to let him out. "See you around, I guess. If not tomorrow, then…some other time." I perked as I remembered something, leaning forward as he left the car. "Hey, don't forget, Kristin's party is this Saturday. Maybe we'll see you then?"

"Maybe." He paused and turned back to me, gray eyes intense. "Thank you for today," he said softly. "I had…fun." Like the word was strange to him. I smiled, feeling a warm glow spread through me from within, even as my dragon hissed in disgust.

"Anytime," I replied, and he was gone.

A few minutes later, I sat in the same corner booth from that afternoon, plowing my way through a jumbo chili-cheese Coney dog, while Lexi slurped her drink and gave me knowing looks across the table. I pretended to ignore her until Calvin got up to stand in line for a second hamburger, and she leaned in, grinning fiercely.

"You are so into him!"

"What?" I nearly choked on my Coney dog as I pulled back to glare at her. Lexi gave me a smug look, and I shook my head. "You mean Garret? You're psychotic. I don't know what you're talking about."

"You're such a bad liar, Em." She rolled her eyes and gestured to the now-empty parking spot where Garret's Jeep had sat minutes before. "Admit it. Whenever he looked at you, you couldn't stop smiling. And when he rode that first wave with you?" She raised her thin eyebrows. "You were about ready to jump him."

"You're crazy," I said. Because it wasn't true. It couldn't be. I was a dragon. I couldn't be attracted to a *human*. A gorgeous, athletic, gifted human, but a human nonetheless. It was impossible. As a race, we appreciated beauty and talent, grace and intelligence, but we did not form emotional attachments, especially with human beings. That was something Talon made abundantly clear: even among our own, dragons did not fall in love.

Lexi snorted, clearly unconvinced. "Whatever. Be the queen of denial, if you want. But I think you know it's the truth. And you know what?" She leaned across the table again, like she was divulging the world's greatest secret. "I think he likes you, too."

# GARRET

"There you are," Tristan said as I came through the front door, tossing the keys onto the counter. "If you're going to be pulling stunts like that, we're going to need a second vehicle. I had to walk several miles down the beach to find this girl's house. It looked pretty normal from what I could see, but we won't know anything unless we can get inside." He eyed my still-damp hair and clothes, arching an eyebrow. "The 'lesson' went well, I assume?"

I stifled a grin, remembering the thrill of the afternoon, the surge of adrenaline the second I caught the wave exactly right and rode it all the way to shore. "You could say that."

"Uh-huh. Well, it must've gone swimmingly, because you're grinning like a moron. The only times I've seen you this happy is when your team wins a month of no KP."

I shrugged, not bothering to deny it, and Tristan shook his head. "So, what did you find out? Is this Ember girl our sleeper?"

"I don't know."

"You don't know. You spent the whole day with her, what do you mean you don't know?"

"We didn't really talk much."

"You had the whole afternoon! What were you doing for six hours?"

"Sorry." I crossed my arms. "Next time, I'll try to hold a conversation while balancing on a plank down a ten-foot wall of water."

Tristan blinked. "Oh, wow, and smart-ass Garret comes out. You *must've* had a good time." I didn't answer, and he sighed, sitting up on the couch to face me. "Look, partner. I'm glad you had fun. God knows you, of all people, deserve it. But this isn't a vacation. We're here for one thing, and that's to find and kill a dragon. You know that. Fitting in and hanging out with these people and learning to surf, that's all acceptable, as long as it gets us closer to the sleeper. If not, then it's a waste of time and we should be focusing our efforts on something else."

"I know." Slumping, I turned away. He was right, of course. This wasn't like me, forgetting the assignment for a fleeting distraction. "I'll stay focused next time."

Tristan nodded, leaning back on the couch. "I assume there will be a next time? You did make plans to meet with her again, correct?"

"Tomorrow," I replied, determined to see the mission through. Find the sleeper. Kill the sleeper. Simple as that. "I'm meeting her and the others at the mall."

# EMBER

"Ember, you're not eating. Are you sick?"

I looked up from where I was poking halfheartedly at my boiled lobster. As a whole, I didn't like seafood. Dragons were carnivores; seventy percent of our diet had to consist of meat, and Sarah made sure we were fed appropriately, but in my opinion, lobsters weren't food. They were big bugs that lived underwater, and ugly ones at that.

Although, this evening, my lack of appetite had nothing to do with giant mutant water bugs. "Um," I said, picking at one of the large claws still attached to the lobster's armored corpse. Ugh, seriously, they expected me to eat this thing? "I do feel a little tired," I hedged, because saying that I wasn't hungry would be a monster red flag, at least to Dante, who would immediately suspect that I was up to something. Stupid twin radar. "It's nothing. I went surfing today and got pounded a few times, that's all."

Liam put down his fork and lowered his eyebrows at me. "You know we don't like it when you put yourself in danger, Ember," he said in a tight voice. "We're your guardians, and I cannot risk you getting hurt or injured on my watch. I've allowed you to continue because you promised you would not pull any more crazy stunts, but if you keep putting yourself at risk, I'll forbid you from surfing entirely."

"What?" I bristled, resisting the urge to bare my teeth at him across the table. "You can't do that!"

"I can't, but Talon can." Liam glowered and pointed at me with his fork. "Don't give me that look, girl. You may be a dragon, and I may be a lowly human, but until Talon deems otherwise, I am responsible for you. All it would take is one phone call explaining that you are a danger to yourself and to others, and Talon would be here the next morning to take you back." He gave me a challenging stare. "You aren't the first reckless hatchling I've had to ship back to the organization. Don't think I won't do it again."

I swelled with fury, ready to tell Liam what he could do with his phone call, but I caught Dante's eye across the table. *Don't cause trouble,* his gaze pleaded. *Don't do anything that will get us sent back. Keep it together and follow the rules.*

I slumped, then pushed myself back from the table. "I'm not hungry anymore," I muttered, not caring what anyone thought right then. "I'm turning in early. Don't wait up."

"You still have training tomorrow, Ember," Liam called as I retreated from the kitchen, heading up to my room. "I'll be at your door at 5:00 a.m. to make sure you're awake."

"*So* looking forward to it," I sang back with as much sarcasm as I could muster, and slammed the door behind me.

I seethed quietly for a few minutes, tempted to slip out the window, head down to the beach and catch a few waves just for spite. Who was Liam to forbid me from surfing? From doing something that I loved? Not only that, riding the waves was the only thing that kept me somewhat grounded; if I didn't have that release, I'd probably be sneaking out every night to go flying with rogue dragons.

I snorted. Maybe I *would* do that again. I didn't need Cobalt to go wing surfing any night of the week; I could do it on my own. It wasn't like Liam could stop me, rules or no.

*Maybe that's why Cobalt went rogue,* I thought sourly, gazing out the window. I could hear the ocean in the distance, shushing against the sand, and my resentment increased. *Because all these stupid rules were suffocating him. Can't Shift, can't fly, can't have any fun, oh, and here's a sadistic trainer to make your life miserable for no good reason.*

There was a soft tap at my door, and I sighed. "It's open, Dante."

The door creaked, and my brother stepped into my room, a concerned look on his face. "Hey," he greeted, closing the door behind him. "You all right?"

No, I wasn't. My anger still hadn't cooled, and now it switched to the only target in the room. "Thanks for sticking up for me in there," I snapped, making him frown. "You could've told Liam I wasn't in any danger from surfing—you know how good I am. Now I'm going to have to watch my back every time I want to go down to the beach. Some twin you are."

His eyes narrowed. "I was more concerned about you mouthing off to Liam and getting yourself sent back to Talon," he retorted. I glared at him, and he gave me a look of exasperation. "You don't get it, do you? This isn't a vacation, sis, not for us. We're not human, and we're not here to have fun. This is a test, and they're watching our every move to make sure we don't screw this up. If we fail, it's right back to retraining. Back to the desert, in the middle of nowhere." He crossed his arms with a grave expression. "Remember that? Remember what it was like? Do you really want to go back?"

I shivered. I did remember. The isolation, the boredom, the same scenery every single day—nothing but dust, scrub and rock, as far as the eye could see. The loneliness. Except for our teachers, the guards stalking the perimeter fence around the facility and the evaluators who dropped by every month to check our progress, we didn't see another living soul. No friends, no kids our age, no company. It was just us, two hatchling dragons against the world.

I did *not* want to return to that. Bad enough when I didn't know any better, when the outside world was nothing more than images on TV or photos in a textbook. Now that I'd actually lived here, I'd go crazy if they sent me back.

I dropped onto the bed with a thump. "No," I growled sullenly, knowing he'd won this round. "I don't."

Dante perched on the corner of the mattress, one leg folded beneath him. "I don't, either," he said quietly. "You're my sister. It's always been just us against everything else. But the rules are different here. Before, we could occasionally slip up and Shift into our real forms and Talon wouldn't care—no one outside the organization would be around to see it. But now?" He shook his head. "We can't afford any mistakes. We can't break the rules, even once. There's more to lose than surfing privileges and getting to stay out late. Talon is testing us, and I am not going to fail."

My stomach felt cold, even though I managed a small smirk. "You know, you were a fun brother, once." *And someone I could trust. Why don't you ever talk to me anymore, Dante? I still don't even know what you* do *with your trainer every day.*

He snorted, looking more like himself. "I grew up. You might try it sometime. I don't *think* it will kill you." He stood, ruffled my hair and yanked his arm back before I could smack it. I glowered as he walked to the door but paused with his hand on the knob.

"It's still just us against the world, sis," he said, quite seriously now, glancing back over his shoulder. "We have to look out for each other, even if that means doing what's best for our future. Even if the other doesn't agree sometimes. Remember that, okay?"

"Yeah." I sighed, mostly to get him out of my room. His words had a strangely ominous tone, though I couldn't put my finger on why. I suddenly just wanted him gone. "I will."

He gave me a brief, somewhat empty smile, and the door closed behind him.

Alone, I flopped to my back and gazed up at the ceiling. Mornings came way too quickly these days. Tomorrow I'd have to be up at the crack of dawn—again—to attend another torture session with Scary Talon Lady. That last exercise, with the soldiers and the guns, had been shocking to say the least. Though it was slightly better than the pointless tasks of before, which, I suspected now, were designed to be pointless on purpose—to break my spirit, and to teach me not to question orders, no matter how stupid they seemed. If I just shut up and did whatever aggravating thing she told me to do, it would be over a lot faster.

Unfortunately, I wasn't very good at staying quiet and following orders, particularly if they made no sense. And now, I wanted to know why my trainer had thrown in these crazy new war games. I'd been curious before, and the encounter with a certain rogue dragon had only intensified my determination. If Talon, my instructor, my guardians and my own brother wouldn't tell me anything, then I would just have to find answers myself.

★ ★ ★

I stayed in my room, listening to music and chatting with Lexi online, killing time until the rest of the house grew quiet. At 11:45, I switched off the computer, tiptoed to the door and cracked it open, peering out.

The house was dark and silent. Liam and Sarah had gone to bed, and from the shadows under Dante's door, he had turned in, as well. I hoped he was truly asleep; maybe that annoying twin radar he had attuned to my every mood would be shut off if he was unconscious.

I crept down the stairs as silently as I could, avoiding the squeaky third step, crossed the moonlight-drenched kitchen and pushed open the door to the basement. In one corner, the door to the secret tunnel sat firmly closed and locked, but that wasn't even remotely interesting anymore. Not when there could be a whole other room somewhere behind these plain cement walls, hiding any number of secrets. About Talon, and my guardians, and me.

I poked around aimlessly for a few minutes, wishing I could Shift into my other form, the one that could see in the dark. I didn't find any panels, levers, touchpads, anything that would indicate a secret room, and after scouring the walls and finding nothing but mold and a couple spiders, I was ready to give up. Maybe Cobalt was wrong, or just delusional.

*Wait a minute.* Annoyed with myself, I paused, turning to scan the room carefully this time. *If Talon did have a hidden keypad, do you think they'd put it in plain sight? Come on, Ember, use your brain and the hundreds of spy movies you've watched over the years. The panel will be hidden, just like the room. Maybe in a wall safe, or under a counter, or behind a picture frame…*

But there were no pictures, or counters, or anything in the room that a switch could hide behind. The walls were bare.

*Except, maybe…*

I turned and padded to the gray electrical box, then pulled back the door. Black switches marched down the center in perfectly straight lines, neatly labeled with the circuits they were attached to.

Except for one, near the very bottom, that was unmarked.

Hoping my hunch was right, and that I wasn't about to short circuit the whole house, I threw the switch.

There was a click, and a tiny section of wall slid down beside the box.

I grinned in triumph. *Well, what do you know? There it is.* A small white panel was set into the concrete, a simple touch pad like the kind you'd see for home security. Numbered buttons sat above a lighted green strip, which currently said *Locked* in digital black letters. My heart began an excited thump in my chest. It was real. Cobalt had been right.

*Let's hope he's right about this code.*

I punched in the eight-number sequence and waited.

There was a hiss, then a section of wall beside the washer shifted and rotated out, like the secret passageway in a spy movie. The room beyond the hidden door was dark, but glowed with a faint green light.

For a moment, I just stood there, gaping at the revolving door like an idiot, until the panel beeped a warning and the wall section began to glide shut.

*Whoops. Move, Ember!* I sprinted across the floor and

ducked through the opening with only seconds to spare. As the panel closed behind me with a hiss, I had the fleeting thought that I might be trapped, but then I saw the rest of the room.

"Holy..." I blinked in astonishment, gazing around. This was definitely not the basement, or even the secret tunnel, with rough cement floors and dim lighting. This looked more like the set of *Star Trek* or *NCIS*. The entire back wall was one gigantic screen, dark for now, but I could tell the images would be nearly life-size when it was on. The floor was shiny black tile and reflected the blinking lights of a long computer console that ran the length of one wall. Against the other wall...

My stomach went cold. What looked like a large metal *cell* sat in one corner. Not exactly a cage, but pretty darn close. It had tiny barred windows near the top, fireproof walls and thick double doors big enough to hold a horse. Or a Shifted hatchling dragon.

"What the hell?" I whispered, venturing farther into the room. My eyes hurt from being open so wide. I could hardly believe this place sat right beneath a sleepy little beach community, and no one had any idea. Talon had never mentioned anything like this.

*So, what else is Cobalt right about?*

My gaze fell on the console and the myriad blinking lights that ran along the surface. A chair sat in front of a smaller screen, with a keyboard below it, and I headed in that direction. If I could get into Talon's files, or my guardian's email, maybe I could discover what they were doing. Or at least figure out what they wanted from me and Dante.

I'd just taken a few steps when I heard the hiss of the door behind me and realized someone was coming in.

*Crap*. Turning, I flung myself at the only visible hiding spot, the open door of the cell, pressing myself against the cold metal wall. The inside of the cage was dark; only a few slivers of light filtered in from the barred windows up top, and I shivered. I couldn't imagine being locked inside this thing, dragon or no. I'd be clawing at the walls to get out.

Peeking through the crack in the door, I saw Liam and Sarah pass briefly through my line of sight before continuing toward the back of the room. The chair squeaked as someone sat in it, and a sequence of taps and clicks soon followed. The light through the windows flickered, becoming brighter, and I realized the huge screen had come to life.

"Report," droned a deep male voice in a brusque tone that reminded me of my trainer. Even through the walls of the cell, it made me jump. "What is the status of Ember and Dante Hill?"

I froze, suddenly afraid to move. I couldn't see the screen, of course. Not unless I pulled myself up to the barred windows and peeked out, and I wasn't going to risk getting caught. But even without seeing him, I knew that the speaker was a dragon. Possibly one of Talon's upper executives, though I'd never met one myself. The dragons that ran the cooperation were very tight-lipped about their whereabouts, for fear that St. George would hunt them down. Why would one of Talon's higher-ups be talking about me and Dante? I pressed against the wall and held my breath, listening hard.

"Dante has adjusted well, sir," Liam said, his voice emotionless even through the wall between us. "He excels at human interaction and is comfortable within the social circle he has built himself. He follows the rules and understands what is expected of him. I foresee no problems with his assimilation."

"Good," said the voice, though there was no praise or pleasure in his tone. "As we expected. What of his clutchmate, Ember Hill?"

"Ember," Liam replied, and an edge had entered his voice, "is a little more…problematic. She has made friends and is adjusting well, but…" He paused.

"She is reckless," Sarah broke in, sounding like she couldn't hold back any longer. "She flaunts the rules and is drawn to dangerous, risky activities. She resists our authority and constantly questions her trainer. In fact, I think Dante is the only reason she hasn't done something drastic. He keeps her grounded, but I fear even he may not be able to control her much longer."

The voice was silent a moment, pondering this, while I bit my lip and ordered my heart to stop racing. Was this the moment they would decide to call me back for retraining? Alone? My stomach heaved. I couldn't do it. I couldn't go back there. Especially without Dante. I would die of loneliness and boredom.

"Has she broken any rules?" the voice finally asked, making my insides clench once more. If Dante had told them, if they knew about that night with Cobalt, I was as good as gone.

"No," Liam said reluctantly, making me slump with relief. "Not to our knowledge. But she could be a ticking time bomb—"

"Then we will observe her more closely," the voice interrupted. "Ember Hill could be a danger to the organization, or she could simply be acting out from the unaccustomed freedom. It is not uncommon with hatchlings. Better that she get it out of her system now, it will let her focus on her training in the long run. It is *not* a viable reason to pull her out, since by your own admission, she has not broken any of the rules."

*Huh.* I blinked in shock. *That's…surprisingly reasonable. Maybe Talon isn't as bad as Cobalt lets on.*

"And what of the rogue?" Sarah asked suddenly, turning my blood to ice. "He could still be hanging around. What if Ember or Dante runs into—"

"The rogue," the voice said, overriding her, "will be taken care of. You need not concern yourself. Our agents moved in last month when he was first reported and determined that he had fled town. He will likely not return, but if you see him, or if either of your charges mentions him, you will inform us immediately, is that clear?"

*Dante,* I thought as both guardians muttered consent. *It* was *you, wasn't it? You told them about Cobalt. That's why he left, and why our trainers arrived early. It was you all along.*

"We will speak with Ember's trainer and see if anything can be done to focus her energy down a more productive path," the voice went on. "Now, are there any other pressing concerns?"

"No, sir."

"Very well." I imagined the speaker pulling back, waving his hand. "Dismissed."

The screen flickered and went dark. Liam and Sarah immediately turned and walked toward the secret door, not glancing in my direction. I peeked from the cage, watched them press a single button to release the door panel, and waited several minutes after the door closed again before I fled myself. Back up the stairs and into my room, thankfully undisturbed by nosy brothers and now untrustworthy guardians. No one had been in to check on me, and I collapsed to the bed, my mind racing with what I'd heard. Talon, my guardian, my trainers, Dante.

And the rogue.

*Okay, Cobalt,* I thought, feeling a shiver run down my back. *You were right. Talon isn't telling us everything. You have my full attention now. I just hope I'll get to see you again to ask about it.*

# GARRET

"So, you have a possible target now."

On the computer screen, Lieutenant Gabriel Martin leaned back in his desk, steepling his fingers in thought. Both Tristan and I stood in the apartment's tiny kitchen, facing the open laptop on the counter. These weekly status reports were routine, keeping headquarters updated on the mission, but tonight was different. Tonight, we actually had a name.

"Ember Hill," Martin mused, drawing his brows together. "I'll have intelligence run another background check on her and her household, see if we can find any discrepancies. You say she has a brother?"

"Yes, sir," Tristan answered. "But they could have been raised together and then planted here to throw us off, knowing we'd be looking for a single target."

"That is a possibility," Martin agreed. "I wouldn't put it past Talon to think of new ways to hide their spawn. Have you spoken to either of her guardians, or been inside their house?"

"No, sir," Tristan said. "But Garret has established a connection with the girl. He's set to meet with her tomorrow."

"Good." Martin nodded and glanced at me. "What about

you, soldier?" he asked. "What are your thoughts on this girl?"

I kept my voice and expression blank. "I haven't discerned anything yet, sir. So far she hasn't given us any proof, only happenstance. Based on that, I couldn't give you a sure answer."

"Forget proof, then." Martin narrowed his eyes. "Sometimes you have to go with your instincts, regardless of everything else. What does your gut tell you?"

"That..." I paused, remembering Ember's smile, the way her eyes flashed when she was angry or excited. That eager, defiant grin that said she wouldn't back down from anything. The unfamiliar twisting sensation in the pit of my stomach when our eyes met. On the surface, she acted no different than anyone else; there were no obvious clues that hinted she was anything but an ordinary girl.

But my instincts, the gut reactions that had kept me alive on the field of battle all this time, said otherwise. Ember was different. Maybe it was her passion, a fiery determination that I'd seen all too often in the creatures I fought. That stubborn refusal to die that made them such lethal enemies. Or that sometimes, when she looked at me, I caught something in that stark gaze that wasn't entirely...human. I couldn't explain it, and I knew St. George would never accept those as valid reasons to eliminate a suspect. But Martin wasn't asking for proof now. He understood that soldiers sometimes had to make choices based purely on intuition. And my instincts had rarely been wrong.

"She could very well be the sleeper, sir," I replied.

Though, for the first time, I hoped I was mistaken.

Martin nodded solemnly. "We'll have to see what comes

of this information," he murmured. "Sebastian, your goal now is to get as close to this girl as you can. See if you can get inside her house. Talon bases will occasionally have underground lairs where they receive intel from the organization. If you find that room, you have the Order's full permission to take out the entire household. Just be discreet about it."

"Should we stake out the house, sir?" Tristan asked, but Martin shook his head.

"No. Talon operatives are trained to notice anything amiss, such as a strange car sitting in the road. We don't want to give them any clues that we could be in the area. Set up electronic surveillance to monitor the exterior, but your primary mission remains. Gain entrance into the domicile—any concrete intelligence will be found inside."

"Yes, sir."

"Good work, both of you," Martin finished, the faintest hint of a smile crossing his face. "We'll follow up on the leads you've provided. But for now, take the night off. You've earned it."

The image disappeared as the video feed disconnected. Tristan blew out a breath and closed the laptop. "Well, that's done," he muttered, stretching his long limbs. "I'm glad we could finally give them a name. They were probably getting a little nervous with the lack of progress. Now we can focus our efforts on this girl, and maybe her brother, until we have an answer."

I didn't respond. I should have been relieved; the mission was back on track, and we had a real course of action. I didn't like the unknown; I wanted a visible plan, orders I could follow, an objective I could reach. I had my orders now. Engage the target. Discern the target to be the sleeper and, if she was, kill the sleeper. Simple, familiar commands. My mind should've been on the mission and how to accomplish it.

But now, all I could think of was Ember. Seeing her again, getting close, learning her secrets. And just a few hours from our designated meeting time, I found myself strangely torn. I wanted to see her, was looking forward to it, in all honesty…but at the same time, I was reluctant. I didn't want to lie to her.

I didn't want Ember to be the sleeper.

Shaken, I grabbed the binoculars from the counter and headed toward the door. I couldn't think like that. Personal feelings had nothing to do with the objective. I had my orders, and I'd never failed a mission yet. I would not waver now.

"Uh, Garret?" Tristan's voice halted me at the door. I turned to find him watching me with his arms crossed, a bemused look on his face. "What are you doing?"

I held up the binoculars. "What we've been doing every night since the time we got here. Why?"

He rolled his eyes. "Didn't you hear the lieutenant? We have the night off. Seriously, put down the damn specs before I hit you with them. Garret, we are in *California.* Beaches, volleyball, bikinis, nightclubs. It can't be missions and training every second of every day." He gave me a look that was sympathetic and exasperated at the same time. "Even the Perfect Soldier needs to take a break once in a while. Hell, you have permission to relax from headquarters itself. Forget the mission for one night."

*Forget the mission.* Forget the Order, and the war, and my objective. Before today, I wouldn't have considered it. My life was the Order; I had to be exceptional, unyielding. The Perfect Soldier. That was what everyone expected of me.

But this afternoon, I'd gone surfing with a beautiful red-haired girl, and everything about the Order and the war had flown out of my head the second my board sliced down that wave. It was the most exhilarating moment in my life. I couldn't remember having that much fun in…ever, really. My free time, when I had it, normally consisted of training—honing the skills that kept me alive. While the other soldiers went to bars and nightclubs, Tristan included, I was usually at the gym, or the shooting range, or studying mission tactics. There were a few non-training activities I enjoyed—reading and action movies, and I could hit the center of a dartboard nine times out of ten—but as a whole, my life consisted of training and battle and little else.

Now I'd begun to wonder—what might I be missing? Tristan had always pressed me to come to bars, clubs or parties with him, and I had always refused, not seeing the point. But maybe there didn't have to be a point. Maybe it was just to experience something new.

"Well," Tristan said, grabbing his keys from the counter, "you can stay here and be the perfect little soldier, if you want. I'm going out. Probably won't be back till sunrise, and there will be a fifty-fifty chance I'll be very wasted, so don't wait up—"

"Hold on."

Tristan paused, blinking in shock as I tossed the binoculars to the armchair and turned back to face him. For a second, I almost backed out, but forced myself to keep talking. "Where are you taking us, exactly?" I asked. "Will I need a fake ID?"

His mouth fell open dramatically. "Okay, sorry. Who are you and what did you do with my partner?"

"Shut up. Are we going or not?"

He grinned, making a grand gesture toward the front door. "After you, partner. I don't know what's happening here, exactly, but whatever you're on, feel free to keep taking it."

*Not "it,"* I thought as I opened the front door. *Who. And you can keep wondering all you like, because I have no idea what's going on, either.*

# EMBER

"Hellooooooo. Earth to Ember. Are you still with us?"

I blinked and tore my gaze away from the glass case and the sparkling collection of diamonds, sapphires, emeralds and rubies within. At my elbow, Lexi sighed, giving me a look that said she'd been trying to get my attention for a while. The well-dressed woman behind the counter offered a polite, I-don't-think-you're-going-to-buy-anything smile, and moved on to a man looking at engagement rings.

"Sorry," I muttered, turning back to Lexi. I hadn't really been spacing out so much as thinking about the hidden room, and the secrets it still contained. In a stupidly risky move this afternoon, I'd snuck down to the basement after my training session, only to discover the code Cobalt had given me no longer worked. Either Talon had it changed or it reset automatically, because after the second time I punched it in, the panel gave an ominous beep and the words *Warning: Incorrect Sequence* had flashed across the screen in red, making me flee back upstairs.

I couldn't get back into the secret room. Which was annoying and left me with only one option. I was going to have to find Cobalt. And I had no idea how I was going to do that.

"Where'd Kristin go?" I wondered, trying to take my

mind off Talon. I was free, I was here with friends and I didn't have to see Scary Talon Lady until tomorrow. I wasn't going to ruin the rest of the day thinking about sadistic trainers and absent rogue dragons.

Lexi pointed. Kristin was on the other end of the jewelry kiosk, admiring a new bracelet while her newest boy-shaped "friend" stuck his bank card back in his wallet. I'd forgotten his name. Jimmy or Jason or Joe or Bob, something like that. Poor guy. None of the core group bothered to remember his name, either. We were all used to Kristin's endless stream of new guys.

"You and your obsession with shiny things," Lexi muttered as we rejoined Kristin, who had sent poor Joe-Bob into a nearby Starbucks for a latte. "You're almost as bad as Kristin, only she gets boys to buy her stuff."

Kristin smiled. "It's not my fault they all want to buy me presents for my birthday." She raised her wrist, where the bracelet twinkled like a thousand stars. Entranced, I watched the light dance off the gemstones, and Kristin shook her head. "Em, you're not using your assets to your advantage. If you really wanted a sparkly, there's not a guy in the world who wouldn't shell out for you. You just have to bat your eyes and let them *think* they're getting some later."

I wrinkled my nose. "That's okay. I'm not, you know… evil."

"Suit yourself." Kristin dropped her wrist and smiled at Joe-Bob, who was approaching with a large, whipped-cream-and-caramel-drizzled latte. He gave it to Kristin with a goofy smile, and she purred her thanks, watching him from beneath her lashes as she took a long sip. I had to turn away to hide my rolling eyeballs.

"So," Lexi announced brightly. "Where to now? Lunch? Is anyone hungry? Besides Ember, I mean."

"Hey." I crossed my arms. "Since I eat more than the two of you combined, my vote should count for twice as much."

"I'm not done shopping," Kristin said, pouting at Joe-Bob. "I wanted to find a top for the party this weekend. Let's go look at one more store, and then we can get food."

I groaned, knowing "one more store" with Kristin meant at least an hour of watching her try on outfits. And while I normally didn't mind, I was starving, restless and getting cranky. Dragon wanted food now!

As if to prove my point, my stomach growled, and I put a hand over my middle. "Kristin, I swear, if I have to watch you try on shoes for an hour, I'm going to eat your boyfriend. With a fork." Joe-Bob blinked at me, but I ignored him. "It's lunchtime, and you don't want to see me hungry. You won't like me when I'm hungry."

"Well," said a new voice behind me, "I guess I'll have to buy you lunch, then."

My heart skipped a beat. I turned, and there was Garret, just a step away, watching me with a faint smile on his face. He wore jeans and a white shirt, and his bright hair glimmered like strands of metal in the artificial light.

I couldn't say anything for a moment, and Garret's gunmetal eyes shifted to Lexi and Kristin, who were also staring at him. "Sorry. Do you mind if I kidnap Ember for a while? Just to make sure she doesn't eat anyone before you leave."

Kristin, appraising Garret with a sly look on her face, hesitated, but Lexi grabbed her arm and stepped away from me. "Hey, Garret! Sure, you two go ahead. Take your time." She gave me a very unsubtle wink, and I frowned at her.

"We'll be around. Text us when you're done, Em. Or…you know…whenever."

They walked off, Lexi nearly dragging Kristin with her, Joe-Bob following behind like a lost puppy, and melted into the crowds. I glanced at Garret, and he smiled. "Looks like it's just us."

★ ★ ★

The food court was a madhouse, as usual. I breathed in the sweet, greasy smell of hamburgers, eggrolls, pizza, corn dogs, waffle cones and cinnamon buns, and sighed. *Oh, yeah. If I could eat General Tso's chicken every single day for the rest of my life, I could die happy.* The crowds were much thicker here, dozens of voices blending into a general cacophony of noise, and Garret seemed tenser than usual.

Still, he was a perfect gentleman, buying lunch for us at Panda Garden, attempting to teach me how to use chopsticks, which I'd never gotten the hang of. After I accidentally launched a piece of the general's chicken at his head, which he impressively dodged, he finally acknowledged defeat and let me have my plastic fork.

Dragons don't eat with tiny sticks.

"How long have you been here?" Garret asked once I'd plowed through most of my food. He probably realized he wouldn't get very far if he tried talking to me while I was starving, and in this, the boy was observant. I took a sip of Mountain Dew before answering.

"Not long." I shrugged. "Just since the beginning of the summer."

"Where did you live before?"

"South Dakota, with my grandparents." I speared a carrot

with the fork and shoved it in my mouth. "Our parents died in a car crash when Dante and I were really young, so I barely remember them. Our grandparents took us in after that."

"What brought you here?"

Questions. For just a moment, unease flickered. Our instructors always cautioned us about too many questions, particularly questions into our history and personal lives. It could be genuine curiosity, or it could be something far more sinister. Many a hatchling had been murdered by the Order because they'd said the wrong thing, revealed too much.

*Garret? Could he be…?* I glanced at him over our plates. Settled back in his chair, he was watching me, a thoughtful expression on his face. The way he was looking at me with those bright gray eyes made my stomach dance. *No way. I'm being paranoid. He's too young to be a ruthless killer.*

Besides, I already had the answer ready to go. "Grandpa Bill developed lung cancer and could no longer take care of us," I said, reciting the script flawlessly. "Dante and I came to Crescent Beach to live with our aunt and uncle until he recovers. I hope he'll be okay, but to tell you the truth, I like it here better."

He cocked his head, adorably puzzled. "Why?"

"There aren't many oceans in South Dakota." I sighed. "There's not much of anything, really. I think I've always been a Cali girl at heart. If I left the ocean now, I might shrivel up and blow away on the breeze. What about you?" I waved the fork at him. "You're from Chicago, right? Won't you miss this when you leave? Or do you get homesick?"

It was his turn to shrug. "One place is as good as another."

I didn't understand that, or the flatness in his voice. "But you have friends, right? Back home? Don't you miss them?"

"I guess."

Now he seemed uncomfortable, as if this conversation hadn't gone the way he'd expected. I let the subject drop, and he fell silent, gazing at his hands. His eyes had gone blank and cold, his expression closed off. I blinked at the change, at the wall lying between us now, wondering what I'd said to shut him down. Morosely, I picked at my food, but then perked up at something over his head.

"Wait here," I told him, rising from my seat. "I'll be right back."

When I returned, I placed a large gooey cinnamon bun on the table in front of him and smiled. "Here. Dessert is on me."

He eyed it curiously. "What is it?"

"A cinnamon roll, duh." I sat and took a large bite out of mine, feeling the warm, cloying sweetness spread right through my teeth. "Just try it. I got you the extra, extra sweet roll, with the caramel-pecan icing on top. You'll like it, trust me."

He took a cautious bite, and his eyes got huge, before his face scrunched up like he had swallowed a lemon. Swallowing, he coughed twice, reached for his soda and took a long sip before leaning back in his chair, like the bun might suddenly leap up and force its way into his mouth again.

"Too sweet?" I asked innocently, biting my lip to keep from cackling with laughter at his shocked expression. "If it's too much, I could help you eat it."

"You go ahead," he rasped, taking another long sip of his drink. "I think I can feel my veins clogging."

Giggling hysterically, I finished mine, snagged his napkin

and pulled the abandoned bun toward me. He gazed back with a slightly exasperated smile on his face.

"You should smile more," I told him, biting into the Sweet Cinnamon Bun of Death. Oh, yeah, this was a diabetic's nightmare. My teeth were screaming for mercy. "You're very cute when you smile, you know."

He cocked his head in that puzzled, adorable way. "Don't I smile?"

"Not very often," I admitted. "Mostly you look like you're trying to decide where the next sniper attack will come from. Some might call that paranoia, but you know…" I shrugged and took another bite of Death by Icing.

He chuckled. "It isn't being paranoid if they're really out to get you."

I blinked at him before I realized he was making a joke. Laughing, I threw my wadded-up napkin at him (he caught it, of course) and shook my head. "See, I knew you had it in you somewhere."

Finishing the last of the bun, I wiped my hands and stood, tossing our trash into a nearby bin. "Well, now that I'm sufficiently hyped up on sugar and preservatives, wanna go shoot some zombies with me?"

# GARRET

I was beginning to reach the point where Ember's sudden, random phrases didn't startle me quite so much anymore, but still, this one threw me a bit. "What?"

It wasn't exactly my fault. This morning, I'd woken with a massive, raging headache, the inside of my mouth feeling like I'd swallowed cotton soaked in vomit. The events of last night were a bit of a blur, but I think it involved Tristan, a karaoke bar and alcohol. Lots of alcohol. When I'd stumbled into the kitchen this morning, red-eyed and bleary with pain, my partner had laughed, slid a cup of black coffee my way and pronounced me a real man. I was too hungover to talk, so I had to be content with flipping him the finger.

Fortunately, I had a high recovery rate, and by this afternoon I'd felt almost normal again. Enough to track down the girl partially responsible for my temporary lapse of judgment, anyway. But apparently, I wasn't one hundred percent recovered from my first experience with hangovers, because I was almost certain Ember had just said something about shooting zombies.

She laughed, taking my hand and pulling me upright. My senses buzzed at her touch. "I take it you've never been to an arcade before, either. Come on. I'll show you."

She led me across the crowded mall, past dozens of clothing stores interspersed with the random phone or jewelry kiosks. Finally, at the end of the mall in a dark little corner, she pulled me toward an entrance lit with hundreds of flashing neon lights. Strange sounds came from within: automated shouts and screams, revving engines and metallic buzzers, bells and whistles.

"What is this place?" I asked, peering through the door.

"It's an arcade," was the reply. "I always see it when I'm here with Lex and Kristin, but they'd rather shop and do boring things, so I've never been inside." Her arm rose, pointing to a boxy black machine near the front, a screen glowing blue in the center. "See that one? It's a zombie shooter. I've always wanted to try it, but the girls aren't interested and Dante is never at the mall, so..."

She looked at me hopefully. I followed her gaze, trying to understand what she wanted. Zombie shooter? At least the "shooter" part was somewhat familiar. "This is...a game of some kind?" I guessed.

"Well, yeah. Of course." Her eyes sparkled as she glanced back, eager and excited. "How 'bout it, Garret? Wanna give it a shot? Or are you scared I'll beat you?"

I smiled. A game that involved shooting things? She didn't know who she was dealing with. "Lead the way."

A few minutes later, I stood in front of a boxy black machine, a flimsy toy gun in my hand, gazing at the screen in the middle. Island of the Hungry Dead, it spelled out in dripping letters, just as a deep, automated voice said the same. Ember grinned at me and hefted her "gun."

"Ready?" she challenged.

"This is extremely impractical," I told her as a dark swampland appeared on the screen before us. "There's no way a firearm like this would shoot anything."

And then a zombie lurched out from behind a tree and lunged at the screen. A bright, fake spatter of blood appeared on my side, and Ember hooted, clicking her plastic gun. The zombie exploded into completely unrealistic clouds of red ooze and disappeared, and the girl blew on the muzzle of her fake pistol like it was smoking.

"That's one for me," she announced as more zombies lurched toward us with arms outstretched. A grin quirked her lips as she glanced at me, smug and challenging. "Come on, Garret, aren't boys good at this kind of stuff?"

I looked back at the approaching zombie horde, raised my gun and smirked. *All right,* I thought, imagining myself back in the Vasyugan Swamps, facing a murderous juvenile dragon and its gang of human smugglers. *You want me to shoot things? Here we go.*

★ ★ ★

"You are a total cheater," Ember announced later that afternoon, after our fourth play through. I grinned at her, the handle of the toy gun smooth and familiar in my palm. She glowered at me, small form bristling with annoyance. "*And* a liar."

I blinked innocently. "What do you mean?"

"There's no way you haven't played this before," she raged, pointing firmly to the screen, where the words *Victory! Player Two* were flashing again. "No one can be that good a shot on their first try. You've done this before. Admit it!"

"I have never played this before," I told her honestly, hoping she wouldn't ask why I was so good at shooting things with a toy gun. *Because I'm very good at shooting things with a real gun.* She gave me a doubtful look, and I held up my hands, grinning. "I swear."

"Okay, fine. I believe you." She brandished another quarter, eyes gleaming. "One more round?"

"You're on."

At that moment, however, my phone buzzed. I dug it out of my pocket and held it up, immediately recognizing Tristan's number flashing across the screen. "Sorry," I told her, backing away. "I have to take this. I'll be right back."

Retreating to a more quiet corner, I ducked behind a flashing crane-type game and put the phone to my ear. "Yes?"

"How's the mall excursion going?" Tristan's voice held traces of amusement. "I assume you found your target, because I know you haven't been walking around for three hours doing nothing."

A bell rang out somewhere behind me before I had a chance to answer. Tristan's voice took on a suspicious tone. "What the heck was that? Where are you guys?"

"Uh, the arcade."

"Well, it's good to know that while *I've* spent the afternoon researching our potential targets, *you've* been messing around at the arcade." Tristan's voice dripped sarcasm. "Did you at least get any useful information out of her?"

"I'm still working on it."

"Fine." Tristan didn't sound convinced, but he backed off for now. "If you say you've got this. I just wanted to tell you a few things I discovered about the Hill residence. Seems the original owner never put the property up for sale. And when the lot did sell, it sold for twice of what it was worth."

"Sounds like somebody bribed him just to acquire the house."

"Exactly. And get this—according to the home owner's association, extreme renovating around the property isn't permitted, but the new owner had a team of contractors at the house for nearly a month, and nothing was changed on the outside."

"So, they might've changed the inside extensively, perhaps to set up a base for Talon operatives."

"That's what I'm thinking." Tristan's voice turned contemplative. "Of course, we're going to have to get inside to investigate. Breaking and entering is out, obviously—if we're wrong, it could spook the real sleepers into moving, and if it *is* a Talon base, they'll likely have a ton of alarms set up. We can't risk alerting the targets. So it looks like it's up to you."

"Anything unusual on the surveillance?"

"No. All clear on this end so far."

"Garret?"

I turned. Ember stood behind me, phone in hand, looking abashed. "Kristin and Lexi are leaving in a few minutes," she announced. "But they want to know if I'll need a ride home."

I was confused for a second, before I realized what she was asking. "Understood," I told Tristan quickly. "Gotta go."

I hung up. Ember still waited, green eyes watching me expectantly. "It's your call," I told her. "If you need to leave with your friends, I understand. Or I can drive you home." And if I drove her home, perhaps there was a way I could get her to ask me inside. Though, if I was being honest, I wasn't ready to leave just yet. And I didn't think she was, either.

She smiled. "You wouldn't mind?"

"Only if you agree to one more game of zombie island."

The grin grew wider, and her eyes flashed. "Deal."

# EMBER

We played three more times. I think he let me win the last one, but I wasn't complaining. I could never get Lexi or Kristin to play games with me, and Dante was rarely at the mall, so having Garret around was pretty great. After we got bored with shooting zombies, we tried a racing game (I won that one), a fighting game where we were pretty evenly matched (I still beat him), and then Garret absolutely stomped me in air hockey. His reflexes and hand-eye coordination were amazing, better than I'd ever seen in a human before. My supercompetitive side would've been annoyed but, unlike my brother, he was so damn humble about it. Plus, he really seemed to be having fun.

Later, we revisited the food court, as I was hungry again and needed a snack after a long day of shooting zombies. As I munched a slice of pizza, Garret sat across from me with a soda, his expression thoughtful.

"What?" I asked at last. "Do I have pepper stuck in my teeth or something?"

He smiled. "You keep surprising me," he said, resting his elbows on the table between us. "I have several things I need to get done today, but I keep getting pulled into zombie games and racing and buying mall food. I've never done that before." The smile twitched into a smirk. "I've decided it's your fault. You're very distracting."

I cocked my head. "Good distracting, or bad distracting?"

"I'm not sure yet."

"Well, when you figure it out, let me know. I'll be sure not to care very much." Finishing the last of my crust, I wiped my hands on a napkin, then noticed Garret's arm resting on the table, lean and tan and muscular.

I blinked. A jagged, pale circle marred his forearm near the elbow, shiny and white against his tan skin. I looked closer and saw another scar near his wrist, like an old, faded puncture wound, and several tiny ones scattered between the pair. They were faint, the smaller ones barely visible, but judging from the larger two, his arm had definitely taken some damage.

"What is this from?" I asked softly, tracing one with a finger before I could stop myself.

He jerked back, drawing in a sharp breath, and I froze. For a second, we both sat there, rigid. Then, not really knowing why, I slowly reached for his arm, cupping my fingers around his wrist. Garret didn't move, his steely eyes trained on me as I gently drew his arm forward again. His skin was cool, and I could feel the strength in his hands, in the muscles coiling back like a spring. But his arm remained perfectly still as I touched the scar again, tracing the circle with a fingertip. "It looks like it hurt."

Garret let out a shaky breath. "It was fairly painful, yes." His voice was tight, as if everything had seized up and he could barely breathe.

"What happened?"

"An accident. I was attacked by the neighbor's Rottweiler

a few years back." His arm shook a little, but he didn't pull away. "I'm told I was lucky I didn't lose any fingers."

Fascinated, I turned his palm over. Another scar marred his forearm, and a thick, jagged line crossed his wrist, making me shiver. As a general rule, dogs didn't like me. I was sure they could sense something wasn't quite right, because they usually fled or barked at me threateningly from a safe distance. I couldn't imagine what I'd do if I had a giant Rottweiler hanging off my arm, but it would probably involve a lot of singed dog hair.

I looked up and found Garret watching me, the intensity of his gaze making my breath catch. Heat rose to my cheeks, and my heart pounded, as he continued to stare at me. The rest of the world faded away, and all I could imagine was leaning forward, meeting him halfway across the table and…

My phone chirped, indicating a new text, startling us both. Abruptly, Garret pulled his arm from my grip and rose, sliding back the chair. I blinked, startled again by how quickly he could move; one moment his hand was in mine, his skin cool beneath my touch, the next he was gone, and I was gazing at an empty seat. Frowning, I dug my phone from my pocket and looked at the screen. There were several missed calls from a number I didn't recognize, so they were probably spam or telemarketers. But the text was from Dante, which almost never happened, and the message was even more ominous.

Where are u? Come home RIGHT NOW. T is here.

"Crap," I muttered. Across the table, Garret watched me with serious gray eyes as I stuck the phone back in my pocket and rose, gazing up at him. "That was my brother," I said.

"There's some kind of crisis at the house—he wants me to come back right away."

Garret nodded. "I'll take you home."

★ ★ ★

There were no strange cars in the driveway when we rolled up to the house, nothing to indicate anything unusual was happening, but my stomach still twisted nervously as we pulled to a stop.

*Why is Talon here? Do they...* My stomach tied itself into a knot. *Do they know about me and Cobalt? Have they come to take me back?*

Forcing my gaze from the house, I looked at Garret, wondering if this was the last time I'd see him. "Thanks," I said, trying to smile. "For lunch and the ride and everything. I guess I'll talk to you later."

"Ember." He hesitated, as if trying to find the right words. "Are you in trouble?" he finally asked. "Do you want me to come in and explain what happened?"

"Um." I cringed inside. Definitely no, and especially not today. Liam and Sarah had made it very clear that they didn't want our friends in the house, for any reason. I always met everyone at the beach, or we'd hang at Kristin's huge sprawling beach house, or head down to the Smoothie Hut. No one seemed to care that Dante and I never invited anyone inside. Lexi and Kristin had never been past the front door, and neither had any of Dante's friends. We'd told everyone that our uncle was an eccentric writer who needed absolute quiet to work, and that was that.

Under normal circumstances, Liam would blow a gasket

if I invited some strange boy into the house. Today, with Talon visiting, it was out of the question.

"You don't have to do that," I told him. "I'll be all right. See you around, Garret."

He looked faintly disappointed, which struck me as a little strange. I couldn't think of any boy who would *want* to come in and take the heat for me. Dante's friends, Calvin and Tyler especially, didn't even knock on the door when they picked him up. They sat in the driveway and honked.

"You still owe me a surf lesson," he said as I reached for the door handle. I looked back, and he smiled. "Tomorrow, if you're up for it," he offered quietly, those metallic eyes never leaving my face. "No Lexi or Calvin or anyone else this time. Just you and me."

"Garret…" I didn't know what to say. I didn't know if Talon would still be here tomorrow, if *I* would still be here tomorrow. Maybe Talon had come to whisk me back to the organization, proclaiming I was rebellious and disobedient, unfit for a life among humans. I didn't want to promise him tomorrow when I wasn't sure I would ever see him again.

But a day with Garret, alone… How could I say no? I liked being with him. I liked his quiet confidence and subtle sense of humor, the way having fun seemed like such a novelty to him. He challenged me, he was easy to talk to and he wasn't bad on the eyes, either. (Okay, so that was an understatement; he was supercute, even my dragon side agreed with that.) I felt he was hiding so much, that I wasn't seeing the real Garret at all, and the more I hung out with him, the more I would learn.

Also, being with him did strange, twisty things to my insides. My dragon instincts did not approve; they still didn't like this human with his amazing reflexes and bright, intense eyes. The eyes of a predator. But there was another part of me that couldn't resist. And the thought of never seeing him again was unfathomable. Even if I knew it was probably for the best.

"Tomorrow," I said, and nodded. "Meet me at the cove at noon. Do you remember where it is? I can give you directions if you need it."

He shook his head. "I remember." One side of his mouth quirked up in that faint, wry smile. "I'll see you then."

*Tomorrow.* Tomorrow I would meet Garret alone on a secluded beach, and we would ride the waves and have fun until evening, and then we might head down to the main beach to hang out with Lexi and Dante and everyone. Just like always. Nothing would be different. I would not let myself think that I'd be gone.

He was still watching me with those bright metallic eyes, and the intensity was back, making my insides squirm. Tearing my gaze from his, I opened the Jeep door and slid out. "See you tomorrow," I replied, a promise to us both, and turned away. I deliberately did not look back, but I could feel his gaze on me as I made my way up the walk, until the front door closed behind me.

★ ★ ★

As I walked into the entryway, something grabbed my upper arm, steely fingers digging into my skin, hard enough to make me gasp. Wincing, I turned and stared into the furious eyes of my trainer, who glared down like she wanted to bite my head off.

"Where have you been?" she whispered harshly, giving me a shake. I bit my lip to keep from crying out in pain. "I've been trying to contact you for hours. Why didn't you answer?"

Too late, I remembered all the missed calls on my phone. The unknown number was probably hers. But she had never called me before; it was just assumed I'd see her again the next morning. "I was at the mall," I whispered back. "I didn't hear my phone ring."

"Get in there," Scary Talon Lady snapped, shoving me toward the living room. "Mind your manners, if you have any." Her poisonous-green eyes narrowed to slits. "I swear, hatchling, if you embarrass me, you'll pay for it tomorrow."

Rubbing my bruised arm, I walked into the living room.

As I crossed the threshold, six people turned to stare at me. Uncle Liam and Aunt Sarah stood in the kitchen, glaring at me over the counter, but they weren't important. Neither was Dante's trainer, who stood along the opposite wall, his hands folded in front of him. Dante, sitting alone in the middle of the couch, shot me a relieved, almost frightened look as the pair of strangers in the room turned their attention to me.

A man rose from the armchair, a smile stretching across his narrow face. The smile looked forced, somehow, not real. As if he had seen pictures of a smile and was imitating them, but didn't understand the meaning. My dragon hissed and cringed back as two pale blue eyes settled on me, ancient and terrifying. An adult, and a really old one at that, the way my instincts were screaming at me to run. He wore a plain gray business suit, and his dark hair was cut close, as was the neatly trimmed goatee.

"Ah, Ember Hill." When he spoke, the entire room fell silent. Not that anyone had been speaking before, but my trainer, Dante's trainer, our guardians and the well-muscled man in a black suit standing beside his chair all went completely motionless, their attention solely on him. His voice was low, confident, similar to the one I'd heard in the secret room that night, and I wondered if this was the same dragon. He gestured to the sofa where Dante sat, rigid and unmoving. "Please, have a seat."

Warily, I sat, giving my brother a quick, nervous glance. "What's going on?" I said, gazing around at the ring of somber adults, all still watching the man in the suit. "Are we in trouble?"

"Trouble? No, of course not." Another blank, empty smile. "Why would you be in trouble?"

"Um…" I decided not to answer that. "No reason. I was just…curious."

"This is a routine visit," the man continued, his pale blue eyes watching me with the unblinking stare of a hawk. "There is no reason to be alarmed. My superiors sent me to check on your progress, see how you are coming along in your new home. So…" He laced his fingers under his chin, regarding us intently. "Have you settled in all right? Are you happy here?"

All attention shifted to us. Scary Talon Lady watched me from across the room, her eyes gleaming dangerously. It wouldn't matter what I said, I realized. I was expected to be happy, settled in and doing fine. Admitting I was anything but would be useless, and probably result in a lot of pain for me tomorrow morning. Talon didn't care about our happiness; they just wanted to make sure we were following the rules. The discussion I'd overheard with Liam and Sarah in the secret room only confirmed that.

"Yeah," I muttered as Dante stated a polite "Yes, sir" at the same time. "Everything's peachy."

As expected, the man in the suit didn't notice my flat tone of voice, and if he did, he didn't care. But my trainer's eyes grew hard and cold and terrifying, making me cringe inside. Oh, I was going to pay for this tomorrow.

"Good!" the man in the suit exclaimed with a brisk nod.

"Talon will be pleased to hear it." His gaze shifted to Dante's trainer and Scary Talon Lady, standing by the far wall. "And their education? How are they progressing?"

"The boy is doing well, sir," said Dante's teacher. I noticed he didn't even look at the other man but stared straight ahead, averting his eyes. I shivered. In Talon society, looking directly into a dragon's eyes and holding its gaze was considered a challenge or a threat. Of course, living among humans with their sloppy glances and wandering eyes, we'd learned to adapt, but you still didn't want to hold a staring contest with an older, more powerful dragon. At best, it was considered extremely rude and asking for trouble. At worst, you'd get your head bitten off.

"And the girl?" The man in the suit looked at Scary Talon Lady. "There are concerns within the organization that your student lacks…discipline. Is this true?"

My trainer smiled, but it was an ominous, threatening smile, directed right at me.

"Oh, she's coming along, sir," my trainer said, her eyes gleaming with dark promise. "There are a few issues we need to work on, but worry not. We'll fix them. We will indeed."

I was *not* looking forward to tomorrow.

The man in the suit stayed a while longer, asking questions, speaking to my trainer and my guardians, occasionally talking to me and Dante. The tension in the room did not go away, and I began to feel very twitchy surrounded by four adult dragons, all their attention directed at me. Not only that, one of Talon's cardinal rules was never to have too many dragons in one place at once, as it attracted St. George like moths to a flame. Some of Talon's higher-ups, the big shots closest to the Elder Wyrm, never ventured into the open. Like the Elder

Wyrm—Talon's CEO and the most powerful dragon in existence—they remained behind the scenes and in the shadows. If the man in the suit was as important as everyone seemed to think he was, having him in Crescent Beach was really weird. Why would someone this powerful pay a visit to two insignificant hatchlings, just to see if they were "happy"?

Something else was going on, but I couldn't figure out what. Just another mystery to add to the big, ominous cloud called Talon.

As the afternoon waned, Aunt Sarah politely offered to cook dinner for everyone, and it was just as politely declined. The man in the suit rose, spoke once more to our trainers, then turned to me and Dante. He didn't say anything, though, just regarded us with those pale blue eyes that were somehow reptilian even in human form. With a nod and a last empty smile, he turned and left the room, his bodyguard following him out. They didn't walk out the front door, but vanished down the basement stairs, probably going to the secret tunnel. The door creaked shut behind them.

I felt a presence beside me and turned to face my instructor, who beamed one of her scary smiles in my direction. She did not look pleased.

"Well," she said in a conversational tone, despite the evilness of her expression. "You certainly made an impression, didn't you? It appears that Talon thinks you have potential but you lack discipline." Her smile grew wider, and her eyes glimmered. "We will have to work on that, won't we? Rest up tonight, hatchling. Tomorrow is going to be…interesting."

# GARRET

Ember was late again.

Parked under the same grove of palm trees from a few days ago, I checked my watch for the third time since arriving at the cove. Eighteen minutes past noon, and still no sign of the girl. I wondered if she'd "lost track of time" again, or had just forgotten. To me, it was incomprehensible. In the Order, punctuality was everything. You were either on time, or you were early, but you were *never* late. If a superior told you to meet them in the chapel at 0400, for no special reason whatsoever, you had better be in that pew when the time rolled around or you'd risk pulling KP duty for a month.

I figured the locals of Crescent Beach didn't worry too much about being on time, at least in the summer. The whole place had a lazy serene feel to it, where you took each day as it came and didn't stress about time, place or anything.

I could never live like that, not on a regular basis. It would drive me crazy. Much like these strange, unfamiliar urges a certain red-haired girl stirred in me. I didn't understand them, and I wasn't sure I liked them. When Ember had taken my hand yesterday, I'd frozen. For the first time in my life, I hadn't known what to do. Looking back, I realized that it was highly unusual that I hadn't responded, that I'd even let her touch me in the first place. In the Order, if anyone grabbed me like that, they would be on the ground. It was reflex, a reaction you couldn't help when your life was constantly on the line.

But I'd let her touch me, let her trace the scars sustained in a fight with a stubborn green dragon that had refused to die. And I hadn't pulled away. Her fingers had sent a rush of warmth up my arm all the way to the pit of my stomach. I'd never felt anything like that before. I…wanted her to touch me again.

Startled by my own thoughts, I leaned back and rubbed my eyes. What was wrong with me? I was a soldier, trained to keep emotions in check at all times. I could face down a charging dragon and show no fear. I could endure two hours of my superior screaming in my face and feel nothing. What was it about Ember that was different?

I shook myself. It didn't matter. I still had my mission, and Ember was still a target. The rest of the group we had pretty much eliminated from the list. Lexi and Calvin had been born in Crescent Beach and hadn't lived anywhere else. Kristin Duff, our other prime suspect, wasn't a local but visited Crescent Beach every summer with her father and stepmother. They had an apartment in New York City, where Kristin's father worked as a stockbroker.

That left the twins, Ember and Dante Hill. Who'd just arrived in Crescent Beach this summer. Who lived with their aunt and uncle in a large house on the beach. Who didn't have any parents.

Nothing was certain, of course. We could be chasing a false lead. Ember Hill could be perfectly normal, but I wouldn't be sure until I knew her better, or she slipped up. Regardless, I had to get her to trust me.

If she ever arrived.

Slumping against the seat, I resigned myself to waiting.

★ ★ ★

At 1331, Ember finally showed up.

Opening the car door, I got out and headed toward the beach, where a lone figure with mussed red hair stood facing the ocean, a surfboard under one arm. She was scanning the waves, shading her eyes with a hand, when I stepped behind her.

"Looking for someone?"

She jumped, spun around and blinked in surprise, as if not quite believing I was there. "Garret? How long have you… I mean… Wow, you're still here." When I didn't say anything, a flush darkened her cheeks as she looked at the sand. "I thought you might've given up," she admitted.

I almost had. I'd told myself I would wait a half hour past noon before calling it quits. That was a reasonable time to give someone who was late. But a half hour had turned into forty-five minutes, then an hour, then fifteen minutes past the hour. I'd finally accepted the fact that she wasn't coming and had shoved the key into the ignition when the girl in question had suddenly gone stumbling down to the beach, not seeing me in the palm grove.

"Lost track of time again?" I asked coolly. She winced, probably thinking I was angry, but I wasn't upset, not really. I was actually relieved to see her; in the hour and fifteen minutes I'd sat alone in the Jeep, my mind had come up with a number of terrible things that could've happened. Illogical, improbable things, but still. Everything from car accidents to shark attacks had gone through my mind, making me restless with worry. It was a new experience, one I found I didn't care for. I'd never worried about anyone before. My fellow soldiers, my brothers-in-arms, it was different with them. We knew that what we did was extremely dangerous. We all knew we could die at any time, and we accepted that. Worry for another's safety was dangerous and could get everyone killed. You had to trust your team to know their orders and follow them through. Casualties were a certainty, a fact of life. That was one of the perks about being in the Order; soldiers of St. George never died of old age.

But… I had been worried for Ember. I'd desperately hoped nothing had happened to her to cause such tardiness. Which seemed rather foolish now. She was obviously okay, though she lacked her usual bounce.

"I'm really sorry, Garret," Ember said, gazing at me with big green eyes. With a start, I noticed dark circles crouched beneath them, a sign of exhaustion that hadn't been there yesterday. "Something came up at home, and I couldn't get away. I wanted to be here—I came as fast as I could. Dante had the car, I had to call Lexi to get her to drop me off…"

She looked miserable, and I spoke quickly to reassure her. "It's fine, Ember. I'm not upset. I'm just glad you came." I smiled, and she seemed to relax. "We're here now, so don't worry about it. But…" I glanced at the single surfboard she held under one arm. "You only brought one board? I'm afraid I don't have one."

"Oh, right." She brushed hair out of her eyes, suddenly embarrassed. "Well, I didn't have time to grab a second one, so we'll have to try something new. If you're up for it."

I started to answer, but as Ember dropped her arm, I noticed something on her shoulder that made my pulse skip. Gently, and without even thinking about it, I grabbed her elbow, tugging her sleeve up.

A mottled purple bruise marred the skin above her bicep. I drew in a sharp breath, not knowing why I was so furious. "What happened?"

Ember squirmed from my grasp and stepped away, not meeting my eyes. "Nothing," she replied, pulling her sleeve down. "Walked into a door. A very rude, boorish door that didn't get out of the way fast enough. It's nothing to be concerned about. If I see it again, I'll be sure to kick it."

"Ember…"

"Garret, trust me. There's nothing you can do." She looked up, forcing a challenging smile. "Now, are we going to go surfing, or what? I hope you're up for what I have planned."

I exhaled slowly, pushing back the desire to find whoever was responsible for that bruise and snap their neck. "All right," I said, nodding. "Let's go. Whatever you dish out, I'm ready."

She grinned, regaining some of her defiance, and backed toward the surf. "All right, then, hotshot. Let's put your money where your mouth is."

# EMBER

"Ready?" I said to Garret. We sat together, straddling the same surfboard, the telltale swell of a large wave getting rapidly closer. I knelt at the front of the board, facing him and the doubtful look on his face.

"This isn't going to work," he told me.

"It'll work. Paddle."

"Ember—"

"Shut up and paddle!"

The rise loomed closer. Garret flattened himself on the board and paddled, while I spun on my knees and crouched low, peering forward like a figurehead. The wave crested and started to break just as we reached the top. I leaped upright as Garret did the same, but I wasn't used to being this far out in front, or compensating for two bodies on the board. It wobbled, I wobbled…and lost my balance.

With a yelp, I toppled off the board. Just before I hit the water, I saw Garret crash into the surf, as well, and then the world went into spin-cycle mode for a few seconds. I closed my eyes and held my breath until the pounding surf ran out of steam, and I staggered upright, looking around for Garret.

He knelt a few yards away in the sand, the water sluicing around him as it returned to the sea. The sun blazed down on his bare, bronzed shoulders as he tossed his head back, flinging water from his eyes and hair. I felt that odd twisty sensation in my stomach, before pushing it down and splashing up to him.

"Well, that didn't work. Ready for round two?"

He peered up at me, a faint smile on his face. "I'm going to get pounded a few more times before this is over, aren't I?"

"Hey, if you're scared—"

"I didn't say that." Still smiling, his pushed himself upright, giving me a half amused, half exasperated look. "Though I must be a glutton for punishment or something. Team Human versus the Ocean, round two."

★ ★ ★

It took us three more tries. The first two were learning experiences, figuring out where to stand with another person on the board. The third wipeout was totally my fault; I flailed wildly to keep my balance, accidentally hit Garret in the face and sent us both into the drink.

I met him back in the shallows, where he was dragging the surfboard toward him by the cord attached to his ankle. When he turned around, his left eye was slightly puffy and red, and I grimaced in embarrassment.

"Sorry about that."

He shrugged. "I've had worse." Seeing my sheepish expression, he offered a reassuring smile. "Ember, it's all right. I know how to take a punch, trust me. This is nothing."

"Lemme see it." I stepped closer and rose on tiptoe to better peer at the wound. Garret didn't move, going perfectly still as I examined his face, his eyes fixed on a spot against the horizon. His skin was smooth and tan, though there was a faint dark circle forming around one eye, making me wince. I also discovered another scar, a thin raised line across his temple, nearly invisible beneath his hair. What did he do, I wondered, to get so many?

That ominous, niggling doubt entered my mind again, and I shoved it back. I would not think of that. He was not part of that murdering cult. He couldn't be.

"Well?" His voice surprised me, strained yet strangely nonchalant. Like he was fighting his own instincts not to back away. "What's the verdict?"

"Um, you might have a black eye later tonight. A small one."

He actually chuckled at that, sending a flutter through my stomach. "And here I thought the waves were the most dangerous things I'd be facing."

My heart was suddenly pounding, and I took a few steps into the water to calm it down. Garret's eyes followed me, his mercury gaze searing the back of my head. My face felt warm, and I peered out over the ocean, shielding my eyes from the sun and his piercing stare. "Well, it's not gonna feel great with all the sand and salt getting into it. Wanna call it quits?"

"Quit?" I heard the challenging grin in his voice, and glanced back at him. He was smiling again, his eyes playful. "Giving up already?" he asked, cocking his head. "I told you I can take whatever you dish out. Or was that last wave too scary?"

I blinked in astonishment. Was he *teasing* me? Where did *this* Garret come from? Maybe that last tumble through the waves had jostled his brain a bit. Whatever it was, I wasn't complaining.

"Okay, then," I said, throwing back my own smirk. "You asked for it. One more time."

We strode back into the ocean, mounted the board and searched the horizon for potential waves. Or at least Garret did. Instead of watching the water, I stared at him instead—his face, his profile, his bright hair and the sculpt of his chest and arms.

*Humans are the inferior species,* Scary Talon Lady had said that morning. *If not for their numbers, we would have subjugated them long ago. Remember this, hatchling—we might look like them, walk among them and have integrated into their world, but humans are nothing but the means to an end.*

"Here we go," Garret murmured, and I peered past his shoulders to where a swell was growing and coming toward us rapidly. He faced me again and smiled, making my heart stutter. "Ready?"

I nodded. The wave rose up and started crashing down, but Garret had already leaped to his feet. I followed, losing my balance for a split second, but then two strong hands came to rest against my sides, steadying me. Heart in my throat, I faced forward as we rode the wave down together, moving in unison. I didn't dare look back, but I could sense Garret's fierce grin over my shoulder, and couldn't hold back a whoop of triumph.

We stayed on the board until the wave flattened out in the shallows, and I whooped again, fist-pumping the air. Unfortunately, that was enough to overbalance the board, and we toppled into the water together, making a loud splash.

Laughing, I stood up, blinking water from my eyes. Garret rose in front of me, shaking out his hair, raking it back with his fingers. His shoulders heaved with silent laughter, his whole face alight with triumph and pure happiness. My stomach flipped, and I softly said his name.

Still smiling, he looked down at me.

Rising on my toes, I put my hands on his shoulders, lifted my face to his and kissed him.

He went rigid, hands coming up to grip my arms, but he didn't push me away. I could feel the tight coil of muscles beneath his skin, the acceleration of his heartbeat, echoing my own. His lips were salty from the ocean, warm and soft, even if they weren't responding.

My insides fluttered, sending curls of heat through my stomach and shivers all the way down my spine. So, *this* was what it was like to kiss someone…and mean it. I'd seen people kiss each other thousands of times before, and I remembered Colin's wet, nasty mouth on mine, forced and disgusting. I hadn't understood why kissing was so popular among humans. Why would anyone want to get that close to someone's face? In dragon society, rubbing muzzles or bumping snouts was a sign of ultimate trust; you rarely wanted your head that close to a jaw that could crush skulls and breathe fire. I'd always thought of kissing as one of those common human behaviors I'd never understand. I hadn't known…it could be like this.

Wait. I was a *dragon.* What the hell was I doing?

Breaking the kiss, I pulled back and peeked up at Garret. He stared at me, his expression hovering between confusion and shock. His hands, still gripping my upper forearms, dug somewhat painfully into my skin.

"Um." Wincing slightly, I drew away, and he let me slip from his grasp. His arms dropped to his sides, and he continued to watch me, metallic eyes suddenly unreadable. I might've been embarrassed, if I wasn't slightly freaking out on the inside.

*I just kissed a human. I* kissed *a human. Oh, man, what is wrong with me?* Raking my hands through my hair, I tried to sort through my jumbled thoughts, but it was hard when I still felt the heat of his gaze. *I have to go home. This has gotten too crazy.*

"Sorry," I muttered, backing away from the still-motionless human. "I, uh, I should probably go. Hang on to the board if you want, I'll pick it up some other time. See you later, Garret."

Garret finally moved, shaking himself as if coming out of a trance. "Didn't Lexi drive you here?" he asked, and his voice, normally so calm and self-assured, shook a bit at the end.

Crap, she had. Damn him and his logic. "It's okay." I waved it off, though I still couldn't look at him. "I can walk back, it won't take too long. Or I'll call Lexi to pick me up. If all else fails, I can stick out a thumb." *I just have to get home, right now.*

"Ember, wait." His voice, low and compelling, stopped me in my tracks. Even though I knew I should keep moving, head up the beach without looking back, I couldn't bring myself to walk away from him. I heard him pick up the surfboard, then splash through the water after me. My dragon instincts growled and shied away as he caught up, even though my stupid traitor heart leaped in my chest. "You can't hitchhike all the way back," Garret murmured, though he couldn't bring himself to look at me, either. "I'll drive you home."

# GARRET

The drive back was… *Awkward* was probably the word for it. Ember remained silent, gazing out the window and studiously not looking at me. I kept my hands on the steering wheel and stared straight ahead, though I could still see the girl from the corner of my eye. Neither of us spoke or looked directly at each other, which was good because my mind was churning like a tornado.

When she'd kissed me…all my senses had frozen. Again. I'd been surprised—shocked, really—when her lips touched mine, but I hadn't responded, not even to push her off. That was crazy. My reflexes were better than that; she should've never gotten that close. No one could lay a finger on me in the Order, and in the space of a few days I'd allowed this girl to not only touch me, but to lean in and *kiss* me. If Ember had been one of Talon's operatives, I'd be dead a dozen times over.

The simple truth was that I'd been dropping my guard around her. She was fun and disarming and easy to talk to. Potential target or not, I…liked spending time with her. But that wasn't the most disturbing thing.

No, what was most troubling was the fact that when the kiss ended and Ember drew back, I'd almost stepped forward to kiss her again. And now, with her sitting just a couple feet away, she called to me. I was acutely aware of everything she did, every little motion, shift or sigh. Even when I wasn't looking at her, I could feel her presence, prodding against mine. And it was driving me crazy.

When we pulled up to her street, Ember was reaching for the door handle almost before the Jeep stopped moving. As her door opened, I wondered if I shouldn't try to stop her, or at least talk to her. But the door slammed before I had finished the thought, and the moment was gone.

Numb, I watched her cross the street and stride up to the beach villa without a single glance in my direction, her surfboard bobbing under one arm. With every step, I wanted to call to her, go after her, but something held me back.

As she neared the front door, I felt eyes on me, and I glanced at the top window of the house. A figure watched me through the glass, the late-afternoon sun gleaming off his red hair, before he turned away and vanished from sight.

★ ★ ★

Tristan wasn't home when I returned to the apartment, which was a blessing, as I wasn't in the mood to talk to anyone. Instead, I went to the freestanding heavy bag in the corner of the living room and hit it hard enough to rattle the chains. I didn't want to think. I needed to find my focus, calm this strange, restless energy coursing through my skin. I slugged the bag again, trying to drive the image of a red-haired girl from my system, erase the feel of her lips on mine.

I wasn't even aware of how much time had passed when Tristan walked in. Stopping short of the living room, he regarded me with a half amused, half concerned look. Panting, I let my arms drop, my knuckles raw from pounding the bag, feeling sweat running down my face and into my eyes. With a start, I realized more than an hour had passed since I'd walked into the apartment, and I hadn't stopped or slowed down since I'd thrown that first punch.

"Soooo…" Tristan began, raising an eyebrow at my sweaty, exerted state. "How was your day?"

My mind still hadn't calmed down. This whole time, I could still see Ember, still feel her hands on my shoulders, the instant when her lips touched mine. I gave the bag one last, resounding punch, then leaned back against the wall and closed my eyes, breathing hard. For a second, I considered not telling Tristan what had happened on the beach that afternoon, but quickly decided against it. I'd never kept anything from my partner before. Absolute trust was required when someone held your life in his hands.

"Garret?" Tristan's voice was cautious now, and I heard him step farther into the room. "What happened?"

I scrubbed a hand over my face. "This afternoon," I muttered, dropping my arm. "On the beach. Ember…she…she kissed me."

Tristan's eyebrows shot into his hair. "Come again?" he asked, as though unable to believe what I just told him. "Ember Hill, the girl we've been following all this time, the one we've pegged as a potential sleeper…*kissed* you?"

I shoved myself off the wall, unable to stop flashing back to that instant. "I'm too close," I said, walking to the window. Beyond villa roofs and the tops of palm trees, the ocean sparkled in the sunlight, only reminding me again. "I lost focus," I continued, "and it wasn't the first time it's happened. I don't think I should see her anymore. It's just going to jeopardize the mission."

"No," Tristan said firmly, and I looked at him in surprise. "No, this is what we want, Garret," he explained. "You *have* to get close. It's the only way to discover anything, to really know if she's the sleeper or not. The more she trusts you, the more likely she is to slip up. You can't stop now. You have to keep seeing her."

*Continue spending time with Ember.* The thought left me relieved and terrified all at once. "How do I proceed from here?" I asked, walking back. I had no frame of reference for this kind of thing, no experience to draw upon. And how was I going to pursue this girl, pretend to like her, if she didn't want to see me again? "After she…kissed me…she almost ran away. It seemed to spook her pretty badly. What am I supposed to do now?"

"Did you ask her out, make any plans to see her again?"

"No."

"Why not?"

"I… I was…"

"Too busy being ambushed?"

I sighed, giving the bag a halfhearted punch. "Yeah."

Tristan grinned. "Well, you're just going to have to suck it up and hunt her down, partner," he said, far too cheerfully, I thought. "Be bold. Don't take no for an answer this time. It shouldn't be too difficult. If she kissed you, she has to like you a *little*."

"If she's the sleeper, she shouldn't like me at all," I protested, crossing my arms. Dragons didn't have those kinds of emotions. They were flawless mimics of the human race, which was what made them so dangerous, but they had no real concept of friendship, sorrow, love or regret. At least, that's what I'd always been told.

Tristan shrugged. "Maybe this is part of Talon's training. Do what the humans do to blend in. Seems like something they would attempt, either for control or to throw us off the trail. Or maybe she is just a normal civilian. In any case, you're going to have to continue the ruse until you find out. Think you can handle that?"

A ruse. That's all it was. Pretend to like this girl. Pretend to have feelings, to pursue some kind of relationship. Earn her friendship and trust, knowing I might have to destroy it, and her, in the end.

It felt wrong. Dirty and underhanded, something *they* would do. But… I was a soldier, and this was my mission. I had to remind myself: if Ember was the sleeper, she wasn't an innocent. She was a dragon, a creature who secretly despised mankind and possessed no empathy, no humanity, whatsoever. Even their young, their hatchlings, were just as devious and monstrous as the adults. Maybe even more so, because they seemed so human. Destroying hatchlings before they became cunning, immensely powerful adults was the fastest way we could win this war.

Even if I had to lie. Even if…if I was honest with myself, a small part of me leaped at the thought of seeing her again.

And even if a smaller part, one I shoved to the darkest corner of my mind, was appalled and sickened by what I was planning.

"I can handle it," I told Tristan, and stepped around the bag, heading toward the bathroom and a cold shower. "I know what I have to do."

"Good to hear. And, Garret."

This time, Tristan's voice was ominous. I looked back warily.

"Don't make the mistake of falling for this girl," he warned, watching me intently. "If she's a normal civilian, you don't have any business getting involved. Not with our life. But if she *is* the sleeper, and this is some new way they're teaching their hatchlings to assimilate…" He shook his head, and his eyes narrowed. "If the time ever comes when you have to pull that trigger, you can't have any doubts. You can't hesitate, even for a moment, or she'll tear you apart. You understand that, right?"

Ember's face flashed before me once more, smiling and cheerful, the memory of her kiss making my stomach tighten. I shoved it away ruthlessly.

"Yes," I said. "I understand."

# EMBER

"Where've you been?" Dante asked as I came up the stairs, intending to go straight to my room to hide out the rest of the night. Unfortunately, my nosy twin stood at the top step, gazing down with wary green eyes.

I snorted. "What are you, my egg nanny? I've been surfing, what's it look like?" I sidled past him and headed toward my room. He followed me down the hall, suspicious gaze searing the back of my neck.

"Who was the human that drove you home?" Dante asked. "I haven't seen him before."

"That was Garret," I replied, hoping he wouldn't see my burning face. "He's the boy I told you about before, remember? The one that we met on the beach with Kristin and Lexi? The one who beat up those trolls for us. He's a nice guy."

*Maybe too nice,* my dragon whispered. I could still feel his lips on mine, the sudden impulse to reach up and kiss him, the flame that had lit my stomach when I did. *What would Talon say if they knew?*

*Talon can eat their own tails,* I thought back. That wasn't the problem. Strictly speaking, pursuing a relationship with a human wasn't entirely *forbidden* by the organization. Making a human fall in love with you was an easy way to control them, an easy way to get what you wanted. Dante was an expert at this; no matter where he was, who was around, he always had someone ready to give him a ride, a phone, the shirt off their back. He didn't even have to try very hard. I thought it was pretty devious myself, but everyone in Talon knew how to manipulate human emotions. The fact that I had kissed a human meant nothing.

The *reason* I'd kissed a human was something else altogether.

I reached my room and turned to close the door, but Dante stepped between the frame, stopping me. His expression hovered between suspicion and concern. "Are you all right, sis?" he asked, watching my face. "I was worried about you. You took off with Lexi right after your training session, and you turned off your phone."

The memory of my sadistic trainer made me bristle. "Jeez, you sound like Uncle Liam," I scoffed, trying to get him off the subject. "I'm fine, so you can dial down your neurotic-twin radar. Garret and I went surfing, that's all."

*And I kissed him. And I want to see him again, badly, so I can do it some more. Lizard balls, I am so screwed in the head.*

"I can't dial down my neurotic-twin radar," Dante said, not moving from his place in the doorway. He stepped closer, putting a hand on my arm. "Not when my twin is upset. Not when I can sense something is really bothering her."

"You know that overprotective twin-brother act? It can go a little far sometimes."

"Hey, you and me? We're all we have here." Dante's voice was completely serious. "If I don't watch out for you, who will? So, come on, Tweedledee." He gently squeezed my arm, then dropped his hand. "What's going on? Did that human hurt you?"

"What are you going to do if he did? Eat him?"

"I'd be tempted, but no." My twin gave me an impatient look. "And you're evading the question. What's wrong, Ember? Something is bothering you, and I want to know what. Talk to me."

I hesitated. I did want to talk to someone, someone who could empathize, another dragon who might understand these strange, new, *human* feelings coursing through me. Feelings that, according to what my trainer had said just this morning, had no place in the life of a dragon. Would Dante get what I was experiencing? I'd always told him everything before.

"I was, um, just thinking about something my trainer said today," I confessed, which wasn't a complete lie. "She told me that humans are the inferior species, that we shouldn't get too attached to any of them, because they're just fodder in the long run. And that they would destroy us if they knew what we really were."

He nodded. "I know. My trainer said the same."

"Doesn't that bother you?" I gestured vaguely down the hall, out the front door. "I mean, we're living with two humans, all our friends are human and we talk to humans every single day. Sure, Liam and Sarah are working for Talon, but I wouldn't consider them *fodder.* That just sounds so…heartless. You don't think that way about Lexi and Calvin and the others, do you?"

"No." Dante immediately shook his head, and I relaxed. "But we have to accept the fact that we're not one of them, Ember. We're *not* human. We live in their world, exist among them, but we'll always be separate. Our trainers are right. We can't get too attached to humans, ever."

I pouted. That wasn't what I wanted to hear. "Why not?"

"Ember." Dante gave me a strange look. "Because we're *dragons.* Humans are… Well, they're not inferior, but they are lower on the food chain. We're stronger, smarter and we live a thousand times longer than they do. All of our human friends—Lexi, Calvin, Kristin, everyone—they're going to grow old and die, and our lives will barely have started. We're just not in the same league, sis. You have to have realized that."

My spirits sank even lower. That clinched it. I was definitely not telling him anything about me and Garret. He probably wouldn't hunt the human down and eat him, but if I mentioned that I'd kissed a boy, he would want to know why. And I wouldn't be able to tell him. I wasn't even sure myself.

"Yeah." I sighed. "I know." Dante continued to watch me, worry and puzzlement shining from his eyes, but I had to be alone to think. "I'm gonna crash for a couple hours." I sighed, reaching for my door. "If I'm not up in time for dinner, come kick my wall or something, okay?"

"Hang on," Dante said, putting a hand on the door as I started to close it. "Kristin's called four or five times," he announced as I looked back. "She wants to know if you're coming to her party tomorrow night."

"That's tomorrow?" Wow, the days rushed by fast. I hadn't even realized it was the weekend already. A small thrill coursed through me. Weekends were the only times when I didn't have to get up and meet my instructor. For the next two days, I was free.

Dante nodded, raising an eyebrow. "We're still planning to go, I take it."

"Of course."

"And I suppose you're going to lose track of the time while we're at this party, and I'm going to have to come up with a believable excuse as to why we're out past midnight."

I beamed at him. "That's why you're the smart twin."

"Uh-huh. And which are you?"

"The pretty one."

He sighed. "Fine. I'll take care of it. As usual." He shook his head and gave me a wry grin. "Only for you, Tweedledee."

After Dante left, I padded farther into my room and flopped on my bed, staring at the ceiling. Well, that had been less than satisfying. I couldn't talk to Dante about my troubles, it seemed. He was my brother, but he was also a dragon. These feelings were as alien to him as they were to me. Strange as it sounded, I needed someone who really understood what I was going through. I needed a human.

I needed…a friend.

Rolling over, I dug out my phone, and scrolled to a familiar name on my contacts list.

"Hey, Lex," I murmured when she picked up. "Are you busy?"

"Ohmygod, Ember!" came the voice on the other end. "No, of course not. Meet me at the Smoothie Hut in fifteen. You still have to tell me everything that happened with hottie Garret!"

"Yeah," I muttered as my stomach twirled again with the memory. "I'll be right there."

Twenty minutes later, I sat at one of the outdoor picnic

tables, two smoothies melting on the table, as Lexi slid into the seat across from me with an eager look.

"Well?" she said by way of greeting, snatching one of the cups, clamping down on the straw like she wanted to bite it in half. "I'm mad at you, Em," she announced without waiting for a reply. "You have me pick you up and drive you to the cove to meet Garret, and then you don't even call to tell me how it went. I've been sitting on pins and needles for hours. So come on, Em. Spill…" She knocked on the table. "You and Garret were in the cove by yourselves, all afternoon. What happened? Anything fun?" She leaned in, smiling like a conspirator. "Did you show him how to skinny-dip?"

"What? No!" I made a face at her, feeling my cheeks redden. "Get your brain out of the sewer, guttersnipe. Nothing like that happened."

"But *something* happened, right?" Lexi watched me carefully, searching my face for the truth. Suddenly self-conscious, I shrugged, and she frowned. "Ember, please. I saw you two at the mall yesterday. I know there's something there. As my best friend, you are obligated to tell me everything in your life that deals with or around gorgeous boys. That's part of the deal."

"I don't remember signing that contract," I mumbled.

"Read the fine print, darling. Did he kiss you?"

My pulse jumped, but I shook my head. "No."

"Did *you* kiss him?"

"Um…"

Lexi shrieked. I shushed her, frowning, and she lowered her voice, grinning like a loon. "I knew it! I knew there was something between you two." She regarded me triumphantly. "Say it! Say I was right."

"All right, yes! Fine, I kissed him. You were right."

"Thank you. See, that wasn't hard." Lexi smiled sagely, and settled back to hear the rest of it. "So, what happened after you kissed him?"

"Nothing." Now that I'd confessed, I couldn't keep the sadness from my voice, the regret of what had followed. "I guess I freaked out a little. I had him take me home after that. We didn't even talk." Sighing, I picked moodily at the table. "I called you just a few minutes after he dropped me off. He probably hates me now, or at least thinks I'm an absolute freak."

"I seriously doubt that." When I didn't answer, she drummed her fingers on the wood, impatient. "You are going to see him again, right? Tell me you're going to see him again."

"I don't know."

"What don't you know? You like him, don't you?"

"I…" I hesitated, thinking. I was a dragon; we weren't supposed to have these kinds of feelings. But whenever I thought of Garret, *something* was definitely there. What did attraction feel like, anyway? Was it grinning every time you heard his voice, or feeling breathless whenever he turned his gaze on you? Was it wanting to see his smile, to hear his laughter because you knew something you said made him happy? I'd never *felt* anything like this before, that sense of just wanting to be near someone, to be close. And if that was the case… "I guess… I do."

I liked Garret. A human.

Lexi nodded. "And he likes you, too. Don't give me that doubting look, Em. Trust me, I've seen it before, and the boy has it bad. Why do you think he keeps showing up and hanging around?" She leaned back and grinned, confident in her analysis. "He's completely smitten with you."

Strangely, that thought made my stomach flutter. That someone like Garret could return my feelings… But this was so new. I never expected I could feel like this. I wasn't *supposed* to feel like this, not according to Talon.

Glancing at Lexi, I gave her a pleading look, my voice coming out kind of desperate. "So, what am I supposed to do now?"

"Oh, Ember." Lexi patted my arm with a confident smile, sixteen years of human experience shining through. "That's easy. When you see him again, you pick up where you left off. And you don't run away this time."

"It might be too late for that." I sighed, putting my chin in my hands, suddenly morose. "I have no idea where he is. I didn't even get a phone number or an email." Ironic, really, that my first real step as a human was also the thing that had driven him away. And now, I was dejected. Over a *boy.* Was this why dragons weren't supposed to have human emotions? They made everything so complicated.

But Lexi was undeterred. "Ember, please. I know this town like the back of my hand, and it's not a big place. We already know his apartment's on the main strip. We'll find him, trust me."

"You're awfully confident about that."

She snorted. "A hottie like Garret kisses you and then vanishes without a trace? I'd be a sucky best friend if I didn't help you get him back."

*Best friend.* Until recently, I thought Dante was my only real friend. It had always been just us against everything. But I couldn't talk to my brother about the human boy I had feelings for. He wouldn't understand. Not only did Lexi understand these crazy, alien emotions, she was encouraging me to act on them.

I gave her a grateful smile. "Thanks, Lex."

She grinned back, looking sly. "No problem. Just remember, when we find him again, I want to hear *alllll* the juicy details from here on. That's my fee for helping you. Leave nothing out, okay?"

I laughed. "You're horrible."

"A girl has to have a hobby. And admit it, you'd be lost without me."

My eyes rolled up. "How did I ever survive so long?"

"I have no idea, but the important thing is, I'm here now." She rubbed her hands together, already scheming. "*And* good news for you. I already know where we're going to look first."

# GARRET

Apparently, parties at seven o'clock didn't really start at seven o'clock.

"Garret? Ohmygod, hi!" Kristin greeted, looking surprised as she opened the door. "I didn't expect you to show. You're, uh, early."

I checked my watch. It read 6:55, barely toeing the line of punctuality where I was from. Let another couple minutes slide, and you'd be begging your drill sergeant to make an example of you. Confused, I glanced back at the girl and switched the case of beer to my other hand. "You said 7:00 p.m. this Saturday, right?"

"Well, yeah, but..." She shrugged and opened the door wider. "Come on in. Nobody's here yet, but make yourself at home."

"Thank you." I stepped through the door into the foyer, taking a quick scan of the room. Bright and airy, with floor-to-ceiling windows that gave a clear view of the ocean, it was large, open and quite expensive looking. Everything was decorated in white. The walls—those not dominated by windows, anyway—were white. The kitchen was white marble and stainless steel. A white leather sofa curled in an L-shape around a black-and-white coffee table, which sat beneath a seventy-two-inch flatscreen on the wall. There were small splashes of color throughout the house—blue pillows on the sofa and fake trees in the corners—but most everything else was a stark, unyielding white.

"You can put the beer in the fridge, and there's more there, if you want one," Kristin called from a half-open door down the hall. "Or soda. Help yourself. People should be arriving soon."

Uncomfortable, I took care of the beer then wandered into the living room, feeling awkward and out of place. Parties and strange houses weren't really my thing. I would adapt, of course, but the only reason I was here hadn't arrived yet and, from the looks of it, wouldn't be here for a while.

"So, where's your cousin?" Kristin asked, still yelling at me from down the hall. I wondered why she didn't come out of her room if she wanted to talk. "What was his name, again? Travis or something?"

"Tristan," I called back. "He came down with something and couldn't make it."

"Oh," Kristin said. That was all. No "That's too bad" or "I hope he feels better." After another few seconds, I heard the door close down the hall. Just as well. My partner wasn't really sick, of course. He was hunched over his laptop, watching the front door of the Hill residence. If the two guardians left the house, he would follow, see where they were going. If they didn't, he would continue to observe. I was glad Tristan was on the computer tonight and not me. He didn't mind long hours of surveillance; it was one of the reasons he was so good at what he did. Nothing escaped his notice, no matter how small or insignificant. If something strange was going on at the Hill residence, Tristan would know about it.

I also had a mission to accomplish tonight, though mine would be very different.

★ ★ ★

"I think we're onto something," my partner had said last night, regarding me over the open take-out cartons on the counter. Outside the window, the sun was setting over the ocean, tinting the sky pink and the clouds a brilliant red. I sat in the living room, carton of Mongolian beef in hand, picking at it with my chopsticks and trying not to think of how the sunset somehow reminded me of *her.* "I think I know what our next move should be."

"How do you figure?" I muttered.

"Simple." Tristan tossed back a carrot, looking thoughtful. "Ask her out."

I nearly choked on an onion, swallowing with difficulty. "Out?" I gasped.

"Yes, out." My partner seemed happily oblivious to my burning face. "On a date, Garret. You do know the word, right? Teenagers do it all the time." He waved an airy hand, still holding the chopsticks. "Dinner, movies, all that garbage. Get her talking. Get her to trust you. It shouldn't be too difficult—she did kiss you, after all, right?"

My face heated even more, remembering. "That doesn't mean anything," I protested. "Dragons assimilate to whatever surroundings they're in. She could have kissed me for any number of reasons."

"Regardless." Tristan shrugged. "I don't see her kissing anyone else, do you? And being asked on a date is common human practice, so there's no reason she should refuse. Eventually, she'll invite you inside, and then we'll be in business. Plant a few bugs around the house, and boom…we'll have them."

"And if she's not our target?"

At least, that's what I hoped it meant.

Lexi nodded.

"Good. Just remember that. Now, one last important thing." She glanced around, then tossed me something small. I caught it—a tiny square of blue plastic that crinkled when I held it up. My face felt suddenly warm, and Lexi grinned. "Just in case."

"Alexis Thompson!" snapped a voice behind us, making my heart leap. Ember emerged from the crowd, giving the other girl a murderous glare as she stalked around the sofa. Lexi *eep*ed and fled, vanishing into the mob, as I quickly stuffed the item between the layers of the couch.

"You are in so much trouble, Lex!" Ember called, scowling at the other girl's retreating back. "And you can forget about that deal we made—I am *not* telling you anything now! Hey, Garret." Ember shook her head and looked down at me, her expression caught somewhere between a smile and a grimace. "Tell me my psychotic, soon-to-be-dead friend didn't just give you what I think she did."

I forced a somewhat pained smile. "I don't think I can answer that without crawling into a dark hole for the rest of the evening."

She laughed, and suddenly everything was okay between us. "Come on." Without hesitation, she reached down, grabbed my hand and pulled me to my feet. "Let's go dance."

*Dance?* I felt a twinge of panic as she tugged me forward, but I forced it down. I'd never done this before—dancing, drinking, letting others touch me. I would just have to adapt. Ember dragged me through a mass of writhing, twisting bodies to the center of the floor, but just as she stopped and let me go, the song faded, and the DJ's voice cracked over the speakers.

"All right, let's slow it down," he crooned, and another song began, slower and much less frantic than the last. Around us, the wild bouncing and twisting calmed, as couples wrapped their arms around each other and began swaying to the music.

Swallowing, I looked down at Ember. She met my gaze, green eyes shining beneath her hair, stepped close and slipped her arms around my neck. My breath caught, and every muscle tensed as she pressed against me, still holding my gaze.

"Is this all right?"

I forced myself to breathe, relax. "Yes." Carefully, not really knowing what to do with my hands, I placed them around her waist, feeling her shiver, as well. She began swaying back and forth with the music, and I followed her lead.

"I'm sorry for yesterday," she murmured after a quiet moment, as we circled in the center of the floor. "I didn't mean to spring that on you. And I didn't mean to take off like I did, either."

"I thought I might've done something wrong," I said quietly.

She shook her head. "No, it wasn't you. I just…" She sighed. "I've never kissed anyone…or dated anyone. I was pretty sheltered growing up, there weren't many boys around. Well, except Dante, and he didn't count. I mean, he's a boy, of course, but he's my brother so I don't really think of him as a boy, not like you… And now I'm rambling, aren't I?" She grimaced, ducking her head to hide her face. "I'm just new at this," she muttered into my shirt. "I've never done anything like this before."

She was so warm. Her body shifted against me, and I closed my eyes. "That makes two of us," I murmured.

"But it can't be that scary, right?" She looked up, cocking her head at me. "I mean, compared to surfing twelve-foot waves and shooting rabid zombie hordes, this should be easy."

That coaxed a tiny smile. "You would think so." I recalled all the battles I'd faced over the years—the fighting, the chaos, dodging bullets and claws and dragonfire. None of it held a candle to what was happening now. "At least I don't have to worry about you wanting to eat my brains," I said, then wondered where that had come from.

She laughed softly, the sound making my heart skip a beat. *Pull back,* the soldier warned. *Don't let her in. This is a mission, and you're getting way too comfortable. Pull back now.*

I ignored it. Having Ember so close, her skin warm on mine, I could feel my resistance melting away, vanishing like a paper held to a flame. It should have been terrifying, made me retreat behind the wall I'd built up over long years of training. That barrier between myself and pain, of watching brothers and comrades killed, torn to pieces before my eyes. The mask I donned, blank and indifferent, when a superior officer was screaming in my face. I should've pulled back, but right now, I was more content than I'd been in a long, long time. I could get used to this, I decided, tightening my hold on the girl. I could, very easily, close my eyes, lower all my defenses and lose myself in her arms.

Ember leaned close, resting her head on my shoulder, making my heart skip. "I don't know what I'm trying to say," she muttered, sounding frustrated. Her breath feathered across my neck, raising goose bumps. "I like spending time with you. I don't want to lose that. I don't… I don't want you to leave."

One hand fiddled with the front of my shirt, tracing patterns and sending little pulses through me. "Of course, if I've read too much into things, go ahead and point out that dark hole so I can get comfortable, 'cause I'm never coming out again."

"I don't think you have to worry about that," I said, my voice coming out rather husky.

She looked up at me, her face inches from mine. Time froze around us, the other dancers fading away, until it was just us in the center of the music and the darkness. Her arms slipped behind my neck and tightened, pulling faintly. But she didn't move from there, just continued to watch me with solemn green eyes, her fingers brushing the nape of my neck. This time, she would let me decide.

Raising a hand to her cheek, I leaned forward.

"Hi."

A new, unfamiliar voice interrupted us, making me pull back. Annoyed, I looked over to face a guy with dark, messy hair and a leather jacket. His arms were crossed, and he wore a dangerous smirk as he stared at me. I frowned, not recognizing him, but Ember gave a tiny squeak and stiffened in my arms.

"Riley?" she gasped, the instant recognition making me tense. "What are you doing here?"

# EMBER

Okay, this night was officially weird.

I'd thought I knew what I wanted. Before we'd come to the party, Lexi had pretty much convinced me that Garret would be there. Kristin had invited him, after all, and her birthday parties were the stuff of legends. Half the town had probably heard about it by now. Even when I pointed out that he might not come, and I had no way to contact him if he didn't show, that hadn't deterred Lexi. She'd already made plans to stalk the beaches and local hangouts every day until we found him.

As Dante and I had pulled up in the car, parking behind the long line of vehicles already in the driveway, my hopes had shriveled a bit. I'd thought Garret probably wouldn't be there; he didn't really seem the party type. I'd steeled myself for disappointment, telling myself that we could look for him tomorrow. All was not lost if he didn't show up tonight.

At the edge of the yard, Dante saw a cluster of his seemingly endless circle of friends and hurried off to join them, leaving me alone. Rolling my eyes, I continued up the steps, planning to track down Lexi so we could cover more ground together. But then, as I'd walked through the front door, there he'd been, sitting on the couch and looking highly uncomfortable as Lexi tossed him what I hoped was not a condom. My stomach had twisted as I'd stalked up. Even through the mortification, all I could think of was kissing him again, feeling his heartbeat under my palm, breathing in his scent. If these were purely human experiences, then I would just be human for a little while. Talon would disapprove, but Talon could go to hell. They'd already taken so much of my summer away. This part of it was mine.

He was about to kiss me, I could see it in his eyes. I could feel it in his hands, flattening over my back, the way his heartbeat picked up, the sudden intent in that metallic stare. My dragon instincts hissed and cringed away, not liking this, even as my own heartbeat thumped in my ears, echoing his own.

And then, I felt a shift in the air, a subtle change that my dragon recognized instantly. Even before I heard his voice, the hairs on the back of my neck prickled, and a sudden heat spread through my insides.

I turned and met the gaze of the rogue dragon.

"Riley?" I said in disbelief. I'd almost blurted out *Cobalt,* but caught myself just in time, remembering to separate the two. My dragon instantly flared with excitement, sending fire and relief singing through my veins. He was safe! He was still hanging around. "What are you doing here?"

The rogue dragon smiled, eyes gleaming. Ignoring my question, he shot a mock-inquisitive look at Garret, though I could practically see the dragon watching the human like he was about to cook him in the middle of the living room. "Mind if I cut in?"

Garret went rigid, his arms becoming steel bands around

my waist, though he gave no outward sign of alarm. His voice was coolly polite when he answered. “I do, actually.”

Riley continued to smile, but his eyes glinted. It was clear he thought the human defying him was amusing, which made me kinda nervous. Riley was a rogue; he didn’t play by Talon’s rules. I didn’t think he’d be stupid enough to Shift here, surrounded by dozens of eyewitnesses, and blast Garret to cinders, but I couldn’t be certain.

Besides, I needed to talk to him. There were so many questions I wanted answers to, so many things about Talon that needed explaining, and he had magically shown up, right here at Kristin’s party. Of course, in true Riley fashion, he had shown up at the worst possible time, but I couldn’t let him get away now. And my own dragon was bouncing against my skin, thrilled that he was here. She hadn’t forgotten that night, soaring the waves with Cobalt, and neither had I.

“Garret,” I said softly, bringing his attention to me. “I know him. Let me talk to him, just for a second.”

He wasn’t pleased. His jaw tightened and his eyes went blank, but he gave a stiff nod and stepped away. Turning, he melted into the crowd without a backward glance, and I was alone with the rogue.

Taking a breath, I was about to suggest we go somewhere private to talk when another song began, faster this time, stirring the dancers into a surging, writhing sea. Riley suddenly grinned and stepped close, moving gracefully with the music, his smile challenging. After a moment’s hesitation, I joined him, pretending to be reluctant, but I couldn’t ignore the excited fluttering of the dragon within. Riley continued to smile, but his eyes were mocking.

"Well, Firebrand, here we are again." His voice was low and cool, meant only for me as we danced close. Not touching, but I could feel the heat that radiated from him, as if a fire blazed near the surface. "And I see you've assimilated quite nicely. You do realize that was a *human,* right? In case you've forgotten, you're not exactly like him."

"Keep your voice down," I snapped back, though with the music pounding the walls and the general obliviousness of the crowd, there was little chance of someone paying attention. Still, it was something Talon had pounded deep into my head; never, *ever* talk about dragon-related things in the company of humans. "That's none of your business, anyway. How did you even know I'd be here?"

Riley grinned. "I told you I'd find you again, didn't I?" he crooned, moving even closer. "You seem surprised, Firebrand. Did you forget about me?" His voice was mocking, but his body moved like liquid, graceful and sure. He wasn't a stranger to this type of scene, that was for certain. My stomach danced, and the dragon surged up like a flame, wanting free.

"Where have you been, anyway?" I asked. He just raised an eyebrow, obviously having no intention of answering that question, and I frowned. "*They're* looking for you, you know," I said, leaning even closer. "They sent agents in last month, because someone ratted you out."

*Dante,* I added in my head, though I didn't say it out loud. Fear suddenly twisted my stomach. Dante was here, at the party. If he spotted Riley now…

Alarmed, I backed away, making him frown. "You should go," I told the rogue. "It's dangerous for you here. If my brother sees us—"

In a blindingly smooth move, Riley slipped behind me. Before I knew what was happening, his hands were on my waist, sending a flare of heat through my stomach as he bent close. "Don't worry about me, Firebrand," he said in my ear as I wavered between leaning into him and shoving him back. "I know how to take care of myself. Question is, do you still want to know about Talon? Who they really are? What they want?" His lips grazed my cheek, breath tickling my skin. "I can tell you, if you're still interested."

I stiffened. He chuckled and slipped his hand into my pocket, very briefly, before pulling back.

"My number is on there," he told me as I felt in my pocket and discovered a scrap of paper, folded over several times. "When you want to talk," Riley continued, serious now. "When they show their true face—and they *will,* Firebrand, make no mistake about it—I'm here. You can always come to me. I want you to come to me."

I didn't know what to say to that. Riley was watching me, gold eyes bright and intense across the space between us, stirring the fire within. Dammit, why did he have this effect on me? Was it because he was a rogue? A fellow dragon, who dared to defy Talon and live his life the way I only wished I could? Or was it something else, something deeper? Something my dragon instincts responded to on a primal level? Riley as a human was charming, mysterious and, yes, if I had to say it, smoking-hot. But when I really looked at him, all I saw was the dragon.

Movement on the other side of the room caught my attention. I looked over to see Garret's lean, bright form gliding across the floor toward the exit.

# GARRET

I had to get out of there.

I'd felt the first prick when the stranger had appeared asking to cut in, a sudden twinge of something odd and unfamiliar. Anger and…something else, something that made me want to shove the stranger back, though I kept myself calm. It flared up again, even stronger, when Ember admitted that she knew him, that she wanted to talk to him. I'd retreated to a corner to observe the pair, feeling grim and irrationally sullen, watching as they danced close. When the stranger suddenly moved behind Ember, putting his hands on her hips, I'd clenched my fists, fighting the burning desire to stalk over and drive a fist into his mouth.

That was when I'd caught myself. What was happening to me? Why should I care what Ember did? It shouldn't matter if she danced with someone else. It shouldn't matter that they seemed comfortable together, that Ember sometimes looked at him with dark, lingering eyes. The stranger was a temporary setback, nothing more. He wasn't important.

But I found myself hating him, wanting to hurt him, to drive him away from the red-haired girl who was supposed to be mine.

Breathless, I slumped to the wall, numb with the realization. This anger, these illogical feelings of rage and possessiveness… I was *jealous.* I was jealous of a girl I was supposed to be stalking, seducing, for the sole purpose of revealing her true nature. This had become more than an objective, more than a mission.

I was falling for her.

*No.* Furious at myself now, I leaned my head back, closing my eyes. This couldn't happen. I was a soldier. I could not let this become personal. Emotions could not ever be a part of the mission. They complicated things, screwed up priorities. If Ember was a human, I'd vanish from her life without a trace, leaving whatever feelings she might have for me broken and shattered in the dust. But if she was our target…

I opened my eyes, just in time to see the stranger slip his hand into her pocket. My trained eye caught the brief flash of paper, tiny as it was, and the urge to leap up and smash his head through the window was almost overwhelming.

Pushing myself from the wall, I fled outside.

# EMBER

"Garret!"

Shoving my way through crowds of people, I followed him through the living room, across the foyer and out the front door.

"Garret, wait!"

The party had spilled outside. Groups of people clustered together on the steps and the long sandy driveway, milling around and talking. Several boys hung around a pickup with an open cooler on the tailgate, drinking from cans and bottles. My dragon growled a warning as I passed them, but I was too focused on reaching the retreating figure ahead and didn't give them a second thought. Garret was leaving, and I had the sudden, panicked sense that if he got away this time, I'd never see him again.

"Hey! Dammit, Garret, hold up."

He finally turned, and for a moment, his expression was tormented, like seeing me was more than he could bear. Only a moment, however, before a wall slammed down across his features, his eyes going empty and cold.

I faced that chilling look, stifling the growl that rose up within. The dragon, baring her fangs in self-preservation. "Where are you going?" I demanded.

"It doesn't matter." Garret's voice was flat, a far cry from the sweet, vulnerable human I had danced with just minutes ago. That icy tone cut into me, making me cringe and bristle all at once. "We're done, Ember. Go back inside and forget about me. You won't see me again."

*"Why?"* I glared at him, torn between anger and desperation. "Just because I danced with Riley? He's a friend, Garret. That's all." The dragon hissed at such an obvious lie, but I ignored her. "Are you really that jealous?"

"Yes," he answered, startling me. "And...that's the problem. I shouldn't care. This shouldn't affect me at all...but it does. *You* affect me." His metallic, gunmetal eyes narrowed slightly in my direction, accusing. Though I still caught a break in his mask, a tiny flicker of uncertainty, even as he turned away. "This is wrong," he muttered, his voice almost too soft to hear. "I can't do this. To either of us."

If I hadn't seen that brief flash of emotion, I probably wouldn't have had the courage to do what I did next. But I took a deep breath, and stepped up to him, reaching out to take his hand. He flinched but didn't yank it back, his eyes flicking to my face.

"It scares me, too," I admitted softly. "When I'm with you, I can't think of anything else, and sometimes I think it's making me crazy. I don't know whether to keep going or run away as fast as I can."

He didn't respond, but I caught something in his expression that hinted that he was feeling the same. "So, yeah, I'm a little freaked out," I went on, determined not to let him go now. "I have no idea what's going to happen here. But being afraid is a piss-poor excuse not to do something, don't you think?" I thought of Scary Talon Lady, of the organization, of my rapidly disappearing summer, and my resolve grew. "So, if you're going to stand there and tell me we're done, because heaven forbid you actually *feel* something, then I'm afraid I'm going to have to call bullshit."

He blinked, his blank mask cracking a little more, and I stepped closer, meeting his eyes. "Garret, if you really want to go, I'm not stopping you. But I thought you were braver than that. I thought someone who could surf giant waves and shoot zombies and kick the crap out of three brainless ogres wouldn't be afraid that someone else…really liked that about him. And that he wouldn't need to feel jealous or afraid, because she's right here. She's standing right in front of you."

His gaze grew dark, smoldering. "Ember…"

"Well, look who it is."

We turned, and my dragon instincts—the ones I should've listened to earlier—rose up with a snarl, bristling and ready for a fight. The boys clustered around the pickup had come forward, and Colin's familiar, leering face was out in front. Behind him, I saw his two pals, Drew and Travis, but also another trio of drunk-looking frat boys, all coming toward us with evil smirks. Six of them. All itching for trouble. The dragon growled, and I bit my lip to keep her in check.

"It's the little slut and her boyfriend," Colin went on, sneering at me and Garret. "Fancy running into you again. I still owe you one, bitch. But I'll get to you after we take care of this tool here." He leered at Garret, who faced the group calmly, his expression now blank. Colin's grin grew more taunting. "Where's your friend now, punk?" he asked sweetly. "Not here to rescue you this time? Hope he doesn't mind if we beat your ass into the ground."

"Coward," I snarled at him. "Afraid to take him on alone? Have to have your buddies back you up for everything?"

He shot me an evil look. "You got a big mouth, little bitch. I hope there's enough to go around."

"Touch my sister, and I'll kill you all," said a voice behind them.

Colin jerked as Dante stepped out from a different cluster of people, his eyes hard as he came to stand beside me.

"Oh, hey, there's two of them," Colin sneered. "I thought I was seeing double."

Smirking, he swaggered forward. Dante stood his ground, as did Garret, moving me behind him even as my dragon snarled in protest, wanting to fight. "Why don't you step away now, pretty boy?" the big human told my brother, whose jaw tightened dangerously. "Or you can stay and get your head stomped in, I don't really care. Two on six doesn't look too good for you, does it?"

"God, do they ever stop talking?" came yet another voice from behind Colin. He whirled to face Riley, who gave him a lazy grin. "Can't *anyone* ever start a fight without all the posturing and cheesy Bond-villain threats? It's not that hard. Here, let me demonstrate." And he smashed a fist into Colin's nose.

Colin flew back with a yell, both hands going to his face, as the rest of the group lunged forward. I leaped away, clenching my fists, as an all-out brawl erupted in the front yard. Riley, Garret and Dante disappeared in a chaotic whirlwind of fists, feet, elbows and knees. Shouts, grunts of pain and the sounds of fists on flesh rang out, overshadowed by the cheers and screams of the crowd.

My dragon roared, frustrated that she couldn't get in there

and rip the humans to pieces, but I wasn't going to stand back and watch this time. When a bulky frat boy swung at Dante, I stepped up behind the human and kicked him in the calf, sweeping his leg out. He staggered, and Dante slugged him in the jaw, knocking him to the ground.

"Ow," he muttered, shaking his hand as if stung. "Damn, it's like hitting a cement block."

I shot a quick glance at Riley and Garret, who, though surrounded by thugs and flying fists, seemed to be holding their own. Riley was grinning demonically as he faced his opponents, taking the blows that landed and swinging back viciously, slamming them into hoods and car windows. Beside him, Garret spun and blocked with his near-inhuman grace, slipping inside an opponent's guard and striking quickly before they knew what happened.

The human Dante had knocked over lurched to his feet and lunged at him again. Dante sidestepped, and the drunk human crashed headfirst into a car door. I grinned, but while we were both distracted, Colin appeared out of nowhere, shoving me aside. I stumbled, caught myself and whirled around to see him lash out with a fist and strike Dante in the temple. My brother crumpled to the ground, and my vision went red.

As Colin raised his foot to kick Dante, I jumped between them with a snarl, baring my teeth. The color drained from the human's face, and he stumbled back, mouth dropping open. I felt the beginnings of the change ripple through me, the dragon rising to the surface, and tensed to pounce.

Something grabbed my wrist, yanking me back, just as Garret slammed into Colin, tackling him. I spun to face Riley, a breath away from Shifting and pouncing on him, too.

"Stop it!" he ordered, his firm voice slicing through me.

It pierced the rage and the heat, the wild snarling of the dragon, and brought everything into focus again. I shivered and drew back, appalled at what I'd almost done. Pulling me away, he maneuvered us to the edge of the driveway, letting me go with a hard look.

"Stay out of this, Firebrand," he ordered, and I took a breath to snarl at him, to tell him I could handle myself just fine. But Dante's gaze met mine across the yard as he pulled himself to his feet, rubbing his head. My brother's gaze was angry and horrified, but not at Riley. At *me.* As if he, too, knew how close I'd been to exposing us all.

Sirens echoed through the night, and everyone's attention jerked to the distant wailing. Almost instantly, the crowd scattered toward cars and vehicles, some even running off into the darkness. I tensed, more annoyed than anything. Stupid cops. Of course their timing was perfect.

Riley's dark head lifted, gold eyes narrowing as the sirens drew steadily closer, then he looked back at me. "Whoops, looks like that's my cue," he said, backing away. "Firebrand, remember what I told you. If you need to talk, you know where to find me."

With a wink, the rogue turned and vanished into the darkness as swiftly as he'd appeared. Somewhere in the sea of cars, a motorcycle roared to life and tore off into the night.

"Ember!" Dante's voice rang out. Glaring at me, my twin stalked to the edge of the driveway, keys in hand. "Let's go!" he ordered, pointing to the vehicle we'd arrived in. "Get in the car, right now! We're going home."

I bristled at his demanding tone. Who was he to order me around? He wasn't my trainer. And I wasn't looking forward to the conversation on the ride home, either. He'd seen me talking with Riley and would probably demand to know how I knew the rogue, something I wasn't about to confess, especially now.

The sirens got louder. Most of the crowd had disappeared, or were in the process of driving off. Unable to stop myself, I looked at Garret, standing alone in the shadows several yards away, his metallic eyes on me. He didn't say anything. He didn't step forward, either to defend me or offer a ride, and hurt flared up to join the anger, confusion and disappointment.

"You know what?" I growled, backing away from Dante and Garret, back toward the house. Blue and red lights flashed in the distance, coming up the road, as I made my decision. "Screw you both. I don't need any of this. I'll find my own way home."

"Ember!" Dante yelled, but I turned and ran, sprinting around the house, down toward the shore and into the darkness. Leaving them all behind.

★ ★ ★

Maybe a hundred yards down the beach, I slowed, kicking up sand as I stalked along the edge of the water, thinking. Small waves rumbled as they rolled onto shore, then hissed as they returned to the sea. Overhead, a full white moon blazed down, turning the beach into a fantasyland of silver and black. I could still hear the sirens from the squad cars, probably at the party right now, breaking it up. Hopefully, everyone had gotten out okay, though I didn't know why I should be concerned. I did feel guilty for running out on Dante, who would call my phone every ten minutes, but who also knew me well enough to know I could get home by myself. I wasn't worried about him. At least he cared. The other boys could fling themselves off a cliff.

I sighed. Riley, Dante, Garret. Three impossible boys who, for different reasons, were making my life very difficult. Dante for being a paranoid jerk sometimes. Who said I could trust him but then agreed with everything Talon said. Who was a perfect model student, didn't bend the rules and expected me to do the same. Riley, a rogue dragon who encouraged me to do the exact opposite. Who flaunted Talon's laws and tempted me with the secrets he possessed, and the freedom he represented. Who called to my dragon and was impossible to ignore.

And Garret. A human. Enough said right there.

I sighed again, tipping my head back. My skin was still flushed, whether from anger or adrenaline or both, and my dragon crackled and snapped in myriad different directions. I needed to calm down. I wished I had my board. It was impossible to stay tense while floating on the surface of the ocean, its cold, dark depths lulling you to sleep. The sea was fascinating. It always amazed me how calm and peaceful it was one moment, only to bear down on you a moment later with the power and savagery of a hurricane.

A wave crawled up the shore, foaming over my toes. Taking my phone out of my pocket, I walked away from the water and set it and Riley's note in the sand. When the next wave hissed over up the shore, I followed it back to the ocean, wading out into the depths.

I stopped when I was waist-deep, feeling the cold seep into my skin, calming the flames that still flickered inside. Hugging myself, I closed my eyes and let the salty breeze cool my face. I should probably go home. Dante had the car, which meant I'd have to take a cab, the bus, or walk back to the house. Flying was, as always, a tempting option. But I'd promised my brother I wouldn't jeopardize our time here, and tempting fate seemed like a bad idea right now. I sighed again, resigned to a purely human trek back home.

"Ember."

My heart leaped at the low, quiet voice, and I turned. Garret's lean silhouette stood on the shore watching me, the ocean wind tugging at his shirt. Seeing him, I felt a rush of happiness and longing; he'd come after me. Quickly, I shut it down. Garret wasn't interested. He'd made that clear tonight.

"What do you want, Garret?" I called, not moving from where I stood. A wave slapped against me, cool on my skin, smelling of salt and foam and the sea. I faced Garret across the dark water and crossed my arms. "Shouldn't you be heading home? The cops have probably broken up the party by now."

"I want to talk to you." He took a step forward, stopping just shy of a wave as it hissed onto the sand. "I don't want to leave things between us as they are."

"So talk."

Those mercury eyes blinked, reflecting the moonlight, as he gave a slight frown. "Maybe you could come onto the beach?" he suggested, nodding to the sand behind him. "That way we won't have to shout at each other."

"I'm fine right here, thanks." I raised my chin, feeling stubborn and insolent. Garret sighed.

"All right," he said...and strode into the ocean, wading through the water in jeans and a T-shirt. I dropped my arms, startled, as he stepped in front of me, the waves lapping at his stomach and chest, drenching the front of his shirt. I felt the heat from his body as he leaned in.

"I'm sorry," he said quietly, his voice just a murmur between us, nearly lost in the rushing waves. "For tonight. For everything. I guess I…"

"Freaked out and turned into a possessive jackass?"

"Yes." His mouth quirked. "So, I'm sorry for that. My head wasn't on straight. But…" He took a deep breath. "I think I see things a little clearer now. I'd like to try again. If you'll let me."

The waves and surf surrounded us, and overhead, the moon glowed fiendishly bright, illuminating the beach and turning Garret's hair silver. The distant lights and sirens faded away, until it seemed it was just the two of us, on a lonely shore hundreds of miles from anything. "I'd like that, too," I whispered.

He relaxed, some of the tension leaving his back and shoulders. "So, we're okay?"

"Yeah."

"Good." He moved closer, sliding his hands up my arms, sending electric tingles through my whole body. "I wanted to make certain, before I did this."

And he kissed me.

This time, I wasn't afraid. This time, my eyes closed, and I leaned into him, kissing him back. His arms slid around me, and I wrapped mine around his waist, pulling us closer. I forgot about Talon. I forgot the fact that I was a dragon, and we weren't supposed to have these crazy, intense emotions swirling through us. I didn't care that my instructor said humans were the lesser species, and that we were higher up on the food chain. None of that mattered. For this one moment, with Garret's cool lips on mine and his arms trapping me against him, I was neither human nor dragon.

Just me.

# PART II

## They're not who you think.

# RILEY

"We've got a problem."

That was *not* the first thing I wanted to hear after returning from a party that, for all intents and purposes, had sucked ass big-time. Granted, kicking around those human yuppies was fun, if not at all challenging, as was getting under the skin of that human kid. They didn't matter, though. I hadn't gone to that party to beat up humans, or to threaten obnoxious mortals who didn't have a clue. I'd gone there for *her.*

"Riley." Wes came into the kitchen as I tossed my bike keys and wallet on the counter. I gave him a weary look. The gangly human looked disheveled—shirt rumpled, brown hair in disarray, normal for him. His English accent grated hard on my nerves this evening. "Did you hear me? We've got a problem, mate."

"This better be important," I growled, brushing past him into the spacious living room. Hell, I was tired. It had been a long night. Through the enormous windows, the moon hung low over the ocean, tempting me to leave the room and head outside, if only to get away from Wes. If I walked out to the veranda, I'd have a great view of white cliffs, sky and, eighty feet below, the pounding surf. The house was built halfway into the cliffs, and the wide, open veranda was a great launching point for those nights that I didn't want to take my bike on the road. Not bad, for a house that wasn't ours. The real owners were in Europe for the summer and had needed someone to house-sit their big empty mansion. Lucky us. With a little online finagling, Wes had made certain they hired him: a responsible, middle-aged accountant with a wife and no kids or pets who wanted to rent a house for the summer. No one would suspect the truth. Or at least, no one would come nosing around, wondering why two college-age guys were squatting in a multimillion-dollar beach house.

Wes followed me into the living room. "Another one of our nests went dark," he said gravely.

My fury spiked. I spun on him, narrowing my eyes. "Which one?"

"Austin." The human raised a hand in a helpless gesture. "Their signal went down this afternoon, and no one is answering. I haven't been able to contact them at all."

"Goddammit!" Spinning, I slapped an expensive vase from an end table, sending a few thousand dollars' worth of porcelain flying into the wall. Wes flinched. Heat flared across my lungs and I breathed deep, controlling the urge to Shift and blast something to cinders. "I *just* came from there!" I snarled. "I spent all last month setting that safe house up. Dammit! What the hell is going on?"

Wes didn't shoot me his normal irritated look, which told me how shaken he was. "I don't know, mate, but it's gone now," he said, and I shoved my hands through my hair, trying to think. Austin. There had been only one dragon in that safe house, a hatchling I'd gotten out just last year. He'd trusted me to protect him; I'd promised I would keep him safe.

Dammit all to hell.

"We should move," Wes added, shoving off the counter. "Let the other nests know we've been compromised. If we leave tonight—"

I lowered my arms. "No," I muttered, and he looked back at me in surprise. Anger and resolve settled around me like a cold fist. The Austin nest was lost, but that just meant I had to succeed here. "Not without the girl," I said firmly, turning around. "I'm close, Wes. She's coming around. I can feel it. Give me another week or two, and she'll be so fed up with Talon she'll be begging me to take her away."

"Right." Wes crossed his arms, raising an eyebrow. "Like the time you swore it would take a week, tops, to convince that Owen chap to join us, and what did he do? We had to spend a month in Chile after he ratted us out to Talon."

"Yeah, but look on the bright side. You finally got a suntan." He glowered at me, and I smirked, remembering his constantly red skin and face as we'd moved from jungle to village to jungle, always on the run. Wes did not like the great outdoors, and the feeling was mutual. "It was a risk," I admitted, "but we both knew that. This is different."

"Why, exactly?"

"Because I say it is."

Wes sighed. "You know that survival instinct that's kept us alive all this time? The one that tells us to move out when bloody St. George or Talon is closing in on us? You're very bad for it."

I smirked and went to my room, knowing we wouldn't be going anywhere just yet. Tossing my jacket to a chair, I flopped back on the satin sheets of the king-size bed and contemplated this newest problem.

*Damn.* I pressed the heels of my palms into my eyes, trying to calm the lingering rage and frustration. Another nest gone. That was the second nest I'd lost in as many months, just vanished off the face of the earth. When the first had gone dark, I'd dropped everything and ridden down to Phoenix, searching for the two hatchlings I'd left there, trying to find answers. Nothing. The house I'd set up for them months earlier was an abandoned shell, deserted and empty. No one could tell me what had happened to the building or the residents. Overnight, they'd just…disappeared.

I'd thought of them on the long drive back, churning with anger and regret. I'd promised to protect them when they left Talon, I'd sworn to keep them safe, and I had failed them. Where were they now? What had happened to them? Of the two possibilities I could think of, I hoped it was Talon who had discovered their wayward dragons and had whisked them back to the fold. The kids I lured from the organization were often young, gullible, inexperienced hatchlings. If Talon had found the nest, the hatchlings had probably been taken back for "retraining." And as much as I hated the thought of losing them to the organization again, at least they'd be alive. The alternative, the other reason for a nest and the hatchlings to disappear, was far, far worse.

The alternative was St. George.

Closing my eyes, I let my arms thump to the mattress. Wes was right to be freaked out. Not that he needed much reason, but staying here when *something* was creeping closer to our location was a bad idea. We'd survived this long by staying on the move and knowing when to run if things got too dangerous. We'd already had to leave the area once. For all I knew, Talon was still looking for us. The longer we stayed, the more dangerous it would become for us both. But I couldn't leave without her.

I had to give it to Wes. He was sullen, pessimistic and drank enough Red Bull to power a freaking blimp, but having an elite, ex-Talon hacker around was extremely useful. He was the one who could track down Talon's hatchlings, discover where and when they were being planted, usually with plenty of time for us to move in and be ready when they arrived. That was the reason we'd come here, to Crescent Beach. Because Wes had discovered Talon was about to send another brand-spanking-new dragon into the world. A hatchling, by the name of Ember Hill.

I'd expected to find what I always did: a green young dragon itching for a taste of freedom, excited, naive and gullible. Easy prey. Show them a mysterious stranger, give them a taste of real freedom, and many were all too eager to jump ship. Of course, the life of a rogue dragon wasn't all bright lights and glory, but the most important thing was getting them out. The technicalities of keeping them hidden and safe came later.

I *hadn't* expected to find a fierce, opinionated hatchling who challenged me, pushed back and who wasn't afraid of me…or of anything. Who defied not only an older, more experienced dragon, but Talon, her guardians, even her brother—a twin, wasn't *that* interesting—to do what she wanted. From the time we'd met, spoken, I'd known I couldn't let her stay with the organization. There was something about her, something that made me determined to get her out, get her away from Talon. Maybe she reminded me of myself at that age, a fiery free spirit, before Talon had systematically broken any hints of independence and original thought. I'd recovered, of course, but I knew what the organization did to their hatchlings. I was damned sure I couldn't let that happen to her.

That's what I told myself, anyway. It had nothing to do with the way my *own* dragon responded to her, nearly surging out of my skin whenever the girl was around. I'd never wanted to Shift into my true form as much as I had tonight, and from the way Ember had looked at me when we danced, I knew she'd felt the same. Though for both our sakes, I'd hidden it well. Ember was decades younger, inexperienced in everything, and she was far too *human* for her own good. Case in point, she'd nearly let a human kiss her tonight.

A different sort of rage heated my lungs, and I growled, remembering the brat she was dancing with tonight. Mortal teenagers were normally a pretty useless bunch—cocky and immature, thinking they knew everything about the world. Easy to manipulate, but not good for much else. But that kid…something about him was different, though I wasn't sure what. Maybe it was the disgust talking, the need to rescue my little Firebrand from the tediousness of human emotion. Or maybe it was my sudden, irrational urge to bite his head off.

I groaned. No good would come from going down *that* path. I had to stay focused. Concentrate on what I'd come to do. Ember *was* starting to come around. My little spitfire wouldn't be content to sit back and let Talon order her around. She would start questioning the organization, if she hadn't already, and when she couldn't get answers from them, she'd come to me. And I'd show her what Talon was really like.

"Riley." Wes poked his head through the frame. "The Austin nest, mate. What do we do about it?"

I sighed, sitting up on the mattress. "Keep monitoring the safe house, but don't try to contact them anymore," I told him. "If whatever caused the nest to go dark is still out there, we don't want to alert it to our presence. After I convince Ember to join us, I'll head to Austin myself and see what's going on. Until then, we sit tight."

"And if Talon or St. George shows up on our bloody doorstep?"

"Well, then *I'm* going out the back window. I don't know what you'll end up doing."

"It's so nice to know you care."

I kicked the door shut. Knowing Wes, he would be up the rest of the night, staring at his laptop screen and drinking obscene amounts of Red Bull. I was tired, cranky and sickened at the news of my safe houses. Annoying human roommates be damned, I needed sleep.

And very soon, I was going to show a certain red-haired hatchling the true face of Talon, and convince her that she belonged with us.

With me.

# EMBER

It was after 2:00 a.m. when I returned home. Garret dropped me off at the corner without a word, and I crept silently down the road, across the yard and up to the front door of the house. All the windows were dark, which was a relief. Still, my heart was pounding as I unlocked the door and eased inside, being careful not to make a sound. I half expected a light to flip on, revealing a pair of angry guardians, or worse, Scary Talon Lady herself, waiting for me. When nothing happened and the room remained dark, I relaxed. Maybe Dante had come through for me, after all. Scurrying up the stairs, I tiptoed to my room, slipped inside and closed the door with a sigh of relief.

"Where have you been?"

I bit my tongue to keep from screeching. "Dammit, Dante!" I whispered, flipping on the light. He leaned against the opposite wall with his arms crossed, looking coldly unamused. "Stop doing that! It's not funny anymore."

"Do you see me laughing?" My twin narrowed his eyes to green slits, and my stomach twisted. "Where were you?" he demanded again. "Why'd you take off like that? I had to lie my ass off to convince the guardians that you were sleeping at Lexi's and had forgotten to tell them. What were you doing?"

"Nothing," I growled, feeling sullen and defensive. "It's none of your business, Dante. Why do you care, anyway?"

"I care that you're going to get yourself sent back to Talon!" Dante snapped. "I care that you keep breaking the rules and don't think about the consequences. I care that there was a rogue dragon at that party, and you two seemed very friendly with each other." His glare hardened, accusing and almost hurt. "You knew he was still hanging around, didn't you? You knew, and you didn't tell me."

"Why? So you could rat him out to Talon again?"

Dante blinked, taken aback, and I sneered. "Yeah, I know it was you. Don't expect me to be forthcoming when you've been keeping secrets, Dante. You didn't have to do that. Riley isn't hurting anyone."

"*Riley?* You know his name?"

I winced. Dante stared at me, aghast, then shook his head. "Dammit, Ember, you don't get it, do you? Rogues are dangerous. They've rejected everything Talon stands for and they'll try to get you to do the same. If you keep talking to this rogue, Talon might see you as a coconspirator, and then the Vipers will come after you both. Is that what you want?"

I shivered at the mention of the Vipers. Dante noticed my hesitation and pushed himself off the wall, coming to stand in front of me.

"I know you're curious," he said in a low voice, "but you're playing with fire, sis. If you keep this up, Talon might label you a traitor. The Vipers will take you away for good, and I can't lose you like that. Promise me you won't talk to him again. Please."

I met his gaze. "If I do, will *you* promise me you won't inform Talon?"

He stiffened and drew back. "It's our responsibility to inform the organization about any and all possible threats," he said. "Rogues put the survival of our race in jeopardy. The rules are clear. I have to tell them."

"Fine." I set my jaw. "Go ahead and tell Talon. But you might be turning your own sister in, as well, so I hope you're okay with that. If the Vipers come for me, it'll be your fault."

He raked both hands through his hair, a very human gesture of frustration. "Ember, please," he groaned. "Don't be like this. I'm just trying to keep you safe."

"I don't need you to keep me safe," I retorted. "I just need you to be on my side for once." He started to protest, but I opened the door, an indication for him to leave. "Choose, Dante. Me or Talon? The organization, or your own blood?"

He stared at me blankly, as if he didn't recognize me anymore. Then he walked across the room and out the door without looking back. I swallowed the lump in my throat and flipped off the light, letting the door swing shut behind him.

# GARRET

I was fieldstripping my Glock when Tristan came home.

"Well, that's never a good sign," he said, placing two full grocery bags on the kitchen counter. I didn't answer. Closing my eyes, I reassembled the pistol again, feeling the comforting metal slide between my fingers. Slide, barrel, spring, receiver. I slid the magazine into place with a satisfying snap and opened my eyes to find Tristan watching me.

He raised a dark eyebrow. "Something bothering you, partner?"

"No." Placing the assembled pistol on the coffee table, I leaned back and prepared to take it apart again, trying to focus this strange, restless energy and calm my mind. Ever since I'd kissed Ember on the beach two days ago, she was all I could think about. I couldn't concentrate on work, training had no appeal and even tasks that had become second nature had grown tedious. I was stumbling through this mission in a fog, and I needed to refocus my mind. It didn't help that tonight loomed over me like a thundercloud, making me nervous and edgy, unable to calm down.

Tonight, I would see her again. I was taking her on a date, as strange as that was for me. At Tristan's repeated prodding, I'd called her last night to ask her out, and she'd accepted instantly, though she had asked me to pick her up at the Smoothie Hut instead of her house.

"I can do that," I'd told her, frowning. Getting inside the Hill residence was one of our main priorities, but Ember had been reluctant to have me close to the villa ever since we met. "But don't you want me to pick you up at home?"

"Um, yes," she stammered, and I could sense she was holding something back. "But…well, it's my brother. He's my twin, and he's a little overprotective. Actually, make that über-overprotective. Overprotective to the nth degree. After I got home from the party, he was pretty pissed. If you show up at the house, he's going to be neurotic and ask questions, and I don't want to deal with that right now." She sounded defensive and a little sad at the same time. "I plan to tell him about us, but after he cools down a bit. Until then, it's just easier for him not to know."

Tristan shook his head, moving the groceries from their bags to the counter. "It's nearly four o' clock, Garret. Don't you have a *date* tonight?" he asked pointedly.

"I haven't forgotten." It had been on my mind the second I woke up this morning. Tristan didn't need to remind me. I was acutely aware of every minute that dragged by. "I'm leaving in a few minutes."

"Oh, yeah. Here." He broke away from the counter and tossed me something tiny and black. I caught it, letting it rest in my palm as I looked down. A tiny, thin square of plastic and metal, lying inconspicuously against my skin. I blinked and glanced back at Tristan. "A bug?"

"Stick that in her cell phone if you have the chance," he said, continuing to put groceries away. "It should go in right behind the battery. Once that's done, we should know in a few days whether or not she's our sleeper."

I stared at the bug a moment longer, strangely hesitant, before slipping it into my pocket. *This is a mission,* I reminded myself, standing to return my Glock to its holster. I certainly couldn't take it with me tonight. *It's nothing personal.*

"By the by," Tristan went on, pausing to grin at me over a Doritos bag. "I'm curious. Where are you two crazy kids going, anyway?"

"Movies, I suppose. Isn't that the normal practice?"

"Yes." Tristan nodded. "If you want to be completely boring and unoriginal. You're not going to get her to talk much by staring at a screen for two hours."

Irritation flared, which was odd for me. "What would you suggest, then, O Guru of the First Date?"

Tristan laughed. "Wow, you *are* nervous. Relax, partner. It's not like this is real. Besides," he added, grinning as he shut the cabinet door and turned to me, enjoying my discomfort far too much, "I have the perfect spot."

# EMBER

The soldiers were on to me.

I'd already been gunned down twice this morning. My scales were spattered with red, and a trickle of paint kept oozing into my eye, making my third lid constantly slide up to protect it. It was getting harder and harder to ambush the sneaky bastards; they were wise to my method of assault now, and ready to defend a sudden attack from above. Still, I'd managed to take several down before being shot to death with paintballs. Tearing away the strip of red cloth at their waist now equaled a successful "kill," and I'd racked up quite the body count. I thought I was doing pretty well, for someone who had to get in close to people with freaking guns. Still, it never satisfied *her.*

I was creeping through the aisles, all senses alert, when a soft groan made me freeze. It came from the other side of the crate wall, and I quickly leaped up top to avoid detection, careful to land silently. Peering over the edge, I blinked.

A soldier lay in the middle of the corridor, facedown on the cement, his gun at his side. I watched, ready to pounce if he got up. Maybe he'd tripped, or maybe he was just taking a nap, I didn't know. But he didn't rise, though his legs moved weakly and faint groans came from his huddled form. Something was wrong.

I dropped soundlessly to the floor, gazing around for his teammates. No one seemed to be around. They were probably stalking different corners of the room, looking for me. The man in the aisle groaned again, tried to get up and failed, slumping back to the cement. He was obviously hurt, and there was no one around but me.

"Hey," I said, trotting forward. I wished I could've Shifted into human form and not look so…targetlike, but as always, I was nude for these little exercises. "Are you all right? Are you hurt?"

He moaned again, and I stepped closer. "Can you walk?" I asked urgently. "Do you want me to get Scary Talon La—"

Quick as a snake, he flipped onto his back, leveled his gun and me and fired point-blank at my chest.

*Dammit!* I flinched back, not bothering to dodge, knowing it was useless. I wasn't even surprised when the rest of the squad appeared from hidden nooks and crannies and fired on me, too. *Dammit, dammit, dammit, I walked right into that one. I'm sure* she *will have all kinds of things to say about this.*

Closing my eyes, I hunkered down until the storm of paint finally stopped, and waited for my trainer to appear.

As usual, it didn't take long. Scary Talon Lady emerged from an aisle, shaking her head, her eyes crinkled with disgust. I growled, curling my lips back, as the soldiers took their guns and vanished again, including the one on the floor.

"I know," I growled before she could say anything. "Pathetic. You don't have to tell me, I know what I did wrong."

Her eyes bored into me. "If you knew," she said in a soft, unamused voice, "why did you do it?"

"I… I thought he was hurt! Really hurt. He's not a soldier of St. George—if he really was injured, I wanted to help him."

"And *that,*" my trainer said in a hard, icy voice, pointing with a sharp red nail, "is exactly why you failed. Who cares if he was hurt? He was still your enemy, and you had no business wanting to aid him." She straightened, giving me a look of contempt. "What is it you *should* have done, hatchling?"

I bit back the snarl rising to my throat. "Killed him."

"Without mercy," my trainer agreed. "Without hesitation. If you are ever in this type of situation again, I expect you to get it right. Because you may never have another chance if you don't."

★ ★ ★

Dante was on the couch watching some kind of action movie when I got home. He lay there looking perfectly nonchalant, with his head on the armrest, one leg dangling off the side and a soda resting on his stomach. I shook my head as I came through the door, on my way up to the shower. Dante never came home looking like a cow exploded on him.

He glanced up at me, and I held my breath. Ever since that night in my room after the party, we'd been walking on eggshells around each other. In typical Dante fashion, he never spoke of the encounter and acted like everything was fine. I knew better. It wasn't fine, *we* weren't fine, but I didn't know how to fix it.

"Good God," he commented as I paused in the frame, feeling hot and sticky and generally cranky. "Were you swimming in it today?"

"Shut up." The response was mostly out of habit, something easy and familiar, and the tension between us eased a bit as I made my way toward the steps. "Why are you home, anyway?" I asked, keeping my voice light, uncaring. "Aren't you supposed to be doing something with Calvin and Tyler today?"

"I'm meeting them at the Hut in an hour," Dante said, taking a swig from the can on his stomach. "Tyler found a new rock-climbing spot just out of town, so we're heading up there to check it out." He glanced at me and offered a wry half grin. "You're welcome to 'tag along' if you like. The guys won't care, and I'm pretty sure you can keep up."

He was extending an olive branch and, another time, I would've gladly accepted. Beating Dante and his friends to the top of a cliff was exactly what I needed to clear the bad air between us. Tonight, though, I had other plans. Plans that made my stomach squirm in a way surfing, dancing or rock climbing never did. Tonight, I would be with Garret.

"No, thanks," I told Dante. "I'll kick your ass some other time."

He shrugged and went back to watching TV. I continued toward the stairs but paused, hovering at the foot of the steps, watching him until he looked up again and raised an eyebrow.

"Yes?"

"Dante…" I hesitated, wondering if I should tempt fate like this, especially when we were still on shaky ground. But I continued, anyway. "Do you ever wonder…what they're training us for?"

"What do you mean?"

Hope flickered. At least he wasn't immediately brushing me off, or pretending he'd forgotten something in his room so he could leave. I raised my paint-drenched arms. "Well, look at me," I stated. "They're obviously not teaching us the same things. I'm running around getting shot at by lunatics with guns, and you're sitting in a nice room learning Tea Ceremony or something."

"Not yet," Dante said, smirking to show he wasn't being serious. "Tea Ceremony is next month."

"Why is our training so different?" I went on, ignoring his last statement. "I'll tell you what I think. I think they're going to separate us. You'll go to some nice academy for important rich students, and I… I'll be sent off to military school or something."

"You're overreacting." Dante swung his feet to the floor, watching me with his elbows on his knees. "They're not going to separate us."

"How do you know?" I demanded.

"Because my trainer told me."

"Oh, well, how great for you," I shot back, not knowing where this sudden anger was coming from. Dante scowled, but the suppressed rage and frustration from this morning, from every session with Scary Talon Lady, surged up with a vengeance. "My trainer doesn't tell me anything. Just lets me know how pathetic I am, that I'll never be a proper dragon, that I'm a waste of time and Talon shouldn't have even bothered hatching me. I hate going there. I hate her, and Talon, and this whole stupid—"

"Ember, that's enough!"

Dante's voice filled the room, sharp and guttural. Stunned, I fell silent, staring at him. "Be angry at your trainer all you like," he said firmly. "Be angry at *me* all you like. But start talking like that, and it sounds like you could be harboring rogue tendencies."

"So what?" I challenged. "Maybe I am. Who would tell them? You?"

He gave me an angry, hooded stare, and didn't answer. Rising from the couch, he vanished into his room, shutting the door behind him, a clear message that he didn't want to talk anymore. Feeling abandoned and despondent, I showered, then wandered down to the beach, walking along the water's edge.

I ached, both from the bruises I'd gotten in training and from my twin's cold dismissal. Nothing had changed between us, not really. The sun warmed my skin, and a breeze fluttered in from the ocean, smelling of salt and the waves I loved so much. Both would normally be a comfort, but not today. I was going to see Garret that evening, and while that made my stomach dance with anticipation and excitement, I couldn't talk to him about dragon problems. And Dante was out of the question, at least for today. Maybe forever.

*If you need to talk, Firebrand, about anything, I'm here.*

Reaching into my shorts, I pulled out my phone and stared at it. After going back and forth with myself several times, wondering if Talon was monitoring my phone, as well, I finally touched the screen and began typing a message, making it as vague as I could.

Can we talk?

I hit Send and waited. The sun beat down on my head and flashed across the phone screen, making me squint and shade it with my hands. The answer came back almost immediately.

When?

I swallowed. Right now, I texted. Meet me at the pier?

Again, only a few heartbeats passed before his message popped onto the screen.

On my way.

# RILEY

*Perfect.* Sending the last text, I lowered the phone and smiled. *Already starting to question things, huh, Firebrand? That didn't take long.*

"I'm heading out," I announced, grabbing my keys and jacket from the counter. "I'm meeting Ember at the pier, so I might come back with a guest. If that's the case, we'll probably leave town in the morning, so be ready to move out fast." I glanced at the only other person in the room and frowned. "Hey, other target who is actively wanted by Talon. Repeat what I said so I know you still care."

Wes, sitting at the dining room table with his laptop, didn't even look up as I paused in the foyer. "Meet a bloody hatchling, get ready to move out, done this a million times, blah blah blah," he said, his eyes still glued to the screen. "Have fun with your hatchling. Oh, and on the way back, if you don't have a chance run-in with St. George, we're out of Red Bull."

⋆ ⋆ ⋆

"Uh-oh," I commented as Ember, perched atop the wooden rails, glanced up and saw me. "I know that look."

She frowned, the sea breeze tugging at her hair. Around us, the long gray boardwalk, stretching out over the water, bustled with activity. Mothers with strollers, sweaty joggers, couples walking hand in hand and fishermen hanging their lines off the edge, all milling around completely unaware of the two dragons standing next to the railing. A woman and her tiny white dog passed us, and the thing stopped peeing on everything long enough to yip at me hysterically before being carted off by its owner. I smirked. Such a noisy little mouthful. One snap, and it would be gone.

"What look?" Ember demanded when the woman and the yappy hors d'oeuvre left. I caught her staring at me while my attention was distracted by the pooch, and bit back a smile. "That 'I hate my trainer and wish he would die' look," I replied. When she gaped at me, I chuckled. "Like I said, I've been around the block with Talon a few times. It doesn't get any easier from here, trust me."

"Great," she muttered darkly. "That's what I wanted to hear."

I caught a tiny flash of color on her bare shoulder, a sliver of red that looked like dried blood. Only, it was too bright to be blood, and memories crowded my brain, making me wince with sympathy. "Oh, Firebrand." I sighed, lightly touching the red splotch. "Soldiers and paintball guns, huh? That sucks."

She jerked up, eyes widening. "You, too?"

"Yup." Stepping beside her, I leaned back, resting my elbows on the railing. Ember watched me, green eyes awed and intense, burning the side of my face. "Only, mine were rubber bullets at first, which you wouldn't think would hurt, but damn, they sting like a mother when they hit. They switched to paintball guns when some poor bastard got his eye put out." I shook my head and gave her a rueful look. "Be thankful you were hatched after the new regime started. It's only a little unbearable now."

She wrinkled her nose and gazed back at the ocean. "So, what happens next?" she asked, kicking one ankle against the railing. "After this training is done? What are they planning for me when I'm finished?"

"I don't know, Firebrand." I hopped onto the railing beside her. "It depends, I guess, on what they have you slotted for. Every dragon has a place in the organization, and your initial training is to determine if you'll excel at where they want to put you. Really, they've watched you since your hatching, trying to decide where you'll fit. If you pass this stage, they'll announce your faction placement, and then your training begins in earnest." I snorted. "Course, they don't tell you what you're going to be until they deem you ready for it."

"What were you?" Ember asked.

I looked at her. She gazed back, and my dragon stirred in response. "I was a Basilisk," I said, and she furrowed her brow, clearly not familiar with that position. "A spy, basically," I went on. "One of the prime factions Talon uses in the war with St. George."

"I've never seen us at war."

"We're always at war with St. George, Firebrand." I remembered those years, the years I was still with the organization, bloody and dark and terrible, and repressed a shiver. "Yes, much of Talon—the Chameleons, the Monitors and the Elder Wyrm's council—never see the war. They hide deep within human society and don't engage the soldiers of St. George if they can help it. They're far too important to the organization to risk discovery. But Talon has elite agents they'll sometimes send against St. George. Never in force, and never in an all-out assault. Our numbers are too small, and the humans in general would slaughter us if this ever became public. There's just so damn many of them.

"But," I continued as Ember listened in rapt fascination, not even caring that there were humans around, "Talon does have a number of trained operatives they send out, striking where they can, usually from shadow. I was one of them. Someone to gather information on the Order, sneak into their bases to steal data or sabotage equipment, discover which of their own agents weren't loyal, basically act against Talon's enemies."

"Sounds dangerous."

"Oh, it was." I grinned. "I can't remember the times I escaped St. George by the skin of my teeth. Took a few bullets, avoided an ambush, dodged a sniper attack, that sort of thing. Fun times."

"Is that why you went rogue?"

The question took me by surprise, and I sobered quickly. Trust Ember to get to the heart of the matter. "No," I replied, shaking my head. Memories flared up again, and I shoved them back. "It wasn't St. George that made me run. It was Talon itself."

She gazed at me, every bit of her attention focused like a hawk. "Why?"

My heartbeat picked up, and my mouth was suddenly dry. This was it, the perfect opportunity. I wouldn't get a better chance. "Because, Firebrand—"

The phone shrilled loudly in my jacket pocket.

"Dammit." Sliding off the rail to the deck, I pulled it out and gazed down at the number. Of course it was Wes; he was the only one, besides Ember, who had this number. "Hang on." I sighed, moving a few feet away. "Lemme take this. I'll be right back."

"Wes," I said cordially when I put the phone to my ear, "for your sake, you had better be halfway down a dragon's throat right now, because otherwise I'm going to kick your ass."

"Where the bloody hell are you?" Wes spat, making my gut squeeze tight. "Get back here right now. We've got another problem!"

I glanced at Ember, then hunched forward, lowering my voice. "What type of problem?"

"The type that has scales and claws and is sitting on our doorstep problem!"

"Shit." I dragged a hand through my hair, cursing his timing. But this could definitely not be ignored. "I'll be right there," I said, and hung up, turning back to Ember.

She hopped from the railing and gazed up at me, concerned. "Problems at home?"

*Dammit, I was so close.* "Yeah," I growled, resisting the urge to kick something. "I have to go. But this isn't over, okay?" I stepped close, putting a hand on her arm. Inside, something flared, a rush of heat through my veins, nearly making me jump back. The same reaction my dragon instincts had had at the party, roaring to life. "I still want to talk to you," I said as Ember's cheeks flushed, as well, making me suspect she felt the same. "I have more information on Talon, and I think you'll want to hear it. Promise you'll meet me again."

She stared back, unafraid. "When?"

"Soon." It was more a promise to myself than to Ember, a claim that whatever this dire problem was, it wouldn't keep me from her. I squeezed her arm and backed away, forcing a grin as I retreated. "Don't worry, Firebrand. I'll be around. See you soon."

# EMBER

I watched Riley jog to his motorcycle, swing aboard and roar off down the street. Part of me wished I could go with him, longed to Shift and fly after the rogue, apocalyptic consequences be damned. My skin still surged from where he'd touched me, the dragon dancing all up and down my veins. She wanted Riley. Not in the way I missed Garret, or thought about him constantly. This was more…primal? Instinctive? I didn't know the exact word, really, but one thing was for certain. My dragon wanted Riley; she almost ached for him. And she would not be ignored.

No, that wasn't entirely true. She wanted *Cobalt.* Which was ridiculous, because Riley and Cobalt were the same. The boy with the lopsided smirk, messy black hair and almost-gold eyes was the same being as the proud blue dragon who had soared the waves with me that night. I didn't understand it. I didn't understand how my instincts, once a seamless part of me, could be so alien now. Almost like I was two different creatures: dragon and human.

I shook myself and started down the pier, back toward the beach. Inner turmoil aside, I did know a little more about Talon now. None of it was *really* bad, though. Not yet. Even the war with St. George wasn't a surprise. The dragonslay-

ers wanted our extinction. Why shouldn't we fight back and defend ourselves?

It wasn't a shock and it just confirmed what I'd always suspected. Talon was training me to be a part of that war. Soldiers, guns, tactical maneuvers, showing no mercy to my prey; I certainly wasn't going to be sitting at a table with high-ranking diplomats. No, I was destined to become one of their elite operatives, maybe a Basilisk like Riley, fighting an endless battle with St. George.

Reaching the end of the boardwalk, I turned and stared out over the water, shivering a little in the warm breeze. So, this was truly my last hurrah. Talon already had my life planned out, where I would go, what I would be. Never mind that I wasn't certain I could do this. Never mind that I hated my trainer and everything she made me do, what she wanted me to become. Talon's decision was law; I didn't have any say in my own future.

My phone vibrated in my pocket. Pulling it out, I clicked it on and saw a new text message across the screen.

We still on for tonight? Smoothie Hut at 5pm, yes?

Garret. I smiled, feeling my crushed spirits rise a little. Screw Talon. Screw their war, their trainers, their plans, all of it. The summer was still mine. I wasn't theirs yet.

Definitely, I texted back. See you then.

# GARRET

For once, Ember was waiting at our meeting place ahead of me.

I spotted the red-haired girl sitting on the curb in the parking lot, legs crossed, foam cup in hand. She looked deep in thought, chewing on her straw, but when I pulled the Jeep into the spot next to her, she bounced up instantly with a smile.

"Hey, Garret!" she exclaimed as I reached over and opened the door, letting her into the cab. She slid into the passenger seat and beamed, and my skin prickled under that smile. "You must be rubbing off on me. Look, I'm on time and everything."

"I see that." I took advantage of the moment just to watch her, noting the dark jeans and top she wore instead of her usual shorts and T-shirt, and the way the afternoon sun fell into her hair and eyes, making them glow.

*Focus, soldier.* I shook myself and put the Jeep in Reverse, pulling out of the parking spot. Ember leaned back and stared out the side window, her gaze troubled. I remembered her earlier call, the warning not to come to the house, and wondered what was happening at her home. If I could get her talking about her family, the twin brother especially, maybe

I could discern something useful. Maybe I would discover she was just a normal teenager, after all.

"I apologize if I got you in trouble this weekend," I offered as we pulled onto the main road. "I didn't mean to make things difficult with your family. I can talk to your brother, if you want me to."

"What? Oh, no, it wasn't you, Garret." Ember shrugged and shook her head in disgust. "Dante is just being a neurotic freak. He gets carried away with the whole overprotective big-brother thing sometimes. And with what happened at the party..." Her eyes darkened a little. "I figured I'd give him some time to cool off before I told him about us."

"You and your brother are close?"

"Well, yeah." She turned back, cocking her head. "He's my twin, after all. We used to do everything together."

"But not now."

"No." Sighing, she looked down at her hands, twisting them in her lap. "He's...different now. It's like he's pulling away from me, and I don't know why. I wish he'd talk to me like he used to."

I knew I should continue asking questions, find out as much as I could about this twin. But Ember looked distressed, and I found that I hated the sight of her unhappy. When we paused at a stoplight, my hand moved of its own accord to gently brush her hair back, tucking it behind her ear.

"I'm sorry," I said as she turned in surprise. "I don't have any siblings, but Tristan is the closest to a brother I have. I know how...distracting it can be, when you don't see eye to eye." She blinked at me, and I pulled my hand back. "Just keep talking to him. He'll come around eventually."

"Yeah," she murmured as the light changed and we moved

forward again. “I hope so.” She brooded a moment more, than shook herself, perking up as we turned onto the highway ramp. “Hey, where are we going, anyway?”

I grinned at her. “It’s a surprise.”

# EMBER

"Movies."

"No."

"Bowling."

"No."

"Ice skating."

He looked at me strangely. "In California?"

"I'm sure there are spots for it. We have a professional hockey league and everything."

"I suppose you're right. And no."

"Concert."

"Not even close."

I let out a little huff. "I'm being kidnapped and spirited off to Saudi Arabia to be the forty-second wife of Grand Sheikh Ramalama."

He chuckled. "You caught me. I hope you brought your camel repellant."

"Smart-ass." I wrinkled my nose at him. "You do realize I have a brother, right? I can keep this up *alllll* afternoon."

He gave me a patient smile, as if he, too, was familiar with sibling tactics and no amount of pestering or torture would make him spill. "Do you have something against surprises?"

"Yes! I don't like secrets. I'd rather have everything up front and out in the open."

Which was, now that I thought about it, a bizarre thing to say. My whole life was a lie. Everything Talon did, everything they taught us, was to maintain that deception. I was tired of it. Not to say that I wanted the world to know about the existence of dragons; even I knew what would come of that, but it would be nice, sometimes, to be myself. To not have to lie to everyone about everything. I used to be able to do that with Dante but, it seemed, not anymore.

Garret blinked, and a shadow crossed his face, as if my statement touched something in him, too. But then he pulled off the road, into a crowded parking lot, and I gasped at the sight of the Ferris wheel and huge wooden coaster, looming at the end of a boardwalk.

Garret swung into an open space and killed the engine, grinning at me. "I thought you might like this more than sitting in a theater for two hours," he said, and there might have been a note of amused triumph in his voice, but I wasn't paying much attention. "Of course, we could still go to the movies, if you want. Turn around and head back—"

"Are you insane?" I wrenched open the door and hopped out, turning to glare at him impatiently. "I will personally rip all four tires off your car if you try to leave now, so come on." He laughed, slid out of the Jeep and followed me across the parking lot as the screams, music and intoxicating smell of cotton candy drew me forward like a siren song.

Past the gates, I paused at the edge of the boardwalk just to take it all in. I'd never been to a carnival before, and didn't want to miss anything. Crowds of people, some with bright stuffed animals tucked under one arm, milled back and forth with no sense of direction. Bells and whistles rang out, things spun, glittered, flashed and whirled so quickly it was almost overwhelming.

This was going to be awesome.

Garret stepped up beside me, gently brushing my elbow. "Well?" he asked, bending close to be heard over the crowd. "This is your occasion. Where to first?"

I gave him an evil grin. Oh, that was an easy one. "Come on," I said, taking his hand. "I know exactly where we're going. This way."

★ ★ ★

"Remember," I told him, gazing at the top of the coaster as the cars inched slowly up the track, "when we start going, you're supposed to put both hands in the air and scream. It's more fun if you scream, at least that's what Lexi says."

He gave me a dubious look from his side of the seat, and did not relinquish his death grip on the railing. "I'll take your word for it."

"Suit yourself." I smiled as we reached the very top of the vertical plunge and teetered there on the edge. For a moment, I could see the whole park spread out before us, and was reminded almost painfully of flying. "Guess I'll scream for us both."

Then the coaster plunged downward, and I did. It was almost better than flying.

Almost.

We rode three more times. The last was at his insistence, and I finally got him to let go of the railing. (Though he still didn't scream.) After that, we moved on to the swing ride, the Tilt-A-Whirl and the bumper cars, with Garret effectively blocking everyone who tried to ram their car into mine. I caught a glimpse of his face once, when he sideswiped a car heading right for me—that same fierce excitement I'd seen while he was surfing. A warm glow of pleasure spread through me, even as I barreled full speed into the back of his car. He was having just as much fun as I was.

"Where to now?" he asked a bit later, when we'd ridden nearly all the fast rides and had finally taken a break to eat. The food tent was crowded and noisy, but at least it was shaded, and a cool ocean breeze blew in beyond the edge of the pier. "I think the only ride left is the Ferris wheel and the little kid's coaster. Did you want to go on either of them?"

Before I could answer, my phone buzzed. Wincing, I dug it out, scowling at the name flashing across the screen. "Dante," I muttered and, feeling surly and annoyed with him, clicked off the phone. "Not interested right now, big brother. Go away."

Setting it on a napkin, I looked back at Garret, who seemed to be awaiting orders, or at least a decision. I grinned at him over hamburger wrappings and the demolished remains of a funnel cake. "Ferris wheel definitely. Kiddie coaster, I don't know. You wouldn't be embarrassed to be seen riding a giant pink caterpillar with four-year-olds, would you?"

He shrugged. "I'm game if you are."

Giggling at the thought of Garret on a giant caterpillar surrounded by toddlers, I stood, pitched our trash into a bin and turned back to the table, dusting sticky funnel cake powder from my hands.

Suddenly, I got a cold, tingly feeling on the back of my neck, and froze, my stomach turning uneasily. Was I being watched? Where? By whom? Was Riley somewhere in the crowd, spying on me, having followed us all the way from Crescent Beach? That was a bit creepy, though. It didn't seem like him. The rogue dragon might be arrogant, defiant and rebellious, but he didn't strike me as a stalker.

Who, then, was watching me?

Garret blinked as I came back, still waiting patiently to hear what I wanted to do. If he noticed that I was distracted, he didn't comment on it.

"Hold that thought, then," I said, gazing around for a restroom, spotting one behind a hot dog stand. "I'm going to wash my hands. Don't go anywhere. I'll be right back."

"I'll be here."

I smiled and left the table, following a gaggle of human girls toward the restrooms, my gaze scanning the crowd for anyone familiar. But almost as quickly as it had begun, the strange feeling vanished, and all was normal again.

# GARRET

Ember smiled and brushed past me, her fingers skimming my arm as she went by. My heart jumped, breath catching, but she had already melted into the crowd.

Leaving her phone sitting on the table.

I stared at it, my smile fading, cold realization settling over me as I remembered. The reason I'd come, the purpose of this date. It wasn't to ride coasters, stand in lines or drive miniature cars into one another. I wasn't here to have fun. I was here to discover, once and for all, if Ember was our target. The bug lay nestled in my pocket, and her phone lay within easy reach. All I had to do was slide off the case, slip the bug behind the phone battery and snap everything back into place before she returned. It would take ten seconds, fifteen tops.

Slowly, I reached across the table, my fingers resting on the smooth black case of her phone. It beeped as I pulled it toward me, indicating a text had come through. I hesitated, then touched the screen, bringing it to life. A green bubble blinked, the new message displayed inside, and I turned the case around to read it.

Hey, Tweedledee. I don't want us to fight. Call me soon, ok?

I paused once more, feeling the bug in my pocket. There was still plenty of time before she came back. This could end our search. This could uncover a nest of dragons and their guardians. Or not. Either way, once the bug had been placed, there was no reason I had to see Ember, ever again.

Reaching into my pocket, my fingers closed around the bug and pulled it out.

# EMBER

When I maneuvered my way back to the table, Garret was in the same spot, his chin resting on his hands as he watched the milling crowd. They watched him, too, or at least I saw several appreciative glances slide his way from passing human females. Bristling, I walked faster, but if Garret noticed the interest, he didn't respond. His expression, though alert and watchful, wasn't the hyperawareness of that day in the mall, when he'd scanned the crowds like he was afraid a ninja would come leaping out at him. He seemed relaxed, more at ease, though as I walked up, a faintly troubled look crossed his face as he glanced at me. It was gone in the next heartbeat, though, so I'd probably imagined it.

Apparently, I was imagining all sorts of things today. There was no sign of any mysterious stalker watching me through the crowds. All seemed normal, though with so many people milling about, it was difficult to spot anything. Besides, if someone *was* watching me, what could they do in this mob?

"Ready?" I asked, bouncing up to the table. My phone lay on the napkin where I'd left it, and I slipped it into my pocket. Garret smiled and rose to his feet with easy grace, tossing his empty cup into the trash bin.

"Lead the way. I'm ready to tame a giant caterpillar if you are."

A couple walked by, a stuffed gorilla under the boy's arm, and I perked up. "Ooh, wait, new plan," I announced, making him arch an eyebrow at me. "Let's go check out the fairway."

"Fairway?"

I pointed to the stretch of game booths up and down the boardwalk. "Lexi says they're all horribly rigged," I explained, watching a skinny guy toss a basketball at a tiny orange hoop, where it bounced off the rim. "But you can win prizes if you score enough points."

"Prizes?"

"Yeah! See, he's probably trying to win her that big stuffed penguin." I pointed to the skinny guy, who was digging through his pockets now, while a dark-haired girl looked on hopefully. "But it looks like he only gets three shots," I explained as the guy handed the booth attendant another bill, "and you have to keep paying for more chances."

"So, I'm paying them to play a game that I'm probably going to lose. To win a prize that I don't even want."

"Looks like it." Now that I thought about it, it did seem pretty rigged. Kristin once bragged that a guy had spent over a hundred dollars trying to win her a giant poodle. "Actually, never mind," I told Garret. "Forget it. I don't want you to lose a ton of cash trying to win something. Let's go check out the Ferris wheel."

I started to turn, but his hand closed on my arm, stopping me. Surprised, I glanced back to see a faint, almost smug grin on his face. "What makes you think I'm going to lose?" he asked, making me blink in shock. "This is part of the date, right? If you want a giant stuffed animal, I'll get you one."

★ ★ ★

And he did. I don't think he missed one target as they bobbed by on plastic waves, even knocking down the tiny, really hard to hit frogs worth three times as much. The kid manning the booth looked reluctantly impressed as he handed him a giant pink bear, the biggest prize on the wall. Garret looked amused as he accepted it, then turned and handed it to me. I grinned and crossed my arms. "Pink looks good on you, Garret. Sure you don't want it?"

"I was playing for you," he replied, smiling back. "Take it. It's yours."

"Oh, fine." I smiled and took the huge toy, hugging it to me. The bear's fur was silky against my skin and smelled faintly of cotton candy. "But only if you let me win you something."

"Deal."

And I did, finally knocking down six questionably sturdy pins with a softball to win a tiny stuffed blue dog. (This was after the ring toss, hoops and dart game, all of which, I decided, *were* horribly rigged.) With the amount of tries it took, I could have probably bought the stupid thing three times over, but Garret accepted the prize like it was made of pure gold, and his smile made me warm with happiness. I did get that strange "you are being watched" prickle on the back of my neck once, but I couldn't see anyone in the milling crowds, and after a few moments of fruitless searching, decided I wouldn't let it make me neurotic. Let them stare, whoever they were. I wasn't doing anything I was ashamed of.

Finally, as the sun began to set over the ocean, we sat side by side on the Ferris wheel bench, rocking gently and watching the crowds get smaller and smaller as we rose into the air. The breeze was cool and the noises of the carnival were muted as the chair took us farther from the ground, the clouds so near I felt I could reach up and touch one. My dragon stirred and fluttered her wings, not satisfied with being below them, wanting to soar overhead. But this was the closest I'd been to the sky since that secret night with Cobalt, and I felt pretty content to stay right where I was.

Hugging my bear, I snuck a glance at Garret. His face, turned toward the distant ocean, was troubled, his eyes far away and dark.

I blinked and bumped his shoulder with mine, bringing his attention back to me. "You okay?" I asked softly.

# GARRET

No. I wasn't.

I'd realized something, maybe while smashing into bumper cars in an effort to protect Ember, maybe while giving everything I had to win her that bear or maybe while just sitting here with her, side by side. I…liked this girl. I wanted to spend more time with her; she was constantly in my thoughts, and right now the only thing I wanted was to lean in and kiss her. Which was, of course, disastrous for the mission, but I couldn't help it. Somewhere between that day on the beach when I'd met her for the first time and the night of the party when we'd kissed in the ocean, she had become something more than a potential target. She had, very inexplicably, become the most important thing in my life.

And that terrified me.

My hand was in my pocket, fingers closed around the bug I hadn't been able to place in her phone. Tangible evidence that I was failing the mission, that I was far too close.

Ember rested her chin on the top of her bear and gazed up at me. Green eyes met mine, open and inquisitive, and a little worried. "You're brooding," she accused softly, sounding very much like Tristan at that moment. "What are you thinking about?"

I shook my head. "Nothing."

"Liar." Clearly unconvinced, she sat up straighter, watching me. "Come on, Garret. One minute you're fine, the next you go all dark and serious. Something is obviously bothering you. What's wrong?"

I scrambled for a response, knowing she wouldn't let it go until I replied. "I…was just thinking about the end of the month," I said, turning to face her. She gave me a puzzled frown, and I gestured vaguely at the amusement park. "Summer will be over soon. In a few weeks, I'll have to go home, back to Chicago and my dad. We won't see each other again."

I gazed out over the railing, surprised by how much that bothered me. Though most of it was a lie, the part about not seeing her again was real. If she was a normal civilian, I'd leave as soon as the mission was over, returning to the Order and the eternal war. And if she was the sleeper…

I clenched my fist around the railing, finally forcing myself to really acknowledge what that meant. I'd always known, of course. It was always there, at the back of my mind; I just didn't want to think about it. But if Ember was the sleeper… I would have to kill her. That was my duty, what the Order expected of me. To put a bullet in her heart, without mercy, and watch her die. It was easy to kill a dragon in human form; they didn't have their armorlike scales to protect them, or the thick chest plates that turned away all but the highest caliber rounds. If you could surprise one before it had a chance to shift, it stood no chance.

A few weeks ago, I wouldn't have given it a second thought. Dragons were the enemy; they wanted to enslave humans, and the Order was the only thing standing between them and global dominion. I knew that. I believed that wholeheartedly.

But before I'd met Ember, I'd never shot zombies in a crowded mall on a random Thursday. I'd never gone surfing and felt that pure adrenaline rush of riding the waves. And I'd never felt anything like what Ember stirred in me when we kissed—that rush of heat that both thrilled and terrified me.

I felt balanced on the edge of something huge, and the earth was cracking under my feet. Everything the Order had taught me about dragons—that they were lethal, conniving, calculating monsters who hated mankind—none of that fit the daring, cheerful girl at my side. Which could mean only two things: that Ember was a normal human being, or that the Order was wrong.

And the second part of that statement disturbed me more than anything I'd ever faced.

A slim hand on my knee jolted me out of my dark thoughts. I looked back to find Ember gazing up at me, still hugging her bear to her chest.

"I know," she said as I struggled to focus on what she was saying; the warm fingers on my leg were fairly distracting. "I've been thinking about that, too. The locals here have a saying—'Don't let your heart leave the beach.' It means you should never get attached to someone who's going to disappear at the end of the summer. If they're going to leave, anyway, why risk it?

"But," she continued, "if we did that, if we never took a chance on anything, we might miss out on something incredible. I don't have a lot of time here, either. When summer ends…" Her eyes darkened a shade. "My life is going to get pretty crazy. But I'm glad that I met you. Even if we have to part ways at the end of the summer, I wouldn't change anything." She paused again, averting her gaze as if in embarrassment. "From the day we met, you've been the person that I look forward to seeing, spending time with, the most. I never really felt like I fit in until you came along. You made me forget…some unpleasant things in my life. You made me feel that I wasn't so different, after all."

I reached up, brushing a fiery strand of hair behind her ear. "We're not…really that different, you know," I faltered. I didn't know why I was telling her this; until now, I hadn't even known I *felt* like this. "I've never fit in anywhere—well, anywhere normal. My life has always been dictated by my dad, and where he thought we should go. The only difference is…you do all the things I never allowed myself to do. Things I never thought I wanted." I looked into her brilliant green eyes and smiled ruefully. "I didn't know what I was missing, until I met you."

Ember's gaze went searingly bright. Dropping her bear, she scooted forward and straddled my waist on the bench, a move that would've normally set off all my alarms, but I had given up on normal a while ago. I wrapped my arms around her small form, holding her tight, letting the heat of her body melt through the last of my armor, dissolving the logic of not getting close. The soldier was still warning me not to do this, reminding me that she was a potential target and nothing else. I ignored him. I was getting good at ignoring him, but today was different. This wasn't me convincing myself I was still following the mission; I knew that was a lie. My emotions had finally gotten the better of me, and I was with Ember because I wanted to be here. Tonight, I didn't care. I'd been a soldier every day for the past seventeen years. Just this once, I wanted to know what it was like…to *live.*

Ember peered down at me, her hands resting on my shoulders, soft fingers gently brushing my neck. Her stare was awed, as if she couldn't quite believe this was real, that it was really happening. I knew, because I was feeling the same.

"Kiss me," I whispered. *Make me forget, for a night, that this isn't real. Make me believe that this could be my life. That I'm not betraying everything I know to be here, to feel like this.*

Ember bent down. Her lips touched mine, and my doubts vanished. The soldier disappeared. Everything disappeared, except her. I felt nothing but her hands on my skin, her lips, her body pressed against me. I kissed her until I was consumed with her, searing this moment into my consciousness, driving away the soldier and St. George and everything about the war. I would get back to it tomorrow. Tonight, I wanted to be normal.

Tonight, Garret the soldier didn't exist.

# RILEY

Two dragons were sitting in my living room when I walked through the door.

I frowned at Wes, who was hovering in the foyer waiting for me. "What happened?" I snapped, looking past him to the pair of teens on my couch. Hatchlings, both of them, looking scared, dirty and exhausted as they huddled together on the floral cushions. Naomi, or Nettle as she was called by nearly everyone, was a dark, thin girl with dreadlocks that stuck out in every direction. Remy, a sandy-haired kid with piercing blue eyes, peered at me over the chair back, solemn and grave.

Wes shrugged helplessly.

"I can't get them to talk, mate. They said they were waiting for you."

Sighing, I stalked to the kitchen, opened a cupboard and yanked out two bags of chips. Walking back to the living room, I tossed them at the hatchlings, who caught the bags and stared at me, unsure of what to do.

"Eat something first," I ordered. Hatchlings were, by definition, almost always hungry, as their metabolism required large amounts of food to keep active and healthy. Shifting, too, took huge amounts of energy, which was why we were always ravenous soon after a change. And a hungry dragon was a nervous, restless, irritable dragon, something I did not need right now. If I was going to get to the bottom of this, I needed them calm.

"It's fine," I assured them as they still hesitated. "Go ahead and eat. Knock yourselves out, really. We'll talk afterward."

Clearly starving, they tore open the bags and plowed through the contents, barely stopping to chew. I left them demolishing the chips and wandered onto the deck, leaning my elbows against the railing.

Damn. Something was definitely up. Nettle and Remy shouldn't be here. I'd left them both at a safe house in Boulder, Colorado, high in the mountains. What had driven them to find me? Something serious. Something that had caused my other safe houses to disappear. It was probably a good thing they'd showed up when they did. Maybe now I could figure out what the hell was going on.

I sighed, looking straight down from the balcony. Far below, the ocean crashed against the rocks, and the salt-laced air tugged at my hair and clothes. Frowning, I scrubbed a hand over my eyes, trying to dissolve the memories that flickered to life again, but it was no use. For some reason, every time I smelled the ocean, heard the crashing waves and felt the wind on my face, I thought of *her.* Of Ember and that brief night of flying the waves. Of racing a fiery red hatchling who called to my dragon, igniting an inferno within. I didn't understand it. Ember as a human was young, naive, stubborn and impulsive. Ember in her true form was all of those things, but also fearless, defiant and beautiful.

I shook my head, pushing myself back from the railing. This was crazy. I couldn't be distracted now. Ember was beginning to come around, but things were moving too slowly for my liking. I should've told her everything about Talon this afternoon. Unfortunately, I would have to deal with this new problem before I did anything else.

"Riley." Wes poked his head out the doorframe. "I think they're ready for you, mate."

Pushing Ember from my mind, I stalked back into the living room. Nettle and Remy perched nervously on the sofa, two empty chip bags crumpled on the end tables. Wes had apparently gotten them drinks, as well, as a pair of open sodas sat dripping on the polished wood.

"All right, you two," I said, sinking into the armchair facing them. "Start talking. From the beginning." They stared at me, clearly not sure where to begin, and I sighed. "What happened to the safe house?" I said to get them started. "And why are you here? Only your guardian was supposed to know of this location. Where is he, anyway? Did you trek all the way up here by yourselves?"

The hatchlings exchanged a glance, then Remy took a deep breath.

"Chris told us to come," he began in a surprisingly steady voice. "He gave us your location and sent us here."

I frowned. Chris was the guardian in charge of the Boulder safe house. All the nests had one: a human who knew about us and who'd agreed to look after one or two vulnerable hatchlings until they were old enough to be on their own. Most of the guardians were ex-Talon servants, already living in hiding; if you were a human employed by the organization, you were in for life. As much as Talon despised having their dragons break away, they were even more fervent about not letting their humans go and risk exposing our existence. The few humans who did escape lived with the fear that St. George or Talon could show up on their doorstep any day, so after years of tracking them down and convincing them I wasn't part of Talon anymore, we'd come to an agreement. I would keep the organization off their backs as best I could, and they, in turn, had agreed to watch over the hatchlings I broke out of Talon.

"Chris sent you here?" I repeated, and they bobbed their heads in unison. "Why?"

"We don't know!" Nettle burst out, making Remy flinch. Her dreadlocks bobbed as she gestured wildly. "He just woke us up in the middle of the night and told us to pack our things. Didn't say what was going on, just shoved us into a taxi and ordered us not to come back!"

A chill settled in my gut. I looked at Wes, who nodded and left the room, probably to check the status of the Boulder safe house. I turned back to the hatchlings. "He didn't say anything to you at all?"

"No." Remy shook his head. "But he did seem really freaked out. Kept glancing out the window and pacing while we packed."

I narrowed my eyes. That house had been located halfway up a mountain peak, isolated and virtually unknown. No one was aware of it except me, Wes and a couple other former Talon servants. In fact, all of my safe houses had been, well, *safe.* I'd had no issues with keeping them hidden before. Why were they being exposed now?

The answer was sobering. I might have a mole in my ranks. With the exception of Wes, who hated Talon almost as much as I did, I really didn't trust humans all that much. They were too gullible, too easy to sway with promises of wealth, power, status or whatever they coveted. I worked with them out of necessity; our numbers were small and I couldn't do everything myself, but if Talon offered them something better, I wouldn't put it past them to betray us.

Which meant we could be in trouble here.

"Riley." Wes appeared at the edge of the hall, his face and eyes shadowed. I rose and followed him into the spare bedroom he used as his office.

"It's gone, mate," he whispered as I crossed the threshold. His laptop sat open and blinking on the desk, and he looked at it as if hoping it would tell him something else. "The Boulder nest has gone dark, and Chris isn't answering the emergency number."

I swore. "We had cameras and communications set up so that even if Talon found the nest, we could still contact them, unless the house was completely burned down." I stared at Wes, hard, and he looked away. "Tell me that's not the case."

He rubbed his arm, his voice going soft. "I don't think this is Talon, Riley."

The cold spread to all parts of my body, and I shivered in rage and growing horror. "No," I muttered, staring at the flickering laptop screen. "It's St. George."

Wes nodded. "Which means they're probably tracking those two right now," he said, sounding grim. "Persistent bastards won't stop if they know a pair of dragons got away from them. So that leaves us with just one option." He walked to his laptop, closing it with a snap. "We have to get out of town, tonight if possible. We're way too exposed here."

*Dammit.* I growled, clenching my fists. "No. Not yet. We can't leave yet."

Wes spun back, eyes widening. "Riley, did you hear what

I just said? Bloody *St. George* is on the way. If they find us here, they'll kill us all."

"I know."

"If we stay here, we're putting those kids in danger, too. We have a responsibility to keep them safe. That's what we promised."

"I know!" I snapped, and raked a hand through my hair. "I just… I'm close, Wes. She's almost ready to leave. I just need a little more time."

"You want to stay because of *her?*" Wes looked at me like I had six heads. "Are you bloody insane? She's just another hatchling, mate. We can't save them all."

Just another hatchling? My eyes narrowed. "Ember will come. She's one of us, she just doesn't know it yet." He started to protest again, and I overrode him. "I'm not leaving without her. So either stay and help, or shut up and leave."

"Fine." He made a frustrated, hopeless gesture. "You want to stay and get us all killed? Great. I bloody hope she's worth it."

I ignored the jab. "We need to secure the house," I said, slipping into safeguard mode now that we weren't leaving yet. "Alarms, cameras, motion detectors, everything. If St. George comes within a hundred feet of the gate, I want to know. How soon can you set that up?"

Wes scrubbed a hand over his face. "Get me the equipment, and I'll have it up and running by tomorrow."

"Good. Start working on that now. I'll get you what you need later tonight." I headed out of the room but stopped when I saw the hatchlings, still huddled on the couch. Nettle had slumped against an armrest and was about ready to fall asleep, and Remy didn't look much better.

"Don't tell them about St. George," I muttered without looking back. "I'll explain what's going on later, but I don't want them panicking without reason. They're scared enough as it is."

"Oh, sure," I heard Wes mumble as I left the room. "Don't want to worry the bloody hatchlings, but the human's heart exploding from stress, that's perfectly okay."

I knew Wes was right. Staying here when St. George was tracking them was stupid and risky, especially if I had a mole. I was endangering the hatchlings, and I was endangering everything I'd worked so hard to build.

But the thought of leaving Ember behind, when I was just starting to sway her to my side… I couldn't do it. I wouldn't lose her to Talon now. Wes would have to suck it up and get used to the idea. Because until I convinced Ember to break from Talon and join the rogues, none of us was going anywhere.

# EMBER

I was soaring the wind currents, the sun warm on my back, the breeze cool in my face. Below me, the white sea of clouds roiled and crashed against one another, smelling of salt and surf and the ocean, and I dipped lower to skim the waves.

Someone dropped beside me, another dragon, grinning a challenge as he swooped ahead. With a strong flap of my wings, I soared after him, following the streaming tail as he rolled and dived through the cloud-waves. I didn't recognize him, though I knew I'd seen him before. Was it Cobalt? Or Garret…?

The alarm clock shrilled in my ear, piercing the fantasy, and I slapped it silent—5:00 a.m. already. Damn. And the dream was already fading, vanishing into the ether as reality returned me to my bed. Had I been flying? And who was that other dragon I was chasing? I tried to hold on to the memory, but it slipped away into the darkness and was lost.

Rolling to my back, I stared at the ceiling, already dreading the day. *Wonder what fun thing Scary Talon Lady has planned for me this time.* Probably another dozen or so rounds of "hunt the dragon," which was still far too realistic for me to enjoy, even in my real form.

I sat up, throwing off the covers, and my bear tumbled

from the mattress to the floor. Smiling, I picked it up, inhaling the faint scent of cotton candy that still clung to the fur, and gave it a squeeze.

*Garret won this for me.* Just the thought of that, of him, made me smile. That day at the carnival had been amazing, especially the part on the Ferris wheel. The way he looked at me, right before I kissed him, made my breath catch. It was like he was seeing me—seeing me for what I really was—and he didn't care.

I knew that was a lie, of course. Garret couldn't know what I was. Our worlds were vastly different. I knew, when the summer ended, I would have to give him up.

But not yet.

"Ember." A knock came at my door, and Uncle Liam's voice drifted through the wood. "It's 5:05. Are you awake?"

"Yes," I muttered, and the footsteps receded. Rising, I set the bear on my unmade bed and dressed into my old, now-paint-spattered shirt and shorts. I didn't bother with a shower, knowing I'd come home dirty, sweaty and covered in bright red paint. (My driver had covered the backseat of his car with a sheet so I wouldn't ruin the upholstery. The sheet now looked like someone murdered a goat on it.)

Dante had already gone ahead when I went down to the basement, and a knot settled in my stomach as I opened the tunnel door. Ever since our fight, my brother and I hadn't spoken, not about anything important. He'd smiled at me when I came back from the carnival and acted as if nothing was wrong, but it wasn't the same. Around our guardians, he was still my friendly, teasing, easygoing brother, but ask him anything Talon or dragon related, and his eyes would go blank, his smile empty. He was slipping further and further away from me, and I didn't know how to get him back.

When I reached the office building, I received a shock. The enormous storage room had been cleared out. Nothing remained of the massive wooden labyrinth except a few crates and pallets stacked in the corner. The floor was empty, except for a square of thick blue wrestling mats in the middle of the cement, making it look more like a gym than a storage room. But that wasn't the biggest surprise.

Scary Talon Lady stood in the center of the mats, arms crossed, waiting for me. She wasn't wearing her normal three-piece suit and heels. She was dressed in a sleek black outfit that hugged her slender form and covered her from neck to ankles. Her blond hair had been pulled behind her and swung halfway down her back, free of its ever-present bun. She was, I realized, quite attractive in human terms. Beautiful and stunning. Though her acid-green eyes, watching me cross the room, were the same: flat, cold and subtly amused.

"Something new today, hatchling." She smiled as I stepped to the edge of the mats. "I think I've been too easy on you, letting humans chase you around with paintball guns and fake bullets. I also think you're depending far too much on your real form to get out of trouble. Sometimes you need to shear through a St. George soldier with claws and fangs and fire. Sometimes it is better to be human. You need to learn to defend yourself as both. Take off your shoes."

Too easy on me? Like dodging paint bullets and playing hide-and-seek with fully trained soldiers was a fun little skip in the park? I eyed her warily over the mats and kicked off my sandals. "So, what are we doing today?"

"Like I said." My trainer cocked two fingers forward, and I stepped onto the mat. The plastic was thick and cool against my soles. "I think it's time to step your training up a notch. Today, you deal with me."

More than a little nervous now, I walked steadily across the flat surface until I was just a few feet away, watching her across the mats. She regarded me coolly for a moment, then pulled a gun from a back holster, holding it up. I jumped.

"Tell me the easiest way to kill a dragon," she said, acid-green eyes boring into me. I forced my attention away from the instrument of death in her hand and tried to focus on the question.

"Um." I racked my brain for the answer, knowing she would expect me to get it right. "When we're in human form. Before we have a chance to Shift. We don't have any protection when we're human."

"Good," my trainer said, though there was no praise in her tone. Her expression was hard as she continued. "The soldiers of St. George know this, too. Which is why secrecy is so important to our survival. If they knew our true identity, they'd have no qualms taking us out with a sniper round to the head from a thousand meters. You wouldn't even know what hit you. If you are ever in a life-or-death situation with St. George, know this—they are not so stupid to engage a dragon in one-on-one combat. If they can, they will shoot you from afar, before you have the chance to get close."

I nodded. Scary Talon Lady held up the gun. "With this in mind, there are times where you might be in close quarters with someone who wants to kill you. And there are times when it is impossible to Shift into your real form, in urban areas or among witnesses, per se. Learning to defend yourself as a human is just as crucial as defending yourself as a dragon. So, the most important thing to remember if you're staring down a loaded gun, or any weapon, is this."

She pointed the gun right at me, the muzzle inches from my face, and I went rigid.

"Don't freeze. If you freeze, you're dead. Just like that." Without warning, she pulled the trigger. It clicked, and I nearly jumped out of my skin. My trainer smiled.

"Not loaded, hatchling. Make no mistake, though, it is real. And it is exactly what you might be facing one day. Now..." She flipped it around, holding the pistol out to me. "Take it. I'll show you the disarm."

I took the weapon gingerly, like I would a poisonous snake. My trainer rolled her eyes. "Stop being twitchy. I told you it's not loaded." She took a step back. "Now, point it at me. Like you intend to shoot me, right through the heart."

Gripping the stock, I raised the gun...and my trainer's hands moved faster than I could see, tearing the gun from my grasp. A half second later, I was staring into the muzzle, now pointed back at my face.

My trainer's cold green eyes stared me down over the gun barrel, her lips curled into an evil smirk. "Did you catch that?"

"No."

"Good. Neither should they." She motioned me forward again, and I took a reluctant step toward her. "I'll show you again in slow motion, and then you're going to try it yourself."

For the next few minutes, I watched her technique as she broke down the disarm step by step. How she angled off to the side when she moved in, making her body a much smaller target for the gun. How she never put herself directly in front of the muzzle. How she forced the barrel up and away before turning it on the opponent. In slow motion, it made a lot of sense; put together at full speed, it happened before you could blink.

"Now it's your turn." Scary Talon Lady took the gun and stepped back a pace, watching me. Nervous and eager at the same time, I took a breath and tried to relax, to stay loose and flowing as I'd been taught. My trainer smiled, holding the gun loosely at her side. "And remember, you must stay focused on your opponent if you want to live. Do not allow anything to distract you. Are you ready?"

I sank down, balanced on the balls of my feet. "Yes."

"Very well. So, how was your trip to the carnival?"

*What?* I faltered, my stomach turning over, and my trainer's arm came up, bringing the gun to my face. The sharp click of the trigger being pulled echoed through the room.

"And you're dead." Lowering the gun, she shook her head in disgust. "What did I tell you about not being distracted? By anything?"

"How…?" I thought back to my date with Garret, and the strange feeling of being watched in a crowd of hundreds. Indignation flared, and gave way to anger. "*You* were the one following me!" I accused, my voice bouncing off the walls. "I knew someone was watching us."

"It's my job to keep tabs on my student," Scary Talon Lady said, unrepentant, and raised the gun again. This time, I dove aside as it clicked behind me, but I didn't have enough time to lunge forward. "When they're distracted by useless human things, I become concerned." She lowered the gun and circled around me on the mat, eyes narrowed to slits.

I circled with her, staying light on my feet, ready to dodge out of the way.

"I thought we were supposed to fit in," I argued as she circled me like a shark. My dragon instincts growled, annoyed with this game of cat-and-mouse, wanting to pounce and claw and bite. But that wasn't the point of the exercise, and I wasn't going to let her beat me again. She wasn't using real bullets, but she would definitely inform me if I wasn't fast enough, if I was shot. "Observe, blend in with society, learn to act like a human—isn't that why we're here?"

"Yes," my trainer agreed, and continued to stalk, keeping the gun pressed against her leg. "It is. Learn to *act* like a human. You must never forget that, first and always, you are a dragon. You are not one of them."

"I know that."

"Really? What's the boy's name?"

Startled, I almost didn't react quick enough when she shot at me again. Dodging to the side, I rolled into a crouch and found myself staring at the gun muzzle again. She didn't pull the trigger, however, just watched me down the barrel with narrowed, poison-green eyes.

"His name," she repeated.

"Why do you care?" I challenged, not wanting this woman to know anything about Garret. He was the part of my life that wasn't bound to Talon and training and all their crazy expectations. When I was with Garret, I could almost forget Talon's stranglehold on my life. I could almost forget… that I was a dragon. "He's just a human," I told my trainer, still aiming the gun at my face. "What's one human to you?"

As if she could hear my thoughts, my trainer's expression went cold and frightening. "Exactly," she said in a steely voice. "He is just one human. One mortal among billions of unimportant, short-lived mortals. You are a dragon. More important, you are a *dragonell,* a female of our race, which makes you even more precious to the organization." She finally lowered the gun, though she still glared daggers at me. "Your loyalty, first and always, is to Talon. Not the humans. They are unimportant. We walk among them, act like them, live with them, but we will never *be* one of them." She gestured sharply with the weapon. "They're a cancer, hatchling. A virus that spreads and corrupts and obliterates everything in its path. The human race is weak and self-destructive, and the only thing they know how to do is destroy. You are part of something far greater than these mortals can ever hope to achieve, and if I ask you a human's name, you had best give me the human's name and not question it!"

She raised the pistol, shockingly fast, but this time, I was ready.

Surging upright, I angled to the side like she'd taught me and lunged in. My hands hit the barrel of the weapon from underneath, forcing it up and twisting it out of her grasp. A second later, I stood before my trainer with the pistol pointed back at her, stunned that I'd actually pulled it off.

"Garret," I muttered as my trainer seared holes into my forehead with her stare. "His name is Garret."

She smiled.

"There, that wasn't difficult, was it?" she said, and I had no idea if she was talking about the disarm or admitting the human's name. Taking the gun from my limp fingers, she stepped back and gave me a hard, assessing gaze. "Yes," she mused, as if coming to a decision in her mind. "I do believe you are ready."

"Ready for what?" I asked, but she spun and walked swiftly from the room, beckoning me to follow. I trailed her back to the office, where she pointed to the chair in front of her desk. I dropped into it warily, noticing on the desk's polished surface a manila folder with my name printed at the top.

Scary Talon Lady didn't sit, but regarded me over the desk, her fingers resting lightly on the folder. I couldn't keep my gaze from straying back to it. My name, in red. What was inside? What did it say about me, and my future with the organization?

"This is a big day for you, hatchling," Scary Talon Lady announced, making me even more nervous. "As you may know, we have watched you from the time you were hatched, assessing your skills, your behavior, what type of position you would excel at. You've completed phase one of your training. Now, we move on to phase two—honing the skills that will serve you in the organization. From now on, you will come to training wearing this."

She tossed something at me, a dark, full bodysuit made of light, stretchy fabric. It seemed to cling to my hands when I caught it, and for a split second, I thought it was alive. Shuddering, I held it away from me. It looked like a normal bodysuit, but it felt almost slimy, and warm. I realized it was the same type of outfit my trainer wore, though I couldn't imagine sliding into this thing.

"This is a very special outfit," my trainer explained as I resisted the urge to drop the creepy thing on the floor. "It's far too complicated to explain, but suffice it to say, your suit will not rip or tear when you Shift into your real form."

I gaped at her. "Really?" Intrigued now, I stared at the fabric, trying not to be repulsed by the way it sucked at my bare skin. "So, if I'm wearing this thing when I Shift, I won't have to worry about running home naked?"

She pointed out the door. "Go try it on," she ordered. "Make certain it fits, then report back here. Go."

I retreated to the bathroom and slipped into the suit, holding my breath as the fabric sucked and oozed over my skin, almost like paint. At first, it was warm and disgustingly slick, but after a few moments it smoothed out, molding to my body until I could barely feel it.

*Creepy.*

I returned to Scary Talon Lady, who gave a tiny nod of approval and gestured to the seat again. "Good," she announced as I perched on the stool with my normal clothes in hand, feeling almost naked. "It fits. I want you to wear it for the rest of the day, so it gets used to your shape and body type. You can put your regular clothes on over it."

I frowned, not entirely certain I'd heard correctly. "Wait, you want me to keep it on tonight, so *it* gets used to *me?*"

My trainer nodded, as if that was a perfectly normal explanation. "Yes, hatchling, but don't worry. After a few minutes, you won't even remember you have it on." She smiled tightly, as if from personal experience. "Only certain members of the organization receive this special clothing," she continued as I squirmed, "so consider yourself lucky. The suits are very valuable and very expensive to make, so *do not* lose it. It will be your training uniform and, later on, it will be your work uniform."

I was still trying to wrap my head around the thought that my suit had to get used to me, like it really was alive, but something about that last sentence caused everything inside me to go still. "Work uniform?" I asked quietly. Maybe I was jumping to conclusions, but I felt the only reason you needed a suit like that was to Shift from dragon to human quickly and quietly. It was, for all intents and purposes, a ninja suit. A magic ninja suit that clung to your skin like it was alive and molded to your body, but a ninja suit nonetheless. And there was only one position in the organization I could think of that came close to that type of "work."

My trainer smiled her most evil smile yet, and pushed the folder at me, flipping it open. Swallowing hard, I looked down at the first line.

*Subject: Ember Hill.*

And below that…

My heart stood still, my veins turning to ice. I stared at those five letters, willing them to go away, to be something else, anything else.

"Congratulations, Ember Hill," Scary Talon Lady mused over the desk. "Welcome to the Vipers."

# GARRET

I was finishing a report to Lieutenant Martin when there was a knock at the door.

On the couch, Tristan straightened and shot me a puzzled look. Two empty pizza boxes already sat open and nearly empty on the counter, so it wasn't the delivery boy. And the Order always called if they were going to show up. There was no reason anyone should be at our apartment at this time of day.

Warily, Tristan pulled his 9 mm and slid into the hallway, gesturing for me to get the door. I reached for the Glock that always sat close by and eased across the room, ready to bring the weapon up if the door flew inward. The knock came again, four rapid blows against the wood, but it didn't sound like whoever was on the other side was trying to break down the door. Hiding the gun against my leg, I reached for the knob and opened the door until the chain caught it, then peered through the gap.

Ember's brilliant green eyes met mine through the crack, and my heart leaped. "Hey, you," she greeted softly. A bike leaned against the wall beside the door, tires firmly inflated this time. "I was, um, just riding around the neighborhood, and I saw your apartment and thought, 'Hey, Garret lives there! I wonder if he's home now?' And…that sounded pretty bad, didn't it? Lexi told me where you were staying—she's good at finding those things out. I'm not stalking you, I swear." She rubbed her arm, looking tired and subdued, unlike her normal self. "Well, maybe a little. Can I come in?"

"Hang on." Shutting the door, I quickly stowed the gun in a closet and closed the laptop, as Tristan vanished down the hall into his room. Unlatching the chain, I opened the door and stepped back. "Are you all right?" I asked as Ember came inside and gazed around curiously. "What are you doing here?" Not that I wasn't pleased to see her; I was, unexpected visits aside. But Tristan would not be happy with a potential target roaming around our base, seeing things she shouldn't see.

He prowled out of the hallway then, thankfully unarmed, smiling stiffly as he walked into the kitchen. Ember jumped when he appeared. "Oh!" she exclaimed as Tristan arched a brow at her. "Tristan, right? I didn't realize you were here. Haven't seen you around lately."

"Sadly, I'm not the party animal my cousin is." He gave me a tight smile. "Garret, come here a second, will you?"

Frowning, I followed Tristan to the living room, where he bent close and hissed, "What is she doing here? You didn't invite her, did you? Did you tell her she could come?"

"No," I replied, glancing back toward the kitchen. "I didn't know she would show up today."

"Well, get rid of her! We can't have her snooping around."

"I'll take care of it."

A soft flutter from the kitchen drew our attention, and we looked back to see Ember leafing through one of Tristan's gun magazines on the counter. Beside it was my laptop, where I'd just sent off that mission report to St. George.

"So, Ember," Tristan said, quickly striding back to the room. I followed warily. "What brings you here? Do you and Garret have something planned?"

As he talked, smiling and holding her gaze the whole time, he smoothly picked up the laptop and tucked it under one arm, like he was going to take it back to his room. Ember flipped the magazine shut and shook her head.

"No, there's nothing. I just, um, wanted to see Garret, that's all." She gave me an apologetic glance, perhaps sensing the subtle tension in the room. "Sorry. Is this a bad time? I could go…"

"No, you're fine," I said as the magazine joined the laptop under Tristan's arm. He gave me a pointed look, raising his eyebrows, and I nodded. "Come on," I said, motioning her out of the kitchen. "We can talk in my room."

As she turned away, Tristan shot me a glare over her head that said, *Call if you need help.* I gave him another tight nod and led Ember down the hall into my room, shutting the door behind us.

"Wow," she mused, turning in a slow circle, observing my shelf, my dresser, the neatly made bed in the corner. "Your room is so…clean. Not even Dante is this neat."

"Blame my dad," I said, turning around as the door closed. "He's a retired sergeant. I had white-glove room inspections for—"

My words were stifled as Ember spun, wrapped her arms around my neck and kissed me.

My mind instantly shut off. Heat shot through me, starting from where her lips pressed against mine, all the way down to the pit of my stomach. I wrapped my arms around her waist, lifting her up on her toes, as my mouth responded furiously to hers. Her fingers dug into my hair, raking over my scalp and setting every nerve aflame. I groaned, clutching her tighter, feeling her tongue tease my lips, making my head swim. I was losing control, drowning in emotion, and I didn't want this to stop.

"Ember," I panted, "wait." With a monumental effort, I pulled back, breathing as though I'd just run several miles with a murderous dragon on my tail. She leaned against my chest, looking up at me, green eyes bright with passion. A part of me, a huge part, wanted to keep going, to forget everything and lose myself to the girl in my arms. But logic had ruled my life for so long, and instinct had kept me alive when I would've been killed otherwise; it told me now that something wasn't right.

Ember's lips were just a few inches from mine, tempting me to lean down and kiss her again. I controlled myself, running a thumb over her cheek. "Why did you come here?" I asked softly, and her eyes darkened. "Is everything all right?"

"Yes. No. I don't know." Pushing herself away, she turned and made a frustrated gesture, not looking at me. "Just… It's been a rough day."

"What happened?"

"I…" She paused. I could sense her struggling with herself, trying to find the right words. "I can't talk about it," she finally whispered.

Suspicion flared, and I narrowed my eyes. "Did something happen with your brother?"

"Garret, please." Her shoulders hunched in misery. "I can't. I wish I could but…" She raked both hands across her eyes, bowing her head. "I'm sorry, I shouldn't have bothered you. I don't even know why I came here."

I should've pressed her. I should've tried to keep her talking, forced her to reveal things about her family, and herself. But at that moment, I found that I didn't care. Ember was upset and had come to me. Not her brother, and not her friends. If I pushed, it might shatter the trust that was slowly beginning to build, but more important, I didn't want her to leave. I might be new to this whole dating-relationship thing, but I was learning, very slowly, to ignore logic and strategy and let instinct guide the way.

Moving behind her, I slipped my arms around her waist and leaned close, holding her tight. "I'm here," I told her quietly, feeling her shiver. "You don't have to say anything, but if you need to talk, I'm here."

She relaxed against me, laying her hands over mine and resting her head on my chest. "It's not fair," she whispered, so soft I barely caught it. "Everything is happening so fast. My life feels totally out of control, out of *my* control. I don't want the summer to end, and…" She paused, the skin of her cheeks warming slightly. "I don't want to give you up."

My breath caught. I didn't say anything but held her tighter, feeling the truth steal over me. I didn't want to let her go, either. When did that happen? When had I become so attached? Closing my eyes, I pressed my face to Ember's neck, feeling us both shiver. It didn't matter. None of this mattered. I was a soldier, my life was not my own, and at the end, no matter the outcome, I would have to return to the war.

Ember reached up, slipping cool fingers into my hair, her voice wistful. "Garret?"

"Mmm," I grunted, not opening my eyes.

"If you could be anywhere in the world right now," she murmured, running her fingertips over my scalp, making it hard to concentrate, "where would you be?"

I frowned. Wishing to be somewhere else was useless. It wouldn't do either of us any good. "Why?" I asked, pulling back to look at her.

"Garret." She huffed and peered back at me. "I'm just curious. Humor me, will you?" She shook her head and leaned into me again, closing her eyes, and gestured vaguely at the ceiling. "Let's say you could fly anywhere you wanted, anywhere at all, regardless of price, time or impossibility. Where would you go?"

I thought about it. I'd been a lot of places. All over the world, from huge cities to tiny villages to lonely corners of wilderness, wherever the war took us. After so long, they all ran together in my mind. Missions, battle, blood, death, repeat. Nothing really stood out.

Except for one.

I looked down at her, seeing my reflection in her eyes as she gazed back, our lips a few inches away. "If I could be anywhere I wanted," I murmured, brushing a strand of hair from her face, "I would choose to be right here. Nowhere else."

Her eyes gleamed. Turning in my arms, she slid her hands up my back and closed her eyes as I kissed her.

Her lips were gentle this time, searching. I felt the lightest flick of her tongue against my bottom lip and shivered, parting them slightly to let her in. She explored my mouth, and I clenched my fists against her back, feeling like I was drowning once more. The end of summer, and the mission, loomed overhead, dark and ominous, but I shoved it away. One more night, I told myself, hesitantly meeting Ember's tongue, feeling like my knees might give out at any moment. Just one more night, to make believe I was normal. To pretend that the beautiful, fiery, unpredictable girl in my arms was mine.

A hollow bang caused me to jerk back, disengaging from Ember just as Tristan threw open the door. His dark eyes swept over us, taking in the scene, and narrowed suspiciously. I gave him a cold look, annoyed but knowing he wouldn't have come in if it wasn't important.

"Something's come up," he announced briskly, confirming my suspicion. "Garret, *your dad* is on the phone and wants to talk to you. Now."

I straightened, my blood going cold. My "dad" was code for the Order, and any communications from them took top priority. "I'll be right there," I said, and Tristan ducked out without shutting the door behind him. I turned to Ember.

"I have to go," I said, already thinking about what the Order might want. Maybe they had found the sleeper dragon and were calling us back to the front lines. The thought filled me with both dread and relief. If they had discovered the sleeper, that meant our target wasn't Ember. But that also meant this was the last time I'd see her before I left Crescent Beach, vanished from her life and returned to the war.

Trying not to think about that, I held out a hand. "Come on, I'll walk you out."

Ember looked confused. "Is everything all right?"

"Yes," I muttered, leading her down the hall, past Tristan's room and the kitchen, to the front door. "It's nothing, don't worry about it. My dad's...kind of important," I temporized. "He doesn't call unless it's an emergency."

The lie felt sour on my tongue. We halted in the entrance,

and I couldn't stop my hand from reaching out, running my fingers through her hair. Maybe for the last time. "I'll...call you later, okay?" I hoped that wasn't a lie, too.

She leaned forward, gently touching her lips to mine, and I closed my eyes. "Talk to you soon," she whispered, and slipped through the door. I watched her walk away, feeling a small part of me leave with her, then firmly shut the door on Ember Hill and a normal life.

Tristan was standing over the laptop when I came into his room, hovering inside the doorway. "St. George just contacted us," he announced, his eyes glued to the computer screen. "We're on a twenty-four-hour alert. Apparently, they're tracking a couple dragons that escaped a raid in Colorado, and they think they're somewhere in Crescent Beach, possibly with the sleeper. They're on their way now. We have orders to join the team when they arrive, so until we hear from mission control, we're on standby. So get ready to head out as soon as they give the word." A shadow of a smile crossed the stern look on his face, and his dark eyes gleamed as he glanced up at me. "Finally, some movement. I was half-afraid they'd forgotten we were here."

I didn't answer. Whirling from the desk, Tristan walked to his closet door, reached all the way to the back and gently removed a long black case, setting it almost reverently on the bed. Clicking it open, he ran his fingers over the polished metal of his sniper rifle, his eyes never leaving the deadly weapon. "Enough with this sitting around," he muttered, "staking out houses and following teenagers down the beach. I was getting tired of it. It's about time we got back to the war."

Normally, I would've agreed. Before I came to Crescent Beach, the news of a raid, where there could likely be several dragons under one roof, would have made my heart race in excitement. Now, I was filled with disquiet, a faint unease that nagged at me and refused to settle. I'd never questioned orders before, never given our purpose a second thought. Before a certain redhead, I'd seen dragons as only one thing: monsters to be hunted down and slain.

Before Ember, everything was far less complicated.

"Garret." Tristan's voice was hard. I glanced at him warily, and he glared back. My partner had this uncanny ability to know exactly what I was thinking, even when I gave him nothing. "This is our job, partner," he told me, his voice firm. "We both knew this was coming. Everything we've done here has led up to this."

"I know," I muttered.

"Then get ready, because the Order is on its way. And when they get here, you'd better have your priorities straight."

"These things killed my entire family," I said flatly, annoyed that he would question it, that he saw far too much. "My priorities haven't changed. I know what I have to do."

"Good." Tristan nodded and picked up his scope, peering down the lens. "Because we move out as soon as they arrive."

I retreated to my room, reached under my bed and pulled out a large black duffel bag. Yanking it open, I quickly changed into my battle dress: flame retardant suit, tactical fatigues, flak jacket, boots, gloves. My helmet and mask I left off for now, but when they did go on, no patch of skin would be left uncovered.

As I slipped my Glock into its thigh holster, I caught a glimpse of myself in the oval mirror above the dresser. A stark, cold-eyed soldier stared back at me, dressed for combat, for dealing death. It was a sudden, harsh reminder; this was who I was. The past few weeks had been a fantasy, a pleasant distraction. But it was time to return to the real world and what I was trained for. I was a soldier of St. George. My purpose was to kill.

Snatching my helmet from the bed, I returned to the kitchen, where Tristan had drawn all the blinds and was standing at the counter with the laptop. He had also changed into combat gear, and gave me a short nod as I came in.

“They’ve located the nest. Get ready. We move in tonight.”

# EMBER

After I left Garret's apartment, I rode aimlessly for a while, my mind still a chaotic, swirling mess. Lexi had called me earlier, wanting to go surfing in the cove, but I knew I wasn't clearheaded enough to tackle giant waves and would just end up getting pounded. Besides, Lexi would probably know something was up, and while she was great with human problems like boys and clothes and feelings, she could not help me with this.

I wished I could've talked to Garret, come totally clean and told him everything. After my training session and the atomic bomb Scary Talon Lady had dropped in my lap, I'd gone straight to his apartment, not really knowing what I would say, just that I had to see him.

That had been a mistake.

Meeting with Garret, stealing those kisses in his room, hearing his whispered confessions, made me realize how much I had to lose when the summer ended. I had thought it was just my freedom, but even that seemed to pale in comparison to losing Garret. He wasn't just a cute human boy who could surf and play arcade games and take me to the carnival. This wasn't a rebellious desire to show up my trainer, to experience human emotions because dragons weren't supposed to have them. No, I really, truly wanted to be with him. And the thought of him leaving, of never seeing him again, made my heart ache in a way I'd never felt before.

So now there were two black clouds hanging over my head, making me even crazier. Or maybe it was just the one big cloud, and all my smaller issues stemmed from it. The suffocating, giant-ass cloud called Talon. Talon said humans were the inferior species. Talon forbade us from flying, or even changing into our real forms, without their permission. Talon sent an evil, sadistic trainer to make my life a living hell.

Talon wanted me to become a Viper.

I shivered, clenching the handlebars of the bike. Of all the factions and positions in the organization, I had never dreamed I would become a Viper. I knew I wasn't big or strong enough for the Gilas, and I didn't have the charm and grace to become a Chameleon. After talking with Riley that afternoon on the pier, I was almost certain I was destined to become a Basilisk. Not ideal, but better than getting lumped with the Monitors, doing boring busywork for the rest of my life.

But Viper. Talon's most elite operatives. Officially, the Vipers were called in as a last resort, a final gamble when everything else had failed. And, of course, they were occasionally dispatched to hunt down rogues and deserters and return them to the organization. That was the official story, anyway. That was why going rogue was as futile as it was dangerous; you stood no chance against a Viper, once it was on your trail. They never gave up once they took a mission.

Was that my calling now? Hunting down my own kind, forcing them back to an organization that was slowly stifling *me?* It didn't seem right. Though I had no idea what else the Vipers actually did. Surely they didn't just hunt down runaways. But when I'd asked Scary Talon Lady about it, she'd just laughed and said that wasn't my concern just yet. That everything would reveal itself at the right time.

I needed to talk to someone. Garret had been a knee-jerk reaction because I was upset and not thinking clearly, but he couldn't help me with Talon problems. I needed another dragon, someone who understood what I was going through. And I knew of only one person who fit that description.

I pulled out my phone as I ditched the bike in the yard and climbed the steps to the house. My heart thumped loudly as I pulled up his number, my thumb hovering over the call button.

Still staring at the screen, I opened the front door, and crashed right into Dante leaving the house.

"Oof. Ow. Again," he complained, taking a step back and rubbing his chin, where he'd banged it against the top of my skull. "Jeez, it's like walking into a bowling ball. But I always knew you were hardheaded."

"Funny." He was acting normal again, like nothing was wrong. But I was tired of pretending, and stepped aside to let him pass. "I guess it's better to have a head like a bowling ball than no balls at all."

"Below the belt, sis." His forehead creased as he peered down at me. "You okay?"

"I'm fine. Besides, what do you care?" He wasn't moving, so I tried sidling around him into the house. "Don't you have things Talon wants you to do? Sucking up, brownnosing, that sort of thing?"

"Okaaay, someone is in a mood." I slipped past him, but

instead of leaving he followed me into the living room. His tone turned suspicious. “Wanna tell me what’s going on?”

“Would you listen?” I challenged, staring at him over the kitchen counter. “Or would you just sell me out to Talon if I said something wrong?”

A hurt, angry expression crossed his face. “All right, that’s it,” he growled. Striding into the kitchen, he leaned over the counter and lowered his voice, speaking in a harsh whisper. “When have I ever not listened to you, Ember?” he demanded. “You keep telling me I’m not on your side, but this whole time, I’ve done nothing but look out for you, lied to our guardians for you, looked the other way when you broke the rules. I lied for you when you went out flying, I covered for us at the party and I didn’t mention I saw you talking to that rogue. I haven’t even said anything about you and Garret.”

I jerked, startled. “How—?”

“Lexi told me.” Dante’s voice was grim. “And it sucked, having to hear it from her and not you. You used to tell me everything.”

He sounded genuinely hurt, and my anger wavered. Maybe I *was* being unfair. As far as I could tell, Dante hadn’t informed Talon that Riley was back. He *had* covered for me at the party, and he’d never breathed a word about my illegal midnight flight with Cobalt. Maybe he was just scared. Maybe he was looking out for me the only way he knew how.

“You accuse me of keeping secrets,” Dante went on angrily, “but you’re the one who’s hiding things. I don’t care what you do with the humans, Ember. We’re supposed to fit in and learn their ways, make them think that we’re one of them. As long as we remember that we’re not. And someday, all humans will know it.”

I jerked up. "Is that what your trainer told you?"

"What does that have to do with anything?"

I turned on him, narrowing my eyes. "Where did they put you?" I demanded. I was tired of beating around the bush, tired of secrets, from both sides. I needed answers, and I hoped I could still count on my twin to come through for me. Dante blinked, confused, and I pressed the advantage. "Faction, Dante. What are you? Where did Talon decide to put you?"

He paused, and for a second I thought he wouldn't answer, stating that he couldn't talk about it. But after a moment, he leaned against the counter with a sigh.

"Chameleon."

I slumped. "Yeah, I thought so. It suits you." I could see Dante in a business suit, smiling and talking to people of power, completely in his element. "You're sure to fit right in."

"What's that supposed to mean?" Dante said, frowning. "It's an important calling." His green eyes flashed as he stared at me. "Why, where did they put you? Monitor? Gila? Somewhere that hot temper won't burn everyone around you?"

"Viper."

The blood drained from his face. His eyes widened, and he took a step back, his red hair a sudden shocking contrast to his white face.

"Viper?" he almost whispered, making my heart skip a beat. "They put you with the Vipers?"

I nodded, a chill going down my spine. Of all the possible reactions, I hadn't expected that. "My trainer told me this morning," I said. "I've been thinking about it all day." Or at least, the times I wasn't with Garret. I snorted and crossed my arms, trying to hide my growing fear. "Of course, they never asked me what *I* wanted, if I even wanted to become a Viper. Why should they decide what's best for me? If this is what I'm going to do for the rest of my life, shouldn't I get some sort of say in it?"

Dante was still staring at me with a faint look of horror on his face, and my resolve grew. "There has to be a mistake," I insisted. "They must've analyzed me wrong, screwed up the system or something. I don't want to become a Viper. I don't want to hunt down our own kind and drag them back to Talon. Because that's what they do, right? If I were to run—" Dante's horrified look intensified "—they would send a Viper to bring me back."

My twin still wasn't answering. I slumped to the counter, feeling cool marble against my heated skin, and closed my eyes. "I can't do it," I said. "This is all wrong." Opening my eyes, I gave Dante a pleading look, willing him to understand, to be my brother again. "Dante, what am I going to do?"

"Ember. Listen to me." Dante came around the counter and took my upper arms. His emerald eyes were intense, fingers digging into my skin. "You are going to become a Viper," he said in a low, firm voice, "because that's what Talon has decided. You can't fight them. If you try..." He trailed off, looking angry as I stared at him, appalled. "Don't fight them," he finished. "Just accept the fact that you're going to be a Viper, and there's nothing you can do about it. Once you accept that, everything will get a lot easier, I promise."

I tore myself free and backed away from him, shaking my head. He didn't follow; just continued to watch me with sad, worried eyes.

"This is for the best," he insisted. "Talon knows what they're doing. You just have to trust them. Stop fighting so hard, sis. This is for the future, to ensure the survival of our race. If you can take out Talon's enemies, that's more than enough reason to become a Viper. You should be proud."

I couldn't answer. I didn't have anything left to say to him. I just turned, walked out of the kitchen and into my room. The door shut behind me with a soft click, a small, insignificant noise to signal the end of a bond that should've been unbreakable. I didn't know my brother anymore. Talon had taken him away from me.

Sitting on my bed, I pulled out my phone again. This time, I didn't hesitate. Dante knew something about the Vipers; I could see it on his face, in the brief flash of horror and fear when I first said the word. But he was a stranger now, someone I didn't know. And if he wouldn't give me answers, then I would go to the one person left who could.

Hey, you free now? I texted, trying to ignore the excited flutters in my stomach, my dragon squirming in joy.

Like the last time, only a few seconds passed before the answer popped onto the screen.

Anything for you, Firebrand. Meet me same place in fifteen.

I watched the screen go dark, and stared at it for a while. I was about to go meet a rogue dragon for the second time that week. I was angry at Dante, disgusted with my trainer and felt a teensy bit guilty about Garret. All of whom might try to call me, and all of whom I didn't want interrupting while I was talking to the rogue.

I made my decision. Clicking off my phone, I placed it on my dresser, turned and walked out of the house, leaving it behind.

# RILEY

I lowered the phone, slipping it into my jeans pocket. Well, that couldn't have worked out better. I'd been planning to contact Ember this evening, after setting up the last of the alarms and motion sensors around the house with Wes. This circumvented things nicely.

Wes came into the kitchen, looking tired. His eyes were dull, and his hair was shaggier and more unkempt than usual. "Well, everything is set up," he muttered, opening the fridge for a soda. "Alarms are in place, motion sensors are ready to go and the system is officially online. If a mouse comes up that driveway, we'll know about it."

"Where are the other two?" I asked.

"I left them watching *The Avengers* on the telly downstairs. After they ate nearly everything in the house." Wes opened the can, guzzled half in one gulp and belched loudly. "Bloody bottomless pits, hatchlings. You're going to the store soon, right, mate? I mean, if we're going to be hunkered down here for a bit while you go sniffing after that girl." He drained the can, crushed it and tossed it in the garbage. "I still think this is bloody stupid, Riley. We need to get the hell out of here, not stand around waiting for some spoiled Talon brat to make up her mind."

I grabbed my leather jacket from the back of the couch, shrugging into it as I left the room. Wes frowned.

"Where are you going?" he called after me.

"To meet with a spoiled Talon brat." I tossed my bike keys in the air, caught them and smirked at the human over my shoulder. "Wish me luck. If everything goes as planned, we might leave sooner than you think."

"Absolutely fabulous," he shot back. "I'm so glad I stayed up all night setting those alarms."

Rolling my eyes, I shut the door on Wes's eternal pessimism and walked to the garage for my bike. This time, there would be no distractions or interruptions. This time, I would take her away from Talon for good.

★ ★ ★

She was leaning against the railing when I strode onto the boardwalk, her hair blowing in the breeze as she faced the water. Even in human form, I could almost see the dragon just below the surface, head raised to the wind, wings half-open to launch herself into the air. I swallowed and forced down my excitement. Every time I saw her, it seemed, this feeling was stronger. The heat in my veins, the yearning to feel her against me, to pull her close and never let go.

Walking up beside her, I rested my elbows against the railing and leaned out over the ocean. "We've gotta stop meeting like this, Firebrand."

She gave me a sideways look, a smile and a faint blush creeping over her cheeks. "Hey, Riley." Her voice was soft, nearly lost in the waves lapping against the posts. "Thanks for meeting me again. I'm sure you have other things you could be doing."

*Like getting ready for an attack? Like leaving town with two hatchlings before St. George breaks down our door?* "Not really. But I'd always make time for you." I half turned, grinning as her blush deepened. "So, what's wrong this time?" I asked, keeping my voice light. "Is your trainer giving you more grief? Did they start using rubber bullets instead of paint?"

"No." She picked at the wood with her fingernails, chipping away a splinter. "I…just found out where they're putting me. What I'll be doing…for the rest of my life."

"Ah. Faction placement. Yeah, that's always an eye-opener. I was certain they were going to stick me with the Gilas, with all the combat training I was getting." She picked at the wood again, not really listening, and I lowered my voice. "So, where did they put you, Firebrand? Monitor or Basilisk? No offense, but you're kinda on the small side to become a Gila."

Ember bit her lip, her eyes darkening. "Viper," she muttered. "They put me with the Vipers."

*Viper.*

My heart nearly stopped. There was a Viper in town. Had been here all along. Dammit, why hadn't I asked Ember this before, when we were talking about her training yesterday? If I'd known Talon had pegged her to be a Viper…

I swore and tried not to panic. Ember blinked, looking up at me in confusion. "Riley?"

"Ember, your trainer," I rasped, leaning forward as she gave me a half wary, half bewildered look but held her ground. "What's her name? What does she look like?"

"I don't know her name," Ember said, still frowning. "She never told me. But she's tall. She has long blond hair, and green eyes—"

"Kiss-ass fighter?"

"Yes."

"Sadistic as hell?"

"Oh, yeah." Ember's eyes widened. "Do you know her?"

I raked a hand through my hair, a lump of ice settling in my stomach. "Lilith," I growled, forcing myself to stay calm, to not look over my shoulder in case she was watching us right now. "Lilith has been your trainer this whole time?"

"Who's Lilith?"

I ignored that question. "Were you followed?" I demanded, and when she frowned, I grabbed her wrist, making her jump. "Ember, did you tell anyone where you were going? Does anyone know where you are?"

"No!" Ember twisted her arm a certain way and yanked out of my grasp, surprising me, but only for a moment. Of course she had Lilith for a trainer. What did I expect? "Riley, what's going on? Who *is* Lilith?"

I took another furtive breath, leaning back against the railing in a show of nonchalance, like nothing was wrong. Casually, I scanned the pier again, searching for the other dragon, though I knew it was useless. If Lilith didn't want to be seen, I'd never catch a glimpse of her. "We can't talk here," I said quietly, hoping Ember would follow my lead and not let on that I knew. "If you want to know who Lilith is, what she really does for Talon, come with me right now. I'll take you somewhere safe. But I need your word that you won't tell *anyone* what you've seen or heard. Do you understand?" I glanced at her from the corner of my eye, my voice turning steely. "Lives depend on it, Ember. This isn't a game anymore. Promise me you won't tell anyone—not your brother, not your guardians and *especially* not your trainer." Briefly, I closed my eyes, hoping it wasn't too late. "If she doesn't already know I'm here."

Ember's face was pale, but she nodded. "I won't tell anyone. I promise."

I gave a brisk nod. "All right. Follow me, and try to act normal."

She sniffed. "You're the one acting like a weirdo."

Without answering, I strode back down the pier, pretending to be casual while on high alert. If Lilith was here, we had to get out of town, fast. Hanging around when St. George could be on the way was risky enough, but staying when there was a known Viper in the area was suicidal. Especially if that Viper was Lilith.

My only hope was that Lilith didn't know about us yet. That she was in Crescent Beach just to train Ember, and hadn't come specifically for me. If that was the case, then we had a chance. There was still time. I could still get everyone out safely.

And hopefully, when we did leave town, my naive little Firebrand—Lilith's protégé, of all things—would be coming with us.

# EMBER

Mental note: Add *riding a motorcycle* to the Almost as Good as Flying list.

Riley's bike tore up the streets, weaving in and around traffic, blasting through stale yellow lights, whipping around corners at top speed. Wind tore at my hair and clothes, stinging the corners of my eyes, the roar of the engine and the occasional honk from an irate motorist echoing in my ears. Riley never slowed down. I think he was making certain that we couldn't be followed, which was probably smart, given my trainer had already confirmed that she liked to "keep tabs on me." I clung tightly to his waist, my cheek pressed to his leather jacket, and watched the world flash by in a blur.

Finally, we cruised up a fairly steep road cut into the side of a cliff, where you could see the ocean and nearly all of Crescent Beach spread out below you. As I raised my head from Riley's back, wondering where we were going, he suddenly turned down a long, gated driveway and pulled to a stop in front of a house.

My mouth fell open. House? More like a mansion. The place was huge, sprawling, much bigger than Uncle Liam's villa or even Kristin's beach house. I gaped at it, then Riley, who smirked back at me, as if expecting my reaction.

"Welcome to my humble abode."

"You live here?" I gasped, and he chuckled, swinging off the bike. "Okay, my entire perspective of you just got flipped on its head. I guess rogue dragon-ing pays better than I thought."

He raked his dark hair back and grinned. "Don't be too impressed, Firebrand. It's not mine. We're just…borrowing it, while we're in town."

"We?"

"Yeah, 'we.' Come on." Jerking a thumb toward the massive front doors, he started up the walk. "I have some people I want you to meet."

The inside was just as massive and sprawling as the outside, and definitely inhabited, judging by the amount of Red Bull and Mountain Dew cans scattered everywhere, the piles of dirty dishes in the sink and the empty pizza boxes on the counter.

A gangly human emerged from a back room, shirt rumpled, brown hair hanging in his eyes. He noticed me standing in the foyer but didn't seem surprised, giving Riley a weary look when he came in.

"This her, then?" he asked with an English accent. "The girl we're all risking our lives for? Oh, sorry, the girl *you're* risking our lives for?" He eyed me from beneath shaggy bangs, arching a brow. "Have to say, I'm not that impressed, mate."

I scowled. "If you've got something to say to me, I'm standing right here."

"You'll have to excuse Wes," Riley said. "He has the bad habit of being a jackass." The human didn't even blink, and Riley's voice turned solemn. "Where are the other two?"

"Still downstairs. Where they've been all morning, probably sulking because I chased them out of the swimming pool. Why?" His eyes narrowed, maybe sensing the nervous tension in Riley's demeanor. "What's going on?"

Riley shot me a glance. I saw him hesitate, wondering how much he should reveal, if he should trust me. I met his gaze head-on.

"You promised me answers," I reminded him. "You said you'd tell me everything about Talon and the Vipers and what they do. I'm not leaving until I know."

"Vipers?" Wes's voice, no longer bored or smug, climbed several octaves. He stared at me with wide eyes, then looked at Riley, dropping his voice to a hiss. "Did she just say bloody *Vipers?*"

Riley sighed. "Lilith is in town," he said quietly. Wes blanched, then shoved away from us, rattling off an impressive list of swearwords. "Keep it together," Riley warned as the human stalked back, his eyes a little crazy. "She doesn't know we're here yet. At least, I hope she doesn't. But she's not here for us."

"Of course she's here for us!" Wes was not doing a great job of keeping it together, I thought. "Why else would a bloody Viper be here? She's bloody well not on vacation!"

"She's my trainer," I said, hoping to calm him down. It did not have the effect I wanted. The human's eyes bulged even farther, and he swung a wild glare at me.

"Riley, what the hell! Are you off your rocker? You brought the snake's new apprentice right into our house? How do we know she's not a plant? She could run off to tell the bitch exactly where we are."

"She won't," Riley said calmly. "I trust her."

Wes shook his head, scrubbing his hands through his hair. "I hope you know what you're doing, mate. I really do."

"Go find the other two," Riley ordered. "Tell them we'll be leaving soon. Get them ready to move out. Remember, we don't want any evidence that we were here. Leave everything as we found it. That means the alarms need to go, too."

"Bollocks," Wes mumbled, turning away. He walked out of the room, still muttering, and I looked at the rogue.

"Still confused as hell over here, Riley."

He nodded wearily. "I know. Come on." He motioned me into the living room, gesturing to one of the sofas, but I was too keyed up to sit. Riley continued to stand, as well, gazing out the window with arms crossed to his chest, seeming to gather his thoughts.

"What do you know about Talon," he asked at length, "and the Vipers?"

I shrugged. "Only what they tell me, which isn't much. I know the Vipers are some sort of special operatives that Talon sends out when things get really messy, but I don't really know what they do. I tried asking my trainer, but she never tells me anything. I didn't even know her name."

"Her name," Riley said, turning to me, "is Lilith. And besides being the most evil bitch to set foot out of Bitchtown, she's the best Viper Talon has. Which makes it *very* interesting that they chose her to train you." His eyes narrowed, appraising me across the room. "That means Talon is very invested in your education—they wouldn't send their best operative to train a hatchling unless they were planning to use you for something big."

"Is she really that important?"

He snorted. "You have no idea. Lilith is sort of a legend

in the organization. Even St. George knows about her. And if you're such a badass that even those genocidal maniacs sit up and take notice…" He shrugged, but he didn't have to say anything else.

"So that's why Wes freaked out. He thinks Lilith was sent here to bring you back to Talon."

"Firebrand." Riley gave me a very solemn look, one that sent chills up my spine. "You still don't know what Lilith is, what the Vipers actually do. If your lovely trainer does come for us, what do you think will happen? She's not going to swat our wrists with a ruler and scold us for leaving Talon, that's for damn sure. If someone like Lilith is sent after you, she only has one thing in mind."

I swallowed as everything—the secrecy, Lilith's training, Dante's reaction to the news that I was put with the Vipers—suddenly became very clear. "No way."

He nodded. "Afraid so, Firebrand. The Vipers are Talon's *assassins.* That's their purpose for the organization. They're sent to kill whoever Talon points them at. Usually, they go after high-ranking officials of St. George, getting behind the lines and into enemy territory where no one else can. But they don't just knock off genocidal maniacs." Riley's lip curled in an expression of pure contempt. "Ever wonder why there are no ex-rogues or deserters in Talon, and why no one ever seems to have a disloyal thought in their heads? Do you think it's because Talon is such a shiny happy place that no one in their right mind would ever leave?" He snorted. "No, it's because Talon uses the Vipers to silence anyone who isn't loyal. Humans and dragons alike, it doesn't matter. They'll take out their own kind if Talon gives the word. That's why the Vipers are so feared." His eyes narrowed. "And that's why I'm determined to get as many dragons out of Talon as I can."

I was still reeling from the news that Talon wanted me to become an assassin, so his last statement took a few seconds to seep into my brain. But then, it did, and I gaped at him.

"Get them out? But you just said the Vipers kill anyone who goes rogue! Why would you want to put their lives in danger?"

"Because it shouldn't be a choice," Riley snapped. "We shouldn't have to choose Talon or freedom. Because I refuse to be part of anything that tries to *kill* me for not wanting what they want." He stabbed a hand through his hair, then gestured at the ceiling in disgust. "They're brainwashed, Firebrand, every one of them. From the very beginning, every hatchling is trained to Talon's standards. They're brought up to want what Talon wants—power, wealth, influence, control. Talon preaches that it's all in the interest of preserving our race, and that's true, but only by maintaining a stranglehold on everything they own. Dragons that have no use in the organization, or who break away and forge their own path, are put down by the Vipers. They might spare a hatchling—it depends on how old they are, how long they've been out of Talon and if they feel the hatchling can still be useful. But rogues like me and Wes, who have been on the inside, who know what Talon is really like..." Riley shook his head. "They'd kill us, no questions asked."

I felt ill and had to sink onto one of the sofa cushions as my legs were no longer supporting me. "I can't do that," I whispered. "I'm not a killer. I can't hunt down and slaughter my *own kind*. How could they expect me to do that?"

"Technically, they wouldn't give you that bit of information," Riley said. "Not yet. Not until you're fully trained to believe whatever Talon says and not question orders. But once your training is complete, there's usually a final exam required to become a full Viper. One that tests not only your skill, but your loyalty to the organization. You might be sent out after another hatchling, or a human deserter. Or you could be sent to deal with a rogue." He smirked then, completely without humor. "Who knows, Firebrand? If you stay with Talon, somewhere down the road, we might meet again. Only you'd be trying to kill me. Or maybe even sooner than that. Maybe that's why Lilith hasn't come for me yet. Maybe I'm your final exam."

"I would never do that," I protested, and Riley shook his head.

"You wouldn't have a choice. Not if Talon orders it. And by that time, you'd be so indoctrinated, you might actually believe you're doing the right thing." He shivered suddenly, a haunted look crossing his face as he stared out the window. "It's insidious, Firebrand," he almost whispered. "You don't realize how much you're changing, how much of yourself you're losing, until it's too late. I fought St. George for years. Never face-to-face, but my actions were responsible for countless deaths. Until one day… I couldn't do it anymore."

"What happened?"

He sank onto the cushion beside me, his face and eyes dark. "I was ordered to rig a building to explode, one of their supposed chapterhouses. Risky stuff—get in, wire the explosives and get out before it went off. Probably the craziest stunt they ever had me do, but I'd been so brainwashed to blindly follow orders, I didn't even realize that it was a suicide mission."

I watched him, engrossed with what he was telling me. His brow was furrowed, his face solemn and grave, different from the smirking, confident rogue I'd met before. I wondered which was the real Riley, the real Cobalt. Or did he have a different identity for every occasion?

"I got into the compound, no hiccups," Riley continued, unaware of my thoughts. "But then, while I was sneaking around inside, I was caught by this little human kid. One of the commander's daughters most likely, couldn't have been more than six or seven years old. We sort of surprised each other." Riley gave a short, bitter chuckle and hung his head. "I knew I should kill her, or at least make it so she wouldn't give away my position, but I couldn't bring myself to do it. I was in the middle of a freaking St. George chapterhouse—I knew if anyone found me, I was dead, but I couldn't stomach the thought of hurting a kid, even a human one."

"What did you do?"

"I…told her I was playing hide-and-seek. It was the only thing I could think of." He sounded embarrassed, and I bit my lip to stifle a grin. "Yeah," Riley snorted. "Not one of my more brilliant moments. But that little kid believed me. She even swore not to tell anyone I was there. And then, she just walked out." Riley sounded amazed, even now. "I could've been killed that day. I was completely alone, in enemy territory, surrounded by armed soldiers who hated my kind. If I was caught, my hide would probably be hanging over some lieutenant's fireplace. But she let me go."

"You didn't blow up the chapterhouse, did you." It was a statement, not a question. Riley made a helpless gesture and shook his head.

"I couldn't do it. I kept seeing that girl's face and thinking there could be more like her, innocent kids wandering around. They weren't part of our war, they shouldn't have to die because of us. But I knew Talon wouldn't accept that. The deaths of a few innocents are nothing to them, not if it benefits the organization. And I couldn't return not having completed the mission." Riley sighed, his face shadowed by memory. "So… I ran. I left Talon, dropped off their grid and I haven't looked back since."

"And they didn't send the Vipers after you?"

"Oh, they did." He grinned humorlessly. "Turns out, I'm a lucky SOB. Dodged a couple Viper attacks before I found Wes, who was looking for an excuse to jump ship, as well. Wasn't long before we realized that there were others like us in the organization. Humans and dragons who wanted to be free of Talon. So now, we do whatever we can to break our kind out of the organization and show them how to live as rogues. How to avoid Viper attacks, how to stay off Talon's radar, how to be free."

*Freedom.* It sounded so appealing now. This was what I'd always wanted, right? Living away from Talon, not having to follow anyone's rules or laws or restrictions. Not becoming a Viper, an assassin who hunted her own kind for wanting to be free.

But the thought of going rogue, much as I hated myself for admitting it, was terrifying, as well. I would be hunted. I would be branded a traitor, a criminal, and the Vipers would come for me. I hated the rules, and I wished my trainer would jump off a cliff—in human form—but Talon was all I'd ever known.

And there was also one other problem.

Dante. I didn't think my straitlaced, perfect-student

brother would turn rogue, even if I did. And if I *did* manage to convince him to run away, he would be branded a traitor and hunted, as well. I wasn't sure I could do that to him.

As if reading my thoughts, Riley paused, and then his near-golden eyes rose to mine, serious and intense. The dragon stared out at me, fierce and primal and beautiful, sending a lance of heat through my insides. "I could show you how to be free, Firebrand," he whispered, a dangerous, alluring croon, "if you want me to."

I stared at him. Riley held my gaze. His nearness was overwhelming; I could feel his dragon watching me, barely contained in his fragile human shell. I felt my own dragon rising to meet his, a surge of heat erupting from the pit of my stomach, spreading to all parts of my body.

"Come with me," Riley urged, shifting closer on the couch. "You don't have to live by their rules. You don't have to become a Viper. You can live your own life, away from Talon and the Vipers and everything they stand for. That's what you want, isn't it?" He didn't move any closer, but I could feel his presence, the dragon, sitting beside me as if he was really there, wings, scales and all. "Wes and I are taking the hatchlings and leaving Crescent Beach tonight. I want you to come with us."

"Leave? With you?" I blinked. "Where would we go? How would we live?"

"Don't worry about that." Riley gave me a careless grin, looking more like himself. "I've been doing this for a while. It's not like we'll be hobos on the street. I have places we can go, where we'll be invisible, where the Vipers will never find us. Trust me."

"I… I don't know, Riley."

"All right." Abruptly, Riley stood, rising from the couch with easy grace, holding a hand to me. "If I can't convince you, then maybe you should hear it from someone else. Get a different perspective on Talon, and what they're really about. Come on."

I put my hand in his, letting him pull me to my feet. My dragon buzzed at his touch, but I ignored it. "Where are we going?"

"Downstairs. I have some people I want you to meet."

# GARRET

I rode in the back of the truck, pressed between two soldiers, feeling every bump and jolt through the metal bench welded to the sides. This vehicle was not designed for human transport, and the interior was hot and uncomfortable, though not the worst I'd endured. Around and across from me, fellow soldiers, my brothers-in-arms, waited with the same quiet anticipation. Some joked and laughed in low murmurs, some dozed with their arms crossed and their heads resting on their chest, some, like me, just waited, lost in their own thoughts.

Beside me, a fellow soldier nudged my arm. He was a few years my senior, with cropped black hair and a nose that had been broken repeatedly. I recognized him as Thomas Christopher, one of the few surviving soldiers of Alpha, the squad that was decimated in the South American raid a couple months back. "Hey, Sebastian, you've been here over a month, right?" he murmured, smiling like a wolf as he leaned in. "Where's the action at? What do you do around here for fun?"

"I wasn't here on vacation," I replied simply.

"Oh, that's right." Christopher leaned back, smirking at me but speaking for the rest of the group. "Our Sebastian is the prodigy, the Perfect Soldier. Nothing ever enters his faultless little head but the mission. Give him a hooker and he'd use her for target practice."

"Shut up, Christopher," Tristan said, sitting across from me with his rifle against his shoulder. "At least he'd have a chance with a woman. She'd take one look at your ugly mug and wonder why there was a bulldog's ass sewed to it."

The other soldiers hooted and ribbed Christopher, who flushed angrily but laughed along with them. More taunts and good-natured insults were thrown back and forth, with Tristan never missing a beat, but I didn't join in. Normally at this time I would be silencing my thoughts, mentally preparing myself for the battle ahead. *Turn off your mind, turn off your emotions, become a blank vessel that acts solely on instinct with no fear to slow you down.* That's what I'd been taught. What I trained myself to do.

Today, that calm, empty silence eluded me. I was filled with a sense of foreboding, a nagging uncertainty that haunted my thoughts the closer we drew to our objective. I'd always been so certain of the Order—what we did, what we protected. Dragons were the enemy and we were meant to kill them. That's what I'd believed, unwaveringly, my whole life.

Until her.

She might not be one of them. We hadn't proven anything. There'd been suspicious happenstance, there'd been strong implications, but there'd been no real proof. Ember might not be a dragon. She could be a normal girl with a normal family, who loved surfing and arcade games and hanging out with her friends. She could be a perfectly ordinary human.

But if she *wasn't*. If Ember was our target, the sleeper we'd been sent to kill, then the Order hadn't told me everything. They never told me that dragons could be kind, that they could be daring, and funny, and beautiful. That they *loved* surfing and arcade games and hanging out with their friends. None of that had been counterfeit. The Order taught that dragons could only imitate emotions, that they had no real concept of humanity. If Ember was the sleeper, then she had proven them wrong at every turn.

What else had we been wrong about?

"Garret."

I flicked my gaze to Tristan, who regarded me through the press of bodies and laughing soldiers, his dark eyes appraising. "You okay? You've been even broodier than normal lately." His tone was light, but his expression was hard and suspicious. "Don't tell me the Perfect Soldier has a sudden case of nerves."

Thankfully, before I could answer, the truck pulled to a stop and the driver craned his neck to look back at us through a small mesh window. "We're two hundred yards out," he told Tristan, who nodded and rose to his feet, clutching his rifle.

"That's my cue." Glancing at me, he offered a devil-may-care grin. "Good luck in there. See you on the flip side, partner."

I nodded. Maneuvering through soldiers, he edged to the back of the truck, opened the doors and hopped out. I knew he would quickly find himself a good vantage point and be watching the house through the scope of his rifle when the raid began. If any of our targets slipped past us and tried to run, they wouldn't get past the driveway. Not with Tristan guarding the front.

The truck rumbled and began to move again, and I took a deep breath, trying to calm my mind. Two hundred yards out. Two hundred yards from the enemy nest. I couldn't have any doubts, not at this stage in the mission. Uncertainties would get me and my brothers killed. I was a soldier of St. George; when the time came and we faced our enemies again, I would do what I'd been trained to do, what I knew I must.

Kill every dragon in sight.

# RILEY

Ember followed me down the stairs, where the crack of billiard balls told me exactly how the two hatchlings were getting ready to leave, which was not at all.

"I'm so glad you two are taking this threat seriously," I stated as I swept into the game room. At the head of the table, Remy jerked up with a guilty expression, raking sandy hair out of his eyes. Nettle quickly put her pool stick on the table, trying to look innocent and failing. I shook my head.

"I thought Wes told you we were leaving tonight. You're supposed to be getting ready to go. Call me crazy, but I don't think this qualifies."

"We are ready!" Nettle protested. Her dreadlocks bounced as she did, vehemently stating her case. "We came here with nothing, remember? We don't have anything to pack. We are ready to go."

"Really?" I crossed my arms. "And what about the whole 'leaving the house as we found it' bit? Are the rooms clean, or do they look like a hurricane went through?" They both dropped their gaze, and I nodded. "Yeah, that's what I thought. You're both going to take care of that, but right now, I want you to meet someone."

I turned, motioning Ember forward. Her eyes were wide

as she stepped around me, staring curiously at the other hatchlings, who stared back. "This is Ember," I told them as the three hatchlings eyed one another over the table. "She might be joining us when we leave town tonight. Firebrand," I continued as Ember glanced at me sharply, "meet two of mine. That's Nettle, and Remy. I got them both out of Talon a year ago."

"S'up," Remy greeted, raising a hand. "Welcome aboard. So, our fearless leader convinced you to join our cause, too, huh?"

"I, uh, haven't decided yet," Ember said, and Nettle's mouth fell open.

"What? Why not?" The other hatchling gaped at Ember, shocked. "Are you stupid? Don't you know what they'll do to you?"

"Nettle," I warned, and the girl backed off. Ember bristled, and I stepped between them before I had a full-on chick fight in the game room. And when those chicks were dragons, it could get ugly real fast. I didn't feel like calling the fire department right now.

"You'll have to excuse Nettle," I told Ember, who gave me a skeptical look. "She has more reason to hate Talon than most."

"Oh?" Ember turned back to the other hatchling, more curious than angry now. Nettle watched her with a sullen expression, and the other girl frowned. "Why?"

Nettle glanced at me, and I nodded. Better to let her tell her story; as one who had lived through the worst facet of Talon, she knew the organization's darkest secret better than most. As awful as her story was, I couldn't imagine what it had been like for her.

"I failed assimilation," Nettle began, bitterness still coloring her voice when she spoke of her past. "My guardian was a real bastard who liked to piss me off, just to remind me that if I ever changed, I'd be sent back to the organization. One day he pushed too far. I lost my temper and snapped at him…in my real form." Her tone became even harsher as she subconsciously rubbed her arm. "I expected to be shipped back to Talon for retraining. That's what everyone tells you, right? Only, it's a big fat lie. Talon doesn't call hatchlings back for retraining. You get one shot, and that's it. According to Talon, if you fail assimilation, you've been 'corrupted by humanity.' You've proven you can't be trusted among humans, ever."

Ember frowned. This was obviously news to her. "Then… what happens if you fail?"

Nettle snorted. "I can't tell you what happens to the male students, but I do know what happens to the females. Remember all that garbage they fed us, about how dragonells were so important to our survival, that we were the future of our race?" She curled her lip. "Well, they weren't lying about that. All female hatchlings who fail assimilation are sent to these special facilities, to become *breeders* for the rest of their lives."

It took only a second for Ember to get what Nettle was saying. Her face went white with shock and rage, and the other girl smiled nastily.

"Yeah, bet they didn't tell you that. You must've passed your tests with flying colors. Me?" She shrugged. "My destiny was to become a broodmare for Talon's future dragons, popping out eggs as often as I could."

I watched Ember's face for her response. She still looked pale and horrified, but her eyes flashed emerald, the dragon reacting to the thought of being a breeder forever. There was no doubt in my mind; if Ember hadn't excelled in both the assimilation process and her training, if she'd "failed" as Nettle had, she would never have stood for what Talon had planned for her. We wouldn't even be having this conversation, because we would've cleared out long ago.

*That's right, Firebrand. Get angry. This is what Talon really is like, this is their true face, and you don't belong with them. You belong with us. With me.*

"And then, I met Cobalt." Nettle nodded in my direction. "And he told me I didn't have to submit to that life, that he could take me away and show me something better. I figured, might as well, what do I have to lose?" She raised her chin defiantly. "I'll tell you now, it was the best decision of my life. I'd rather be on the run from Talon, the Vipers and St. George forever than ever go back to the organization."

"That's horrible," Ember whispered. "They'd really do that to you?"

"It's one of Talon's dirty little secrets," I said. "And one of their best kept, too. I've tried to find the place they keep the breeder females—only the top dragons in the organization are aware of them, and even fewer know where they're located. The females never leave the compound except to breed with a specially chosen sire, and then they're sent back. I've looked everywhere for those damned facilities and have gotten nil. If Nettle hadn't come with me when she did, I wouldn't have had any hope of getting her out."

"I'm never going back," Nettle said again, even more fiercely, as if Ember would be the one to drag her away. "Never. I'd rather die."

Still lounging at the head of the pool table, Remy snorted. "Jeez, Nettle. So dramatic. It's not like you're the only one

Talon has screwed over." He turned a rakish grin on Ember, shoving shaggy sandy bangs from his eyes yet again. "Nettle might've been destined for broodmare-dom, but they were planning something even worse for me."

"You don't know that," I said. True, I hated Talon, but we didn't need to invent any horrible tales to win Ember over. And Remy tended to exaggerate when he was telling a story, particularly when it was about himself. "All we've heard are rumors and speculation. No one really knows what goes on in there."

"Where?" Ember asked, and Remy grinned.

"A secret underground lab," he said in a dramatic voice. "Where they experiment on the male dragons unfit for Talon." He thumped his scrawny chest. "Dragons like me. I was 'too small,' my bloodline was 'undesirable' for the gene pool, so they were going to ship me off to the lab to be sliced up and poked and prodded and turned into something new."

"We don't know it's a lab," I said again as Ember's brows shot up. "There is no evidence to suggest Talon has a secret lab, and there is certainly no evidence to suggest they do all the things Remy just said. But," I continued as Remy pouted, unhappy that I had undermined his claim, "Talon does have a place where they send 'undesirables.' Dragons that are scrawny or crippled or sickly, whose genes will weaken the breeding pool. Poor saps are sent off to a heavily armed facility in the Appalachian Mountains—"

"And no one ever sees them again," Remy finished dramatically. "Because they're sliced and diced and prodded and turned into something new. A superdragon with three heads."

I rolled my eyes. "Get out of here," I said, jerking a thumb at the door. "Both of you. You have a room to straighten.

Out." They scurried through the door and vanished down the hallway, leaving me alone with Ember.

I turned to find her watching me with an amused smile on her face. "What?" I asked, crossing my arms. "What's that look?"

She shrugged. "Nothing. Just… I've never seen this side of you before."

"What side?"

"The big brotherly side." She glanced down the hall, where Remy and Nettle had disappeared. "You really care for them, don't you? I wouldn't have expected it."

"Well, to paraphrase a famous fictional ogre, dragons are like onions—we have layers."

She laughed, and I grinned with her, before she sobered again. "It's true, isn't it?" she whispered, a troubled look crossing her face. "Talon really does all that."

"Yeah, Firebrand, they really do. Sorry to burst your bubble, but they're not who you think they are."

"And if I stay, they'll turn me into a Viper." She shivered and rubbed her arms. "I'll be forced to hunt down rogues like Remy and Nettle." She bit her lip, averting my gaze. "And you."

My heart beat faster. I was close, so close, to convincing her to jump ship, to turn her back on Talon and join the rogues. "Could you do it?" I asked. "If Talon gave you the order to take us all out, no mercy, no questions asked, would you be able to carry out their wishes, knowing what you do now?"

She didn't answer, still battling some inner torment, struggling with the choice. I watched her, filled with that strange yearning, fiery and terrible. It was like I could almost feel her heartbeat, feel the breath that filled her lungs, mirroring my own.

Taking a gamble, I closed the distance between us, reached out and gently took her arms. Her emerald gaze shifted to mine, pinning me with a fierce, direct stare. My heart turned over, and my dragon roared to life, wanting to sweep his wings down and enveloped us both.

"Come with us," I said, holding her gaze. Her dragon stared out at me, eager and defiant, and my resolve grew. "You don't belong here. You're not one of them, and I think you've known something was wrong from the beginning. But—" I slid my hands up her arms, feeling her tremble "—it's not just Talon, is it?"

She drew back, though not very far. "Riley, I don't..."

"Don't pretend," I insisted, pulling her closer. Her hands went to my chest, and the contact seared the skin through my shirt. My heart sped up, and my voice became raspy. "Not with me. There is something between us, Firebrand. I've been fighting this since the day I saw you in the parking lot, and I know you feel it, too."

She shivered but didn't deny it. I actually saw relief flicker through her eyes. Relief, perhaps, that she wasn't alone, that maybe this was just as confusing and torturous for me as it was for her. But then she gave her head a small shake and pushed on my chest. "No," she muttered, dropping her gaze. "Let go, I can't do this...."

She tried pulling back, and I grabbed her wrists before she could leave. "Look at me," I demanded as she tried yanking out of my grip. My dragon roared in frustration, and I dragged her close, lowering my head to hers. "Look me in the eyes and tell me you don't feel anything," I whispered.

"Tell me that, and I'll let you go. You can go back to your guardians and Talon and your trainer, and you'll never see me again. Just tell me, to my face, that there is nothing between us. That this is all in my head."

"I can't." Ember stopped fighting me, though she didn't meet my stare. "I can't say that, because every time I see you, I feel like I'm going to explode. And that *scares* me, Riley. But I can't go with you yet."

"Why?" I demanded, trying to catch her gaze. "Something is telling us we belong together, you just said so yourself." Releasing her wrists, I grabbed her by the shoulders, bending slightly to see her eyes. "I would protect you, Firebrand. I'd keep you safe, I swear. What are you afraid of? There's nothing keeping you here."

"There is," she whispered, and finally raised her head. "Dante. I can't leave Dante behind. I have to go back for him."

Her brother. Dammit, I'd forgotten about him. "Ember," I said as gently as I could, "he won't come. He's Talon's all the way—I've known it since the night of the party. If you tell him where we are, he'll probably inform the organization as soon as he can. Hell, he might even go to Lilith himself. I can't risk that."

"He'll come," Ember insisted. "I know he will. I just have to talk to him, convince him of what Talon is doing. He'll listen to me." My skepticism must've shown on my face, because her expression hardened, and she took a step back. "I'm not leaving without him, Riley. We've been through everything together. I have to try, at least."

She glared at me, stubborn and unyielding, and I sighed. "I'm not going to convince you otherwise, am I?" I muttered, and she shook her head. “Dammit. All right, Firebrand. What do you want me to do until then? We can’t stay here. It’s too dangerous for Nettle and Remy. Even if I’m willing to risk an attack, I won’t do that to the hatchlings. I promised I’d keep *them* safe, too.”

“We could meet you somewhere,” Ember suggested, green eyes thoughtful as she gazed up at me. “After you leave. Just give me a call when you find a place, and we’ll meet you there in a day or two. That’ll give me time to convince Dante…and say goodbye to a couple people here.”

Her face fell at that last statement, making me frown. For a moment, she’d sounded incredibly sad. Suspicion reared its ugly head; I’d been a rogue awhile now, and knew how hard it was to leave everything behind, how frightening it was for some. What if she was too attached to Crescent Beach, her friends and her old life? What if she went back, and discovered she couldn’t say goodbye, even after everything she’d learned about Talon?

Or was there another reason? I remembered that boy from the night of the party, the one she’d danced with, smiled at. Almost kissed. I stifled a growl and crossed my arms, watching her.

“I don’t know if I like the idea of leaving you here, hoping you’ll catch up to me later. What if you have a change of heart?” She didn’t answer, and I narrowed my eyes. “Or is this just a ploy to get me to leave town, and you don’t have any intention of showing up?”

“No,” Ember said, looking up quickly. “That’s not it. I’m not going to become a Viper. I refuse.” She paused, clenching her fists, and took a deep breath. “I can’t stay with Talon anymore,” she whispered fiercely, “not with what I know

now. This isn't about stupid rules and hateful trainers and not getting to live my life the way I want anymore. This… this is about *killing* my own kind. And knowing exactly what Talon is like. I can't be a part of that. I won't.

"But…" She faltered, the shadow of some memory crossing her face, turning her eyes dark. "I've made connections here, people who are my friends, even if they are human. And they'll wonder what happened to me if I just up and vanish into thin air. I want to say goodbye." For a second, an agonized expression flickered through her eyes, before she closed them briefly. "I have someone I want to see, one more time. And then, we'll go with you, Dante and I. Turn rogue or whatever you call it, and leave Talon for good."

"Promise me." I took a step forward so that we were a breath apart, close enough to see my own reflection in her pupils. "Swear that I'll see you again."

"I swear." Her voice was barely a whisper, even as her gaze held mine. We had both gone perfectly still, standing at the edge of a vast precipice, afraid to be the one to take that first step. Or maybe just gathering the courage for the plunge. My heart pounded in my ears, my stomach turning backflips, as I reached out and took her wrists again, holding them to my chest.

"Make me believe it, Firebrand."

Ember licked her lips. "Riley…"

The alarms blared overhead.

# EMBER

A shrill beeping cut through the silence. My dragon, already dangerously close to the surface, nearly sprang out of my skin when I jumped. I pushed her down, both relieved and annoyed at the interruption, and backed a couple steps away, looking up at the ceiling.

Riley leaped back, too. With a curse, he fled upstairs, leaving me in the game room with Nettle and Remy peering curiously down the hall. We blinked at one another, then followed him upstairs to a bedroom, where he and Wes stood before his open laptop, glaring at the screen.

The alarm, whatever it was, continued to sound. Wes and Riley were bent over the computer, their faces intense.

"What's going on?" Nettle asked as we came into the room. "Is someone coming?" Wes and Riley ignored her, still completely focused on what was on the computer. I edged forward and peeked over Riley's shoulder.

The screen showed a black-and-white image of the driveway up to the house. I could see Riley's motorcycle parked off to the side. As I watched, feeling the tension lining his back, a large brown delivery truck pulled up to the front and lurched to a stop about fifty feet from the door.

"Bloody hell." Wes sighed, collapsing into the chair. "I

wish these blighters would stop using our driveway as a turnabout when they get lost. That nearly gave me a bloody heart attack." He shook his head at the image on the screen. "GPS, mate. Use it, love it."

"They're not leaving," Riley growled, still staring at the screen. Wes blinked and scooted forward again, narrowing his eyes.

We all crowded closer. No one seemed to breathe, staring at the lone truck in the drive. Then, without warning, the door flew open, and several humans spilled out onto the cement. My heart gave a violent lurch. They were armed and armored, and looked very much like the soldiers in my training sessions. They wore helmets and masks that concealed their faces, and carried huge, deadly-looking guns. Only, this time, I knew it wasn't a drill, and those guns weren't filled with paint.

St. George had come. This was the real thing.

"Shit!" Wes leaped up, overturning the chair as he did. "Bloody St. George! We're dead. We're fucking dead."

"Shut up!" Riley snarled as Nettle screamed and Remy bolted toward the door. His voice boomed out as he whirled around. "Remy, freeze! Nettle, hush! Right now! Listen to me," he continued as both hatchlings stopped and gazed at him with huge eyes. "We're not going to panic. Follow me, do exactly what I tell you and we'll be okay." His near-golden gaze shifted to me, intense and determined. "I swear, I'll get us out alive."

"Riley, they're surrounding the house," Wes exclaimed, right before he slammed the laptop and stuffed it into a shoulder bag. "We have about twenty seconds before this place becomes a war zone."

"Wes, take everyone out through the main bedroom," Riley ordered, pointing down the hall. "Get to the balcony, we can launch from there. They'll likely have all other exits covered, and at least one sniper watching the front. Now, listen to me, you two," he continued, snapping his fingers at the other hatchlings. "This is just like we talked about. Go off the balcony and head for the rendezvous point. You're going to be out in the open until you can get around the cliffs. Fly low, hug the mountain and don't panic if you're shot at. A moving target is difficult to hit, even for St. George, so keep going and don't break from the cliff wall. Wes, do you remember where to go? Can you get them there?"

"Yes," Wes answered, hefting the bag to his shoulder before glaring at Remy. "If the little blighters don't drop me, that is."

"Good." Riley ignored that last part. "Don't stop until you've reached the fallback point. I've stashed money and supplies in the cave. If you can get to it, it'll give you a head start. Wait for me there, but if I don't make it, stay together and get as far away from here as you can, understand?"

They nodded. Nettle seemed on the verge of panic, but Remy was calmer now. Riley looked at Wes, who waited solemnly with the book bag over his shoulder. "Get them out of here. I'll try to give you a head start, keep the bastards from shooting you out of the air. If we get lucky, I'll see you at the rendezvous."

Wes nodded gravely. "Be careful, Riley. Don't get dead."

Riley jerked his head at me as the human and the two hatchlings raced off down the hall. "Ember, you, too. Go with Wes and the others."

"No," I shot back, my heart hammering against my ribs.

Doggedly, I followed him into the hall, toward the living room, though my instincts were screaming at me to go the other way. "I'm not leaving you."

"Dammit, Ember!" He spun, grabbing my arm. "This isn't one of your training sessions. This is St. George, and they *will* kill you!"

A crash shattered the tense silence, the sound of breaking glass, as something small came hurtling through the window, followed by a blinding flash of light. A second later, a massive boom rocked the house, and a wave of energy slammed into me, knocking me away from Riley. At the same time, the front door flew inward, and a trio of armed, masked soldiers spilled into the room, sweeping their guns toward us.

# GARRET

In combat, everything slows down and speeds up at the same time.

The door exploded inward with the force of my kick, and we lunged inside, the muzzles of our M-4s leading the way. I took in the room in a split-second glance—bright, airy, expensive looking—before movement to the right demanded my attention.

A body dove behind the kitchen counter, and we opened fire. The M-4s chattered in sharp, three-round bursts, filling the room with noise and smoke, shattering glass and tearing chunks out of the marble. Rubble flew everywhere, ceramics exploded and wood splintered as we edged toward the kitchen, concentrating fire on our target.

"No!"

The scream came from the hall, from someone at the edge of the living room. I whirled, sweeping my gun up and sighting down the muzzle, my finger tightening around the trigger.

I froze.

Ember's small frame filled my sights, green eyes wide with horror and fear as she stared at me. For a single heartbeat, I faltered, unwilling to believe, and the gun wavered. For a split second, I hesitated...

…and watched as the girl I had kissed, who had taught me to surf and play video games and laugh at myself, shifted and reared up with a roar, her body exploding into wings and talons and crimson scales. I realized my mistake and brought the weapon up again, too late. The dragon's jaws opened, and a blast of flame seared toward us, engulfing the floor and setting the furniture ablaze.

I dove away from the roaring dragonfire, feeling the scalding heat even through my armor. Rolling behind a sofa, which was now completely engulfed in flames, I leveled myself to a knee and returned fire. The red dragon gave a defiant screech and ducked back into the hall as a bullet storm peppered the entryway, tearing chunks out of the walls.

There was another roar, and a second dragon, even bigger than the first, rose up from behind the counter and sent his own blast of flame into the fray. The once-pristine living room swiftly became a roaring inferno, tongues of fire licking the walls and floor, as the blue dragon whipped his head back and forth, catching everything ablaze. The heat was incredible, and smoke stung my eyes and mouth, making it hard to see. Squinting through flames and smoke, I caught a gleam of scales through the firestorm, ducked out of cover and fired several rounds at the dragon-shaped blur.

There was a screech of pain over the bark of gunfire, followed by an angry roar. I couldn't tell which dragon it came from, but the smaller red one suddenly reared up, jaws gaping, and sent a fireball streaking for the couch. As I ducked behind cover to avoid the fiery explosion, both dragons spun and bounded for the glass doors leading to the balcony. I leaped upright, sighting the gun after the retreating targets, but the blue dragon hit the doors first in an explosion of glass, going right through the flimsy barrier with the smaller one close behind. We raced after them, knowing that once they took flight it would be nearly impossible to catch them again. I leaped through the shattered frame, bringing up my gun, only to see the red dragon dive off the balcony into empty sky. We hurried to the railing, a few of my teammates firing after the escaping dragons, but the pair swiftly vanished around a cliff face and out of sight.

# RILEY

"Cobalt!"

Ember's cry echoed behind me, nearly swallowed by the wind and the pounding of the surf below us. She sounded frantic, but I ignored her, concentrating on staying aloft, keeping my wings moving, beating. I couldn't stop now because if I did, I wasn't certain I could get off the ground again.

We followed the cliff face for a couple miles, until it dropped off and became a rocky shoreline, waves crashing against the rocks. I felt exposed out here, gliding over the water in plain sight. Thankfully, this side of the cliff wasn't friendly to humans or tourists; there were no beaches or docks or good surfing areas, only jagged coastline and rock. Humans rarely ventured down this shore. Which was exactly why I'd chosen it.

I glided low, following the coastline, until I finally saw what I was looking for: a tiny patch of sand, too small to be called a beach, even a private one, in the shadow of a cliff face.

The second my claws hit the sand, my strength gave out and I collapsed at the edge of the water, the waves hissing over my heated scales as they returned to the sea. Blood oozed in vivid red streams from a pair of holes right above my stomach plates, bullet wounds I'd taken just before we fled. Thankfully, it was more of a graze than a direct hit, and that part of my body was well armored, but still. Seawater foamed over me as a wave rolled onto the beach, rushing into the wounds and setting them on fire. I clenched my jaw in pain, panting through my nostrils, as Ember splashed over, wings outstretched, pupils dilated in fear and alarm. The sun glinted off her metallic crimson scales, her eyes blazed emerald, and even through the pain, the sight of her real form made my blood sizzle.

"You're shot!"

"Yeah," I growled, digging my claws into the sand, wishing it was the face of the soldier with the gun. "One of the bastards got me. It's not as bad as it looks."

She stepped closer, folding her wings over her back. She didn't Shift, but gently nudged a wing aside to peer at the wound. I watched her, my body coiled around hers, fighting the desire to reach out and drag her close, wrapping us both in my wings.

"You were incredible back there, you know," I said quietly. "Looked St. George in the eye and didn't back down. You would've made an awesome Viper."

"Yeah, well, I was terrified the whole time, so don't think I'll be doing that again anytime soon." Her voice caught, and she drew back slightly, shivering. "They were really trying to kill us," she whispered. "Why do they hate us? We haven't done anything to them."

"You know the answer to that, Firebrand." I closed my eyes as another wave flowed over us; it hurt like a mother but at least it would clean the wounds. "Talon taught you just as well as me. They hate us because we're different, and mankind always fears what they don't understand." I shrugged painfully. "Course, our ancestors might've started that grudge with the whole burning towns and eating villagers thing. Or it might've started when the first slayer killed the first dragon for his treasure hoard, who knows? The point is, this war is nothing new. Humans and dragons have been fighting each other for centuries, and it's not going to end anytime soon. Not until one of us destroys the other. And with all the humans on the planet, who do you think will go extinct first?"

Ember shook her head, nostrils flaring. "But it's so pointless," she raged, baring her fangs. "Has anyone tried *talking* to each other?"

I snorted a laugh, wincing as it sent a stab of pain through my ribs. "You just saw what St. George is like. If you think you can get through to them, by all means, go back tonight and try to have a conversation. But I bet you won't get within a hundred yards before they start firing." She scowled, and I raised my head, bringing my muzzle level to hers. "You can't reason with fanatics, Firebrand," I told her gently. "St. George hates us because we're dragons, and that's the only excuse they need to wipe us out. They see us as monsters. That's why they want us extinct."

She blinked, slitted green eyes gazing into my own, sending heat singing through my veins. In human form, I'd felt drawn to her, but it was nothing compared to the almost savage pull I felt now. Firmly, I shoved it back. There was no time.

Gritting my teeth, I planted my claws and pushed myself upright, hissing at the sharp lance of pain. Ember quickly stepped forward and leaned into me, bracing herself as she took some of my weight.

"Cobalt, don't. What are you doing?"

"We can't stay here and risk St. George finding us. I have to get to Wes and the others, but I don't think I can fly very far." Setting my jaw, I limped up the beach, cursing as my talons sank into the sand, slowing me down. Ember stayed with me, walking close, her shoulder touching mine to steady us. "Fortunately, I come fully prepared for these kinds of circumstances."

We reached the rock face, where a pile of branches and driftwood sat in the sand against the cliff wall. At my nod, Ember raked the pile aside with her claws, until she revealed the plastic crate beneath. Inside was a single change of clothes, a new wallet with duplicate fake identities, money, a burner phone and a small first-aid kit.

I grinned at her astonishment. "Like I said, I've been doing this awhile, Firebrand. And the first thing you learn when you go rogue is that you *always* have a backup plan." I might've said more, but at that moment, I shifted my weight the wrong way and my leg gave out from under me. I caught myself with a hiss, but it seemed so much easier to slump into the cool, dry sand, so I did.

Ember was beside me in an instant, eyes worried as she leaned in. Beautiful, dangerous, the other half of me. And the urges within became too strong to ignore.

My wings swept down, wrapping around us both, drawing her against my body. She reared back, startled, but I hooked my talons into her scales and pulled her close. Ember resisted for a moment, then gave a low growl and pressed forward, twining her neck with mine. Flames roared through me, a fire exploding through my core, consuming and intense. I closed my eyes, wanting her closer, wanting to twist and writhe and coil in the sand, tails and wings thrashing, until we had become one.

With a start, Ember hissed and pulled back, breaking from my embrace and the cocoon of wings. Her entire stance—wings flared, pupils dilated, nostrils flaring—spoke of desire and alarm. Shaking her head, she backed away, looking like she might launch herself into the air and flee.

"Cobalt, I don't—"

"No," I interrupted, half rising. "Don't say anything. Don't fight it, Firebrand. We belong together, you know it as well as me. Say you'll come with me. Tonight."

"We just met." Ember sounded very human then, like she was trying to convince herself. "I don't even know you, really."

"So what? We're not human. We don't play by the same rules." I switched to Draconic, my voice low and soothing. "This is instinct, plain and simple. Human emotion has nothing to do with it. Stop fighting it. Stop fighting me."

She wavered, still wary and uncertain, and I growled, clenching my talons in the sand. The moment was gone, but I still needed her to leave with us. I'd have all the time in the world to convince her then. "Firebrand—" I nodded toward the ocean and the sun, sinking into the horizon "—you can't stay here, not with St. George sniffing around. They'll be looking for us, and the bastards are stupidly persistent. You'll be in danger if you stay here, and so will that twin of yours."

Ember blinked, her gaze darkening at the mention of St. George and Dante, and backed away. "Dante," she muttered, as if just remembering. "He still doesn't know St. George is in the area. I have to go." She looked at me, pleading. "I have to go home and convince him to come with us. I can't leave him, not now."

I sighed out a curl of smoke and nodded. She was still planning to leave with us, that was all that mattered. "Go on, then," I murmured, jerking my head toward the ocean. "Do what you have to. Get your brother, meet us at the rendezvous point later tonight and let's get the hell out of Dodge."

"Where will we meet you?"

"I'll call you later with the location." At her betrayed look, I softened my voice. "It's not that I don't trust you, Firebrand. But if I'm caught, I don't want them surprising you at the meeting place. It's safer if you don't know where it is. I promise I'll call you when the time comes. Just focus on being ready to go when I do."

"What about you?"

"Don't worry." I smirked and flicked my tail at the crate that held the burner phone. "I'll call Wes, and he'll come and pick me up, provided he and the hatchlings got to the bolt hole safely."

"You're still hurt." Ember's gaze went to my still-oozing ribs. "I don't want to leave you."

I ignored the way my heart leaped at that statement. "Firebrand, I'll be fine. Trust me, this isn't the worst situation I've been in. My surly hacker friend has patched me up many times before. Only bad part is listening to him bitch the whole time he's doing it." I clenched my jaw and struggled to my feet with a grimace, splaying my legs to remain upright, panting. "But we need to leave, and we need to leave soon. I'll wait for you both as long as I can, but if you and Dante don't meet us by midnight...we'll have to go without you."

Ember nodded. "We'll be there." Looking at the sun,

she nodded grimly, nostrils flaring. "I'll see you in a couple hours, at most. Be careful, Cobalt."

I staggered forward and pressed my muzzle beneath her chin, closing my eyes. "You, too," I whispered.

She gave me an unreadable look as I pulled back, then turned and padded gracefully away. I watched her go, feeling a part of myself leave with her, until she paused at the edge of the ocean, silhouetted against the sun. Her wings cast a dark shadow over the beach as they unfurled, and I felt an almost painful longing to go with her, to spring forward and follow the red hatchling into the sunset, but I kept myself grounded and under control. Ember's wings flapped twice, sending up whirlwinds of sand and foam, as she launched herself skyward. Still, I watched as the crimson dragon climbed rapidly into the air, scales glinting in the evening sun, until she soared over the cliff face and disappeared into the blue.

# EMBER

I didn't fly far. Just to the top of the cliff, where I found the road back to town, and quickly Shifted back to human form behind a pile of large rocks. I was barefoot, phoneless, penniless, dressed in what appeared to be a black wetsuit and nothing else and several miles from any place familiar. I wished I could just fly home, but of course that wasn't an option. Especially now that St. George was in town and on the warpath. I couldn't linger in any place for long. At least one of those soldiers had seen me right before I'd changed, and knew what I looked like in human form. If they spotted me now, I was dead meat.

A car came down the road, a white Camry with tinted windows and music blasting from inside. Halfheartedly, I stuck out a thumb, and the vehicle cruised right on by without slowing down, giving me a honk as they zipped away. I stuck my tongue out as it passed, tossing dust in its wake, and fantasized about meeting them with a flat tire on the side of the road. Glancing at the last sliver of red peeking over the ocean, I sighed.

*Well, looks like I'm hoofing it.*

With limited options, I began jogging down the road toward home. Away from the cliff, and the beach, and Cobalt.

*Cobalt. Riley.* That moment on the beach, when he'd yanked me to him, still lingered in my mind. I didn't know what to think of it, though my dragon had no such doubts. Even now, she was urging me to turn around, to fly back to Riley and never leave his side.

But there was someone else. Someone who made my chest ache at the thought of never seeing him again. Someone I'd have to leave behind. Guilt, a new, unpleasant emotion, gnawed at me as I thought of Garret. I knew our time together was already short, that he would leave at the end of the summer, but right now it felt like my heart was being torn out. And not just because of Garret, though I would miss him terribly, I realized. I would also have to say goodbye to Lexi and Calvin, to surfing and the ocean, and everything I'd come to love in Crescent Beach. My summer was truly at an end.

My throat felt tight, a strange sensation, and the corners of my eyes stung. I shook myself and jogged faster, shoving thoughts of Garret and everything else to the back of my mind. I couldn't stay here, that much was certain. I had to fetch my brother and leave town with Riley, before St. George found us all.

The sun had set and the stars were starting to come out when I finally staggered up the sidewalk to the villa, knowing this would be the last time. One of the cars was gone from the driveway, so hopefully I'd gotten lucky and both guardians were out of the house. Even so, I'd have to move quickly. No telling where St. George was right now, if they were scouring Crescent Beach for us, and I didn't want to keep Riley waiting. I'd promised to meet him and the others as soon as he called with their location; that didn't give me a lot of time.

Dante wasn't in the living room or the kitchen, but light and music seeped out from the crack beneath his door. Relieved that he was home, I hurried down the hall and banged hard on the wood.

It opened, and my brother frowned at me over the threshold, looking perfectly normal in a sleeveless shirt and black trunks. His frown grew more confused as he saw me, barefoot and panting, in a single dark suit that covered my whole body.

"Ember?" His green eyes widened. "What's wrong? Are you hurt? And what the hell are you wearing?"

"St. George," I gasped, and his eyebrows immediately shot up. "St. George is here! They've found us. We have to leave town, Dante. Right now!"

"What? Whoa, slow down a second." Dante grabbed my wrist and pulled me inside, slamming the door behind him. "What do you mean, St. George is here?" he demanded, spinning to face me. "How do you know? Talon hasn't said anything about possible St. George activity, and I think that's something they would mention."

"No, listen to me." I glared at him, wishing he would just trust me for once. "I've seen them, okay? They're here. They *shot* at me! I was with Riley, and a squad of them kicked down the door—"

"Riley?" My brother's eyes narrowed. "You were with that rogue dragon again? *Dammit,* Ember, what are you thinking? Why were you at a *rogue's* house? No wonder St. George came for him. You're lucky you weren't killed!"

"I almost was!" I snapped. "We barely made it out alive.

But even before that, I learned some very interesting things about Talon, and what they really want from us."

"You can't believe anything a rogue says. They're traitors and criminals. They'll lie through their teeth just to—"

"You knew the Vipers were assassins, didn't you?" I interrupted. Dante blinked, surprised, and I nodded. "You knew, and you didn't tell me. Why? We're supposed to look out for each other, isn't that what you've said all this time? You're my brother, and you didn't think it was important to tell me I was destined to hunt down and slaughter my own kind?"

"It's Talon's decision to tell you when," Dante said, crossing his arms. "Not mine. And none of this would've happened if you just stopped fighting them." He huffed and gave me a look of supreme exasperation. "Talon is only concerned about our survival, Ember, and you act like they're the devil incarnate! They're not the bad guys, can't you understand that? They're the ones keeping us safe from St. George."

"Dante." I scrubbed my hands over my eyes, weary and frustrated. He wouldn't listen; he wouldn't hear anything I had to say about Talon and the rogues and St. George. Riley had been right.

Still, he was my brother, and I had to try. "I'm leaving," I said softly, my voice hoarse and resigned. "Tonight. Riley offered to take me with him when he leaves town and… I'm going with him."

Dante stared at me a moment, the blood draining from his face. "You're going rogue?" he whispered, his voice choked. "Ember, you can't! They'll hunt you down. You know what Talon does to traitors, you said so yourself."

"That's why I can't stay." I gave him a pleading look, needing him to understand. "I can't become a Viper. Not with what I learned tonight."

"Is this because you're upset with your trainer? With me?"

"No!" I scrubbed both hands down my face again. "It's not about my trainer," I whispered. "It's not about you, or breaking the rules, or anything like that. Dante, I'm not going rogue because I'm tired of Talon telling me what to do. This isn't about not getting to fly, or not liking training, or having the organization constantly run my life. None of that matters. I'm leaving because… I can't stand by what Talon believes. What they expect me to do."

Dante sank to the bed, running his hands through his hair. I watched him a moment, then said, "I'm going. I don't expect you to understand. Not yet. But Riley and the others are waiting for me and I… I want you to come with us, too. You'll see, Dante. Once you meet them, you'll see why we have to go."

Dante closed his eyes. For a moment, he sat there, head and shoulders bowed, thinking.

"If I don't come," he said at last, his voice low and grim, "you'll go without me, won't you?"

I bit my lip. I really, really didn't want to leave my brother. We'd been through everything together. But I couldn't stay and let Talon change me into something I was not, something I didn't want to be. Dante would be safe here; St. George wasn't after *him,* they wanted Riley and the other rogues. And me.

"Yes," I answered, though that one word was the hardest thing I'd ever said. Dante flinched, as if he, too, wasn't expecting it.

"And nothing I say will change your mind."

It was a statement, not a question, but I shook my head all the same. "No," I managed. "I'm leaving. With or without you."

"All right." The words were so soft, I barely caught them. With a shaky breath, he let out a long sigh and looked up at me. "I'll come," he murmured, making my heart leap to my throat. "I don't like it, and I think this is a huge mistake but… you're my sister. I can't leave you to face this alone. I'm coming, too."

The breath exploded from my lungs in a rush. I'd hoped he would come, that he would choose family over Talon, but until this moment, I hadn't been certain. Crossing the room, I threw my arms around his neck and hugged him tightly. He held me a moment before gently pushing me away, looking embarrassed, anxious and slightly guilty all at once.

"Where are we meeting this rogue?"

"I don't know. He said he would call me later."

Dante nodded. "Better get packed, then," he said, averting his gaze. "I assume we'll want to take a few things before we're hunted all over creation."

Numb with relief, I nodded and walked toward the door, but his voice stopped me at the frame. "Ember," he said very somberly, and I turned. His eyes were troubled as they met mine. "You know what we're doing, right? How serious this is? This isn't like breaking curfew, or forgetting to call when we'll be late. This is treason. Once we go rogue, there's no turning back."

"I know," I said. "But we have to do this, Dante. If we don't go now, we'll never be free."

He didn't say anything to that, just turned away without a word, and I hurried to my room.

I threw on pants and a shirt over my ninja suit, not knowing if I would need to Shift and wanting to be ready if I did. Digging a backpack out of my closet, I began stuffing it with clothes. I threw in my hidden roll of cash and my little box of treasures, then noticed my phone sitting on the dresser, where I'd left it before going to see Riley. It blinked at me, indicating new messages had come through. I picked it up and switched on the screen.

Eight missed calls. All in the past twenty minutes. All from Garret.

My stomach turned over. After tonight, I wouldn't see him again. I wouldn't see any of my friends again. Lexi I'd planned to call later tonight, when we were well away from Crescent Beach, just to tell her goodbye, and to thank her for everything. For teaching me to surf, for encouraging me to pursue a boy I liked, for being a friend. I'd miss her, and I knew that a phone call was a sucky way to end things, but there was nothing else to be done.

But Garret…

I hit his name and held the phone to my ear. After two rings, someone picked up. "Hello."

I swallowed. "Hey, you."

There was a very long pause on his end, so long I thought we'd lost the connection or he'd hung up. "You still there?" I prodded.

"Where are you?"

His voice sounded strange, dull and flat. Had something happened with his dad? Was he upset that I hadn't been here when he called? "Home," I answered. "I was hanging out with a couple friends this evening and didn't bring my phone. Sorry."

"I need to talk to you," he went on, as if I hadn't said anything. "Will you meet me somewhere?" Another pause, and he added in an even softer voice, "It's important."

Now I hesitated. I had to meet Riley later tonight; as soon as he called to let us know where he was, we would leave Crescent Beach and not look back. But…this was the last time I would see Garret. I didn't want to just disappear on him, with no explanation of where I had gone. I wanted to say goodbye, at least.

And right then, standing in my room, listening to the voice that could make my heart soar, ache, jump and melt, a small part of me wished I was normal. If I was normal, if I was *human,* I could be with Garret. I wouldn't have dragonslayers kicking down my door, wanting to kill me. I wouldn't be standing here, feeling like the ground was opening under my feet, and I was seconds from plummeting into the void.

"I don't know, Garret," I whispered, my throat suddenly tight. "Now isn't really the best time."

"Please." His voice didn't change, but I caught a hint of desperation beneath the quiet surface. "It won't take long. Meet me at Lover's Bluff in twenty minutes. I just… I have to talk to you, tonight."

My phone buzzed before I could reply. I glanced quickly at the screen, my skin prickling as I saw an unfamiliar number. Riley.

"Ember?"

"All right," I said, putting the phone back to my ear. "Lover's Bluff, twenty minutes. I'll be there."

"Good." It was almost a whisper. "See you then."

I ended the call with Garret, and switched to the one coming in. "Riley?"

"Hey, Firebrand." The voice on the other end sounded tired. "We made it. Still planning to leave with us?"

I swallowed the lump in my throat. "Yes. And Dante is coming, as well."

"Oh, well, color me shocked. I didn't think you'd be able to convince him." Riley sounded reluctantly impressed and disappointed at the same time. "We're at Lone Rock Cove right now, back in the cave. Had to scare a couple potheads off the beach, but its empty now. Wes has a car waiting. We leave as soon as you and Dante get here."

"Give us an hour," I told him, ignoring the sudden gnawing guilt, the feeling that I was betraying him. "I… I want to say goodbye to a couple people first. It'll be fast."

"We can't wait too long, Firebrand," Riley said. "We'll be here, but come as quickly as you can."

"I will. See you soon."

Dante was standing in the doorway when I hung up and turned around. His backpack hung from his shoulders, a baseball cap perched on his head, and his face was solemn as he eyed the phone in my hand.

"Was that the rogue?"

I nodded. "They're at Lone Rock," I said, lowering my arm. "We have to meet up with them soon, but…"

Dante frowned. "But…?"

"Garret called." I slipped the phone into my jeans pocket. "He wants to meet with me, said that it was important. I said that I would meet him at Lover's Bluff in twenty minutes." I chewed my lip, torn in two directions. "We shouldn't keep Riley waiting, not with St. George still out there," I murmured. "I just wish I could see Garret one more time, say goodbye."

"Why don't you do that?" Dante said, surprising me. I blinked at him, and he shrugged. "The rogue isn't going anywhere," he said casually. "I'll go ahead to the cove, let him know that you're on the way. You should go talk to Garret."

"Dante." Still stunned, I could only stare at him. "I…are you sure?"

"Take the car," Dante insisted. "You'll get there faster. Don't worry about me—I'll catch a cab or have Calvin drive me up. But you should go." He shrugged, and a tiny smile crossed his face. "I know you liked that human. If it will make you feel less guilty, you should tell him goodbye."

I wanted to hug him again but didn't this time. Instead, I snatched my keys from where they sat on my desk, threw my pack over one shoulder and gave Dante one last, uncertain look.

"You're sure you're okay with this?"

"Yes. I'm fine."

"And you'll be at the cove when I get there, right?"

"Ember." Now he sounded impatient, though he wouldn't meet my eyes. "Just get going. I'll see you soon, I promise."

I nodded. "Tell Riley I won't be long."

Brushing past him, I hurried down the hall, out the front door and sprinted to the sedan waiting in the driveway. Tossing the backpack to the front seat, I hopped in and turned the key in the ignition, bringing the car to life. It had been a while since I'd driven, but I remembered how it worked, more or less.

Backing onto the road, I caught sight of Dante, watching me from the window, right before I hit the gas and sped off toward the bluff and Garret.

★ ★ ★

The tiny parking lot close to the bluff was deserted, except for a single black Jeep that I instantly recognized. By now, the sun had set, and a shimmering full moon was climbing into the sky. It was very quiet as I climbed out of the car, looking around for Garret. I didn't see him, but the sign pointing up the steps to Lover's Bluff was easily visible in the darkness.

My stomach fluttered. It wasn't long ago that I'd snuck out to meet Cobalt here and spent the night flying the waves with him. So much had happened since. Meeting Garret. Training with Lilith. Discovering things about the Vipers and Talon I wished I'd known earlier. Facing down St. George. Deciding to go rogue, leave everything I knew behind and not look back. Who could've guessed that one fateful meeting would lead to this?

Now, there was just one more thing I had to let go of. One last goodbye.

Taking a deep breath, I started up the narrow, twisty path to Lover's Bluff.

He was leaning against the railing with his back to the sky, the moonlight blazing down on him, as I climbed that final step. Silvery light glinted off his pale hair and washed over his lean form, dressed head to toe in black. His arms were crossed and his head was bowed, but I saw the gleam of gunmetal eyes as he spotted me and pushed himself off the railing.

A warning tickled the back of my brain as I crossed the flat rock toward the lone figure waiting at the edge of the cliff. Something about him seemed...wrong. This wasn't the same Garret I'd met before, the boy I'd kissed in the ocean, whose smile could turn my insides to mush. This was a cold, remote stranger, and my heart began to crash in my chest.

"Garret?" I asked softly, peering into his face as I got closer. His expression was blank, completely closed off. "I'm here. Are you all right?"

He didn't answer, but a flicker of anguish went through his eyes as he looked at me. He looked completely lost, then, like something horrible had happened, and he didn't know what to do. Worried, I stepped closer, and he stiffened, almost like he was…afraid of me. "Garret." Confused, I tried again, wanting him to talk, to tell me what was going on. We didn't have a lot of time. Seeing him now, even though he was acting so strange, made my throat ache with longing. He could never come with us; he could never be part of my world. And no matter my feelings, I knew better than to bring him into it. He would return to Chicago and live a normal life, free of genocidal dragon killers, shady organizations and Viper assassins hunting him down. The best thing I could do for him…was to let him go.

I just wished he would tell me what was going on.

"I'm glad you're here," I offered, feeling time slip further away from us. "I'm glad we could meet like this, because I have something to tell you, and I wanted to do it face-to-face." He continued to watch me, metallic eyes glimmering in the darkness, still giving nothing away. "I'm leaving," I said, and a tiny furrow creased his brow. Well, at least *that* got through to him. "Something came up," I continued, "and I have to get out of town. Tonight. Please don't ask what's going on, I can't tell you that. I just… I wanted to say goodbye."

Garret's expression went hard and cold. Without warning, he raised his arm, and pointed a dull black pistol at my face. The click of metal echoed loudly in the looming silence.

"You're not going anywhere."

# GARRET

The raid that evening had been disastrous.

Not only had our targets escaped, they had left chaos behind them. By the time the fire department arrived, the mansion had burned nearly to the ground, billowing black smoke into the evening sky. Of course, we'd vacated the premises long before anyone knew something was wrong, and no one had seen us enter or leave. But now, a smoldering ruin sat where a multimillion-dollar house once stood, three of my teammates had suffered major burns and there were two escaped dragons who could be anywhere at the moment.

And all of it could have been avoided, if I had done my job.

Because I'd hesitated. I'd seen Ember in the lair of my enemy, and I'd faltered, instead of gunning her down like I'd been taught. I'd seen her change and shift before my eyes, turn from the girl I'd known into one of the monsters. And, like all her kind, she was at her most dangerous cornered and trapped, and responded as all dragons would. With fire and savagery, giving her and her companion time to escape. Surprise was always our best weapon; now that the dragons knew we were here, they would become even harder to track down. We could lose our quarry forever.

And it was all on me.

No one said anything about my failure on the ride back. Stunned, wounded, furious soldiers filled the van, smelling of smoke and burned armor, but no one blamed me. When our livid commander demanded to know what had happened, we took the blame and the dressing-down as a unit. Not even Tristan, whom we met back at the safe house, could guess the truth.

But I knew the real reason we'd failed. And I knew something no one else did.

Ember Hill *was* the sleeper.

Ember, the girl I'd kissed in my bedroom, who'd made me wonder what a normal life was like, who had been on my mind every single day from the time we met, was the enemy.

And now, I had to kill her.

I wasn't sure what I'd been thinking, calling her so many times, hoping and dreading she'd pick up. What I should have done was tell the captain immediately, reveal her identity, where she lived, where we could find her. If Ember was the sleeper, that meant her brother was likely a dragon, as well. There might be numerous dragons in Crescent Beach, not just the pair they'd been tracking. It was my duty to tell the Order everything I knew.

But I couldn't do it. Not yet. Though I didn't know *what* I was going to do. Especially when she called me back. Hearing her voice, familiar and strange at the same time, I'd frozen up. What did I want? To talk? To demand she explain what I already knew? She was a dragon. I was St. George. What was left to discuss?

"Meet me at Lover's Bluff in twenty minutes," I heard myself saying. It was a good spot to do what had to be done—isolated yet fairly close to where we were now. No one would hear the gunshots, or the screams of a dying dragon. And she agreed, though it was fairly obvious she was in a hurry. Planning to leave town, most likely. But when she promised to meet me there, alone, I believed her.

After we hung up, I stood there for a moment, debating with myself. The smart thing would be to tell Tristan, have him back me up. The smarter thing would be to inform my captain where this meeting would take place, and have the whole squad ready to take down a known dragon when she finally showed.

I went alone. I didn't tell anyone where I was going, not even Tristan. He would have stopped me if he knew. Going after a dragon yourself, with no partner and no backup, was strictly forbidden by the Order. It was crazy, risky and stupid, but I wasn't thinking rationally at that moment. I just took the Jeep and drove away. To a lonely bluff in the middle of nowhere, to meet a dragon, alone.

"Garret?"

At the sight of the gun, Ember's eyes went huge. Frozen, she stared at me over the muzzle of the Glock, more confused than fearful, pleading for an explanation. I ignored her questioning look, ignored the trembling in my other arm, and kept the pistol aimed right between her eyes.

*Pull the trigger, Garret.*

The Perfect Soldier's voice echoed coldly in my head. *Kill her. She's a dragon, and this is your duty. This is what you were sent to do.*

"Garret, what are you doing?" Ember stared at me, her eyes glimmering with hurt, betrayal. "Why..."

She trailed off, the blood draining from her face. I saw the moment where everything clicked in her head, the confusion shifting to horror as she realized. The broken whisper that followed made my stomach clench. It was an accusation, a cry of despair and a plea that this was a terrible mistake, all at once.

"You…you're St. George."

She took one staggering step away from me, stopping as I pressed forward, her face going blank. I forced myself to speak, my voice soft and cold, a sharp contrast to the swirling chaos inside. "Where are the others?"

Green eyes flashed, and she raised her chin. I followed the tiny movement with the gun, keeping the muzzle level with her face. She set her jaw and remained silent. "Tell me," I insisted. "Now. I *will* shoot you if you don't."

"You'll shoot me, anyway," Ember retorted, and now I heard the rage in her voice, the furious betrayal. "That's what you've been after all this time, isn't it? You're with St. George, and you came here to kill us." Her voice trembled, and she swallowed hard. "That's why you were so interested. That's why you hung around. Everything we did, everything you told me—it was all a lie."

*Not everything.* My other hand was shaking violently, and I clenched my fist, trying to calm myself. This was it, the end of the mission. I had to focus. I couldn't let myself think of those "everything" moments. Slow dancing, surfing on one board, riding the Ferris wheel with her beside me, not wanting to be anywhere else.

Kissing her in the ocean and feeling my entire world stop. Wishing I could be normal, if only to be with her. Because she hadn't just taught me how to surf and shoot zombies and to scream while plunging down a roller-coaster drop. She had shown me how to live.

Ember was still staring at me over the pistol, her gaze defiant. "Go on, then," she whispered, and I saw she was shaking, as well. "Shoot me. I'm not telling you where the others are so you can kill them, too."

*Do it.* The soldier's voice returned, and I took a deep breath, straightening my arm. The gun sight hovered at her forehead; it would take only one tiny motion to end this. *She's a dragon, and this is what you were sent for. Why are you hesitating? Kill her now!*

I set my jaw, my finger tightening around the trigger. Ember still watched me, unwavering, but for the first time since I'd known her, I saw a tear slip from her eye, crawling down her face. It gleamed in the moonlight, punching a hole right through my stomach, and the hand that held the gun started to shake.

*I… I can't.*

I relaxed, not lowering the pistol, but everything inside me slumped in defeat. *I can't do it. I can't kill her.* Stunned, I stared at her over the weapon, at the girl I knew was a dragon, knew was the enemy.

And I couldn't kill her.

Dazed, I let my gaze drop, my focus wavering for just a moment.

As Ember moved.

In the split second before I would've lowered my arm, the girl lunged, crossing the space between us in a blink. My attention jerked immediately to the danger, but by that time, Ember hit my arm from below, forcing my wrist and the pistol skyward, wrenching it from my grip. Stunned, my body still reacted on instinct, even when my mind was elsewhere. As the weapon was stripped from my grasp, I lashed out with a kick, striking the hand that held the gun as Ember drew back. The pistol was hurled away, skittering over the rocks, and came to rest a few feet from the edge of the cliff.

Unarmed, Ember backed up, eyes glowing with an eerie, ominous light. I saw the air around her ripple, felt the shift of energy between us, and spun, hurling myself at my weapon. Behind me, there was a soundless explosion, an enraged snarl rang out, turning my blood to ice. Diving for the edge of the cliff, I snatched up the gun, whirled around—

—and felt the breath explode from my lungs as something big and red slammed into me, knocking me off my feet. I hit the ground on my back, seeing snarling fangs, wings and crimson scales fill my vision, and brought the gun up for one last, desperate shot.

A clawed foot hit my elbow, forcing it to the ground. Another struck my chest, sinking curved talons into my shirt, as five hundred pounds of hissing, furious red dragon landed on me, pinning me down. Hot wind blasted me, whipping at my hair, as the monster bared its fangs and roared in my face.

I slumped, the gun dropping from my nerveless fingers. I couldn't move; the dragon had my weapon arm pinned, its whole weight pressing me down. I could feel its claws pricking my chest through my shirt, though they hadn't sunk in all the way. Its breath fanned over my face, smelling of smoke and ash, and the narrow jaw, filled with lethal, razor-sharp teeth, hovered inches from my throat. Briefly, I wondered how it would kill me. Would it rip me apart, sink those claws into my chest, tear out my throat? Or would those jaws open all the way and blast me with dragonfire?

But the dragon didn't do any of those things. I'd been holding my breath, waiting for the pain of being torn apart or incinerated, but it only stood there, front claws pinning me down, just watching. As if it couldn't decide what to do with me. I looked up, past the jaws and teeth and flaring nostrils, and met its gaze.

Its eyes were the same emerald green, bright and intense, though they were slitted and reptilian now. Very inhuman. Its wings were flared to either side for balance, leathery membranes casting a dark shadow over us both.

"What are you waiting for?" I gritted out, making the dragon blink. I sucked in a breath, my lungs flattened and abused from the huge creature on top of them. I wanted this done. I'd lost this battle, and the price for failure was death, like everyone in the Order. Fate, it seemed, had finally caught up. "Stop toying with me," I panted, glaring at the creature overhead. "Just get it over with."

The dragon's eyes narrowed. Shifting its weight, it drew its muzzle back, nostrils flaring, and I turned my head, bracing myself for the sheet of dragonfire, hoping it would be quick.

The dragon's head snaked forward, and I flinched despite myself. But those deadly jaws went for my arm, for the hand that once held the gun, and closed over the muzzle of the pistol. Raising its head, the dragon gave an almost disgusted snort and hurled the gun away, where it sailed over the railing, glinted once in the moonlight and dropped into the ocean far below.

As I watched my weapon vanish over the edge of the cliff, the weight on my chest and arm disappeared. The dragon reared onto its hindquarters, flaring its wings, and backed away. Stunned, I levered myself to my elbows, watching it retreat, wondering if this was some sort of trick. If it was just toying with me further.

The dragon closed its eyes. Its form shimmered, rippled like a mirage and began to shrink. It grew smaller and smaller, wings disappearing, scales and claws melting away, until I was staring at Ember once more. She wore a dark suit that hugged her body like a second skin, outlining her deceitfully slender form. Her green eyes shone as she gazed down at me.

I didn't move. I was unarmed, and the slight girl standing over me was just as dangerous as she had been a moment ago. It would take half a second for her to pounce on me again and tear me apart. But she didn't move, either, just continued to watch me with sad, angry green eyes, and slowly, my muscles began to unclench. The thought was ludicrous but… it seemed this dragon, the target I'd been sent to kill, the girl I'd pursued with the intent to destroy, was going to let me go.

*No,* the Perfect Soldier protested. *Don't believe it. That's insane. Dragons don't show mercy, not to us.* But what else could I believe? I'd been helpless a second ago, pinned under a creature three times my weight. One breath, one slash, would've ended my life. I didn't know why it hadn't. I was a soldier of St. George. It should have killed me just for that.

Looking up, I met the gaze of my enemy and muttered a single word, my voice coming out raspy and harsh. "Why?"

She took a deep, shaky breath. "If you have to ask that," she whispered, glaring at me, "then you don't know me as well as you think." She paused, then added in an even softer voice, "You don't know *us* as well as you think."

"Ember…"

"Goodbye, Garret." Ember stepped back, her eyes hard. "Don't follow me. Don't come near me. If I see you or anyone else from St. George again, I won't hold back. Stay the hell away from us."

Turning, she fled barefoot across the rock without looking back, reached the stairs on the other side and was gone.

★ ★ ★

Alone, I dragged myself to my feet, feeling like I'd been sucker-punched in the head, and leaned against the railing. The ocean breeze tugged at my hair, cooling my heated skin, as I closed my eyes and tried to make sense of what had just happened.

I was still alive. I'd met a dragon, alone, fought it without any backup, lost and… I was still alive. I put a hand to my chest, feeling something warm seep through my shirt. My fingers came away red and sticky from where the dragon had dug its claws into my skin, but it could've done worse. It could've ripped me open like a paper sack. Charred the skin from my bones with a single blast of flame. But it hadn't. It—*she*—had let me go.

*You don't know* us *as well as you think.*

"We've been wrong," I whispered. It killed me to say it, to finally realize, after years of believing dragons were evil, could only *be* evil, but tonight's encounter left no room for doubt. Dragons, at least *some* dragons, weren't the vicious, calculating monsters we'd thought. Not all dragons hated mankind. If they did, I wouldn't be standing here, feeling like the world had been tipped on its head. I'd been wrong, and the Order had been wrong. Ember had *known* I was St. George, that I was her greatest enemy, and she'd spared my life.

In a daze, I stumbled back to the parking lot, my mind spinning. What did I do now? Return to the Order? Rejoin the war as if nothing had happened? As if hunting down and killing more dragons wouldn't remind me of *her,* and what I learned here tonight?

As I reached my Jeep, still unsure of my next move, my phone buzzed. I pulled it out, wincing as Tristan's number blinked across the screen. I'd already ignored one call from him, but I couldn't ignore him forever.

Sighing, I put the phone to my ear. "Where are you, Tristan?"

"Where am *I?*" the furious voice on the other side answered. "Where the fuck are you? What the hell do you think you're doing? If the captain finds out you ran out like that, you'll be lucky to get fifty lashes in front of the whole squad."

"I…had to think."

"Well, get your damn head back in the game, partner. We've got orders. Where are you?"

"I'm coming back now."

"No, I'm already moving. Meet me at the corner of Palm and Main. I'll explain everything then. St. Anthony, out."

Seconds after I arrived at the rendezvous point, a white van screeched to a stop at the curb, and Tristan flung open the door. "Come on," he ordered, and I obeyed, sliding into the passenger seat. Tristan hit the gas almost before I closed the door, and we sped out of the lot.

"What's going on?" I asked, snapping the seat belt into place. Tristan flashed me an exasperated glare and shook his head.

"New orders," he said, gunning the engine and speeding through an aging yellow light. "Headquarters wasn't pleased when they heard about the raid. There's not much time before the targets leave town and drop off the grid again. But we know one of them is injured, and will probably have to hole up for a few hours, at least. They're sending out all available soldiers to search every potential bug-out spot, cave or abandoned building. Any place these dragons could hide."

"Is that what we're doing?" I asked, clenching my fist against my leg. Tristan shook his head.

"No. We have a special mission." He nodded to the dashboard, where his laptop lay open between us. On the computer screen, a blinking red dot was moving through a grid of streets, toward the ocean. "That's our target. Ember Hill."

My stomach twisted violently. I forced myself to speak, to remain calm. "Why her?"

"We don't have any idea where the other targets could be," Tristan said, glancing at the computer screen, following the dot as it moved swiftly across the map. "Right now, she's our best and only suspect. When you were at the carnival with her that day, I went to her house and put a tracking device on her car, so we could follow her if she went anywhere suspicious. When I received orders tonight, I knew exactly how to find her." He tapped the computer screen with a grim smile. "It sure looks like she's on the run, doesn't it? If we're lucky, she'll lead us right to the other targets."

The walls of the vehicle were closing in, and the seat belt felt suffocatingly tight. I stared at the red blip on the screen, willing it to stop, to turn around and head back home. It didn't. It sped unerringly toward the ocean and the edge of town, driving me closer to a looming, inevitable choice.

# RILEY

*Where was she?*

I stood on the beach facing the ocean, the cliff wall at my back, waiting for her. My ribs throbbed; Wes had patched me up as best he could, the bandages tight around my waist, but it was still painful as hell. Remy and Nettle were hunkered down in the cave behind me, and I'd told them not to leave, not to show themselves, until I gave the word to move out. Wes had already taken the car to a safe location, and was waiting for my call to return and pick us up. It was better that way, in case there was trouble. I was taking a huge risk myself, standing in the open like this, wounded and knowing St. George was still out there, searching for us. But I couldn't risk not seeing Ember when she came. If she came. From our last phone call, she should've been here by now.

*What if she doesn't come?*

She'll be here, I told myself. I had to believe that. St. George was probably scouring Crescent Beach for dragons, that twin of hers would be reluctant to turn rogue and Ember herself had grown to love this town and everything in it, but I had to believe that my fiery hatchling would keep her promise and return. Because I was one hundred percent positive I couldn't leave without her.

*This is stupid, Cobalt. What's happened to you? You're acting like those weak-willed humans you always made fun of. You're acting like a sap who's fallen in love.*

I snorted. Love. That was ridiculous. Dragons didn't love. Living things, anyway. Gold, wealth, power, influence—*those* we loved. Even dragons out of Talon were drawn to shiny things and treasure. It wasn't the same. I'd seen plenty of humans "in love." It was messy and annoying and complicated. What I felt toward Ember…that was pure instinct, something as natural as flying or breathing fire. I didn't know what this was quite yet, but I knew it was something far purer than the mortal's definition of *love.* Muddled human emotions had nothing to do with it.

"Riley!"

My heart didn't jump as much as it sagged in utter relief. All my senses came to life again, sending heat through my veins, as Ember sprinted over the sand in her black Viper suit and threw herself against me.

I grunted, the impact sending a sharp twinge through my middle, but it was almost instantly forgotten. Ember was shaking, gasping for breath, her hands clenched in my shirt. Alarmed, my arms tightened around her. "Firebrand? You okay?"

No answer, just a noise that sounded half growl, half sob, and my alarm grew. "Hey, look at me," I said, pulling back, though not enough to let her go. "What happened? What's wrong?"

"St. George," she whispered, and I couldn't tell if she was grief-stricken, terrified or really, really pissed. "He's one of them, Riley. Garret is part of St. George."

"Shit." This day was getting better and better. "Did he

hurt you?" I asked, swearing that if I ever saw that human again, I would fry him to cinders. "Are you all right?"

"I'm… I'm fine." She pulled away, raking hair from her eyes, and gazed around the beach. "Where's Dante?"

I frowned. "I thought he was coming with you."

"We split up. He said he would meet me here…" Ember broke off, walking a little ways down the beach, searching. "Where is he?" Her eyes, her stance, everything, was hopeful, and I sighed, hating what I had to do next.

"Firebrand," I said as gently as I could, walking up behind her. "He's not coming. I've seen his kind before. If he hasn't sold us out to Talon by now, I'd be surprised. We have to go now, before Talon or St. George finds us."

"No." She spun on me, eyes flashing. "You don't know him. He'll come. He'll be here, he promised he would."

"Talon has him now." I shook my head sadly. "He's theirs, Ember. He'll betray his own blood if the organization tells him to."

"He's my brother, dammit!" She glared at me, both the dragon and the human girl of one mind. Both stubbornly resolved. "You're wrong," she insisted. "I'm not leaving him. Something might've come up, slowed him down. We have to wait a little longer. He'll be here."

"No, hatchling," purred a new voice, one that turned my blood to ice. "I'm afraid he will not."

# EMBER

"Lilith," Riley growled, backing away, as my trainer, Scary Talon Lady herself, sauntered toward us. She was dressed like me, a tight black suit hugging her slender body, her blond hair pulled behind her. Her "work" outfit. My breath seized up with the implication.

"Where's Dante?" I demanded, suddenly terrified. "What have you done to him? If you've hurt him, I swear—"

"Don't worry, my dear." Lilith smiled at me, evil and predatory. "Your brother is fine. He's at home, in fact, waiting for me to bring you back to the fold."

Riley swore. I looked at him, then at Lilith, confused. "I don't understand."

"Dante informed me where you'd be tonight," the Viper went on. "He said you had been coerced by a rogue dragon that had been hanging around the area, telling all kinds of nasty lies about the organization. He was very concerned about your state of mind, so he contacted me. Smart boy. He knows where his loyalties lie." Lilith gave me a mock-sorrowful look. "You, however, hatchling, I am *very* disappointed in you."

"You're lying," I breathed, shaking my head. "Dante wouldn't sell me out."

"Sell you out?" Lilith sounded shocked. "He saved you, hatchling. Because of him, I can bring you back to the organization tonight. Because of his actions, you won't be leaving with this traitor, and I won't have to kill you for collaborating with a known rogue."

"What about Riley?"

"Riley?" Lilith frowned a moment, then turned to him with an evil smile. "Is that what you're calling yourself these days, Cobalt? How very…human. Setting your sights a little high with my dear protégée, aren't we? You should've known I would find you eventually."

"Ember, run," Riley growled, every muscle in his body coiled for a fight. "Don't worry about me. Just get out of here, now."

"Stay where you are," Lilith ordered, her voice sharp and cold. "When I'm finished here, we are returning to the organization, where you belong. And you will wait right there until I am done. This won't take long." She flexed her nails, smiling a vicious, demonic smile. "But I suggest you turn around now, hatchling, and close your eyes. You probably don't want to see this."

*She's really going to kill him.* I glanced at Riley, and he gave me a small, resigned nod that made my stomach clench. Whatever I did, whatever I chose, he understood. If I went back to Talon, he wouldn't fault me, but he wouldn't run, either. He couldn't beat Lilith, especially wounded, but he would fight for me, for Nettle and Remy and Wes, and all his other rogues. He would fight Talon's best Viper to give them a shot at freedom.

I swallowed my fear and stepped away from Lilith, backing up to face her with Riley. "No," I said, making her eyebrows arch. "You want him, you'll have to kill me, too."

Lilith smiled.

"How unfortunate," she mused, taking one step back herself. "I was hoping you would see reason tonight, but I see that Cobalt has polluted your mind beyond repair. Very well." Her eyes began to glow, an ominous, poison green. "If your choice is to turn your back on Talon and side with these criminals, that makes you a traitor, as well. So, now you can die with them!"

And she surged into the air, almost faster than I could see, rising up to engulf us in her shadow. Her wings spread to either side, huge green membranes fanning the air, making me feel tiny, insignificant. An arrow-shaped skull rose on a long, snaking neck, spines bristling down her back to the slender, lashing tail. Slitted eyes glared down at us, eager and merciless, as twenty feet of full-grown, venomous green adult dragon screamed a terrifying battle cry and pounced.

Already in dragon form, Cobalt lunged in front of me, snarling a challenge as the adult twice his size bore down on him. Sand flew as Lilith's arrow-shaped head darted forward, terrifyingly quick, snapping at Cobalt's neck. The rogue twisted aside, wings and tail beating the air, and struck out with his claws. His talons raked along the poison-green scales of his enemy but didn't pierce through, and Lilith spun, hissing like a furious snake. Moving insanely fast, she came at him again, lashing out with a flurry of claws and fangs, giving him no time to recover. Snarling, Cobalt was driven back toward the ocean, trying to avoid the savage whirlwind of strikes, but he stumbled, and Lilith reacted instantly. Her talons scored a nasty hit along his shoulder, the blow almost too quick to see. Blood spattered the sand in vivid red drops, and Cobalt howled in pain.

But she had forgotten about me.

Sprinting through the sand, I leaped at my former trainer, Shifting in midair, intending to land on her back in full dragon form and sink my claws into her neck. But as I left the ground, her tail came up, whipping through the air and smashing me aside. I hit the sand, and she immediately turned and pounced, sinking curved claws into my side, pinning my wings down. She was *so fast.* It was like battling a snake, a huge, intelligent snake with claws and wings and lashing tail. I shrieked as her weight crushed my wings and her talons pierced through my scales, drawing blood.

With a roar, Cobalt hit her from the side, golden eyes blazing and furious. Claws flashing, he would've raked her open from spine to belly if she hadn't moved, releasing me in an instant and leaping back. Growling, the blue dragon placed himself between me and the Viper, wings partially open, muzzle pulled back to show his fangs.

I struggled to my feet, wincing, as the Viper chuckled, the sibilant noise making my skin crawl. "Well, well," she hissed in Draconic, circling us in the sand. She moved like a shark, lithe and graceful, and we circled with her warily. "A bit overprotective, aren't we, Cobalt? Aren't you even the slightest concerned my student is going to stab you in the back? After all, she was handpicked by the Elder Wyrm to become a Viper."

"Don't listen to her," I snarled, glaring as Lilith continued to stalk. "She's just trying to throw you off balance, get you to lower your guard. She does that." Facing my former trainer, I curled my lip in a sneer. "You already showed me that trick, remember? I'm not falling for it again."

The Viper laughed. "Well, it's good to know my lessons haven't completely gone to waste," she said, regarding us coolly. "But I think I'm done toying with you now." Her acidlike gaze fastened on me. "Hatchling, this is your final chance. You would be an amazing Viper—it's in your blood. You and your brother were destined for greatness from the beginning. But you're throwing it all away if you stay with this traitor." Her voice dropped, becoming low and soothing. "Return with me, and all is forgiven. You can come back to Talon, and everything will be as it should. You and your brother will never be separated, I can promise you that."

*Dante.* I hesitated, and Lilith smiled. "Yes, hatchling. He's waiting for you at home. Forget this insanity and come back to us. You can't fight Talon. Dante knows this. It's time you accepted that, as well."

I curled a lip. "And all the dragons who didn't fit Talon's standards? The female breeders and the undesirables? Have *they* accepted it, too?"

"That is no concern of yours." Her eyes narrowed, and her voice changed, becoming ugly as she lowered her head. "I am growing impatient, hatchling," she warned. "Continue this fight and you will die. I will destroy you, Cobalt and those pathetic hatchlings hiding in that cave." Cobalt jerked up at this, and the Viper smiled. "Did you think I was unaware of those disgusting weaklings? No, I will show no mercy to traitors, hatchlings or not. They will die, and you will share their fate as I tear them limb from limb, making certain they suffer every moment of it. I will skin them alive, crush them in my jaws and bring their shattered bones back to the organization as a reminder of what will happen to those who betray us."

Cobalt roared, baring his fangs. "Heartless bitch!" he snarled, flames licking at his teeth in rage. "You won't touch them. I'll kill you first!"

He lunged at the Viper with his jaws gaping wide, going for that long, graceful neck, now temptingly close to the ground. Lilith grinned, and I realized too late that's what she wanted. As Cobalt went for her throat, her head darted back, quick as a snake, and his jaws snapped shut on empty air. Lilith half reared, wings snapping out for balance, and drove the full weight of her body onto the smaller rogue, crushing him to the sand. I saw Cobalt's head and neck snap up, a breathless cry escaping him, before he dropped motionless to the ground. His wings flapped once and went still.

With a shriek, I hurled myself at the Viper, not knowing what I would do, only wanting her away from Cobalt. Lilith stepped over the fallen rogue to meet me, fangs bared in an eager, bloodthirsty smile. Snarling, I raked at her; she dodged aside, smirking. I went for her again, snapping at a foreleg, hoping a broken bone would slow her down. She whipped it out of my reach and flung a stinging backclaw across my muzzle, making my eyes water. My temper snapped, and I leaped at her with a scream, intending to claw and shred and bite until there was nothing left but a pile of bones and scales.

The Viper met me midspring, driving her horned head into my stomach and chest. It felt like I'd been hit by a speeding Mac truck and, without my chest plates and armor, probably would've snapped every rib in my body. Nevertheless, the air left my lungs in a painful explosion, and I was flung backward, hitting the sand at the water's edge and rolling several feet in a tangle of wings and tail. Dazed, gasping for breath, I felt a stinging pain in my hind leg as the Viper's talons closed around my ankle. Snarling, I tried getting up, but fell back as she dragged me through the sand, turned and hurled me away a second time. The world went upside down for a dizzying moment, just before I slammed into the lone rock with enough force to nearly knock me out.

I crumpled to the sand with a gasp, blackness hovering around my vision like fuzzy clouds. The world still spun frantically, and there was a fiery ache in my side where I'd hit the boulder. I tried getting to my feet, but my legs gave out and I slumped back with a hiss of pain.

"That's it?" The Viper's voice echoed weirdly in my head, hollow and ringing, but still amused and smug as hell. Through my darkening vision, I saw the deadly green dragon prowling up the beach toward me, her eyes glowing in the shadows. "That's all the fight you have, hatchling?" she crooned in Draconic. "Perhaps I've underestimated you, after all."

Gritting my teeth, I pulled myself around the boulder, my tail and wings dragging behind me. My claws slipped through the loose sand, making progress difficult, and pain flared through my side. Panting in fear, I heard the Viper's approach, getting ever closer, and I clawed frantically at the ground.

"Running away now?" Lilith called. "You should know you can't escape me. Give up, little hatchling. Let me kill you now, and I'll make it quick."

Hugging the boulder, I tried to be calm as the killer dragon's footsteps shushed through the sand on the other side of the rock. "What pathetic little prey you are," she mused, dangerously close. "I am quite disappointed indeed."

I took a deep breath and felt the heat in my lungs ignite.

*Dragons are never prey,* I thought as a long neck snaked over the rock, the arrow-shaped head smiling down at me. *Dragons are always predators.*

"There you are," Lilith purred. "I see you, hatchling."

I raised my head and blasted the Viper above me with fire. Flames couldn't hurt us, of course, as our scales were fireproof, but the sudden explosion caused her to snort and flinch away. Surging upright, I leaped to the top of Lone Rock and hurled myself at the Viper's back.

I hit her side, between wing joints and neck, sinking my talons into her scales to stay on. Her spines poked at me as I clawed and scrabbled for a better grip, raking and snapping as best I could. Lilith hissed and spun, bucking wildly, but I clung to her with the last of my strength. Biting down hard, I felt the sharp tang of blood fill my mouth, and Lilith screamed in fury.

Her long neck whipped around, jaws closing on a wing joint, ripping me from her back. I dangled in the air a moment, before she reared up and flung me to the ground, hard. I landed on my stomach, and before I could move, one clawed forepaw pinned me down, and another fastened around my throat. Claws sank into my skin, pricking me through my scales. I gagged and looked back into the face of the Viper, who was no longer smiling.

"Now you've annoyed me," she growled as I struggled desperately, clawing at the sand beneath me, whipping my tail. It was no use. She was too big. "Don't worry, my dear.

I'll make it quick. Once I tear your throat out, you won't feel a thing."

Her claws tightened, digging into my throat, drawing blood. I thrashed frantically, beating my wings, but I couldn't move the murderous dragon holding me down. "A shame, really," Lilith said, shifting her weight to a better position. "You had so much potential. I suppose we'll have to rely on Dante now."

Dante? "Wait," I choked, feeling the claws loosen the tiniest bit. "What do you want with Dante?"

Lilith smiled once more. "That is not your concern any longer, hatchling," she said, and squeezed my throat again, making my world erupt with pain. "Because in a few moments, you won't be alive. Now, why don't you go ahead and die like a good dragon? It's what Talon would want."

Her claws pierced my neck, sinking through scales, and I knew this time they wouldn't stop. I closed my eyes and braced myself for the end, hoping it would be as painless as Lilith said.

Shots rang out behind us.

# GARRET

"There's her car."

Tristan yanked the van off the road, pulling to a stop behind a familiar white sedan on the shoulder before killing the engine. I stared out the window, fighting a sickening sense of dread. There were no landmarks out here, just an empty road, sand and rock, but I recognized this place. I knew what lay beyond the narrow, nearly invisible trail snaking off toward the cliffs. Lone Rock Cove, the place where I met Ember for the first time.

"She's probably down in the cove. Come on." Tristan stepped out and slid open the door to the backseat, where his rifle lay nestled in its case on the floor. Picking up his gun, he swung it to one shoulder and handed me an M-4 as I stepped around the front. I took it numbly, trying to clear my thoughts, to decide what I was going to do. I couldn't kill Ember, and I couldn't go against the Order. I was trapped between two impossible choices.

"What's the plan?" I heard myself ask.

Tristan shoved a 9 mm into a side holster, first checking the cartridge to make sure the gun was loaded. "We scout the area, see where the suspect is, what she's doing and, if necessary, hold position until the team arrives. If she is here, my guess is she'll be in that cave on the beach." He eyed my civilian attire, as I'd left my vest and uniform behind when I went to meet Ember, and frowned. "That's not going to be much protection against dragonfire, partner. If we do get into a fight, be careful."

Without waiting for an answer, he turned and began making his way toward the cliffs, moving quickly over the rocks and sand. I hesitated a moment, then followed, the sick feeling in my stomach growing stronger the closer we got to the cove.

Tristan disdained to take the path between rocky walls that would lead to the beach, instead seeking out the high ground at the top of the cliff. Lying down near the edge, he peered through a pair of night-vision goggles, while I knelt and waited uneasily behind him, desperately hoping she wouldn't be there.

"Bingo," Tristan breathed, and my heart sank. He motioned me forward, holding out the binoculars. Feeling like my chest was squeezed in a vise, I took the goggles from him and gazed over the edge.

The cove was already well lit from the enormous silver moon directly overhead, so it was easy to spot the three figures in the sand along the water's edge. Ember I recognized immediately, causing my heart to thud against my ribs. She was with the young man I'd seen at Kristin's party, the boy who'd danced with her and fought off Colin's friends with us. They were both talking to a slight, slender woman in the same black bodysuit that Ember wore. I couldn't see their faces very well, but by Ember's posture and quick, angry movements, it looked like they were in a heated argument.

"Well, we found her, and some of her friends," Tristan

muttered, taking the goggles back to stare through them again. "All human, for now, anyway. I wonder if she's going to do anything interesting—"

She didn't, but at that moment, the woman surged up in the blink of an eye, making my stomach leap into my throat. I tensed, hardly believing my eyes, as a monstrous adult dragon unfurled dark leathery wings and shook the cliffs with her roar.

"Shit!" Tristan scrambled back from the edge. "Well, that answers my question, doesn't it? Looks like the girl was our sleeper all along!" I didn't answer, unable to tear my gaze from the scene below. I watched the green dragon lunge at Ember with teeth bared, watched the boy shift into the blue dragon from earlier that night and attack the much larger adult.

"We found them." Tristan's voice rang with urgency as he spoke into his phone. "Three targets, Lone Rock Cove. One of them is an adult. Should we hold position until the squad arrives?" He paused, listening, as my heart beat faster with alarm. "Understood."

I spared one more glance at the battle below. Ember, now in her true form, leaped at the adult's back, but was smashed aside by the green dragon's long, whiplike tail. My heart skipped a beat as she flew back, tumbling to the sand, and the huge adult pounced on her viciously. My insides seized up, but the blue dragon lunged in with a roar, driving her away, allowing me to breathe again. But it was obvious they were both outmatched. The adult was bigger, faster and more vicious than either of them. If I went down there now, I would be a traitor to my Order. But if I stayed here, Ember could die.

"Yes, sir. St. Anthony, out." Tristan put away the phone and took the rifle from his shoulder, lying on his stomach at the edge of the cliff. My heart lurched as he lowered the gun and gazed through the sight, pointing it at the three dragons below.

"What are you doing? I thought we were waiting for the rest of the squad."

"Change of plans," Tristan muttered without looking up. "I told headquarters the three targets are on the move. They want me to take down as many as I can before they have a chance to fly off. This might be our only opportunity."

A cold fist seized my gut. "That's against protocol. There're only two of us and three of them, one of which is an adult. We need the whole squad to fight it."

"Don't worry." Tristan smiled, his finger sliding around the trigger. "I can take out the hatchlings before they even know what's happening. This was our mission, Garret. We can't let them get away. If we can bring down even one, it'll be a victory. Now, shut up and let me kill a dragon."

I spared one last glance at the fight below. The adult was circling the other two like a wolf, lashing its tail against its flanks as they crouched in the center, watching it. Both looked hurt, while the green dragon was obviously playing with them.

"Stop moving," Tristan breathed, his entire focus on his targets. "Just for a second." The adult paused, giving him a clear view of the two hatchlings, and Tristan smiled. "Yes."

I made my decision.

I lunged, grabbing the barrel and forcing it down, just as a shot rang out. At the same moment, a shriek of pain rose from the beach, making my heart clench, thinking one of the dragons had been hit. But that wasn't the case. The adult had reared up and crushed the smaller blue one into the sand,

and the dragon's scream had masked the gun retort. They hadn't noticed us yet.

But Tristan whirled on me, eyes blazing. "Garret, what the hell?" he snarled, trying to yank the gun back. I held on and refused to relent. "Are you crazy! What are you doing?"

"I can't let you do this."

He stared at me like I'd spoken Swahili. "These are orders," he finally snapped. "I'm doing my job, what the captain told me to do."

"The Order is wrong," I said. His face blanched, and he gaped at me like he didn't know who I was. "This is wrong, Tristan. Dragons aren't completely evil. Some of them are just trying to get by. We don't have to slaughter them wholesale."

"What the hell are you talking about?" Tristan finally yanked the gun away and surged to his feet, his eyes wide. I followed, muscles tensing, as my partner staggered back, shaking his head. "Garret, you can't be serious. They'll kill you."

"I don't care." I stood with my back to the cliff, hearing the roars and cries of the dragons behind me, and faced my partner's accusing gaze. "I'm not letting you shoot them, Tristan. If you want to kill them, you'll have to get past me."

For a moment, he stared at me, disbelieving. For a moment, I thought he would let this go. But then, I saw the instant his expression changed, cold anger and loathing flashing through his eyes, before he went for his sidearm.

I was already moving, grabbing his wrist as the pistol came up, forcing the muzzle away from me. Tristan dropped his rifle and lashed out with his other arm, throwing a fist at my temple. I raised an arm to block it, then brought my knee up, striking him in the stomach. He grunted and bent forward; I wrenched the gun from his hand and brought it smashing down to his skull, hitting him right behind the ear. Tristan crumpled forward, collapsing to the rocky ground, and didn't move.

Stepping over my unconscious partner, not daring to think about what I'd just done, I grabbed my M-4 and ran for the beach, the roars of desperate dragons ringing out behind me.

# EMBER

I opened my eyes as gunfire boomed over the sand. Lilith shrieked, and the weight pinning me down vanished, the claws around my throat jerking away.

Panting, I rolled to my side, staring in amazement. Lilith was backing toward the ocean, shaking her head, blood and sparks erupting along her side and armored chest. Walking down the beach toward us, his gun level and firing short, controlled shots as he came, was *Garret.*

At the sight of her most hated enemy, the Viper screamed. Opening her jaws, she sent a line of dragonfire roaring at the human coming toward us, and Garret dove away before the flames could engulf him. Rolling to his knees, he fired at her again, but Lilith was already moving. Lightning fast, she darted to one side, then the other, racing in a zigzag pattern up the beach. The soldier tried following her with the gun, but her quick, frantic movements were difficult to track, and she drew ever closer to the lone human, jaws gaping to bite him in two. Horrified, I struggled to my feet, shouting a warning to Garret, knowing I'd never reach them in time.

And then, a scaly blue body flew at her from the side and slammed into her ribs, knocking her off balance. Lilith stumbled and nearly fell as Cobalt spun, hissing and snarling, to stand between her and Garret. Lilith roared and turned to face him, but flinched back as a storm of bullets sped through the air, some sparking off her horns and chest plates, but some hitting home.

Ignoring the pain in my side and neck, I charged my former trainer, leaped at her back and sank my claws into her flank. She shrieked again and kicked me in the stomach with a hind leg, sending me tumbling through the sand. Winded once more, I still bounced to my feet, ready to continue the fight—

But it seemed the Viper had had enough. Now faced with St. George, as well as two stubborn dragons, she crouched and leaped skyward, her wings blasting us with sand as she rose into the air. I watched her go, meeting her gaze as she soared overhead, seeing the acid-green eyes narrow hatefully.

"This isn't over, hatchling," she warned in Draconic. "You cannot escape Talon. I will return for you all, soon."

With a few strong downbeats, the Viper rose up the cliff wall, shoved off the rock face and glided away over the ocean. Within moments, Talon's best Viper assassin became a distant blur against the night sky and disappeared.

I exhaled and sank to the cool sand, feeling like I'd been run over by a herd of elephants in cleats. My ribs throbbed, my side burned and my throat ached from where Lilith had tried to rip it out. I was bruised, battered and bloody, and wanted nothing more than to go home, take a long shower and curl up in my bed.

Only… I couldn't do that. Ever again. Dante was home. The brother who'd abandoned me, who'd turned his back on his twin in favor of Talon. He was part of the organization now. And I, especially after tonight, was most definitely a rogue.

Sick and disheartened, I slumped even farther, wishing I could bury myself in the cool sand until I figured everything out, but a sudden, angry growl made me jerk up. Cobalt was on his feet, body tense and lips curled back from his fangs. His eyes glowed, and he took a threatening step forward.

Glaring at the soldier a few yards away.

# GARRET

By far, that had been the stupidest thing I'd ever done.

I should be dead. By all logical statistics, I shouldn't have survived that fight. Challenging even a single hatchling, alone, was a good way to get yourself killed. You might get lucky, but even the smallest of Talon's offspring were quick and dangerous, armed with fire and claws and teeth. You could kill them, but they could tear you apart just as easily.

Taking on a full-grown adult dragon without an entire squad backing you up was suicide, plain and simple. There was no way around it. Adults were far too powerful for a single human to challenge alone. Even with a pair of dragons on my side, I'd gotten very, very lucky. If it hadn't been for Ember and the other juvenile joining the fight when they did, I wouldn't be breathing.

*Although,* I reflected as the adrenaline began to wear off and the full realization of what I'd done hit me full force, *I probably won't be breathing much longer.*

I'd betrayed the Order. Disobeyed commands, struck down my partner and charged the enemy without backup, which had allowed it to escape. Reckless and undisciplined, but not the worst thing I'd done. If that was my only crime, I could be court-marshaled and thrown into St. George's prison for a few months, even years. But my betrayal went far deeper than that.

I'd helped the enemy. I'd knowingly engaged in battle with the sole purpose of aiding the fiery red dragon who'd spared my life. I'd fought *with* them against their enemy. It didn't matter that their foe was another, more powerful dragon, and I had no idea why it was trying to kill its own. My interference had probably saved their lives.

*Was it worth it?*

I glanced at Ember, lying in the sand a few yards away, sides heaving. *Ember,* not "the dragon." She had a name, a personality, a normal life. Or she'd *had* a normal life, before tonight. Before we'd kicked down the door and tried to kill her for existing.

A heavy weight settled over me. If there had been time, I would have told her I was sorry, that we'd been wrong. Though any apology was grossly insufficient for the things I had done, the numbers slaughtered and the blood on my hands. Ember would hate me, she deserved to hate me, but I couldn't return to the Order and blindly kill her people like I used to. She had opened my eyes, and I couldn't… I *wouldn't,* return to what I had been.

A growl cut through the silence, raising the hair on my neck. I jerked up to see the blue dragon glaring at me with teeth bared, looking decidedly hostile. I tensed, fighting the instinct to raise my weapon. Of course, it saw only its greatest enemy, a soldier of St. George. I might have helped drive off the adult, but when Talon and the Order stood face-to-face, the only outcome was death.

I forced myself to lower the gun, keeping it at my side,

as I raised my other hand. "I'm not here to fight," I told the dragon, who snorted in obvious contempt.

"Bullshit," it spat at me, the word sounding strange coming from a dragon's mouth. I'd rarely heard them speak in their true forms; hearing one snarl an expletive was a weird sensation. "I suppose you didn't mean to kill us earlier tonight, either." It stalked toward me, eyes narrowed, lips pulled back in hate. "Way I see it, you came here expecting one dragon, not three. And now that you have no squad to back you up, you're trying to beg your way out. Well, it doesn't work that way, St. George," the dragon hissed. "Don't expect us to play nice when you tried to kill us all."

I raised my weapon, backing up as the dragon pressed forward menacingly. "I don't want to shoot you. Stand down."

"I've already been shot once tonight," the dragon answered, the murderous gleam in its eyes growing bright as he backed me toward the cliff. "If you think you can kill me, do your worst."

It tensed to spring at me. I tightened my grip on the trigger—

And Ember lunged between us.

# EMBER

Cobalt stopped short as I leaped in front of him, blocking the path to Garret. Growling, I lowered my head and spread my wings, sinking into a crouch. The dragon's gold eyes blinked in surprise, then narrowed angrily.

"Ember, what are you doing?" he snarled in Draconic. "He's St. George, Firebrand. Move, before he shoots you in the back."

"I know what he is," I retorted. "And I'm not going to let you do this." Planting my claws, I stayed where I was. "He helped us, Cobalt. He drove off the Viper. Lilith would've killed us both."

"That doesn't matter!" Aghast, he stared at me, confusion and disgust written over his reptilian face. "He's still part of the Order. He's killed dozens of our kind! The only reason he's not trying to murder us now is that we outnumber him." I stubbornly set my jaw, and Cobalt snarled impatiently. "You think he would've spared us tonight? If those alarms hadn't gone off, they would've slaughtered us. You, me, the hatchlings, Wes—they would've killed us all."

"So we're going to kill him in cold blood now? How does that make us any different?"

"Dammit, Ember!" He started toward me, but I bared my

fangs at him and hissed, making him stop. I wasn't screwing around. I was not going to let Cobalt kill Garret, even if he was St. George. He'd saved our lives. *Why,* I had no idea. He knew I was a dragon. He knew St. George tried to kill us tonight; hell, maybe he'd been there, too.

But he wasn't firing on us now. He'd helped drive off Talon's notorious Viper assassin. And when I spared a glance at him, the human standing quietly on the beach was a different person than the soldier I'd faced earlier tonight.

My heart sank. We were enemies. I knew that. But I couldn't let Cobalt attack him now. There had been far too much fighting and blood already. I'd had enough.

"Ember."

Garret's voice, low and grim, echoed at my back. I glanced over my shoulder to find him watching us, a grave look on his face. From the faint crease of his brow, he hadn't understood the snarled, hissed conversation between two dragons, but he'd probably gotten the gist of it.

I wanted to talk to him, but not like this. Not as lifelong enemies, dragon to St. George. Turning slowly, keeping my movements calm and unthreatening, I Shifted back, hearing Cobalt's warning growl echo behind me. But as I shrank down, my human form kneeling in the sand between the soldier and the dragon, Garret stepped forward, earning a hiss from Cobalt.

"Don't," he said urgently, and I glanced up at him, puzzled. "Don't change back, Ember, there's no time. You have to leave now." He shot a wary look back at the cliffs, at the path he'd come in. "St. George, the rest of my team, is on their way. You should go."

I blinked, but Cobalt gave a snarled curse and backed away. "I knew it," he growled with a furious look at Garret.

"I knew we shouldn't trust him. Come on, Firebrand. Before they get here and start shooting anything that moves." Whirling, he bounded toward the cave, his lithe body flying over the sand, moving like a huge scaly cat. But I hesitated, looking back at the soldier.

"Why?" I asked, needing to know. "Why did you save us? Did St. George send you? Or was this just to repay me for earlier? Clear your conscience before you start shooting us again?"

"No." He quickly shook his head. "Never again. I…" He broke off, raking a hand through his hair, before looking up. His gray eyes were haunted as they met mine. "I'm done," he said firmly. "No more missions. No more raids or strikes or killings. No more deaths. I'm not hunting your people anymore."

Stunned, I could only stare at him. "Really?"

He didn't smile, but his eyes softened a touch as he gazed at me. "How could I," he almost whispered, "after I met you?"

A lump rose to my throat, and I swallowed hard. "What about St. George?"

"It doesn't matter." His voice was resigned now, weary. "I can't follow their beliefs, and I can't condone what we've done. I knew what I was doing when I came here tonight." For a moment, his expression clouded with what might've been fear, before he shook himself with a deep, steadying breath. "I knew the consequences. I would do it again if I had to."

"Ember!" Cobalt's impatient voice rang over the sand. I looked back to see him at the edge of the water, wings half-open and ready to go. Behind him, a whip-thin black dragon and a smaller male with dusty brown scales bounded toward him from the cave. Nettle and Remy in their true forms, staring at me wide-eyed. "What are you waiting for? Come on!"

"Go," Garret said, nodding toward the other dragons. "Forget about me. I'm already dead. Just go."

"Garret..."

A shout echoed from the other direction, and we turned. Figures spilled onto the beach from between the cliffs, guns leading the way as they came toward us in a black swarm. I cringed, and Garret spun back, eyes narrowed.

"Ember, go! Now!"

I bit my lip, turned and sprinted away, seeing Nettle and Remy already taking flight, rising into the air. Cobalt waited for me, holding his ground, even as the first shots rang out behind me. Shifting midstride, I hit the ground running, already pumping my wings as I launched myself skyward, seeing Cobalt do the same. As we soared up the cliff wall, bullets zipped by me, sparking off the rocks, and there was a stab of pain as something punched a hole through my wingtip, making me falter in midair. I hissed in fear, beating my wings and scrabbling my claws down the rock face, expecting a bullet in the spine at any moment.

Cobalt soared over the top of the cliff, landed and spun back, peeking over the edge even through the bullet storm around us. Shots echoed around me, sparking off rock and sending jagged chips and dust into the air. With a defiant snarl, I gave my wings a final thrust and half flew, half clawed myself over the edge. Staggering several feet from the dropoff, finally clear of St. George and their deadly weapons, I collapsed to the dusty ground.

* * *

"Ember." Cobalt's gold eyes peered down at me, worried and anxious. From where I lay, panting, his horns and wings seemed to frame the moon, and the light shimmered off his metallic-blue scales. Maybe it was the adrenaline, or maybe it was living through yet another near-death experience, but I decided I preferred his real form far more than his human one. I wished he could stay in this body forever.

"Ember," he said again, his tail thumping a panicked rhythm in the dirt. "Are you hurt? Did they hit you?" He nudged me, anxious yet gentle. "Talk to me, Firebrand."

"I'm fine," I rasped out, and struggled to my feet. My right wing, down near the last finger joint, throbbed where the bullets had torn through the membrane, but it wasn't serious. I stretched it out, gave it a couple flaps to make sure it still worked and folded it to my back again. "Looks like I'm still in one piece."

Nettle and Remy crept forward, a slinky black dragon with a crown of spines bristling from her head, and a runty brown dragon with stripes down his neck and tail. They both had backpacks looped around their necks, and it would've looked ridiculous if the situation wasn't so dire. "What now?" Nettle asked, her sibilant voice tight with fear. "Where do we go now?" Cobalt pulled away from me and turned, facing the desert.

"We run," he said simply. "Far away from here. As far from St. George and Talon as we can. Let's find Wes, and get the hell out of Dodge. I have a place in Nevada where we'll be safe, at least for a few months while we decide what to do. It's not the nicest place, but it's better than nothing. Firebrand?" He turned to look at me, offering a brave smile. "You ready to go?"

Go. Leave Crescent Beach. My stomach twisted. This was it. I was going rogue, leaving Talon for good to go on the run like a criminal. With Cobalt and two others of my kind, but still. Would I see my brother again? Or any of my friends?

No. No, I wouldn't. My time as a normal human was done. I had chosen my path, and the consequences that came with it. No more surfing, volleyball, parties or hanging with friends. No more kissing boys in the ocean, feeling butterflies in my stomach, wishing the whole world would just stop for a while. Summer had come to an end, as I knew it must, and I had to move on.

After I took care of one final thing.

"Not yet," I told Cobalt, watching his eyes widen in surprise. "There's one more thing I have to do."

# GARRET

She'd escaped.

I watched Ember fly away, heart in my throat, as my squad swarmed around me, guns raised, and opened fire. I watched, not moving from where I stood, as Ember fled across the sand, leaped into the air with the blue dragon and soared up the rock face, struggling to get out of range. My heart stopped once when it looked like she'd been hit, wavering in the air, clawing frantically at the cliff. But she recovered, surged over the top in a flash of wings and crimson scales and vanished from sight.

I exhaled slowly in relief. *Get out of town, Ember,* I urged silently. *Run, as far away from us as you can, and don't look back.*

"Sebastian!"

The squad was returning, filing back over the sand, weapons lowered in defeat. There was no use waiting for the dragons to return; they were long gone, and everyone knew it. The squad leader was striding toward me, long legs carrying him over the sand, every muscle tense with controlled fury. I snapped to attention as he marched up and brought his face very close to mine, glaring holes in the side of my head.

"Explain yourself," he ordered in a low, tight voice as the rest of the team clustered around, angry and confused. Most of them I'd known for years, my whole life. Teammates I'd fought beside, stood shoulder to shoulder with on the battlefield, saved from certain fiery death, and vice versa. None of them looked friendly now. A few seemed bewildered, uncertain what was going on, but many of them were glaring at me with suspicion. I wasn't supposed to be here, alone, and at the very least my recklessness had caused the targets to escape. They hadn't figured out the real reason, not yet.

"I asked you a question, soldier," the squad leader continued when I didn't reply. His name was Michael St. Francis, and he was a good man: patient, fair and easy to get along with. I'd had no problems with him before tonight. "I assume you have a good reason for being out here alone," St. Francis continued, still glaring at me. "I assume you have a good reason two hostiles didn't fry you to a crisp before we could get here. And I assume you have a *damn* good reason for letting them escape and blowing this entire campaign back several months." He leaned forward an inch or two, his voice softer but no less furious. "And you're going to give me your damn good reason right now, because it sure looked to me like you were *talking* with the hostiles right before we came in." His hot breath blasted my ear, and a mutter went through the soldiers around us. I continued to gaze straight ahead, my expression blank, as St. Francis stepped back. "Is that what you were doing, soldier?"

"Yes, sir."

The muttering ceased instantly. For a second you could've heard a pin drop.

"Sebastian," St. Francis said, his voice completely without emotion. "You just admitted to speaking with the enemy and allowing them to escape. I would think very, very carefully about the next words out of your mouth, because you are seconds away from the firing wall." A cold lance went through my stomach, but I stared straight ahead, my expression blank as St. Francis continued. "What, exactly, were you doing out here?"

"I can tell you that," said a new voice outside the circle.

The cold spread to all parts of my body as Tristan stepped out of the shadows, moving people aside as he approached us. I winced inwardly. A dried trickle of blood streamed from his nose, and a massive purple bruise stood out on his temple, spreading to the corner of his eye. He stepped into the circle, shooting me a hard glare, before turning to the squad leader.

"Garret is a traitor to the Order," Tristan announced in a clear, firm voice. "He deliberately prevented me from taking the shot on one of the targets, targets I had orders to kill. I tried reasoning with him, but he said the Order had been wrong to kill dragons, that we were mistaken. When I tried to stop him, he attacked me."

I held my breath, knowing I was trapped, but wondering how much Tristan would reveal. This was no longer a simple case of reckless behavior, and the mood of the circle had definitely changed. Soldiers were staring at me now, some in disbelief, some in pity, contempt and rage. St. Francis, to his credit, remained calm, emotionless, as he nodded at my former partner.

"Is that all?"

Tristan hesitated, then nodded. "Yes, sir."

"I see." St. Francis turned to me, his eyes and voice cold. "And do you have anything to say in your defense, soldier?"

*Nothing that you would accept. Nothing that would assuage my guilt, only compound it. Tristan didn't tell you everything.*

"No, sir," I muttered.

"Take his weapons," St. Francis ordered, motioning to the soldiers closest to me. They stepped forward, seizing the M-4 and stripping me of my sidearm. I didn't move, and the soldiers stepped back, keeping their own weapons trained on me. "Garret Xavier Sebastian," St. Francis went on, "I'm taking you into custody. For collaboration with the enemy and treason against the Order. We'll escort you back to headquarters, and then your fate is out of my hands."

I met Tristan's eyes, and he turned away. Even after everything between us tonight, I couldn't blame him. He knew, as I did, what that fate would be. I would be taken back to our chapterhouse, where my case would be presented to a jury of commanding officers, leaving them to mete out punishment. If I was found guilty of treason, I would be marched to a long brick wall behind the training compound, offered a blindfold, and then the line of soldiers standing fifteen feet away would shoot me. A fitting end to one who sympathized with dragons.

So be it. I had always known death would come for me, sooner rather than later. And even if my death was execution before a firing squad and not in the jaws of a dragon as I'd always thought, at least, this time, I knew what I believed. I would die saving someone instead of ending a life.

As I was led away, I glanced once more at the top of the cliff, where Ember and the other dragons had vanished into the darkness. They would be long gone by now, free of St. George, and that, too, gave me some small comfort. I hoped she would think of me sometimes, though we were enemies and she would never realize that the reason for everything—

every choice, every understanding, every decision I'd made tonight—was because of her.

*Because St. George fell in love with a dragon.*

A faint smile tugged at my lips. Tearing my gaze from the sky, I followed my former teammates through the cliffs and into the shadows, leaving behind the beach where I first met a fiery, green-eyed dragon girl.

# EMBER

I lay on my stomach behind a sand dune, watching the line of soldiers move toward the big brown truck parked behind a boulder. My heart slammed against my ribs, echoing loudly in my ears, making me wish I could silence it. I was human again, still wearing my sleek black outfit, and I knew from this distance the human soldiers would have a near-impossible time spotting me among the rocks and sandy hills, but the sight of them still filled me with dread. They were my enemies, I understood that now. Before tonight, the war had been a distant thing, something intangible and unreal, never solid.

I'd been naive before; I would not be that foolish again. St. George would show us no mercy, no quarter. They would kill us just for existing. From here on, they could expect the same from me.

Except for one.

I saw him almost instantly, walking between two armed soldiers, head slightly bowed, following them down the path. Seeing him made my heart ache with longing, and sadness, and guilt. Because I'd wanted to be human for him, if only for a little while. Because those few moments we'd shared had been perfect, even though they were a lie. And because I remembered the look on his face when he saved us from

Lilith, the knowledge that he'd just betrayed everything he knew. Just as I had with Talon. And his final words to me, right before I'd flown off with Cobalt and the others, finally made sense.

*Forget about me. I'm already dead. Just go.*

They would kill him. St. George would kill him for helping us. And he'd known. He'd known the consequences, and he'd still chosen to help. He'd chosen to save his sworn enemy, face death at the hands of his own people…for what?

*I can't follow their beliefs, and I can't condone what we've done. I knew what I was doing when I came here tonight.*

"I still can't believe you talked me into this," growled a voice at my side.

I looked away from Garret long enough to grin at the human beside me. Sprawled on his stomach, Riley wore a pair of black jeans and a gray shirt that had been stuffed in one of the backpacks, and looked distinctly unhappy about being so close to St. George. He did not return my smile.

"I thought you were a Basilisk," I whispered to him. "Isn't this the type of thing you used to do all the time?"

"For Talon, yes," Riley shot back. "Not for fun. And definitely not to rescue some St. George bastard who shot at me earlier tonight. That doesn't seem good for your health."

"He helped us, Riley," I reminded him. "He knew the consequences, and he still helped us. St. George will kill him because of it."

"I don't care about that." Riley's voice was heartlessly blunt. "Let them kill one another—the more, the better, I say. The only reason I agreed to this insane plan was because I know I can't talk *you* out of it." His hand rose, lightly brushing my cheek. "So, here I am. With a death wish, apparently."

The roar of an engine jerked me out of my thoughts. I looked up just in time to see Garret enter the truck with the soldiers, and the doors slam shut behind him. The headlights flicked on, the truck bounced several times as it pulled forward onto the road and then sped off into the darkness.

"They're moving." Leaping upright, I swiftly changed, shedding my human form once more, letting my dragon self uncurl into the sand. Wings fluttering, I looked at Riley, who got to his feet a bit slower, looking reluctant. "Riley, come on! We can't let them get away." He sighed, and I bared my fangs, impatient. "Stay or come, but make your choice. I'm getting him out, with or without you."

With a roll of his eyes, Riley disappeared, Cobalt rising up to take his place. His gold gaze narrowed in exasperation. "Fine, Firebrand. You win. Let the suicide mission commence."

Spreading my wings, I let the warm night air tease the membranes and breathed deep, filling my lungs with heat and fire. Gazing down the road, I let a savage grin stretch my muzzle, and I hissed a challenge into the wind. St. George had hunted dragons their entire life. Let's see how well they fared when the dragons decided to fight back.

*I'm coming, Garret. Just hold on.*

With a blast of wind, I launched myself skyward.

# EPILOGUE

# DANTE

“Do you know why we have brought you here, Mr. Hill?”

I nodded stiffly. Across the desk, the blond man I’d met once before watched me with a cool blank expression, his hands folded in front of him.

“Yes, sir,” I said calmly, politely, as I’d been taught. “I assume it has something to do with my sister.” niño

His lips thinned. “Your sister, Ember Hill, has betrayed us,” he stated, making my heart sink. I’d known, of course. The moment Talon came for me that night, I’d known, and it still made me sick to my stomach. “She refused to return home with Lilith, and left town with a dangerous rogue, a former Talon operative named Cobalt. Where they are now is anyone’s guess.” He paused, gauging my reaction across the polished surface. I held my breath and waited, until he smiled.

“Ember Hill is now a rogue, a traitor in the eyes of Talon. If she will not see reason and return to the organization, she will be killed. However, the Elder Wyrm would like to avoid that if necessary.” His cold blue eyes narrowed, appraising me, even as I guessed his next words. “Therefore, Dante Hill, we would like *you* to be in charge of bringing her back.”

★ ★ ★ ★ ★

# ACKNOWLEDGMENTS

First and foremost, a massive thank-you to my editor, Natashya Wilson, who has been the biggest cheerleader for Talon ever since she heard my fledgling idea for a dragon series many moons ago. For all her hard work, dedication and excitement. For all the emails going back and forth on tiny details I would've missed. Basically for being the most awesome editor on the planet. Thanks to Laurie McLean, the best agent out there, who wouldn't take no for an answer. To Brandy Rivers, for getting *Talon* noticed by the right people; you are a queen of your field and an all-around fabulous person.

A huge shout-out to the team at Harlequin TEEN—Amy Jones, Melissa Anthony, Lisa Wray, Michelle Renaud, Nicki Kommit, Larissa Walker, Reka Rubin, Christine Tsai, the sales team and everyone at Harlequin who has worked so hard on my books. Publishing a book takes a village, and I wouldn't want to be anywhere else. To the talented artists and designers of *Talon*'s gorgeous cover, Kathleen Oudit, Erin Craig, Bora Tekogul, Fion Ngan, Natasa Hatsios. And to Chris Parks, for the gold dragon emblem. Thank you for one of the most striking covers I've ever seen anywhere—you all outdid yourselves.

Thanks to Jeff Kirschenbaum, Sara Scott, Ainsley Davies and Chris Morgan for all your support and excitement. And for making a tiny Kentucky author feel like a movie star.

And, last but definitely not least, thanks to my family, who never doubted for a second that I would become an author someday. And to my husband, Nick, my real-life knight in shining armor, who knows me well enough *not* to slay the dragon, but to look into fireproofing the house and buying a dragon saddle instead.

# QUESTIONS FOR DISCUSSION

1. When the story opens, Ember and Dante have one idea of what Talon is and what it does for dragonkind. How does Ember's view change and why, and how does Dante's change? Why do they end up with different opinions about Talon? Point to characteristics shown by each in the story to back up your position.

2. The Order of St. George believes it is right about dragons. Talon believes it is right about what it needs to do to survive. Riley/Cobalt believes he is right to have left Talon. In what ways is each of them right and in what ways is each shortsighted? Is anything ever completely "right"? Discuss.

3. Why does Talon believe that dragons are superior to humans? What impact might that have on the organization in the future? Discuss using examples from the story.

4. Why does the Order of St. George believe that killing all dragons is acceptable? What other approaches might they use to protect humans from dragons?

5. Ember has been taught that dragons do not form emotional attachments the way humans do. Why do you

think Ember herself forms attachments to Garret and Lexi? Is she different from other dragons, or is something else at work? Use examples from the story to back up your point of view.

6. Going rogue means that Ember will have to be on guard against both Talon and the Order of St. George. Which is the bigger threat and why?

7. Ember and Dante are the only brother and sister known to dragonkind in recent memory. How does the relationship they have influence each of them? Point to examples from the book. What do you think will happen if they do meet again?

8. If we were to discover today that, yes, dragons actually do exist and live among us, what kind of reaction do you think humankind would have to this news? How would dragons be treated?

*Turn the page to read an excerpt from*
*ROGUE*
*the second book in* THE TALON SAGA
*by* New York Times *bestselling author Julie Kagawa.*
*Only from Harlequin TEEN!*

# EMBER

Three hours on the back of a motorcycle, the sun beating down on your shoulders and the wind whipping through your hair, though exhilarating, reminds you why flying wins every time.

"You okay back there, Firebrand?" Riley called over his shoulder. I peeked up from behind his leather jacket and caught my reflection in his dark shades. My hair whipped and snapped like a flame atop my head, too short to tie back but just long enough to be horribly tangled when we stopped. Before us, the highway stretched on, an endless strip of pavement heading east. Around us, the Mojave Desert provided much the same scenery: sand, scrub, cactus, rock and the occasional hawk or turkey vulture. The air shimmered with heat, but heat never bothered me. My kind was well adapted to dealing with blistering temperatures.

"My butt has gone numb!" I called back, making him smirk. "My hair is going to take hours to untangle, and I think I've eaten like four bugs. And I swear, Riley, if you tell me I should keep my mouth closed, you're going to be riding the rest of the way sidesaddle."

He grinned. "We're about forty-five minutes out. Just hang on."

Sighing, I laid my chin against his back, watching the eternal sameness flash by around us, and let my mind wander.

It had been three days since we left Crescent Beach. Three days since my world had been turned upside down, since I'd learned Talon was hiding things from me, since I'd fought the Order of St. George and discovered that Garret wasn't who I thought he was. Three days since I'd made the decision to go rogue and leave town with Riley, abandoning my family and my old life and branding myself a traitor in the eyes of Talon.

Three days since I'd last seen Garret. And Dante.

I clenched a fist in Riley's jacket, my emotions churning with anger, sadness and guilt toward them both. Anger that they'd lied, that I'd trusted them, only to have them betray that trust. Garret was part of St. George; he'd been sent to Crescent Beach to kill me. Dante, the brother who'd promised to have my back no matter what, had turned me in to Talon when he'd discovered I was going rogue. But at least Garret had redeemed himself somewhat, saving me and Riley from a Talon assassin, then warning us that his own people were on their way. It was because of him that I was here now, on the back of a motorcycle with Riley, flying across the Mojave Desert. I didn't know where my brother was, but I hoped he was okay. He might've abandoned me to Talon, but I knew Dante. He thought he had been doing the right thing.

Idiot twin. He still didn't know the truth about the organization, the dark secrets they kept, the lies they told us. I'd make him see, eventually. I would get him out of Talon soon.

After I took care of this other thing.

The sun was beginning to drop toward the horizon when

Riley slowed and pulled off the highway into a large, nearly empty lot on the side of the road. A sign at the edge of the pavement cast a long shadow over us as we cruised by, making me squint as I gazed up at it.

"Spanish Manor," I read, then looked at the "manor" in question, finding a boxy, derelict motel at the end of the nearly empty parking lot. Peeling yellow doors were placed every thirty or so feet, and ugly orange curtains hung in the darkened windows. Exactly one car, an aging white van, was parked in the spaces out front, and if not for the flickering Vacancy sign in the office window, I would've thought the place completely abandoned.

Riley cruised up beside the van and killed the engine, and we both swung off the bike. Relieved to be able to move around again, I put my arms over my head and stretched until I felt my back pop. Gingerly, I tried running my fingers through my hair and found it hopelessly tangled, as I'd feared. Wincing, I tugged at the snarls and tore loose several fiery red strands while Riley looked on in amusement. I scowled at him.

"Ow. Okay, next time, I get a helmet," I said, and his grin widened even more. I rolled my eyes and continued my hopeless battle with the tangles. Of all the human beauty traditions, I found hair the most time-consuming and obnoxious. So much time was wasted washing, brushing, teasing and primping it; scales never had this problem. "Where are we, anyway?" I muttered, separating a stubborn knot with my fingers, trying to ignore the dragon beside me. It was hard. Lean, tall and broad-shouldered, clad in leather and chains, Riley certainly cut the figure of a perfect rebel biker boy leaning so casually against his motorcycle, the breeze tugging at his dark hair. He took off his shades and stuck them in a back pocket.

"We're about an hour from Vegas," he said, and nodded to the ramshackle Spanish Manor squatting at the edge of the lot. "Wes told me to meet him here. Come on."

I followed him over the parking lot, up a rusting flight of stairs, and down the second-story hall until we came to a faded yellow door near the end. The curtains were drawn over the grimy window, and the interior of the room looked dark. Riley glanced around, then knocked on the wood, three swift taps followed by two slower ones.

A pause, and then the door swung open to reveal a thin, lanky human on the other side, dark eyes peering at us beneath a scruff of messy brown hair. He scowled at me by way of greeting, then stepped back to let us in.

"About time you showed up." Wes slammed the door and threw the locks as if we were in a superspy movie and there could be enemy agents lurking outside, hiding in the cactus. "I thought you'd be here hours ago. What happened?"

"Had to make a quick stop in LA for a few things," Riley answered, brushing by him. He did not mention the "things" in question, namely, a duffel bag full of ammo and firearms. Both he and Wes ignored me, so I turned to gaze around the room. A quick glance was all that was required; it was small, rumpled, unremarkable, with an unmade bed against the wall and soda cans scattered everywhere. A laptop sat open and glowing on the corner desk, nonsensical words and formulas splayed across the screen in neat rows.

"Riley…" Wes began, a note of warning in his voice.

"Where are the hatchlings?" Riley asked, overriding whatever he was going to say. "Are they all right? Did you find the safe house?"

"They're fine," Wes answered, sounding impatient. "They're holed up near San Francisco with that Walter chap, with strict instructions not to poke one scale out of the house until they hear from you. They're bloody peachy. *We're* the ones we have to worry about now."

"Good." Riley nodded briskly and walked across the room to the desk, then bent down to the screen. "I assume this is it, then?" he muttered, narrowing his eyes. "Where we'll be going tonight? Did you get everything you needed?"

"Riley." Wes stalked after him. "Did you hear a word I just told you, mate? Do you know how crazy this is? Are you even listening to me?" The other ignored him, and with a scowl, Wes reached across the desk and slapped the laptop shut.

Riley straightened and turned to glare at the human. In the shadows, his eyes suddenly glowed a dangerous yellow, and the air went tight with the soundless, churning energy that came right before a Shift. Riley's true form hovered close to the surface, staring out at the human with angry gold eyes.

To his credit, Wes didn't back down.

"Listen to yourself, Riley." The human faced the other in the dingy light, his voice solemn. "Listen to what you're trying to do. This isn't stealing a hatchling away from Talon. This isn't walking up to a kid and saying, 'Oy, mate, your organization is corrupt as hell and if you don't leave soon you'll never be free.'" He stabbed a finger at the laptop. "This is a bloody St. George compound. With bloody St. George soldiers. One slipup, one mistake, and you'll be hanging from some corporal's wall. Think about what that means, mate." Wes leaned forward, his gaze intense. "Without you, the underground dies. Without you, all those kids you freed from Talon will be helpless when the organization comes for them. And they *will*, Riley, you bloody well know they will. Do you even care about that anymore? Do you care that everything we've worked for is about to go up in flames?" He gestured sharply at me. "Or has this sodding kid got you so wrapped around her finger that you don't know what's important anymore?"

"Hey!" I protested, scowling, but I might as well have shouted at a wall. Riley clenched his fists, nostrils flaring, as if he might punch the human or Shift into his true form and blast him to cinders. Wes continued to glare, chin raised, mouth pressed into a stubborn line. Both of them paid absolutely no attention to me.

"What are we doing, mate?" Wes asked softly, after a moment of brittle silence. "This isn't our fight. This isn't what we said we would do." Riley didn't answer, and Wes's tone became almost pleading. "Riley, this is crazy. This is suicide, you know it as well as I do."

Riley slumped, raking a hand through his messy black hair, the tension leaving his shoulders. "I know," he growled. "Trust me, I know. I've been trying to convince myself I haven't completely lost my mind since we left town."

"Then, why—"

"Because if I don't, Ember will go without me and get herself killed!" Riley snapped, and finally looked in my direction. Those piercing gold eyes met mine across the room, the shadow of Riley's true form staring at me. I shivered as he held my gaze. "Because she doesn't know St. George like I do," he went on. "She hasn't seen what they're capable of. She doesn't know what they do to our kind if we're discovered. I do. And I'm not going to let that happen. Even if I have to sneak into a St. George base and rescue one of the bastards myself."

I swallowed, feeling something inside me respond, a rush of warmth spreading through my veins. My own dragon, calling to Riley's, like he was her other half.

Wes scrubbed a hand down his face. "You're both completely off your rockers," he muttered, shaking his head. "And I'm no better, since it seems I'm going along with this lunacy." He groaned and plopped into the chair, then opened the laptop. "Well, since you appear to have lost your mind, let me show you exactly what we're up against."

Riley turned from me, breaking eye contact. I knew I should go see what Wes was talking about. But I could still feel the heat of Riley's gaze, feel the caress of the dragon against my skin. I needed to get away from him to clear my head, to cool the fire surging through my veins. Leaving them to talk, I slipped into the small, only slightly disgusting bathroom and locked the door behind me.

Wes's and Riley's voices echoed through the wood, low and urgent, probably talking about the mission. Or, in Wes's case, trying to convince Riley, once and for all, not to go through with this. I sank onto the toilet seat and ran my hands through my hair, letting the words fade into jumbled background noise.

I knew Wes was right. I knew what I planned to do was stupid and risky as hell. I knew I hadn't considered all the threats, didn't realize what I was getting into. What I was planning flew in the face of everything I'd been taught, and if I voiced it out loud, it sounded insane, even to me.

Break into a compound of St. George, the ancient enemy

of our race, the Order whose sole mission was to see us extinct, and rescue one of their own. Sneak into a heavily armed base full of soldiers, free a sole prisoner who could be anywhere and get out. Without getting blown to bits in the process.

It sounded crazy. It *was* crazy. It was downright suicidal, like Wes said. I didn't fault him, or Riley, for being reluctant. They had no stake in this, no reason to want to undergo a mission that could get us all killed. They had every right to be afraid. If I was being completely honest, it terrified me, too.

But I couldn't leave him behind.

I went to the sink to splash water on my face but paused when I caught sight of my reflection. A skinny, green-eyed girl stared back at me from the mirror, red hair standing on end, eyes ringed with dust and dark circles. I didn't look remotely Draconian. I looked tired, and dirty, and very mortal. Nothing fierce or primal lurked inside my gaze to indicate that I was anything more than I seemed.

Was that why he'd hesitated, that night on the cliff? When he'd pointed that gun at my head, and I'd finally realized what he really was? When he ceased to be Garret and became the enemy, a soldier of St. George?

He could've killed me. I'd been in my human form, taken off guard, and had been too stunned to do anything at first. He'd had me at point-blank range, alone and trapped on a bluff miles from anywhere. All he'd had to do was pull the trigger.

But he hadn't. And later, he'd betrayed his own people to save me and Riley from Lilith, my sadistic trainer and Talon's best Viper assassin. Lilith had come for Riley that night, and when I'd refused to leave him and return to Talon, she'd tried to kill me, too. She'd nearly succeeded. We'd survived only because of Garret's unexpected arrival, and his help in driving off the Viper. Otherwise, Lilith would've torn us apart.

But, by helping us, Garret had damned himself. To aid a dragon was treason in the eyes of his Order, and the punishment for such betrayal was death. He'd told me that himself. Garret had known the Order would kill him, and he'd still chosen to save us.

Why?

I'd tried to follow him that night, hoping to somehow get him away from the soldiers who were now his captors. But there had been no opportunity for a rescue, and Riley had finally convinced me that falling back and planning our next move was the best option. So, here we were.

I turned on the sink and splashed cold water on my face, washing away the dust and grime. When that was done, I attempted to tame the snarled bird's nest atop my head, wincing as I ran my fingers through the knots and tangles, finally combing them out. I had a brush in my backpack, along with a change of clothes and other essentials, but primping seemed like a giant waste of time right now. Besides, who was around that I wanted to impress? Wes hated me, and Riley… Riley was interested in my other half.

My dragon perked at this, sending a curl of warmth through my stomach, and I squashed it, and her, down. I didn't know what I was going to do about Riley, but there were other things to focus on. Hopefully Riley and Wes had come up with a brilliant plan, because other than knowing I couldn't leave Garret with St. George, I didn't have a clue what to do.

When I came out of the bathroom, Riley and Wes were bent over the laptop, talking in the same low, urgent tones. Riley glanced up, and our eyes met once more, making my skin flush. Then Wes snapped his name, and he turned his attention to the computer again.

Edging up behind them, I peered over Riley's shoulder at what looked like an aerial map on the screen. The surrounding area seemed barren—desert and dust and flat, open ground—but in the very center of the map sat a cluster of small buildings. No roads led to it, no other buildings or landmarks stood nearby.

"Is that where Garret is?" I asked softly. Wes shot me a dirty look. "That," he stated, narrowing his eyes, "is St. George's western chapterhouse, and it took me a bloody long time to find it, thank you very much. It's not like the Order advertises where they are—technically those buildings don't exist on any map or sightseeing brochure. But yes, the bastards that tried to kill us in California have likely returned there, your murderous boyfriend included." He snorted and turned away, and I resisted the urge to slap the back of his head.

"I had no idea it was so close," Riley muttered, staring intently at the screen, his face grim. "Right on the Arizona/Utah line. I'm going to have to relocate a couple safe houses farther east."

"There's nowhere completely safe, mate," Wes said quietly, slumping back in his chair. "Not since they caught on that Talon moved a lot of its business to the States. They're bloody everywhere now."

"Where were they before?" I asked.

"England," Riley answered without looking at me. "St.

George's main headquarters is in London, where it's been for hundreds of years. They're very traditional, and they don't like change, so it took them a while to spread out. That's why Talon does a lot of business in the US and other countries—the Order doesn't have such a strong presence here. Or it didn't for a long time." He leaned over the laptop. "This is a fairly new base," he stated, staring at the tiny white squares on the screen. "It wasn't here ten years ago." One finger rose to trace the perimeter, his face shadowed in thought. "There's the fence, and that's probably the armory, barracks and mess hall, officer housing...so this big one has to be headquarters." He tapped the screen, tightening his jaw. "That's where he'll probably be."

"Bloody fabulous," Wes muttered. "The most heavily guarded building of them all. Tell me again why we're doing this? If it was a hatchling we were all getting ourselves killed for, I'd understand. I wouldn't like it, but I'd understand. That's more your type of loony." He continued to glower at Riley and ignore me, as if I wasn't standing not three feet away. Well within singeing distance, I thought. "Even if we do get this blighter out, what makes you think he won't run straight back to St. George to tell them where we are? Or shoot us in the back himself?"

"He won't," I snapped, glaring at Wes. "I know Garret. He's not like that."

Wes turned a disgusted sneer in my direction. "Really?" he drawled. "Then answer me this, if you know the blighter so very well—how long did it take you to figure out he was part of St. George?"

I flushed. I'd never guessed the truth, never let myself think Garret could be the enemy, not until he'd aimed a gun at my head, and even then I hadn't wanted to believe it. Wes gave me a smirk. "Yeah, that's what I figured. You only *think* you know him. But the truth of it is he was lying to you that whole time. He would've told you anything to get you to reveal yourself, anything you wanted to hear."

"He saved us from Lilith—"

"He shot at a bloody adult dragon," Wes interrupted. "Because it was clearly the bigger threat. And when it was over and his squad hadn't arrived to back him up, he told you what was necessary for him to stay alive. He told you exactly what you wanted to hear."

"That's not true!" I remembered Garret's face that night, the intense way he'd looked at me, the remorse and determination and guilt. *I'm done,* he'd told me. *No more killing. No more deaths. I'm not hunting your people anymore.*

Wes snorted. "Leopards can't change their spots," he said with maddening self-assurance. "St. George will always hate and kill dragons because that's what they do. It's the *only* thing they know how to do."

I looked to Riley, standing silently beside the desk, hoping he would back me up. To my dismay, his mouth was pressed into a grim line, his jaw set. My heart sank, even as I turned on him, frowning.

"You agree with him," I accused, and his eyebrows rose. "You think this is a huge mistake, even though you were there. You heard what Garret said."

"Firebrand." Riley gave me a half weary, half angry look. "Yes, of course I agree with him," he said evenly. "I've seen what St. George does, not only in the war, but to all our kind, everywhere. How many safe houses do you think I've lost to their cause? How many dragons are murdered by the

Order every year? Not just the Vipers or Basilisks or the ones directly involved in the war." His gaze narrowed. "I've seen them slaughter hatchlings, kids younger than you. I once watched a sniper take out an unarmed kid in cold blood. He was on his way to meet me, riding his bike through the park, and the shot came from nowhere. Because I couldn't get to him in time." Riley's eyes flashed gold, the dragon very close to the surface, angry and defiant. "So no, Firebrand, I'm not completely thrilled with the idea of rescuing one of the Order," he finished in a near growl. "Any excuse for another of the bastards to die is a good one in my book. And don't think your human is innocent just because he fought Lilith and let us go. He has dragon blood on his hands just like the rest of them."

I cringed inside, knowing he was right. But I still raised my chin, staring him down. "I'm not leaving him to die," I said firmly. "He saved our lives, and I won't forget that, no matter what you say." He crossed his arms, and I made a helpless gesture. "But you don't have to come, Riley. I can do this alone. If you feel that strongly—"

"Firebrand, shut up," Riley snapped. I blinked, and he gave me a look of supreme exasperation. "Of course I'm coming with you," he growled. "I told you before, I won't let you take on St. George alone. I'll be with you every step of the way, and I'll do my damnedest to keep us alive, but you can't expect me to be happy about it."

I swallowed. "I'll make it up to you, Riley, I promise."

Riley sighed, running a hand through his dark hair. "I'll hold you to that," he said. "When this is over, I fully expect you to do whatever I say, no hesitation, no questions asked. But first, let's concentrate on getting through the next twenty-four hours. Come here." He motioned me forward. "You'll need to see this, if you're planning on sneaking into the base with me. You *are* planning on coming, I assume? No chance of talking you out of it?"

"You know me better than that."

"Sadly, I do."

I eased in front of him and gazed down at the screen, suddenly very aware of his presence, his hand on my arm as he peered over my shoulder, the smell of his leather jacket. Wes grumbled under his breath, something that included the words *sodding* and *bollocks*, and Riley gave a grim chuckle.

"Yeah," he muttered, his deep voice close to my ear, making my skin prickle. "Just like old times."

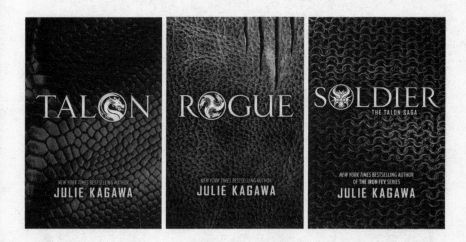